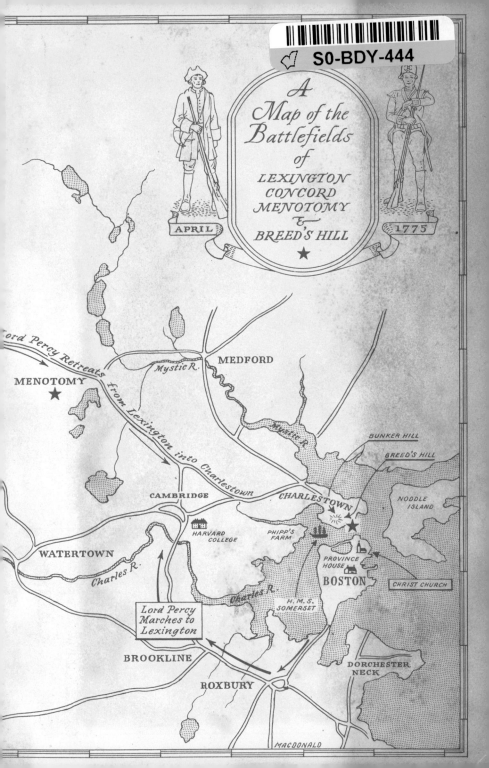

A
Map of the
Battlefields
of
LEXINGTON
CONCORD
MENOTOMY
&
BREED'S HILL

APRIL

1775

Lord Percy Retreats from Lexington into Charlestown

MENOTOMY

Mystic R.

MEDFORD

Mystic R.

BUNKER HILL

BREED'S HILL

CAMBRIDGE

CHARLESTOWN

NODDLE ISLAND

HARVARD COLLEGE

PHIPP'S FARM

WATERTOWN

Charles R.

PROVINCE HOUSE

Charles R.

BOSTON

CHRIST CHURCH

Lord Percy
Marches to
Lexington

H. M. S.
SOMERSET

BROOKLINE

DORCHESTER
NECK

ROXBURY

MACDONALD

CONCORD BRIDGE

Concord Bridge

By HOWARD HORNE

THE BOBBS-MERRILL COMPANY, INC.

INDIANAPOLIS   *Publishers*   NEW YORK

First Edition

For Ivy Wilson

affectionately

CONTENTS

BOOK ONE

The Fortress

CHAPTER **I**

The World Turned Upside Down

THE GENERAL was shaving. Having been bathed and massaged by his Negro servant, he put on a pair of flowered knee breeches and was busily lathering his face when the young colonel blundered into the bathroom with the request that he should do something quickly. General Gage had little patience with people who wanted something done quickly.

"It's no use," he said, his face hidden in a crust of creamy lather. "I've finished with impulsiveness. All this talk of erecting fortifications and arresting the leaders . . . "

"But the leaders are dangerous and the rebels are out of hand," Colonel Lord Percy exclaimed. "You cannot be cool about them."

"I intend to be as cool as is humanly possible," the general answered, stropping the razor and feeling along the thin edge. "Indeed, I have to be cool. I heard this morning that during a convivial feast at the Green Dragon two days ago Hancock said the best thing that could happen to me is that I should be hanged on the yardarm of the *Somerset*."

"You let them talk like that?"

"Yes."

"And you don't arrest 'em?"

"Why should I? I don't like arresting 'em. It's too easy, and it solves nothing."

The general returned to contemplate himself in the mirror. He was not angry. He was simply bewildered by Lord

Percy's impetuosity. It occurred to the general that the colonel at thirty-three was really too young to be his brigadier. Peering into the bluish mirror, the general began to open his mouth wide so that the skin would be stretched out; then he twisted his neck, made grimaces at himself and began to draw the steel-back razor down through the thick white mess of lather. Lord Percy was still talking—something about the rebels. The general turned sharply, glared at the colonel and said in a muffled voice, for some of the lather was trickling into his open mouth: "It's all mystery, the mother of mysteries, the whore of Babylon." He was surprised to hear himself saying these words; he could not remember ever having employed them before.

Long ago the general had come to the conclusion that the business of shaving was one to be performed in complete silence, without disturbance of any kind. He was annoyed with Lord Percy. He was also annoyed at the thought of the ball he was giving at Province House that evening. He found balls dull affairs, though it was pleasant to see the Boston women. Also he liked the conviviality, and it pleased him to walk down the ballroom while "God Save the King" was being played by the Negro orchestra. What he did not like was the hour of preparation and the wearing of the immaculate uniform appropriate to a royal governor. There were other things on his mind. His youngest child was tossing in bed in a fever, and his wife Margaret was almost out of her mind with worry. In the middle of all this disturbance Lord Percy chose to invade the most sacred place in the whole of Province House—the bathroom.

While Lord Percy talked on, the general concentrated on the face that was beginning to emerge in the mirror. Underneath the mountains of lather there was a good red skin, the color derived more from grog and rum than from exercise. The lips were long, broad and well shaped—a fine mouth, good ears, broad cheekbones, a firm chin and what the general himself liked to call "a damned sturdy and upstanding nose." It was a good face, and part of it was at last being revealed in that dull mirror which he had once decided to throw away but kept for no better reason than that he was accustomed to it.

Now he pinched the end of his nose and held it up so that he could draw the razor down the whole length of the long upper lip. Since this was the most delicate operation of all and every ounce of concentration was needed to carve off those resistant hairs, he held his breath until his glassy eyes began to protrude from their sockets. Lord Percy, seeing that intense look of apoplectic concentration, thought something was wrong, but he did not dare approach the general too closely. When the upper lip was shaved the general went on to shave the chin. This was easy. It was a square chin pitted with small pocks, and he was accustomed to shave it in three quick strokes. One side of his face, his chin and his upper lip were now shaved. He turned round and barked, "Boy, bring me the hot water!" and then glared glumly at the remaining paste of lather on his face which, in the bluish light coming through the window, resembled some kind of enormous toadstool growing out of his face.

He was deliberating on the kind of strategy to be employed when Lord Percy said, "We must get to work and show the rebels there's a limit to their impudence."

"Get to work!" the general roared. "Can't you see I'm shaving, you blithering fool! I like to perform my ablutions in privacy, sir. All you do is mumble about the sins of the Americans. Get to work indeed!"

It was the last straw. The general's anger, never well controlled, now blazed savagely. To prevent himself from telling Lord Percy what he thought of him the general glared into the mirror, cursing under his breath, and suddenly, with renewed fervor, began to shave himself violently—so violently that he sliced his cheek. It was one of those cuts which penetrate very deeply but do not bleed at once. Having shaved himself to his satisfaction, the general turned to strop his razor, unaware of the broad splash of blood along one side of his face. Lord Percy, obeying the instincts of any young colonel in the presence of a superior officer, said nothing, though it occurred to him that a half-naked general bleeding to death was not something you would come upon every day of your life.

"Damned fine razor," the general said. "I've had it ever since I came to America—twenty years now—and it's still as sharp as the day I first used it."

In a kind of daze, standing in the middle of the bathroom, the general pondered what he would wear to the ball. He came to the conclusion he would wear a peruke of silver wool, a crisp and curly peruke which he had not worn recently, one that Margaret admired. He went to the cupboard, pulled the peruke off the peg, and then caught sight of Lord Percy gaping at him.

"What the dickens are you gaping at me for?" the general exploded. "It's a good peruke, isn't it?"

"Yes, sir."

"So it should be. I paid eleven pounds for it. You ought to pay more attention to your peruke, young man. It's a sign of good taste. Your father had an excellent collection." The Negro servant boy came in, and the general shouted after him: "Where's that damn towel? Yes, and bring my stockings in!" Turning to Lord Percy, he went on: "I've seen perukes in France you wouldn't believe! But a good, tight, reasonable peruke——"

It was then, for the first time, that the general observed he was bleeding. The blood, as so often happens with cheek wounds, flowed thickly, splashing on his chest and ruining his flowered knee breeches. There were spots of blood on the floor and on the towel. "Lord save us," he said and went once again to look at himself in the blue mirror where the blood was a reddish-purple color. Then he raised his fist and sent it crashing against the mirror.

For a moment Lord Percy thought the general had gone hopping mad. He had never heard the general curse before. Now there came a flow of voluble cursing which surprised by the richness of its vocabulary. The general did not curse as most soldiers curse; it was a general's cursing, and it included words from the boudoir as well as from the gutters. Lord Percy was shocked, and he began to beat a retreat.

"You might as well hear it, Colonel," the general said sternly. "It clears the air. Better than a fumigatory. Got to let the boil burst, eh?" He began to mop the blood on his face, cursing in an undertone, wondering what Lord Percy would say years later when he recounted the story of coming upon the general in the bathroom. Meanwhile he was glad he had smashed the mirror. It never had given an accurate representation of him, and he admired accuracy. Accuracy and precision were words constantly on his lips; he liked to say the English were less learned than the French because the French at least possessed a passion for accuracy. He liked clear outlines, but he also genuinely liked people, with the result that he had no faith in cut-and-dried solutions. It was one of his boasts that he did not have to leave Province House to know the temper of the Bostonians: it was something you could feel in the air around you—a glance out of the window at the passers-by was enough. Lord Percy, like a good brigadier, believed in exact calculations, straight lines drawn on maps, great lists of figures.

"I wish to God I knew what the devil you had come to see me for," the general said. "Was it only about fortifications?"

"Well . . . yes."

"You seem dubious. Are you sure it's not gambling debts? I hear the subalterns are gambling advance pay and losing it to the Americans. God's pity, must we lose everything to the Americans, even the currency of the realm? I don't mind my officers running after American women, but I do object to them losing the pay they may not live long enough to earn. I hear my officers think nothing of wagering a hundred pounds. It's a fine kettle of fish when my army is heavily in debt to its mortal enemies."

"There are only three or four officers in debt, sir."

"Three or four officers, five or six hundred soldiers—and that's not the end of our indebtedness. They keep coming to me with their claims for the damage done by our men on tours of inspection. I'm paying 'em. I don't believe we've done the damage, but I won't have it said of us that we reneged on our debts. I'll tell you this. You think in terms of fortifications—and no doubt they are necessary—but I think in terms of keeping their friendship. If we are ordered to keep 'em down, we've got more in our hands than we can carry. We'll need to build a ring of fortifications round every American house. I trust the Americans will behave themselves, and I trust in God and the wooden walls of England——"

"I still believe——"

"I believe you have a right to your own opinions, but I'm cursed if you have a right to an endless repetition of them."

Lord Percy was in despair. He had hoped to obtain a reasonable answer on the subject of fortifications. Instead, General Gage had scoffed at the idea when it was first broached, and he was still scoffing at it.

"Then in God's name, sir, what is there left to do?" Lord Percy exclaimed. "Do we just sit in Boston on our arses?"

"We do indeed—if we are lucky."

"You mean . . ."

"I mean what I say. I'm a general, sir, and I know the part luck plays in a campaign. I know as well as the next man what will happen, but when I draw up a list of my reinforcements and plan an attack I remember the imponderables. You should read Pascal. He has a deal of sense about how the length of a woman's nose changed the destiny of a great nation. There may be such a thing in America. I'm looking out for it. I don't hate the Americans. Upon my soul, I've shown my love for them by marrying one of them. No one could say I was indifferent to their desires or their just claims. I won't tolerate rebellion against the king, but short of that I'll tolerate any damfoolery that may enter their heads and I'll look out for their wisdom. I don't complain against them."

"I do."

"I know you do, but you're young and you'll grow older. . . . Where the devil's my servant?"

The general shouted at the top of his voice, and when the small black boy came running in, dressed in beautiful wine-red knee breeches with a wine-red coat embroidered with gold, he thought he knew why the boy had delayed. He was very handsome, this boy, with his round cheeks and glittering eyes and wide mouth—a mouth which was split apart in a perpetual grin. Evidently the boy had also been bathing and scenting himself, preparing to cut a good figure for the ball.

"Wait for me in the anteroom, Percy," the general said, taking the towels from the boy. "You're quite sure it was only fortifications? I have a feeling that there is something on your mind?"

"Well . . . yes, sir."

"Out with it!"

Stammering a little, Lord Percy said, "We've received intelligence that the *Nautilus* is due to arrive this evening." He was not in the least surprised when the general's mouth opened wide and a look of extraordinary apprehension appeared on his face; for both of them knew that the *Nautilus* carried secret dispatches from the government, and they had long ago suspected that the dispatches would lead to—the word they used was "difficulties."

The bathroom door closed, and the general found himself

gazing absent-mindedly out of the window. The window was of dark crown glass, and though you could look out, no one could see what was happening inside. He had a clear view of the whole length of King Street to the wharf and the fluttering sails of frigates in the harbor, the dim streets nearly empty now in that hush which precedes supper. He knew his peruke was askew, but he did not care. He kept absent-mindedly patting the cut on his cheek with the towel, and all the time he was thinking of H.M.S. *Nautilus,* which had sailed—Heaven knows how long ago—from Plymouth with its little black metal box. He could guess at the contents. There were rumors enough, and the Americans seemed to know everything written in it. "The cursed box," he said to himself, and then he lighted his long silver-stemmed pipe and sucked noisily at the mouthpiece.

He had time to spare, and he kept gazing out of the window as though attracted by the silence of the deserted streets and the fluttering of the pennants in the harbor. The *Nautilus* had not come in yet, but at any moment it wound round the headland. He heard the clear silvery bell of Christ Church ringing, and from somewhere down below there came the smart pacing of the sentries, the smack of rifle butts against stone. The room filled with blue tobacco smoke. He could hardly breathe, so thick was the smoke, and he could hardly see the objects in the room. He thought of all the work he had done during the day from the time when, in the early morning, he had watched Lord Percy drilling his men on the Common to the time when he had completed the last of the eighteen letters all written in his own hand. There were orders concerning food, timber, fishing rights. There was the endless poring over maps. There was the death sentence on a deserter which he had commuted in the afternoon, saying, "I don't want blood on my hands. We've had to shoot some, but on my oath we aren't here to put people up against the wall." He kept saying, "I'm an American in my bones, but I don't expect them to love us, though they would love us well enough if they only knew."

He began to peel off his knee breeches. The blood on his thigh made him feel sick. "Christ," he said. "Where the devil is everything coming to?" At the same moment he heard a subdued roar from the direction of the harbor. The *Nautilus,* with long pennants waving and the cross of St. George at her bow, was riding past the headland and every one of her white sails was stiff in the westerly wind.

When a young army officer, straight from the *Nautilus,* bearing a black dispatch box, was taken to the Blue Room at Province House, it was already dusk, but no candles had been lighted. In the half-darkness the general sat alone at the head of the table. Long ago he had guessed at the contents of the box. He watched the clouds floating by and for a few moments he pretended not to notice that there was an officer standing by the door, a man wearing a scarlet coat, white knee breeches and thigh boots. For a while longer the general gazed at his hands lying on the green baize tablecloth; then he turned to the officer, and he was about to say, "Put the box before me," when he saw that the officer was someone he knew.

"Good God, boy, don't stand there gaping!" the general exclaimed, and then stood up suddenly—so suddenly that he very nearly threw the chair over and only succeeded in catching it by a miracle. "How should I know, my dear Oliver, that they would send you?"

"Captain Oliver De Lancey reporting to the royal governor," Oliver said, smiling.

The general immediately forgot the black dispatch case which Oliver placed gingerly on the table. All his weariness, all his anger and sense of frustration had gone from him. He threw one arm over Oliver's shoulder, laughed and said, "I don't believe it even now. I must tell Margaret at once." He was about to drag Oliver into the private rooms which he occupied with his wife when it occurred to him that he had not yet had a good view of his nephew. He found some flint and struck a light, and soon all the candles were blazing.

"You're a handsome devil, Oliver," the general said, looking approvingly at the youngster who filled out his uniform and stood there at attention, his face lighted with smiles. "You still had milk on your mouth when I saw you last, and now, by God, you're a man—and a captain, too. It's not a bad mustache either."

The general was so delighted that he burst out laughing and clapped Oliver several times on the shoulder. Now, instead of the weariness which had assailed him previously, there was a look of extraordinary youthfulness on the general's face. He was dimly aware that his own sudden youthfulness had been communicated to him by Oliver. In the candlelight Oliver shone like some glossy animal, full of young eager life. The yellow mustache shone like gold wires, and the eyes, which were the most striking thing about Oliver, filled with light. But most of all the general was attracted by the energy in the man. There was something about Oliver which reminded the general of a young leopard.

"We'll have a great deal to talk about, my dear boy," the general said. Then suddenly he caught sight of the dispatch box resting on the table, and his face fell. With Oliver by his side he opened the box with his own key, nervously removed the papers and then sat down heavily in his chair. As he read the instructions of the government in London the blood drained from his face.

Once Oliver said: "May I leave now, sir?"

The general, without moving his head, said, "Stay here, my boy," and went on reading, so absorbed in the papers on the table that he had almost forgotten the presence of his nephew. Pale, miserable, his hands shaking as he held the papers up to the light, the general would sometimes walk

absent-mindedly toward the dark uncurtained windows. At
last he said quietly, "I'm sure Margaret will want to see you.
Go, my boy—go and pay your respects to her, and then of
course you must join us at the ball tonight."

As Oliver stood at the door before leaving the Blue Room
he saw an old man hunched over the table, where all the papers were scattered as though snow had fallen.

On his way down the stairs the general reflected that all
the arrangements for the ball were in order. The candles were
lighted. Every lackey stood in place. Through one of the tall
doors painted white and gold he caught a glimpse of a young
woman in flowered blue brocade, wearing a turban of the
same material from which rose a plume of perfectly white
feathers; and then she moved away, yielding her place to an
officer, brilliant as a gaming cock in red, white and gold. It
was like a scene from a play. The fiddlers were tuning up,
and he could hear the black bearers as they brought the
chairs of arriving guests to the alleyway; then there would be
the soft sound of the chair legs falling on marble. It was like
a play he had seen many times before, all familiar to him,
every detail in place, the actors perfectly rehearsed. He fingered
the cut along his cheek.

When they were halfway down the stairs he turned to
Oliver and said, "Mind, don't breathe a word of it."

"I won't, sir."

"I don't want to spoil their appetites," the general explained. "They'll have enough to worry about."

Oliver De Lancey swayed a little and held onto the banister for support.

"Still got your sea legs, I see," the general commented.
Taking Oliver by the arm, he led him straight into the ballroom, where the women were admiring themselves in the
mirrors and the officers were grouped in the center of the
floor. The chandeliers blazed. The Negro servants were

continually moving in and out. On the curved balcony the
Negro musicians, dressed in such splendid array of colors
that they resembled the officers, were still strumming their
instruments or earnestly setting the music pages in order on
the little iron stands that resembled nothing so much as grid-
irons. But what was more important was the atmosphere
of hectic excitement in the room—the flushed cheeks of the
young women and the loud, bright conversations of the officers whose epaulets glittered like diamonds under the lamps.
And among them all, the general commented to himself, there
was hardly anyone to compare with young Oliver De Lancey.

As he paused at the entrance of the ballroom, wearing his
silver peruke, the blue watered-silk ribbon across his chest,
the heavy blue coat with embroidery of gold wire, his spotless flowered knee breeches, the general was content with
himself. He was sorry that Margaret would be late, but then
she was always late; and besides, she had been in the sickroom
with the boy. They had lost a child six months before. It had
shaken him and reduced Margaret to a ghost of herself, but
somehow she had recovered. "Poor Margaret," he whispered, and nodded absent-mindedly to a man in a coat of
lilac poplin who was bowing from the gilt doorway.

Then something very curious happened to the general. He
was about to enter the ballroom when everything began to
swim before his eyes. His officers were standing there—
Smith, De Bernière, Pitcairn, Kemble, Small, all excellent
fellows—but they were all swimming in front of his eyes.
He pulled himself up sharply with a great effort, and then—
he did not know how it happened—he found himself leaning against the doorpost, Oliver holding him up by the arms.

"Are you all right, sir?" Oliver said, breathing hard, his
slightly puffy cheeks looking more puffy than ever. There
were little bubbles of silvery sweat on his fair yellow mustache.

"Quite all right," the general answered gruffly. "It's
damned hot, though."

"Yes, sir."

"It's the heat, isn't it?"

"Yes, sir."

"Never knew it to be so damned hot in April before."

"You're quite right, sir."

Something in Oliver's tone made him look up sharply. It dawned on him that he might have had a heart attack. He wondered what they were all thinking about him, for he must have been leaning for an unconscionable time against the doorpost.

"I tripped, Oliver, do you hear?" the general said in an unnaturally loud voice, his mind moving quickly. He decided to limp a little as he crossed the room. His blood had congealed in his veins. Now it seemed to be springing free, and there was nothing in the world to compare with the sudden exhilaration which came over him. He entered the room, pretending to be in deep conversation with Oliver, his head bent low, and all the time he was looking up at the people in the ballroom through his bushy eyebrows. The officers bowed as he passed. The young women half curtsied to him, and the fiddlers struck up "God Save the King"; for was he not the royal governor? He pretended to dislike such ceremonies, but secretly he was pleased by them. His fine, slightly protuberant blue eyes flashed a little as he glanced round the ballroom—flashed with fire and tenderness when they alighted on the glossy shoulders of the young women and with a humorous sternness when he caught the gaze of his officers. He was absurdly proud of them all, and it was his custom to say that he had never known a better bunch of soldiers. Weren't they exquisitely polite to the women, cheerfully loud-mouthed when they gambled and roaring mad when they were drunk? There was not one of them who would not be taken for a man of good breeding. "God bless you all, God bless you all," the general said as the last chords of the anthem faded, and it pleased him to think he had spoken these words in the appropriate tone of gruffness expected from him.

Swinging round in the center of the floor and addressing first the ladies and then the officers, he said, "I take pleasure in presenting my nephew, Captain Oliver De Lancey of the Grenadiers, who has arrived in Boston on the *Nautilus* to procure—" and here the general paused, looked searchingly at his audience and then said quickly—"to procure horses for his regiment."

"An excellent reason," responded an officer with enormous silver epaulets and with a French accent.

Everyone knew that Oliver was the general's favorite nephew, or rather the nephew of the general's wife, and everyone knew also that Oliver had not come solely to procure horses. They were pleased to see the thickset youth. He possessed a tendency to fat, but a slight plumpness was regarded as a sign of excellence in a man; and besides this, his delightful innocence and awkwardness pleased them. The ladies in particular were delighted, for they saw at once that nothing would be easier than to make him blush.

"I pray you enjoyed a good journey." Lord Percy, wearing a shimmering wine-red silk coat, advanced toward Oliver and smiled with that particular smile possessed by the Percys for generations, a gentle and secretive smile that put everyone at ease.

"Oh, I did indeed."

Lord Percy turned immediately toward the general and said quietly and apparently with the utmost sincerity, "You do us a great honor, m'lord, to bring such a brilliant officer to our camp." And then, seeing that the general's interest had been taken by a young woman who had immediately plucked at his sleeve and begged for an introduction "at once, on this very moment, my dear Lord Governor, otherwise I shall surely perish," he took Oliver by the arm and said, "Look, do you know anyone here? I'm Percy, and there is Sir Frederick Haldimand, and this is Colonel Smith. We're the best of friends. Upon my soul, you would hardly believe it when we go winebibbing, but we are frolicsome. It is a habit of ours. . . . You are staying?"

"A few days."

"A pity. You may miss the fun," Lord Percy said darkly, and all the time he was steering Oliver toward the wall, from where he would be able to observe the general without being himself observed. Though he was delighted to meet Oliver, of whom the general had occasionally spoken, he was infinitely more interested in observing the general's expression. He could guess what had happened. There had been an interval of about an hour between the time when Oliver arrived with the dispatch case and the time when the general descended the spiral staircase. Lord Percy had trained himself to observe the changing features of men. He alone in the small ballroom had seen the general falling into a faint when he reached the bottom of the stairs. He had seen Oliver supporting him, and he had observed how the general limped painfully as he entered the room and immediately afterward forgot to limp; for the fiddlers had struck up and it was one of the general's minor faults that he could never prevent himself from blushing with the utmost pleasure when the anthem was played and everyone bowed or curtsied to him as the representative of the king, the Lord Governor of the Province of Massachusetts. And Lord Percy was particularly pleased because the news appeared to be good. He liked the general, and he had completely forgotten the incident in the bathroom. Indeed it was impossible to recognize in the handsome, masterly general with the heavy upper lip and the bushy eyebrows the squat, nearly naked figure streaked with blood who had been his companion a little more than two hours before.

Turning toward Oliver, Percy said, "The ladies are all of a dither, of course. They rarely see strange faces. Now, which one may I have the honor of presenting to you? And remember, I insist that you call me Percy."

"You are excessively kind," Oliver said, gazing earnestly

at the beauties ranged against the wall, for the general, with
his hands behind his back, was stomping along the parquet
exactly as though he were reviewing them—passing along
the line, peering down into their faces, sometimes so close
that it must have been possible for him to see well down into
the region of their stomachs. Sometimes he would cock his
head to one side with all the air of a wise priest listening at
the confessional.

"As you observe," said Lord Percy, "the lord governor
adores the ladies."

Oliver bridled. There was the faintest suggestion that the
general did more than adore them.

"He is a man of sentiment," Lord Percy went on. "There
are depths to his nature which none of us has ever fathomed,
and I can see that you share those depths. I am not flattering
you, my dear Oliver. It is simply that I have come to feel
for your uncle the most blessed affection. He rules sternly,
but wisely. The rebels are respectful to him. He has a claim
on our hearts and on our affections."

"No, no, you are going altogether too far, Percy." It was
the general's voice. Lord Percy had plunged so deep into the
confidential description of the general's qualities that he had
failed to observe him swinging swiftly across the room, to
take Oliver by the arm with the words: "You must come to
meet Sir Frederick. He is an absolute military genius. Another Gustavus Vasa." Immediately Oliver found himself
confronting a tall, thickset man in a brilliant scarlet uniform
a little too large for him, and there was something curiously
disturbing in the way he wore his uniform. He was more
showy than the others. The buttons were a little too large,
the cravat a little too florid, the epaulets nearly twice as large
as any other officer's. He had a heavy peasant face, with a
long jaw and piercing black eyes. "General Sir Frederick
Haldimand," the general said gravely, "may I have the honor
to present my nephew, Captain Oliver De Lancey?"

"Ah! So he is the young man with the dispatch case?" Haldimand said, and there was something keen and determined in those small black eyes. He spoke English slowly and with difficulty, yet always grammatically. "And what is in the dispatch case?" Haldimand laughed, going as usual to the root of the problem.

General Gage shrugged his shoulders, and for one instant his eyes looked heavy, blurred, without life. It was as though some appalling weight of doom had suddenly fallen on him. "We'll talk about it later," he said. "The Blue Room—at eleven o'clock."

That was all, for immediately afterward General Gage went on his way to talk with the Boston Tories and their wives. Haldimand had detected his misery and guessed that Gage had spent only a few minutes with the letters from London. He turned to Oliver, sized him up—first a penetrating look at the face, then a study of the eyes and chin, then a prolonged observation of the way in which he held himself, from the brightly polished boots to the yellow hair tied at the nape with black ribbon. Oliver, in turn, was puzzled by the tense stare of Haldimand, and he was surprised to come upon a general in the British Army who spoke with so foreign an accent and wore so extravagant a uniform.

"And what are your views of Boston, Captain De Lancey?" Haldimand asked.

"I have no views," Oliver answered honestly enough. "I left the ship but an hour ago in the dark. I did see a few pretty faces as I rode up to Province House."

"Then you are interested in women?"

"I saw a forest of church steeples, too," Oliver said, avoiding the question. "And the town's clean—I observed that— and well lighted, and a commendable place, but I prefer New York." He wondered how long this ridiculous conversation with Haldimand would last. He knew that Haldimand was testing him.

Haldimand in turn was irritated because he could never make a junior officer talk naturally. He lacked Gage's grace, his air of naturalness. Still, he felt a sensation of pity for the young officer who had stepped off the *Nautilus* and found himself immediately whirled into the bedlam of a ballroom where no one was dancing, the governor appeared without his wife, and there was a taut look on the faces of the officers.

Oliver had not seen the letters from London, but he could guess their contents. He was the messenger of ill tidings, and though he had never been in Boston before, he knew enough about the situation to realize that the British garrison was hopelessly outnumbered by the American militia and minutemen. Some officers paused to nod at him. Their scarlet trimmings, gold epaulets, white knee breeches were carefully laundered; they held themselves well; there was not one of them who did not look as though he were in full command of himself. This puzzled Oliver a little, for he knew that the port of Boston was now idle, that the rebels refused to work for the British and Boston was already almost a besieged city. "Damned fine-looking men," Oliver told himself, "and they're all sitting on a volcano."

The general, most uncharacteristically, had forgotten to introduce Oliver to the guests. That strange moment at the entrance to the ballroom had left him in a peculiar dreamlike state. It was, the general kept telling himself, not a heart attack, but the first intimations of one. He must be careful. Meanwhile he would pretend that nothing had happened.

Lord Percy took Oliver in hand. "Come," he said, "let me introduce you to some of the beauties of Boston," and he searched the gathering for some particularly splendid creature he would offer to Oliver. Soon Oliver found himself bowing to a young lady whose name, he learned, was Eugénie de Malmédy-Armagnac. She wore a blue flowered dress with black lace; her hair was the color of corn and her eyelashes were very dark. She spoke English with the faintest of French accents. Oliver was wholly captivated.

"A treasure. The most perfect treasure in Boston," Lord Percy whispered. "And she is not married, my dear Oliver."

Beautiful as she was, Oliver could not gaze at her for more than a moment at a time. Her eyes were the color of morning seas, but there was something curiously dangerous about the darkness of those lashes; and though the mouth was wanton enough, there was the strangest expression on her face, as if she intended to convey affection and distance at the same time. She smiled perpetually—almost a wooden smile or else she was so completely delighted with the wild world that she could not prevent herself from offering this perpetual smile of benediction.

"Oliver De Lancey has just come off the *Nautilus*," Lord Percy explained unnecessarily. "He knows nothing of Boston, my dear. Absolutely nothing. And so I shall place him at your mercy. I beg you to show him the sights. He has come to buy horses, but I assure you he will have time on his hands."

"Indeed, ma'am," Oliver said haltingly, "it is a great pleasure."

"Don't talk about pleasure, Oliver. This is one thing which Eugénie cares nothing for, isn't that so? Yes, she is cool to all pleasures, but she makes amends by her adoration of music. She plays the harpsichord divinely. She is a gifted painter. She understands sculpture. . . ."

He was about to go on to elaborate on all Eugénie's virtues when there occurred a sudden hush in the ballroom. Margaret Gage was entering. She had come very slowly down the stairway, more like a queen than the wife of the governor of a province, very tall and stately, dressed in a gown of royal purple, superbly in command of herself, although she had left the sickbed of her youngest child only a moment ago.

Her husband advanced to take her hand. Again the musicians struck up, the officers and notables of Boston bowed and the women curtsied; then the huge Negro in the scarlet-and-gold uniform of a major-domo announced: "My lords, ladies and gentlemen, the dinner is served!"

Sitting at the head of the table, watching the play of candlelight on the bare shoulders of the women and the decorations of the men, General Gage felt profoundly at ease. Gone was the sense of terror which had swept over him at the entrance to the ballroom. He had always liked acting the host. Today he liked it more than ever, for the wine was excellent, the dishes though few were admirably cooked, and conversation flowed. No one spoke about the rebels; the subject was delicate and besides, it had been discussed so often that there was nothing left to be said. The general smiled at the portly Tory merchants, but it was a smile without warmth; he reserved his warmth for his officers. In this room hung with portraits of himself and his wife, with Italian statues on the highboy, he felt, as he often felt toward evening, that there were few pleasures greater than the sight of his officers in candlelight, to listen to them, to take no part in their conversations—simply to be *there*. Oliver was sitting beside Eugénie. Well, he could ask nothing better. Eugénie was the daughter of the richest of the Tory merchants; she was beautiful and high-spirited, an ideal match for Oliver if the boy had sense enough to throw her off her feet. Margaret was smiling at him from the other end of the table. He winked at her and then turned to Haldimand, who was sitting by his side.

"Well, Haldimand, a toast between ourselves," the general said, raising a glass of port.

"Between ourselves, eh?" Haldimand replied. "Is this a time for toasts?"

"There couldn't be a better."

Haldimand gave his little barking laugh. "Then I'll drink

to you, and a pox on your enemies! You have enough, Tom."
He paused and said very seriously, "More than enough."

"Damme, let's just drink between friends. Our enemies
can care for themselves. I'm in no mood to give hostages to
fortune tonight. Fortune's a knave. I've been through too
many wars. Now I want to kick off my shoes and sit with
my dogs and Margaret before a fire. I'm fifty-three. It's a
damned good age to be. And you're a damned good friend."

Haldimand could never remember a time when Gage had
spoken so close to the nerve. In the candlelight the long
curving cut on his face showed bleakly, the little white lip of
the wound throwing a shadow like a scimitar. Gage's hands
had been trembling when he clasped them over the plate and
said grace in a firm, commanding voice. Perhaps the strain
was beginning to tell: Haldimand didn't know. He drank
the toast in claret and automatically reached out to replenish
the cup.

"I'll drink another one," Haldimand said. "You're worth
a damned sight more than two drinks, Tom."

"That's good of you."

"I'd drink a tubful if I thought I could honor you more."

The general laughed and started to put out his hand in a
gesture of affection, but he took hold of himself in time. He
heard Margaret's pleasantly high-pitched voice. Lord Percy
was discussing the history of the first settlers with his neighbor, Countess de Leslie, and Henry De Bernière, the general's
favorite among all the young officers, was describing with
excited gestures the fighting in Canada. All the time, at the
back of Gage's mind, like faint warning shadows, was the
thought of the dispatch case. He said under his breath, one
eyebrow cocked, "The decisions must be made tonight."

"What decisions?"

"God knows. We must make them together. Upon my
soul, there never was a time when I had less heart for the
things we are going to do. I am hoping for some news from

Dr. Church, but I do not hope too much. We work in the dark, eh?"

"Forget the dark," Haldimand said. "I'll drink to your honor."

Haldimand poured himself another glass, not waiting for the Negro to do it for him, and suddenly he was aware that there was silence down the whole length of the table. It happened often, those curious moments when every thought, every word is held in suspense—the goddesses have entered the room, they said in Switzerland—and he wondered whether anything of General Gage's whispered conversation had somehow been communicated to them. . . . There was the faintest look of fear on Haldimand's face, a sagging at the corner of the lips, a curious thrust of the jaw. But no, the conversation went on, the Negro servants were perpetually attending to their desires, and very distinctly he heard the guards tracing out their eight steps in the courtyard below.

Oliver was not so much captivated as completely enthralled. Eugénie's bare shoulders, the way she tilted her face a little to one side, the mockery in the veiled eyes—all these delighted him; and as often happens when you are entirely enthralled by the presence of someone, you become aware of the dreadful moment when it will be necessary to leave the beloved presence long before that moment arrives. Oliver was cursing himself for a fool for being able to spend only three or four days in Boston.

"Dear heart," he murmured. "Is it some fatality of the stars which has brought me to your feet?"

Eugénie laughed. "How earnest you are! And then, you are not at my feet. You are nibbling cold salad, my dear, and I will say this, you are nibbling heartily."

"Lovers are always hungry," Oliver replied, gazing into her eyes.

He hardly knew what he was saying, and he hardly believed she was sitting beside him. It was too much to hope for. It was incredible that he was talking to her at all. A strange day: arriving in Boston at sunset, with a blustering westerly wind, and the opening of the dispatch case; then this strange creature who spoke English with a ravishing French accent. He glanced briefly to the head of the table. The general was leaning forward, deep in conversation with Haldimand. Lord Percy was leaning back in his chair while two Boston beauties hung on his words. The colonel had a passion for hunting. He was discussing a hunt on his estate in England. There was a pleasant hum of conversation all round the table, the clink of glasses, the silent footfalls of the impassive Negro waiters.

"I drink to your eyes, dear Eugénie," Oliver found himself saying. "To your eyes and the light shining in them."

The stiff words came from his heart. Eugénie blushed prettily. She was more than a little taken by the young captain, and it amused her to observe his eagerness. Afterward they would dance, and he would escort her to her sedan chair. . . . How could he learn to please her? He must know more about her, much more than she would ever tell. And so it would be necessary to discover a confidant, someone who knew Boston well and would plead his case if necessary. He dared not even glance at her any more. Her address? This surely was easy: the general's secretary would know, since presumably she had been invited to Province House. How young she was! He felt feverish, and the wine was beginning to make him dizzy. The general was deep in conversation with Haldimand, and Margaret Gage was talking to a young officer of Marines. There were perhaps thirty people at the long table. To Oliver they were all delightful, and all of them behaved with cultivated manners.

Eugénie was secretly amused by the young officer, who was so demonstrably at her mercy. She would look up suddenly and find him watching her; his eyes would melt, become confused, cloudy with the pain of love. He was thickset and

perhaps a little too fat, but there was a quality of gentleness
in his attentions to her. She spun out her fan, held it to her
face, peered over the lacy rim and said, "But you have paid
me altogether too many attentions, Captain De Lancey. I
must hope they are honorable."

"They are indeed, ma'am!"

"And it were better if they remain so."

"Surely, ma'am."

"Then I shall permit you to see me during the days you
spend in Boston." She smiled behind the fan and gently
lowered her lids.

Oliver did not know what to make of this demonstration
of affection. Perhaps she was playing with him. He trusted
no woman. He desired her more than he had ever desired
anyone else; and in the confused moments while he waited
for the dinner to end he undressed her, clothed her again and
undressed her in his imagination. All the time he was careful not to show by any outward signs that he was determined
on nothing less than possession. In this he failed, for she
moved a little closer to him and said, " 'Twere a greater
cunning to conceal the emotions of tenderness, my dear Captain De Lancey."

"They are concealed well enough, ma'am. The only emotions I have are of the most devout respect."

"Well said, but the eyes say something altogether contrary. I do not say it is a fault or a virtue. I only say that it
is there. You have the most revealing eyes, for a man."

It was useless. He gave up in despair, looked at her
frankly. There was something in his bold look which suggested that she need have no fear, for like so many lovers he
was incapable of calculation or secrecy.

She leaned still closer. "Then I am bold to declare that I
shall not fear you, Captain De Lancey. You are all kindness
to women, that I know. Upon my soul, I believe I can trust
you."

"You can, ma'am, of that you may be sure."

"Yes, because you are the soul of discretion and decorum I shall trust you. I shall trust you to the extent that I shall let you dance with me."

He couldn't quite make up his mind about her. There was malice somewhere, though the malice was gentle enough. She loved to hold the fan lightly over the pure swelling curve of her white breasts, or over her shoulders, or over her face. Her beauty was the sort that would be enhanced by jewelry; it surprised him that she wore so little of it.

The sweets were being served, the dinner was coming to an end, there would follow the inevitable interval when the women departed into another room and the men remained to smoke their pipes and drink liqueurs and tell stories. Oliver dreaded this moment, but like so much that he dreaded, this interval never came to pass. Mrs. Gage rose, and at the same moment her husband rose. The whole company made its way to a small anteroom near the ballroom. Coffee was served. More candles were lighted. Through the open doorway they saw the white pilasters and the gold leaf gleaming in the ball-room. The whist tables were already being set out. The fiddlers were strumming again. From time to time the general and Mrs. Gage, sitting in high-backed golden-brocade chairs, summoned one of the guests. First came a merchant, then another. The general asked them about conditions in Boston, and always these talks were carried on in whispers. After the merchants and notables came the turn of the officers. Vice-Admiral Seymour spoke to the general at length, but there was nothing secret in what they said to each other; they shook with laughter. And often it was observed that the general would gaze tenderly in the direction of his Margaret and whisper some nonsense to her, whereupon they both laughed and exchanged those enviable glances of comprehension which come only to those who have been happily married for many years.

"And here's young Oliver," the general said. "He is already captivated by Boston," he went on, glancing at Eugénie, whom Oliver led by the hand. "Four days in Boston, and how, pray, will you spend your precious time? You must see all the sights, of course. We must make an itinerary for you."

"I am sure, my lord," Eugénie declared, "that he will be too busy rounding up blood mares to have time to see our small city. Besides, one can see all Boston in an afternoon."

The general frowned. He liked Boston, and it pained him that she should think that everything could be so easily seen.

"Nonsense, dear Eugénie. I have been here more than a year and I have yet to learn the most elementary things about Boston. You have lived here all your life and you know it well. It would be a pleasing service if you showed Oliver a little of this city."

"Then you like our city, my lord?"

"I have a passion for Boston," the general replied. "God knows, I would love to settle here and end my days in it."

Once again the strange weakness that had overcome him at the entrance to the ballroom returned. He put out his hand for support. The mantelshelf was near. He smiled to hide his confusion. For an instant he saw Eugénie swimming toward him, then she swam away. Everything became instantaneously brighter, and the sound of music—the musicians were striking up again—became unendurably loud. The weakness passed, leaving him pale and shaken, and Eugénie was surprised to see his face turn white as a drumskin except for the long red gash where he had cut himself.

"My lord, you are not well," Eugénie said, going to his assistance.

With a pure effort of will the general swung back into full consciousness. "Nonsense, nonsense! You will delight me . . . dear Eugénie . . . dance with Oliver."

The dancers were beginning to flock over the recently

powdered floor. The horns and fiddles grew louder. Plumes, powdered wigs, bare shoulders, scarlet coats and brocaded dresses caught the glittering light of the candelabra; and sometimes there would come from a jeweled headdress or a diamond necklace brilliant gleams which raced across the ballroom. The general beat time with his hands, sitting on the gold-brocade throne of an armchair, leaning forward, unable to take his eyes away from the young couple dancing together. Sometimes he even beat time with his foot. He suddenly felt very old. He was shivering, wondering when he would feel faint again. Little shivers were running up his spine; the memory of the black box came like a dark shadow. Where would it end? Soon, much sooner than anyone expected, there would be changes. How great the changes would be no one would know till the time came. The orchestra was playing for the quadrille a lilting song, and very soon the dancers found the words:

> *What happy golden days were those*
> *When I was in my prime!*
> *The lasses took delight in me,*
> *I was so neat and fine;*
> *I roved about from fair to fair,*
> *Likewise from town to town,*
> *Until I married me a wife*
> *And the world turned upside down.*

The general observed that they sang the song superbly, while retaining the measure of the dance, and their faces were very bright. Eugénie and Oliver were singing louder than the rest. "God bless them," he whispered, and then he made a sign to Captain Kemble, who came out of the throng and bent low to hear the general's whispered commands. "Tell them to come to the Blue Room at eleven o'clock." There was no need to say anything else. Kemble would know exactly whom to whisper to. He turned away, making the faintest of smiles, and went slowly round the room, whispering the message casually—so casually indeed that the merchants could not fail to notice that something was afoot. All the time the general was beating time to the song with his foot. He leaned over and whispered to Margaret. "You are looking so beautiful tonight, my dear."

"And I vow you are the handsomest lover," Margaret said, but she did not face him. She, too, was looking toward Oliver and Eugénie. "Do you think it is a good thing?" she asked a moment later.

"You mean Oliver and Eugénie?"

"What else could I mean? After all, Oliver is here only for a day or two. It is hardly fair to disturb him so greatly."

"He is English and she is American, or if you like, both American and French. They are the best marriages," the general declared. "Let them have their enjoyment, Margaret. Tell me, have you ever seen two people so demonstrably in love? It warms the cockles of the heart."

Margaret was silent, reserved, a little statuesque. She was thinking of the child tossing in bed upstairs, hating fever, hating even the thought of fever: the pale face on the damp pillows. It was all pretense. She had no right to be here, and yet, such was her position, she dared not be anywhere else. Little did they know what she went through, day after day, worrying over her children, all her reserve coming from this: She wanted continually to cry out in pain, and at the same time refused to show her feelings. When she thought of Oliver and Eugénie she thought of the years of marriage ahead.

Long before eleven o'clock the dances came to an end. The officers would go to the taverns or their barracks, the merchants would return to their porticoed houses, the ballroom would once again be deserted. The general stood in the doorway, bowing as the guests departed, smiling casually and discreetly, very warm and gentle to the women, unconsciously reserved toward the men. Phrases came from the courtyard below where the chairs were moved up to take the guests.

" . . . an excellently good dance . . . the general was looking
well . . . of course Margaret always is a little pale . . . I'll say
this for the British governor, he knows how to entertain. . . ."

Well, he was doing his best. It pleased him to stand beside
the huge white-and-gold-painted door with the lion and unicorn emblazoned in gold and to see the flares throwing immense shadows on the damask curtains of the chairs. His
officers were behind him. They would be the last to leave.
Eugénie curtsied and smiled up at him, and once more he
heard himself saying, "How beautiful, how beautiful!" He
hardly knew what he was saying. He was thinking of those
merchants who had come to dinner. Most of them were loyal
and good men, and some of them were spies for the rebels;
but it was better not to think of that. Oliver was accompanying Eugénie to her chair. He saw them holding hands, and
he thought he saw Eugénie slipping a note—a little twist of
paper—into Oliver's hand, but he wasn't sure. He was happy
with Oliver. It would be pleasant to have him at Province
House, and perhaps they could arrange, before Oliver left for
New York, another social evening—perhaps some kind of
entertainment. The presence of Oliver helped him to forget
his responsibilities. As he went up the spiral staircase with
Margaret on his arm, a tune bothered him. His mind went
running after it, as a hunting dog will go after a wounded
hare. Suddenly his free hand went to the wound on his cheek
and he said to himself, "Well, that's true enough—'The
World Turned Upside Down.' It's a good name for Boston,
I declare." He turned to Margaret and asked quietly, "How's
the boy?"

"Poorly, dear."

"Oh, he'll get better."

"You always say that," Margaret answered with a note of
hysteria in her voice.

"We must do what we can," he answered softly. "It's all
we can ever do."

Then arm in arm they went to the boy's bedroom.

CHAPTER 2

A Journey in the Dark

Follow me quickly. Eugénie.

Oliver read the message scribbled on a slip of blue paper, and then all his blood seemed to mount in a wave to his face. He could hardly breathe. His hands shook, and he was afraid the strange trepidation might have been observed. But no, the officers were standing on the steps bowing and smiling at the women as they entered the chairs. The great red flambeaux were smoking, and there was a smell of pitch on the air. The moon had not yet risen, but the church spires glinted with occasional blue flickers of lightning. It was pleasant to stand there, looking down the street, the chairs, with their flambeaux, making little splashes of colored light. He could feel the soft sea wind coming in.

"I declare you've made a conquest already," a young lieutenant was saying at his elbow. "I'm De Bernière—Ensign De Bernière."

"Wearing the uniform of a lieutenant," Oliver remarked with his lips pouting. He was not accustomed to being addressed so familiarly by younger officers.

De Bernière laughed, his frank young face suddenly catching the candlelight. "Oh, there are special reasons."

"What are they?"

"Mostly secret," De Bernière answered, "and no worse for being secret. As for the young lady, I'll wager she's the most beautiful woman in this town. Well, beauty is dangerous."

It was on the tip of Oliver's tongue to say, "Damn your impertinence!" but instead he said, "I'll ask your opinion whenever I want it," and was about to turn away when the young ensign gripped him by the arm.

"I meant no offense, Captain. We're in the devil of a mess. I want to help. Don't you believe me?"

"Yes, I believe you," Oliver said ironically, and once again he made an effort to escape.

"Then I beg you to excuse me a little longer. She gave you a message, didn't she? I could swear she gave you a message which spoke of a rendezvous somewhere. I want to tell you it's dangerous to accept."

Oliver's temper was rising. Another word and he thought he would be inviting the impertinent young ensign to meet him at swords; but there was something authoritative in De Bernière's manner. "By God's grace——" There was a curse on his lips already formed, but it died as quickly as it had arisen. De Bernière took him by the arm and led him to an alcove. Through the corners of his eyes Oliver saw the general already making his way up the stairs.

"Oh, you don't know the half of it," the ensign went on, oblivious of the rage mounting in Oliver's face. "Will it make things easier to understand if I say we are trapped— trapped like dogs, and we daren't fight it out? There's not a thing we can do with good consciences except to sit here and wait for an explosion, and God help us all when it occurs! Does this mean anything to you?"

Oliver nodded, and fished in his pocket for his pipe. It was not there, and he made a childish gesture of annoyance. He was more than ever annoyed with De Bernière. "Go on," he said.

"I could go on for a month of Sundays, but what's the use? You're not attending to me. You're thinking of your conquest." He looked straight into Oliver's eyes. "Now aren't

you? And you're thinking, What the devil has this impertinent ensign to do with me on a night like this?"

"Blast you to hell!" said Oliver.

"Will you listen to me?"

"I'll give you one minute."

"That's better. . . . You are new to this town, but you
ought to know there are spies everywhere—spies and worse.
They'll throw you into the tidewater with chains round your
ankles if they catch you. They've done it before. The general has given orders that not one of our officers is allowed
to be in the streets at night without what he calls a 'sufficient
guard.' The general treasures the honor of the British name.
He won't allow us to do a thing which isn't in General Orders. He'd prefer that a loyalist should be tarred and feath-
ered than that any rebel should come to harm. That's how
we live here."

There was a hint of bitterness in the ensign's voice. Oliver
kept thinking of the general slowly making his way upstairs,
the weight of his immense responsibilities, the suffering
which twisted the corners of the general's mouth. *The general treasures the honor of the British name*—that was true
enough!

"Do you still want to go after her?" De Bernière said in a
low voice. "There's nothing to prevent you except the danger—it's real danger. I'm not trying to prevent you, sir."

Oliver was silent. He could still smell the perfume which
hung about Eugénie, still see in the eyes of his imagination
the soft light glittering on her bare shoulders, the strange
look in those pure blue eyes shaded by black eyelashes.

"It's up to you, sir," De Bernière was saying. "If you're
determined to go, I'd advise you to carry a brace of pistols."

By this time the Negro servants in Province House were
beginning to douse the lamps, but none came near the tran-
quil corner where the captain and the ensign were talking in

hushed tones. Through the window Oliver caught a glimpse of a small yard where a red-coated sentry wearing a high, pointed Grenadier's hat was pacing to and fro. The soft peal of a church bell striking the quarter told him that ten minutes had passed since he last caught a glimpse of Eugénie pulling up her skirts as she bent low to enter the chair. "It's devilish hot," he said, for the storm, which had long hovered over the bay, was drawing closer.

"Then you'll not go, sir?" De Bernière came closer, until Oliver could see every little drop of sweat on the man's forehead.

"I haven't made up my mind yet," Oliver answered, delighted because he was keeping the ensign in a state of uncertainty. "I've a right to do as I please. Even if she is a rebel—— I've thought of that, too, and I've thought of being knifed in the back, and a hundred other things. I'm still not sure of your arguments. A man must make up his own mind." Oliver thrust out his jaw, pulled his coat down, rubbed his knuckles against his buttons.

The storm was coming closer, and the house was silent except for the creaking of some timbers. Oliver was trying to think what to do, and at the same time he was oppressed by the gathering heat, the excitement of his talk with De Bernière, the odd sense of disaster which had been with him ever since he saw the general faltering outside the ballroom. A little more than a year before, in England, he had visited General Gage, then on holiday. The general had been gay and charming, a great red-faced bulldog of a man surrounded by his adoring family, with a permanent twinkle in his eye. Now the twinkle had gone, the cheeks sagged, there were blue lines under his eyes and a terrible razor cut along his cheek. Obviously he was losing his cunning, plagued by the miseries of being cooped up in Boston, plagued by responsibilities.

"I'll go now," the ensign was saying.

"Yes, go to the devil!" Oliver said abruptly, and without glancing in which direction De Bernière went, he made his way up the stairs.

The candles were lighted, the bed was made, the room smelled of fresh paint. Sea-scented wind came through the open window. Everything in the small bedroom delighted Oliver except the smell of paint, which made him dizzy. There were lace pillows. As he sat on the edge of the bed absent-mindedly gazing at the polished floor boards, he said: "Damnable things, lace pillows. They leave a mark on your face." He laughed to himself, but the laughter did not ring true. Somewhere, not far away, he heard Margaret Gage stepping into the room where the sick child lay. He heard whispers, the creaking of a cradle as it was being rocked; then more footsteps, heavier this time, for evidently the general had gone to join Margaret. Oliver threw himself down on the bed and kicked off his boots, being careful that they should make no noise. He would have gone to sleep with the candles still smoking if the window had not rattled in the wind. He went to the window, breathed in a great draft of the fresh stormy air and was about to close it when he saw, deep in the shadow of a wall below, a sedan chair standing there. At first it did not occur to him that it might belong to Eugénie. He was aware only of the silence of the evening, the beauty of the spires, the calm blue-silver stretches of the sea with the frigates bobbing in the waves at anchor; and sometimes there were inexplicable black patches on the moonlit sea—perhaps the wind caused them, or perhaps they were the shadows of clouds. All Boston lay before him, a small town of hills and gardens, silver in the moonlight, with soft shadows playing over walls and leaden roofs. As the moon rose higher the small town began to glitter with a blinding radiance, and all the time the wind was blowing stronger. "God help us all!" he murmured, thinking of the extraordinarily hurt look he had observed in the general's eyes, and he made a movement to close the windows; then, for the first time, he observed a long slender arm waving from the chair. Even then he did not connect it in his mind with Eugénie. He thought someone was signaling—a spy perhaps: the arm kept waving slowly up and down. It was not a man's arm. There was something altogether too graceful in those movements. He stood to one side, hiding among the curtains, and peering through the gap between the curtain and the wall, he saw the arm suddenly withdraw into the darkness. He stood at the window again. The arm came out and began slowly waving again. He stood within the curtains a second time, and once more the arm was withdrawn.

"Well, she's a damnably persistent young woman," Oliver said, and for some reason he strode across the room in his stocking feet to blow out the candles.

His mind was leaping wildly. Everything De Bernière had said was now flashing through his mind in no recognizable order. Moonlight flooded the room. The trunks were piled neatly against the wall—three tin boxes with his name written on them in white paint—and he knew there wasn't a good butcher's knife in any of them. On a night like this a butcher's knife might be more valuable than a pistol. But he found his pistol at last, and having found it, he searched for his cloak. He threw the cloak round his shoulders, and then decided to go to the window. The chair was still there. There was no sign of any bearers. She must have seen him through the slit in the damask covering, for the arm immediately appeared again. His mouth was dry. He moistened his lips with his tongue.

He was wondering how he would get down the stairs of Province House undisturbed when he heard a gentle tapping at the door. The tapping did not frighten him, but he was puzzled by it. Perhaps it was Margaret Gage coming to see whether everything was to his liking and to bid him good

night, but for some reason it occurred to him that it might
be Eugénie. Somehow she was both in the chair and outside
his room. Somewhere far away there came the hum of conversation: the general and his advisers in the Blue Room.
The moon was three quarters full, making every roof a shining mirror, and there was no sign of movement in the town—
only the silver roofs and the silver arm. The tapping went
on. Oliver stepped silently to the door and opened it quickly.
De Bernière stepped in.

"I was just going to bed," Oliver muttered.

"In your cloak?" The ensign smiled and thrust a small
pistol into Oliver's hand. "She's waiting for you," he went
on. "You'd better go. God knows what she's up to, but
you'd better find out."

Oliver was a captain receiving orders from an ensign, and
he gasped at the assurance in the young man's voice. He
gasped again when De Bernière suddenly went on all fours
and crept toward the curtains. He peered out, and then returned in the same manner.

"This is the maddest thing I ever set eyes upon!" Oliver
exclaimed.

De Bernière laughed. "Oh, there are madder things. In
our time we've gone out disguised and searched the whole
countryside. And we've seen evidence of treachery everywhere. They're poor mad devils—and so are we!"

"Don't you trust the king's army?" Oliver asked. It had
suddenly occurred to him that he had no reason to trust De
Bernière. He knew nothing about him, and there were reasons enough for believing that De Bernière himself might be
a traitor. Why the secrecy? Why the long whispered conversation in the alcove? And then he looked down at the little
silver pistol in his hand, glinting in the moonlight. Though
he was confused, he still had enough presence of mind to say,
"What company are you?"

"Light Infantry company of the Tenth—Henry De Bernière

at your service." The ensign smiled. "And for God's sake come quickly. She won't wait much longer."

Oliver put on his boots, dropped the pistol into the inner pocket of the cape and followed De Bernière down the stairs. Nearly all the candles were out. The air was still full of the bitter smell of burned wicks and candle grease. De Bernière led him down a long corridor. At the end of the corridor a guard was dozing, but he jumped to his feet when he heard their quiet footsteps. "Those damnable guards have got a sixth sense," the ensign muttered. "They can sleep on their feet, but if they hear a mouse creep, they're instantly awake. You can see we're well guarded." Beyond the guard they came to a small iron-studded door. De Bernière flung it open, waved his hand and said, "Find out what you can— that's the important thing."

Oliver found himself in the dark street alone, dazed and a little frightened, wondering how on earth he had come to this place where the damp leaked from the walls. "It's a fool's errand," he told himself. At that moment a church tower began to ring the half-hour, and soon afterward the other bells began to ring their solemn strokes. He whispered to himself: "Dear God, if I am a fool, let me be wise in my folly." He slipped across the street, keeping to the shadows, and it was only then that he recognized where he was: he saw the little alleyway with the waiting chair. Once again there was a long white arm stretched out, waving gently.   .

There was no one else in the chair, no one hiding behind it, only the four Negro bearers hiding in the shadows in their full livery. Eugénie pulled the curtains aside.

"At your service, ma'am," Oliver whispered, seeing her face pale against the dark.

"Step in quickly," Eugénie said softly. "For God's love, don't stand there!"

He pulled the black door open and sat beside her, listening quietly to her breathing. She was out of breath, as though she had been running. But of course she had not been running; she had been waiting, and she had almost lost hope that Oliver would come with her. Grunting, the Negroes began to lift the heavy chair, the handles creaking under the weight. They moved slowly, all the while keeping close to the walls. It was dark in the chair—dark and musty and scented. The curtains were thick with dust; they were always flapping against him. He could not make out the pattern of them, and he could not even make out the outlines of Eugénie's face. But he could feel the warmth flowing from her, and he knew by the sound of her voice that she had turned her head toward him. His uneasiness remained. He expected at any moment that the chair would be set upon by armed thugs. Why not? If Boston was, as De Bernière said, in a state of "prepared rebellion" against British arms, nothing could be more likely.

"Well, ma'am, since I am at your mercy and pleased so to be, there should be no secrets between us. They say that Boston is half in rebellion against the king."

"That's true, and they have reason to be."

"Then you are a rebel, ma'am?"

There was a long silence.

"I'm not a rebel, Oliver," Eugénie said quietly. Now her head was turned away from him, for her voice came from another direction altogether. "You arrive at conclusions too quickly. And you have another fault: you call me 'ma'am' when I would prefer to be called Eugénie. And you have still other faults."

"An endless list of them, I dare say, ma'am, but did you invite me on this strange errand to discuss my faults?"

"At least you show some spirit." Eugénie turned and faced him. "I have told you I am not a rebel. Don't you believe me, Oliver? How can I make you believe me?"

"There's no way, except by deeds," Oliver said hopelessly, feeling like a trapped animal in a cage.

What was it all coming to? She was young and beautiful and desirable, and she was taking him to her own house—or to some house where the rebels had gathered. There was no other explanation for the journey: he would become the hostage of the rebels. He cursed himself for not remaining on the bed. He was a damnable fish who had swallowed the bait, and it was a story as old as the hills. De Bernière was right to speak of danger : there is nothing more dangerous than a woman in the dark. He was thinking in this way when he felt her fingers against his face and heard her low voice saying, "By deeds, Oliver, is it by deeds that a man is made safe?" and he was about to brush her hands from his face when she kissed him on the lips. Then he knew he was more trapped than ever, for he felt helplessly at the mercy of her kiss. Her head fell against his shoulder and she whispered, "You asked for a safe-conduct?"

"I asked for certainties," Oliver answered softly.

"What else is a kiss?" Eugénie said. For the first time he put his arms round her. He shivered a little because he felt, through the thin silk, how loudly her heart was beating against his. Then he was silent, for there was nothing he wanted to say to her : only to remain there forever beside her, stroking her arms and her face, while the poor Negroes grunted and the chair handles creaked under their weight. He had forgotten how many corners they had swung past, though he knew they had slipped across one of the roads leading to the sea: a breath of sea air had entered the chair.

"I vow, you have little mercy on me!" Eugénie exclaimed when he kissed her again.

"Did you expect mercy?" Oliver asked quietly. "It's too much to be hoped for, surely, and yet you shall have all you require. I shall not kiss you unless you demand it, Eugénie, and—O God, what a pleasant name it is to say in the darkness, Eugénie, even when——"

"Even when?"

"Even when I don't know the end of the journey, and I confess I am in dread of coming to the end."

"Then you prefer being with me?"

"I prefer being with you to anything else. This is all that matters, and nothing else can ever matter so much."

Once again Oliver felt an obscure sensation of being led into a trap; but now, even if he were to enter a trap with his eyes open, he no longer cared. If Eugénie was acting a part, she was, he told himself, a prodigious actress. No, they had fallen in love, while the volcano prepared to explode, and the heavens had favored him.

She said: "You will leave for New York in the *Nautilus* in five days. Let us at least have those five days for ourselves."

"They are all yours, Eugénie," Oliver answered.

She was silent for a long while. He heard footsteps. They were quick and alert steps, such as are made by men on patrol. Suddenly the chair came to a stop. The steps grew louder, then passed away. Evidently they had hidden in the shadows while a patrol passed. It occurred to Oliver that those four heavy-set Negroes must have been well trained.

"How are you now?" Eugénie asked tenderly.

"No more and no less in love with you than I have been since I set eyes on you."

"Then you feel safe with me?"

"Of course."

"Did it ever pass your mind that I would take you to the headquarters of the rebels?"

"It did once, but no longer. I wouldn't have cared where you led me, Eugénie." He heard her laughing quietly in the dark. "Tonight," he said, "everything is wonderful and everything is beautiful, and I am in love with you. And above all, it is unbelievable."

Soon Oliver knew by the sound of the Negroes' footsteps that they had left the street and were winding down a flagged pathway. A gate shut quietly. He heard voices. A lamp shone through the curtains, throwing patterns of damask on Eugénie's cheeks. There was a grating sound as the chair legs came to earth on gravel. Immediately the curtains parted.

"You were a long time, Eugénie," a voice said.

Eugénie stepped out, pulling up her skirt, revealing a gleam of white, unstockinged legs.

"My God, and what have you brought?" the voice went on. "A British officer, eh? That's a strange kettle of fish!"

Oliver stepped out of the chair to find himself confronted with a thickset man who wore a long blue cape buttoned at the neck. The man was about thirty, but his eyes looked younger. They were very clear and penetrating, and since he was holding a lantern on a level with his eyes, Oliver was able to see them clearly. As the man leaned forward, examining Oliver closely, the lower part of his face in shadow, Oliver also saw that he possessed a peculiar grace of movement and gesture.

"So you have brought a prisoner?" the man whispered.

Eugénie laughed. "Oliver's no prisoner. Besides, he comes under safe-conduct."

"I never did understand you, Eugénie," the man said. "Is this some caper? An English officer, I declare. I suppose you brought him here, my dear, simply for a change of air, or is there some more important reason?"

"I brought him here to talk with him. He leaves in a few days on the *Nautilus* for New York, and we'll have little enough time together."

A moment later Oliver found himself alone in the chair while Eugénie and the stranger with the lantern withdrew a short distance away. They whispered together, the girl's voice urgent, the man's steady. In the moonlight Oliver saw that he was in a bare garden, where there were some elms against the wall. A small house hardly larger than a summer-house stood against the sky. While Eugénie spoke, the man

kept nodding his head. The Negroes had disappeared. It
was very quiet in the garden. The lantern was resting on the
stone paving of a pathway, and sometimes he could see
Eugénie's dress gleaming in its light. Then Eugénie disappeared into the house, and the man came up to Oliver.

"I'm not Eugénie's guardian," the man said. "It's her own
affair. She says she wants to talk to you, and she hopes you
will have time to talk with me. You must forgive me for
being so contrary. The truth is that we are all a little contrary tonight."

Oliver stepped out of the chair, glanced around him, saw
the lights coming up in the house and said stiffly, "I have the
honor to address—?"

"If I tell you my name," said the man, "it won't help you.
I'm a doctor by trade. My name's nothing. My fame is less.
Eugénie admires you—isn't that enough?"

Saying this, he led Oliver into the small house and then
blew out the lantern. Eugénie had evidently gone round
lighting the candles, for the house was now brilliant with
lights. Oliver was led into a large, plainly furnished room
where there were small sofas, a harpsichord, three low book-
cases, and a table set in the corner.

The man laughed. "You must not place the blame on my
shoulders. She, not I, kidnaped you."

"Kidnaped?"

"You must admit that Eugénie has kidnaped you quite
successfully. For myself, I respect the king's uniform, though
I dare say you would regard me as a rebel."

"Then you're an enemy of the king!" Oliver said hotly, and
his hand went to his pistol.

At that moment Eugénie entered. She had removed her
turban, and her dark hair now fell to her shoulders. She still
wore the blue brocade dress with the black lace. She smiled,
put her face up to the doctor's, brushed his cheek with her
lips, turned to Oliver and said, "There must be no arguments

between you. You must believe me, he has only the best intentions toward you." Oliver was angry because she had kissed the man, though it was such a kiss as a sister might give to a brother. Then she went up to Oliver and removed his cape from his shoulders. All the time he was wondering what would be the next stage of the drama. What strange purposes did she have? Why, after all, had she brought him here? He was a little closer to an explanation when the man said: "It is like Eugénie to bring a rebel and a king's officer together."

"What do you want of me?" Oliver asked quickly with some heat in his voice, staring straight at the man.

"I want nothing except friendship. Why should I want anything else?" The man laughed. "There are not fifty people in the province who desire war. It's the king's ministers who want war with us. They forget we have rights."

"The right to rebel against lawful government is not one granted to colonials," Oliver answered heatedly. "You're a rebel, and the government hates rebellion and always will!"

"How would you like it if the colonials possessed armed garrisons in England?" the man asked out of the blue.

"It's not the same thing."

"No, by God, it isn't, but how would you like it, eh? Oh, we are keeping our powder dry. We know what to expect, and we'll fight back at the first sign of provocation. We've had enough, I assure you!"

"Who is making threats now?" Oliver asked calmly. "Provocations are easily made, surely."

"That's true, but there's something worse than a provocation—it's the standing, eternal provocation of having the British Army on our soil, here in Boston, and I tell you on my honor none of us will rest easily while it remains!"

"Then what do you want me to do?"

"I'll tell you. I want you to report that there's only one solution. Have done with it! Tell General Gage that we

want peace, an enduring peace between the English and the
Provincials, but it will come about only when the Redcoats
have left our shores, or joined with us. Tell *that* to General
Gage. Tell him we would welcome them with open arms.
Tell him we want no blood shed between us. And tell him
something else: tell him he is powerless. The will of the
British Government doesn't affect our shores. Do you under-
stand that?"

Oliver whistled under his breath. He realized now that
this wasn't an ordinary rebel, but a man who spoke with
authority. The doctor's voice was very low and earnest; his
eyes, of a soft, almost feminine blue, were blazing quietly.

Oliver could not take his eyes from the young doctor's face.
His hair was powdered. He wore a blue coat with gold buttons, and his knee breeches were of the same color, but more
faded. There was something careless and at the same time
deliberate in his manner. He smiled rarely, but when he
smiled you felt an intense pleasure radiating from him. A
Negro came in with a tray of hot toddy, but Oliver hardly
noticed the presence of the Negro; he saw only the broad
pleasant face of the young doctor.

"You underestimate the power of British arms," Oliver
said after a pause. "It isn't an easy thing, I dare say, to throw
the Redcoats into the sea."

"I didn't say it was easy, but I know it can be done."

"How could it be done?"

"By fighting them, sir! Why, we can maneuver where
we will, display our forces according to our whims, lead the
Redcoats a merry dance wherever we wish; and what can
you do? That's why I tell you the best thing of all would be
for General Gage to declare his allegiance with us!"

"That's treason, sir!" Oliver answered hotly. Before he
could go on to denounce the doctor in even stronger terms he
was interrupted.

"Call it what you like," the doctor said grimly. "I'm giving you some home truths. They may not be palatable now, but they're good medicine. Think on it!"

"Oh, stop quarreling!" Eugénie exclaimed. "I brought you here, Captain De Lancey, for no purpose except friendship." She smiled at the doctor, and there was something in the smile which made Oliver shiver; it was as though a secret understanding had passed between them.

"A strange hour for friendship," Oliver answered, "but I am grateful to you." He turned to the doctor, rose, and said: "You ask me to take a treasonable message to General Gage, but I won't!"

"It would be better if you did."

They were silent for a while. The toddy was getting cold. Eugénie smoothed down her long silken dress, and there was something in her manner which suggested that she was out of humor with the young doctor.

"Did you bring me here to talk treason with this blood-letter?" Oliver asked bitterly.

"I vow I did not know he was here," Eugénie said without a change of expression.

"That's true enough," the doctor answered. "I've known Eugénie for many years, and it's not my practice to interfere in her private affairs. I came by accident."

"Then why not go by accident, and leave us in peace?"

"Because these are serious matters, Captain De Lancey. The destinies of nations are held in the balance tonight. I tell you, the fate of America lies in your hands!"

Oliver laughed. He was genuinely amused by such high-flown sentiments. He had a due regard for his own vanity, but it had never been stretched so far as this.

"The fate of America?"

"Exactly. And the fate of Britain as well."

"Let's be brief," Oliver said primly. "Let's say the fate of the whole world."

"It might come to that," the doctor said slowly. There

was a long silence, the Negro hovering near, Eugénie pluck-
ing at invisible folds in her skirt, her eyes lowered, her face
composed and grave, with no hint of anxiety. She had not
expected to find the doctor here, but now she was perfectly
willing for the drama to play itself out.

"I've heard some nonsense in my time, but that's damned
nonsense, sir," Oliver said seriously. "The fate of America
and Britain isn't in your hands or mine. I don't suppose
either of us knows where the decisions lie, but they are not
made by young officers like me or young doctors like you.
I've told you there's nothing I can do."

"Then you want us to be slaves forever?" the doctor said,
and for the first time there was harshness in his voice.

They were almost at each other's throats. There was a
hard smile at the corners of the doctor's lips. Eugénie was
sitting a little away from them, her head inclined to one side.
She seemed now to be enjoying their quarrel.

"I'll tell you this," the doctor went on. "A musket shot
somewhere, fired by accident most likely, may begin it. We're
as near to war as we have ever been. They say General Gage
is warmhearted, decent and honest. Let him do his best to
prevent the war. As for the rebels, they can't help their rebellion. They'll fight to the last."

The doctor's voice had grown very low. He was bending
forward, peering into Oliver's face. He was troubled, angry,
reserved, and he paid no attention to Eugénie. He marched
to the curtained window, and then marched back again; then
he jammed one heavy fist into an open palm and cried out:
"I trust in God and in people! There's good sense among
men, isn't there? If there's a clear danger ahead, why, people
don't rush ahead, do they? But you don't see it! A state of
rebellion—more restrictive orders—doesn't it ever occur to
you that we want our freedom more than our daily bread?
Think of the people sleeping in Boston. Think of them
wherever they are, their pistols and fowling pieces by their

beds. They're all waiting for the war—they feel it coming. It's something they smell in the very air they breathe, and there's no need for it, by God, there's no need for it!" He turned sharply to Oliver and said in a lower voice, "There's history flowing through your hands, Captain De Lancey, and you're throwing it away! Don't you believe in goodness?"

"Of course I do, and so do you, but what do you expect me to do?"

"I've told you. We can save this war, but there's only one way now: come over to our side, Captain De Lancey."

"And if we don't?"

"Then you must take the blame for whatever happens. If you attack us, if you so much as lay a finger on a single one of our men, then it's all over—the fuse is alight!" He turned to Eugénie. "It's Providence that brought him here, my dear. I've thought and thought. We can't hold them back much longer. It's hell-fire, to live in this age. Oh, they don't know what is going to happen, what terrible things are going to take place. Murders and killings and whole cities in flames!"

"It may not happen," Eugénie said quietly.

"Only a miracle can prevent it," the young doctor said, and for the first time Oliver noticed the sweat streaming down his face. There was a passionate urgency in his voice, and he gave Oliver a look of entreaty. Then he did a strange thing: he went straight up to Oliver, threw his arms round Oliver's shoulders and stood very close to him while looking deep into his eyes, as though he were attempting to find an answer to his anxieties there. He said quietly and with a kind of deliberate calm, "Let us both work for peace, and let there be God's grace on us." That was all. A moment later he was gone, closing the door behind him.

In all his life Oliver was never to experience an expanse of time longer than that which followed the doctor's disappearance. He sat down with the empty glass in his hand. Eugénie was beside him, staring straight in front of her with her bare arms laced round her knees. "I love you—there is always that," she said, seeing the look of misery on Oliver's face. The curtains shook in the wind.

At the end of an ageless interval Oliver walked across the room and blew out the candles. In the faint moonlight coming through the curtains he could see Eugénie standing and facing him, and her face was white and bathed with tears.

CHAPTER 3

A Treasonable Doctor

AT THREE O'CLOCK in the morning Ensign De Bernière was awakened by one of the guardsmen at Province House with the news that Dr. Church had suddenly arrived with important information for the royal governor. De Bernière had never seen the middle-aged doctor, but he knew enough about him to dislike him heartily. Immediately after hearing of the doctor's arrival, De Bernière had gone to the Blue Room. He told General Gage that the doctor had come, but to his surprise he was told to keep the doctor waiting. It was quite evident that the general had as little liking for the doctor as anyone else.

"Please be patient. They are in conference," De Bernière reported to the doctor, who stood facing the wall.

"Patience is not one of my virtues," Dr. Church answered. "Tell them I have important news. If they knew why I am here, they would break up their conference to hear me."

De Bernière returned to the Blue Room, gave this message to General Gage and received the same answer as before. A few moments later he was explaining to the doctor that there was absolutely nothing to be done. They were deep in conference, but they would see him at the first opportunity. He felt certain that the general was employing a deliberate strategem: if you kept the doctor waiting, he would grow nervous and would talk more freely. It was a game De Bernière understood perfectly. He was glad he had thrown himself on the bed fully clothed, and he hoped he would be allowed to witness the doctor's entrance into the Blue Room. Twenty minutes later the doctor was still there, his face still turned to the wall.

"Patience! Patience!" the doctor exclaimed suddenly, making a clacking noise with his fingers, his back still turned to the wall.

"Go to hell," De Bernière said, looking with distaste at the doctor, and then he began to walk up and down the carpet, wondering what had happened to Oliver De Lancey. He had thought he had said "Go to hell" in words so low that the doctor would not hear them. He was mistaken. The doctor had heard them perfectly.

"If you have a mind to swear at me, or revile me, sir, do it in the open," Dr. Church said. "I won't be treated in such manner, and I'll take it upon myself to report your detestable language to the royal governor himself."

"I was talking about the weather, sir," De Bernière answered lamely.

"Have the goodness to tell the governor I have been kept waiting forty minutes," the doctor went on relentlessly. "I'm not accustomed to being kept waiting, sir."

"I've been into the Council Chamber once."

"Then go again. . . . Did you hear me?"

De Bernière was almost at the end of his tether. The doctor was a spy, and he distrusted spies, even when they brought intelligence from the rebels. The doctor stood with his legs apart, his heavy shoulders stooped, his black coat coated with dust—not shabby, yet the back of the coat was oddly repulsive. He was breathing deep breaths; every time he inhaled, his shoulders rose a little. He had thin legs and a heavy squat body, but his hands were almost feminine, with slender ivory fingers.

Suddenly the doctor swung round and faced him. De Bernière was so startled that he jumped. It was the first time he had seen the man full face. When the doctor came into the room he wore a heavy scarf round his chin and his hat was pulled over his eyes. It was a strong face, not brutal or weak, with the bristling look of a terrier, and blue-jowled— a heavy face which at any other time might have appeared perpetually ironical and good-humored.

"I've waited long enough," the doctor said. "Have the goodness to tell General Gage I can wait no more! I have brought important dispatches. His life—my life—depends on them, and I've known him long enough to know that he wouldn't willingly keep a man in my lamentable situation waiting."

"What's all this damfoolery?" a voice said from an open doorway.

De Bernière sprang to attention. "The doctor is complaining of being kept waiting, sir," he said slowly, licking his lips. The general, tired and angry, with blue lines under his eyes, looked like an avenging demon, blazing with gold epaulets and white facings.

It was only then that the general caught the doctor's eye. His face, furious and swollen with anger a moment before, became suddenly gentle, and he went straight up to the doctor, wrung his hand and said: "Have patience, my dear Dr. Church. I hope to present you to the Council, but there's so much to be done. . . . A few more minutes, and we'll be through."

"I've waited fifty minutes already."

"And I promise you that within the hour we shall request you to attend on us. Have a drink. De Bernière, have the goodness to bring Dr. Church a drink."

"I'm not to be fopped off with a jug," the doctor said in an alarmingly loud voice. "Do you realize my position, sir? I must get to my home unobserved, or all will be up with me. Ten minutes with you alone, sir, that's all I demand. My work in the past has surely given me the privilege of making these occasional demands."

The general smiled pleasantly, said something about the lateness of the hour, apologized for having kept the doctor waiting and murmured, "If you insist, Dr. Church."

The doctor breathed a sigh of relief. "I see that your lordship is busily occupied through the night," he said. "Well, I can understand that there is a great deal of work to do. Where shall we discuss matters?"

"Anywhere you please. Perhaps you would like to discuss them with my staff. I beg you to wait just a moment—no more than a moment."

With a pleased expression on his face the general mounted the stairs and went straight to the Blue Room, which he had left only a few minutes before. Quite deliberately he had hoped to reduce Dr. Church to a state of extreme apprehension. He had succeeded admirably, but he was not in the least delighted with his success. For news of the rebels he depended on the doctor to an extent he hardly dared to admit to himself. Church knew all the rebel secrets; posed himself as one of the rebel leaders; had brought complete details of the conferences of the illegal Provincial Congress; knew intimately all its members. It was not in the general's plans that the doctor should be put completely out of countenance. . . . Returning to the Blue Room and carefully closing the door, he said: "Gentlemen, the doctor is in attendance upon us, and I fear he will suffer a distemper if he is kept waiting any longer." There were quick smiles from the men gathered round the table, and immediately afterward there was a shuffling of maps, which were gathered together and carefully concealed under the green baize cover. Then the officers round the table rose to their feet, smiled grimly to one another, nodded, whispered among themselves. When the general summoned the doctor into the room it was as though the spy was being received with all the honors due to a rebel leader. With Dr. Church at the door, they all bowed and held themselves in respectful silence, waiting for him to speak. Mean-

while an extraordinary look of triumph appeared on the doctor's face. No longer irascible, he smiled pleasantly and even
youthfully at the officers who had spent four hours round the
table and were now exhausted by their long deliberations.

"You have our most earnest apologies," General Gage
murmured, "for keeping you waiting so long. You understand our difficulties?"

"Indeed I do, my lord."

Saying this, the doctor nodded toward Lord Percy and
exchanged a smile with the young colonel.

"Yes, I understand your difficulties, gentlemen," he went
on, "but let us get down to business." He sat down beside
the general, and it occurred to him that he was now assuming the chairmanship of the Council Chamber. "You know
where my sympathies lie, gentlemen. I profess a consummate affection for the king's majesty, and I am here to dis-
charge my obligations to the Crown." He was warming up.
He possessed a passion for words like "consummate" and
"obligation," and rolled them on his tongue. He was behaving naturally, at ease among his peers, his domed forehead
shining in the light of the chandeliers. There was Admiral
Graves, lean, red-faced, with a sailor's deep-water-blue eyes
and expression of petulance; Lord Percy, long-nosed and
delicate, his pale, aristocratic face held a little to one side;
General Haldimand, shaggy and overdressed; Colonel Smith,
a fat man bursting through his clothes, awkward in his movements, with a brain like a knife; Vice-Admiral Seymour, his
face so sharp and distinctive and a little morose, as though
the cares of managing the frigates and the effort to restrain
his natural anger against the rebels were wearing him out. He
could be explosive, the doctor reflected, if he allowed himself.
There were ten or twelve others. They kept nodding and
murmuring approvingly as the doctor explained his own
position, his "relentless determination to follow the public
welfare," his "deep and approving interest in the benefits

conferred on the province by the gentlemen who are here present." And then quite suddenly he explained that he had himself come from the Provincial Congress, which had met during the afternoon, and had risked his life in order to put their treasonable discourses into the hands of the representatives of the Crown. As he said this the doctor looked straight into Lord Percy's eyes, and he was amused to detect a flicker of deep recognition, a gleam which suggested that he had penetrated all the nobleman's reserves and could now count himself among his lordship's friends.

"Yes, yes, gentlemen, at the risk of my very life. We are living in dreadful times, and the best of us cannot be assured of the safety which is surely part of that eternal benediction vouchsafed by God." Here the doctor looked up at the ceiling and paused for a moment while he uttered a silent prayer of thanksgiving. "Yes, God watches over us, gentlemen. He surely approves those of us who are in His service. But what shall we say of those who, in league with Satan, attempt in their ignorance to defeat the laws of Providence? Gentlemen, the Provincial Congress has determined to raise an army. This is the important matter I have to tell you. They intend to raise an army and to seek the co-operation of the other New England states. So they decided to send delegates to the New England colonies to discover their sentiments on the subject, but everyone knows what their sentiments are." He paused, shuffled in his pocket for some scraps of paper, put on his spectacles and said: "I have here the precise figures of the army they intend to raise. It will number altogether 18,000 men. Of these, 8,000 are to be raised in the Province of Massachusetts, 5,000 in Connecticut, 4,000 in New Hampshire and a further thousand in Rhode Island. A goodly number, as you can see, gentlemen."

It pleased him to observe that they were all craning forward with deep interest.

"These figures I have related by no means cover the potentialities of the rebels," he went on, lowering his voice. "No, there is sad news to come. The rebels are not content with these numbers. They intend to raise six companies of artillerymen, each company to consist of thirty men, and they will be raised in Massachusetts to assist the army in the field. There is worse news yet. They decided today to evacuate Boston, and next Monday the order will be issued commanding all the peaceful inhabitants of the town to remove themselves. The poorer sort will, of course, be assisted financially. Finally, Mr. Hancock and Mr. Lincoln have ordered that moneys for the waging of armed rebellion shall be collected in the name of Mr. Gardiner, Receiver-General of the Congress. So you see, they have come to some mighty dangerous conclusions, and their deliberations are not to be held lightly."

It is deplorable, thought the general, that there should be so much fat to so little meat. Silence had descended on the table. Yes, it was good honest meat, he would have to admit that. And was it such little meat? He had known they were arming, and he had long suspected that they were preparing to muster. He said: "So the Congress of rebels has declared for war?"

"Yes, sir. They have voted on it. They have prepared for it. They have set their minds to it."

"And there's no turning back?"

"No."

At this moment the doctor had suspected that the high officials gathered round the table would have expressed their satisfaction in his own extraordinary perspicacity. They would have thanked him, formally and informally, and perhaps General Gage would have expressed some such sentiment as "my intense satisfaction in your good works, which must be brought to the knowledge of the king." Nothing of the kind happened. Instead, there was an audible sigh of relief,

and no one could have said whether he was relieved because
the doctor had come to the end of his speech, or because the
die was now cast.

"Thank you," the general said, gazing down at his gold
ring. "Have you any further news for us, Dr. Church?"

"Yes, sir. Congress is adjourned this day for a fortnight."

"So nothing will happen for a fortnight? Is that your
opinion of the matter?"

"Yes."

"That gives us a fortnight to prepare our strategy?"

"Yes."

"And after that we may expect a general declaration of
war. They will have removed the people of Boston, and presumably their armies will be prepared."

"Yes."

The general was quiet for a moment, then he gazed straight
at the doctor, smiled and said, "Dr. Church, you are among
friends. Is there anything you can suggest which will delay
these foolhardy actions by the rebels?"

"I do not know what can delay a matter so long prepared,
but I know this: They are not all unanimous, sir. There is
division among them. I might say there was great irresolu-
tion shown during the course of the debates this week. There
were many who opposed the creation of an army."

"How strong are they?"

"There are hotheads stronger than they are who can sway
Congress."

"But is Congress swayed already?"

"I wouldn't say it was swayed. I would say it was preparing to be swayed. There is unanimous feeling against
the British."

"But they are not sure how to express that feeling?"

"Certainly there are many who are unsure. When the
motion was taken to consider the appointment of officers for

the army, there were some who resolutely set their minds
against it."

"And what happened to them?"

"Nothing of consequence. They were listened to, and
they will be listened to again, but in the end they will be
overcome."

"You're sure of it?"

"Yes, I am sure of it."

General Gage had the curious feeling, while Dr. Church
was talking, that he was himself present at the Congress.
How earnestly they discussed their plans! With what rhet-
oric they called on the name of freedom! He had only to
shut his eyes to be able to see them in their tawdry wigs,
their homespun clothes, their terrible solemnity. It would
be untrue to say he did not fear them, but he felt more certain
of himself now. The news from the doctor fitted in strangely
with the instructions received from the British Government.

"Well, sir, what do you make of it?" The general leaned
over the table and smiled at Lord Percy. "A pretty kettle
of fish!"

"Very pretty," Lord Percy answered. "I think we all owe
a debt of gratitude to the courageous doctor."

It was the remark Dr. Church had been waiting for. It
fell very sweetly on his ears, and his face, which had shown
signs of strain for so long, suddenly glowed. His lips formed
into a smile of pure pleasure, and he made a profound in-
clination.

"The great courage of the doctor should be signally re-
warded," the general intoned, not without a shudder.

"Oh, dear Heaven, dear Heaven!" the doctor murmured
under his breath. Beads of sweat, dripping along his nose,
slid over his heavy chin and fell on the white lace of his
cravat.

General Gage, thinking the doctor was overwrought and

might burst into tears, placed a protecting hand on the doctor's knee.

"You must face the world bravely," the general said. "Yes, always bravely."

"Under Providence I have faith in God and the king," the doctor returned.

"You are a credit to your great profession," the general said.

"I am hoping I shall not be entirely forgotten by—by the king's majesty."

"Oh, I can assure you the king will be made aware of your contributions, your—may I say?—indispensable contributions. You will receive your reward, Dr. Church."

"I was not thinking of a pecuniary reward, Your Excellency."

"Of course not."

"A mark of the king's favor—a small attentiveness on the part of His Majesty, if I may be so bold."

"You can be assured of it," the general answered. "You have my oath on it. Your services are such that the king could not overlook them. I shall make a special report to Lord Dartmouth, and if some small pecuniary assistance . . ."

"If you insist," the doctor answered. "Only if you insist, my lord."

"Then it shall be as you say. I know that you have no high regard for money, that your services are beyond monetary recompense, and we all know how much you have labored under the gravest difficulties—yes, the gravest difficulties."

For a moment Dr. Church suspected that the general and all the high officers round the table were playing with him. They smiled generously and delicately.

There were infinite gradations of politeness, infinite delicacies and ruses, when it came to deciding how much money to give the doctor. The general whispered to his aide-de-camp; Lord Percy whispered to Haldimand, who was gazing up at the ceiling. When at last a small bag of gold was prepared and the aide slipped it into the doctor's pocket, the general said quite calmly, "Think nothing of such rewards, my dear doctor. There will be more—there will always be more." And the doctor was left with the impression that he was closer than ever to the knighthood he coveted above everything else.

After the doctor had gone there was a brief silence. The wine was passed round. Haldimand lighted a churchwarden pipe and Colonel Smith took a pinch of snuff. Once more the maps were brought out and placed solemnly on the table. They were beautiful maps, the pride of the general's cartographer and of the general himself, but he could no longer take pleasure in them. The strain of being polite to the doctor had given him a headache.

"We have heard what the doctor has to say, and now we must get to business," the general said. "I hope none of us will dispute the fact that we are inordinately lucky to have him on our side. The important thing is that he has given us these advices, and it is clear that the rebels are ready to fight. As you know, most of their guns and ammunition are in Concord. If what Dr. Church says is true, we must capture the American guns and ammunition at the earliest possible moment." Saying this, the general drew a straight line across the map from Boston Common to Concord. "Each one of you will have to decide whether he believes the doctor," he went on. "We depend on that. We hang on the thread of his words. I do not pretend to trust him."

General Gage looked round the room. Haldimand, wide awake now, was nodding in agreement. Vice-Admiral Seymour was mechanically buttoning and unbuttoning his coat, and Lord Percy was humming under his breath. All of them had rings under their eyes. It was past four o'clock, and every single one of them would have to be out of bed before seven.

"Have you any comments, gentlemen?"

Only the vice-admiral responded. He asked about disposition of his ships.

"I may need your boats to ferry my men across," the general answered.

"And the prison ships?"

"I don't want to think about them. If it can be managed, I'll take no more prisoners. I agree with the rebels in this. The citizens of Boston must make their own choice, either to stay or to go. And I'll make sure that those who stay can be trusted."

"You're taking a risk," the vice-admiral said quietly. "An unnecessary risk, if I may say so. If I had my way, I'd throw the lot into the prison ships. They're rapscallions, the whole lot of them!"

"You must allow me to disagree," the general answered pleasantly.

There were smiles round the table. Everyone knew that the vice-admiral disapproved of all Americans and that the general disapproved of only some Americans.

"God help you, then!" the vice-admiral went on, his face reddening. "God help you! Show 'em force, it's the only way. Why, sir, that was the whole content and meaning of Lord Dartmouth's letter, and you have the temerity to disobey. I'd shoot every man jack of 'em! Do you know what it costs to feed the prisoners on the prison ships? Why do we trouble to feed 'em, sir? I'd open the sea cocks if I had my way. I'd drown every living soul of them, and why? Because there isn't any treatment except death which is good for rebels!" His veins swelled at his temples. He struck the table with his fists, and a heavy groan came from his thick, fleshy lips. "Damme, must we fill their bellies when we can hardly find enough food for our own sailors! What kind of war is this? We let them go scot free, don't we, except for occasional hangings at the Neck? There's not enough hangings in my estimation, and not half enough shootings! I'd hang Dr. Church! I'd hang Dr. Warren! I'm not so sure that I wouldn't hang every damn doctor in the place. You can't trust doctors, especially American doctors. I offer you the suggestion, General. Open the sea cocks. *That* will teach 'em a lesson."

"One they won't forget?" the general commented, cocking his brow.

"Exactly. One they won't forget. They'll remember it."

"I dare say they'd remember it for a very long time, wouldn't they, Seymour?"

"That's my intention, sir."

"And do you know what the consequences would be?"

"Most excellent consequences, sir. We'd ha' put the fear of God in 'em, and there's nothing debatable about the need of putting fear in their hearts. We've got to find the way, and sea cocks, in my estimation, is the best way."

"Then do you know what would happen, sir? Can you guess? Can you realize in what detestation the name of Britain would be held? Don't you think of honor, Seymour?"

"I think of it well enough, but what honor is there in rebellion against the king's majesty?"

"We're not discussing rebellion. We're discussing your plan of opening the sea cocks of the prison ships. The *Preston* and all the others. I'll tell you what would happen. We would find ourselves facing an army of 100,000, and it wouldn't be an ordinary army, sir. It might not even be armed. There would be women and children in this army, young children, even children two or three years old, providing they could walk. And it would come upon us like a wave, like an Atlantic roller, and we'd drown under it, and they'd stamp us down with their boots and their cotton slippers. There wouldn't be a single one of us alive the day afterward. They'd burn us out; they'd smoke us out; they'd come like vengeance straight out of Heaven! No, Seymour, there are no easy solutions. We've got to do it the hard way or not at all." He paused, sipped some wine and went on. "It comes to me, gentlemen, that I have kept you too late. We've got many heavy days ahead of us, and I suggest that we sleep on the matter."

Haldimand leaned forward and whispered. "I don't think we dare sleep on it, Tom. We ought to make our conclusions now. We can't wait for the reinforcements."

The general smiled. "I was hoping we could." There was a look of mingled fear and perplexity in his face. He went on in a louder voice: "We have a fortnight in which to act— perhaps longer. But I don't think we have any right to expect them to delay their muster. They know when our reinforcements are due, and it's their thought, as it is ours, to strike soon, before preparations are made. They know where we are weak and where we are strong. We needn't hide it from ourselves. Having thought about the matter, and taking into consideration Dr. Church's advices, I conclude that we must act within the next week—better, within the next five days. We *must* prevent their stores from reaching their armies, and there's only one way in which it can be done: their stores must be destroyed. If we can do that without hurting a man, without the loss of a single life, then we shall have a victory such as we never dreamed of a month ago. Remember what Church said. They are preparing to evacuate Boston next Monday. We shall have to strike at once. Tomorrow night is the best. It would be better if we could wait until there is no moon, but we can't wait."

"Do we arrest their leaders?" Lord Percy asked, leaning across the table.

"You keep saying that. I can see no immediate advantages

in arresting them. I'd like them to show their hand. And then, too, if we arrest them, there is the danger that the arrests, unless they were carried out in complete secrecy, would act like a tocsin—a call for battle. We would have to arrest Church, too, and *then* where we would get our advices? No, my dear Lord Percy, I can see no real advantages in arresting them. We must seize their stores—that's the important thing. Everything Dr. Church has told us leads only to that. We must do it secretly, if possible, with the best men we have, and we must count on them to behave with scrupulous and exemplary regard for orders. I want the rebel stores captured without a shot fired." The general looked across the table at Colonel Smith, who was sitting with his eyes closed and his chin buried in his high collar. "Where shall we find our best men, Colonel?"

Colonel Smith's hands were wrapped round his ample stomach. Now he slowly lifted his hands to the table, and without looking up he answered, "Grenadiers and light infantry."

"Exactly," the general replied. "I propose that we send out our Grenadiers and Light Infantry at the time and occasion which seems most suitable for the purpose, such time and occasion to be communicated to you later. I ask for your agreement, gentlemen."

To his astonishment, everyone agreed, perhaps because everyone desired to go to bed.

"You understand the gravity of our decision, gentlemen?"

They all nodded, yet no one except Colonel Smith had thought for a moment about the gravity of the affair.

"Thank you, gentlemen," the general said. But when they rose he was still sitting in his chair, still busily turning his gold ring, still forming words with his lips, and he was now more wide-awake than he had been at any time since late afternoon. They walked out in silence. Only Lord Percy,

General Haldimand and Colonel Smith remained behind.

"God bless your designs!" Lord Percy said quietly. "Is there anything more tonight?"

"Yes. General Orders. Grenadiers and Light Infantry to be relieved from all duties. They'll have to learn new exercises and new duties, and they'll have to learn 'em secretly. That's all." He let his eyes fall on each of them in turn. "I'd like you, gentlemen, to drink one more glass with me." He watched while Colonel Smith poured out the wine; then in silence he rose, said, "To the king's majesty!" drank the wine, and then tossed his glass to the wall. One by one the officers followed the general's example, and pleased expressions appeared on all their faces when they heard the sound of smashing glass. It was a sound that brought new life into them; it was as though there had suddenly flowed through them a new and intoxicating electricity.

"Good night, sir," Lord Percy murmured, and with a little wave of his hand the general answered, "Good night all!"

Left to himself at last, the general walked straight to the window, opened it and gulped in a long draft of air. At this hour the air was sweet and pure. The streets were deserted, white in the coming dawn even though the sun had not yet pierced the clouds. The phrases of Lord Dartmouth's letter poured through his mind, and now he no longer felt any particular horror of those letters written in bold, copperplate handwriting, signed with the ferocious signature. *The authority of the kingdom must be supported, and the execution of its laws enforced.* Well, there was no harm in that. He had expected it all along, but it was a phrase which allowed many interpretations. There were other phrases less innocuous, but they too could be interpreted according to the ways of a peaceful solution. *The first and essential step would be to arrest the principal actors in the Provincial Congress.* But this was impossible. *You must use force and strike down the opposi-*

tion to His Majesty's commands. Yes, he would use force. He would come in the night and remove their stores and they would be unable to fight. Not a man would be hurt, not a woman would have cause to grieve.

The sun caught the sails of the frigates in the harbor, fell on the silk hood of a calash on the quay, and then flashed on windows. A farmer's straw-filled cart came slowly down the deserted road; a bugle blew; he heard a guard's voice down below; and then against the white sunrise he saw puffs of blue smoke rising from the chimneys. Hunched up, sucking at his empty pipe, he left the window and went to see his sick son.

CHAPTER 4

The Fiddler on the Green

LIGHT CAME flooding through the curtains. Oliver looked down at the sleeping face beside him on the couch. How gay she had been at the ball! How serious during the night! But now she was neither gay nor serious, but curiously childlike in her sleep. Sometimes, even while she was sleeping, a smile would appear on the corners of her lips. And then as he watched her, seeing the light flooding all round her, she began to tremble with the cold of the early morning. As she trembled, the heavy greatcoat he had thrown over her fell away, and she lay naked in the sun.

He could not take his eyes away from her. Everything in the room was unfamiliar, and she herself was unfamiliar. The girl lying there was curiously unconcerned and remote. She was so pure, so white, so incredibly distant. She opened her eyes, smiled up at him; then she slipped gracefully off the couch, drew on a white cambric petticoat, and then the dress she had been wearing the night before. They had been one body; now they were hopelessly separated. When she slipped into her dress he felt the shock of separation like a blow between the eyes.

"Where are you? Where are you? You have gone from me!" he exclaimed, and took her hands and pressed them against his face.

"I love you, Oliver," she answered, bending over him. "Isn't that enough? I don't know why I love you. I don't know why I should have asked you here. It simply happened, and that is good, isn't it? We must never regret it—never!"

"Come to my arms!"

"Do I have to be in your arms to be loved?"

"Yes," Oliver answered, surprised by the strength and composure of her young voice. "Yes, you must be. There is no other way."

For a long while she simply gazed at him. His hair was in disorder, his lips were swollen from too much kissing, a thin golden stubble appeared on his chin; he looked calm and exhausted, a little silly and boyish. But when she kissed him again, he held her wrists and there was a look of sudden desperation in his eyes, as though he feared she would leave him that moment. She said: "Whatever happens, I will never leave you. You are in my heart."

"Yes, but I must see you, I must keep on seeing you, I must always see you, Eugénie."

"Why?"

"Oh, what a silly question! How can I live without you?"

It was strange how much he loved her, how terrible it would be to leave her. Nothing like this had ever happened before. She was very quiet, gazing at him. Questions arose in his mind: How was it that he had come here, into this house where everything was unfamiliar? Was it her house? Was it a house she had borrowed? He shivered in the cold air and said, "It is morning, and you are wearing your ballroom costume." Immediately afterward the thought crossed his mind that once he had left the house, he would never see her again.

Eugénie must have been thinking the same thoughts, for she shook her head slowly from side to side and said, "There are only four days, Oliver, and some part of those four days you must be about your business. Do you think I haven't thought of that? You'll leave on the nineteenth, and where will you go? New York? Maybe you'll never come back

here again. And what shall I do while you are away? Have
you thought of that?"

"Yes, I have thought of it, and I dread it," Oliver answered, avoiding her eyes. Then, remembering that he wore
a heavy gold signet ring with the arms of the De Lancey
family on it, he took it off and quickly placed it on her finger.
He said softly: "Let this be a sign, Eugénie. I shall come
back. Let me come back to you."

"If you want me," she said. Shortly afterward she left
him, saying she would prepare breakfast and then he must
return in the chair to Province House.

Oliver dressed hurriedly. She brought a bowl of hot water,
towels, a mirror, soap and a razor blade. As she came in he
saw one of the Negroes standing in the doorway, dressed in
livery, but what was extraordinary was that the Negro was
carrying a fowling piece. He looked threatening—a great
black head in the sunlit doorway.

"Eat, my dear," Eugénie said. "As soon as you have
shaved, we'll eat."

It was a strange way of saying things—telling you to eat
when you were about to shave. Oliver smiled and wondered
what plots were afoot. She wore a neckerchief now, and she
had thrown some kind of lace apron over her ball dress.

"Do you live here?" he asked, for it occurred to him that
if she lived in this house, she would have been able to change
into a housedress. It was strange in the early morning to see
her appearing in the beautiful blue silk ball dress.

"You mustn't ask questions, Oliver," she answered. Her
voice, fresh, cool and very young, sounded as if it had secret
rivulets of laughter running underneath it, ready to come to
the surface without warning.

"I see. I am a prisoner, then, at your mercy?"

"At my mercy."

That was all. She was gone a moment later, and there
came the smell of eggs and boiling milk. He looked round

the room—the embroidery frame, the enormous gilded harp,
the silhouettes in medallions on the wall—everything in order: no trace of the quarrel with the doctor, no trace of their
love-making. And when she swept in with the tray, he felt
obscurely that they had been married for a long time, at least
three or four years, so intimate was his knowledge of her
behavior and gesture.

After they had breakfasted she said, "The chair is ready,
my dear."

For some reason he had thought she would accompany him
in the chair. The knowledge that it was waiting outside had
no effect on him. After breakfast one goes home, he
thought. It was as simple as that. He smiled to himself,
stroked his mustache and behaved exactly as he would have
behaved if they were married and would see each other again
in the evening, after they had gone about their affairs. It
occurred to him that the institution of marriage was blessed
for this reason: every day one returned to one's beloved.
"How splendid you were . . . and are," he said, and he could
not take his eyes away from hers. "Oh, dearest, dearest, how
good you are!" he kept saying stupidly. When he took her
in his arms it did not occur to him that it might be for the
last time.

She said softly, "You must go now, Oliver. They are waiting for you."

"When shall I see you?"

"Soon, soon, Oliver." She lowered her eyes; it was almost
a confession of weakness. She was trying to think up some
answer, and at the same time she dared not. "I'll come to
you," she said. "Not here."

"Why not here?"

"You must never know where you are. Promise that.
When you leave the house you must promise to have your
eyes closed."

He was almost angry, but he knew he would perform

whatever office she might desire. He said: "Blindfolded?"

"Yes, it's better. You mustn't know. You must never even guess. Will you promise?"

"On one condition: you promise I can see you again and again?"

"Yes, my darling, as many times as you like."

She blindfolded him, and then he kissed her. As they walked out into the garden, he was conscious of the presence of the Negro with the fowling piece. They stood for a while, breathing the scents of the garden, and he heard the chair being brought nearer. Somewhere, not far away, was the sea.

"I have one more request to make of you, Oliver. Your friend of last night wanted you to take a message to the governor. Beg the governor to join the rebels. They will honor him. Oh, it is not treason. Will you believe that, Oliver?" As she said this, she slipped something into his pocket. "It's a letter. Please give it to him."

"When shall I see you?"

"Tonight."

He kissed her once more, settled in the chair, held her hand for a moment, breathed deeply and contentedly. It was some time later before he realized that the Negroes were already taking him into the crowded streets. He was still blindfolded. He tore the handkerchief away, and then, because it was close and hot in the chair, pulled the curtain aside. Written on one of the walls was the name: Summer Street. He knew then that he would be able to find her, but this knowledge gave him little consolation: if he found her, she would know he had disobeyed her.

It was a street like many others in Boston, shaded by trees, with knots of workmen walking about, and barefoot Negroes. A trap with red wheels flew past. An officer, bowing and removing his three-cornered hat to some women emerging from a house, rode by on a small chestnut horse.

Oliver sat back in the chair and thought only of Eugénie.

He was still deaming of her, imagining her laughing and talk-ing beside him, when they reached Province House. He gave each of the Negroes a guinea, and made no effort to follow them back or have them followed. None of them resembled the huge Negro with the fowling piece. What a strange bloody world this is! Oliver told himself as he went running up the steps of Province House, where everything was gleaming with fresh paint.

In the hallway Ensign De Bernière was waiting for him. "So you have come, sir. Thank God! We were going to send the army to search every house in Boston for you."

Oliver's first impulse was to curse the man for impudence, but De Bernière was not laughing. On the contrary, he had the expression of a man who has been under great strain.

"You haven't been wounded—no fights?" De Bernière went on solicitously.

"Why the devil should I get into a scrape?" Oliver an-swered. "Why the devil——"

"The devil, indeed!" De Bernière said sharply. "Yes, the devil—the very devil. Pray, sir, do not speak to me of devils. I am haunted by them. I see them in every face I meet in Boston. They have cloven hoofs, if only one could see them without their boots and stockings. Tails, too."

"I don't doubt it."

"And tongues of fire—their tongues are the worst. Have patience. You will see them."

"I haven't seen them yet."

"No, but you will! Oh, you will! There's no doubt about it. I wouldn't trust one of those devils out of earshot. I hope you held your sword handy, sir." Saying this, De Bernière led him into an anteroom, threw himself down on a chair, took out a pipe, lighted it and said, "You must excuse me. We have been sitting up all night over one of their damned traitors—a more wretched face I never saw. Am I a jailer? Conferences till sunrise. I envy you, sir. His lordship drowned himself in a mess of maps, surrounded by all the other lordships."

"I don't know what the devil you are talking about."

"But you will, you will! The fires are burning. Very slowly, but they are burning!"

Oliver was mystified. There occurred to him again the thought that the young ensign was being impudent, atrociously impudent; at the same time he was aware of an underlying gravity in the youth's manner, a hint of exhaustion, as of a man who has spent the whole night dealing with important and insoluble problems.

"We know now more than we ever knew," De Bernière said, suddenly changing his expression to one of deep concern. "The fat's in the fire. There may be other ways of putting it, but that one is as good as any other. They are arming for war."

"Are you sure?"

"Bless my soul, I have been guarding the very instigator of it all night. Creeps in and out of here dressed in widow's weeds. Plays poker with dummies. A doctor of medicine, he calls himself. He'll physic the country by bloodletting!"

"A doctor?" Oliver asked, wondering what all this amounted to. "A doctor, did you say?"

"I did, sir, and I've never set eyes on a bigger ruffian. Oh, he's useful. He comes and spies for us."

"A young man?"

"Young enough. I wouldn't say he was old, anyway. He has eyes that pierce into you, a flabby jaw, well-cared-for hands and a good deep, chesty voice."

Oliver was turning pale. It occurred to him that the young doctor he had spoken to in Summer Street had gone straight to Province House.

"Why, what's the matter?" De Bernière looked steadily at Oliver and held out his hand. "Have you ever met the man? A Dr. Church?"

"I've met a doctor."

"Where?"

"God knows where. A handsome fellow, broad-faced, fine forehead, everything you'd desire in a man. Kept quoting the gospel at me—*his* gospel."

"I wouldn't say Dr. Church was handsome," De Bernière commented, puzzled for the first time since his encounter with Oliver. "I just couldn't believe that a man of your pronounced taste and ingenuity would ever pronounce him handsome. It just isn't in him to be handsome. Now would you say a toad was handsome?"

"No."

"Then I don't believe you've set eyes on Dr. Church, and that's a pity. He's an excellent specimen of a toad. He wants to kiss the king's hand. I know better things he could kiss. Handsome, eh?" De Bernière began counting on his fingers. "There's Adams, but he isn't handsome. He has a mouth like a slit, and beady eyes. And Hancock, you wouldn't say he was handsome, either. There's only Warren. Warren's handsome enough, God knows, and he's got a square head on his shoulders. Do you think you saw Warren?"

"God knows whom I saw," Oliver said.

"Did he have fair hair, blue eyes and two ivory teeth?" De Bernière went on relentlessly.

"Fair hair and blue eyes and a ruddy complexion. He wore his clothes well, and spoke well."

"Yes, but the ivory teeth?"

"I don't remember the teeth. What the devil have teeth got to do with it?"

"Because Joseph Warren has got two ivory teeth. It's as simple as that."

Oliver attempted to summon up the image of the doctor. Some officers came into the anteroom; then, seeing it was already occupied, they went out. They stayed long enough for Oliver to observe that they looked worn out, as though they hadn't slept. "Doesn't anyone sleep here?" he asked.

"We've given up any thought of it," De Bernière answered. "Don't you remember the teeth?"

"I've tried to, but I'm damned if I do! Are teeth so important?"

"He dressed well, didn't he?"

"Yes."

"Carried himself well?"

"Yes."

It was at that moment that Oliver remembered the letter. He wondered why he had not looked at it during the journey in the chair. It was addressed to General Gage, and right across the envelope there was scrawled, as though hurriedly and at the last moment: *In the sacred name of compromise.* De Bernière took the envelope and shook his head. "It's not Warren. I know that. He's too much of a firebrand even to dream of compromise. Was there anyone else there?"

"No, only the doctor."

"And I suppose they locked you up in an attic, and put a guard outside your door, and left you there."

"Yes," Oliver answered, lying, and his face flushed. He remembered that he had had about two hours of sleep. Whenever he had insufficient sleep, bright lights blinded him and the top of his skull felt drawn and tight.

"They're cunning dogs," De Bernière went on. "Up to all the tricks, damn 'em." He rose and paced the floor, first slowly, then faster, till his quick little steps were moving almost at a trot. He halted, glared out of a small window set high up in the wall, and then resumed his pacing. "I'd like to get my hands on Eugénie," he said.

"If you do, I'll blow the top of your head off!" Oliver shouted.

To his surprise De Bernière seemed in no way incommoded by the outburst. De Bernière had, in fact, expected it. He was testing Oliver. He had a feeling that time was slipping through his hands, that something deliberately dramatic was necessary to prevent a war, and at the same time he regarded war as inevitable. Nothing had shocked him so much as Dr. Church's words, when the livid doctor had said the rebels were arming, and he was shocked only because it was something he had known all along. He had been listening outside the door. He had heard Dr. Church's inflated speeches, and he had been amused by the gentle, provocative tones of Lord Percy. Afterward it had been his duty to prepare a cot for the doctor and to stand guard over him while he slept, snoring like a pig. In the morning he had been by the doctor's side when a washbasin was brought to him; it was odd how many times the doctor washed his hands, as though aware of an obscure guilt. Then the chair, and then helping the doctor to disguise himself, all the time behaving like a *valet de chambre:* the very thought of it made him feel sick. He said: "I wish you would remember about the teeth. It's awfully important."

"I don't remember."

"Then it's probably not Warren. You'd remember Warren's teeth. He's proud of them." He went on a moment later: "He carries a swordstick. Surely you saw his swordstick?"

Oliver shook his head.

"And very proud of his hands; likes gesturing with them. About your height—broader shoulders, though—and speaks well. Oh, well, it's all wasted time. We'll probably find out who he was when we have seen the letter, though the handwriting looks uncommonly like a woman's. The curse of it is that the general's asleep. We can't open it, though I've half a mind to. . . . You may accept my apologies. We're all disorganized. Lord Percy's drilling his ragged crew on the Common, but the rest of us are scatterbrained this morning. . . . You don't remember anything else—anything that would be worth while to tell an officer who desires information ardently?"

De Bernière looked extraordinarily serious, and his youthfulness made his gravity all the more alarming. Oliver had long ago become reconciled to being questioned by him. He felt no pride in his own rank. The ensign was genuinely anxious and perturbed: there was something in his manner which suggested that he knew more than he told, was closer to General Gage than he would admit, and knew the risks involved.

"So the general's asleep?" Oliver said.

"Yes, and we have orders not to wake him unless something of very great urgence arises."

"Don't you think a letter from Warren would be a matter of urgence?" Oliver said, desperately trying to solve the problem that was tormenting him. "I'm pretty sure of one thing: whoever it is, he is high up in the rebel organization."

De Bernière gazed at the envelope, turned it over, examined the handwriting again and shook his head.

"And there's another thing," Oliver went on obstinately. "He is someone I would be prepared to trust."

"You can't trust any of them," De Bernière answered. "And even if you could trust one individually, there would be no guarantee that you could trust any of the others. They don't agree among themselves. Warren could promise peace, and sue for it, and show his hand. Adams will talk of war because he likes the sound of his own speeches. A plague on demagogues! No, there's no hope that way. If only they were organized! If only they knew what they wanted! What's so terrible is that no one really knows what he wants." He was holding the letter in his hand and shaking it as though he thought its secrets could be shaken out of it.

Oliver snapped: "We have to trust someone."

"There is absolutely no one," De Bernière said helplessly.

Oliver had no desire to argue further. He took the letter back and ran up the ornate staircase, searching the faces of the officers coming down the stairs for some sign of what was going on in their minds. Most of them looked as though they had not slept. They were all pale, and the embroidery of their uniforms only made them appear more startlingly listless. In the street a small column of Grenadiers was marching to the Common with fifes and drums playing. Birds were shrilling in their nests under the eaves. It was a clear day with a cold wind coming from the open sea. Oliver found a sentry posted outside the governor's bedroom. The sentry refused to let him go in. A little while later Oliver met Haldimand coming out of the Blue Room. The huge Swiss was unshaved and glared at the white-and-gold stairway with a lorgnette held up to his eyes: the lenses were nearly half an inch thick.

"I have an urgent letter for General Gage," Oliver announced.

The general, his uniform all creased and ill-fitting, looked Oliver up and down. At that moment he seemed to Oliver a symbol of all the obstructions he had met since the moment he walked up the steps of Province House.

"Where is the letter?" Haldimand said in a strangely loud voice which echoed through the corridors.

Oliver handed it to him nervously, but still held his hands on it.

"Haff the gootness to leave it in my hands," Haldimand said impatiently.

"No, sir," Oliver answered, holding on to the letter.

"Impertinence!"

"I beg a thousand pardons, sir, but I am under instructions to deliver this to the general's hands."

It was absurd, and it was ridiculous! The white-and-gold

stairway was wheeling in the sunlight. A clock chimed. The
scarlet-uniformed sentries were marching across the parquet
floor below. In refusing to give Haldimand the letter Oliver
had not the slightest idea he was committing a gross im-
propriety; and Haldimand, surprised by the action and not
seeing Oliver too clearly, let the letter go, but not without a
sigh of regret. He had served in the British Army for twenty
years, but he had never understood the British.

"Who's it from?" Haldimand muttered.

"I don't know, sir," Oliver answered honestly. "I think—
from Dr. Warren."

"Take this officer to see General Gage," Haldimand said
to the sentry outside the Blue Room. "If the general is sleeping, it is advisable to wake him. Afterward, Captain De Lancey, come down to me." It was only then that Oliver realized
that Haldimand spoke English well enough when he had a
mind to it.

General Gage was sleeping alone in the immense pink bed.
He had fallen asleep around five o'clock in the morning while
reading Polybius' account of the destruction of Carthage,
and his square spectacles were still on his nose. He had not
pulled the curtains; the sunlight fell on him. He breathed
heavily like a man who sleeps exhausted.

When the sentry knocked on the door there was no sound,
only the heavy echoing of the knocks.

"Are you sure he is in the bedroom?" Oliver asked.

"I saw him go to bed," the sentry replied. "Poor man, he
hasn't enjoyed a good sleep for weeks. If it's not his child
being sick, it's worry."

There were more knocks, and still there was no answer.

"So you're sorry for him?" Oliver asked, alarmed at the
turn of the sentry's words.

"I wouldn't say I'm sorry, sir. He's a martinet, and it's

not in me to be sorry for a martinet. But he has a good heart when he cares to show it, and he has an American wife, as we all know. What should he be doing giving orders to cut the throats of the rebels?"

Oliver had not expected the sentry to speak so openly. The man's eyes were bloodshot.

"I've been here two years," the sentry said, "and I'll tell you this: someone's going to put a light to the powder keg. It's not in human nature when you have a light and a powder keg not to have a blaze."

The sentry talked in whispers. They could hear something moving inside the bedroom.

"Well, what is it?" the general asked in a complaining voice.

"Oliver De Lancey, sir, with a letter for your attention, sir."

"Can't it wait?"

"No, sir."

"All right. Come in, Oliver."

When Oliver entered the bedroom he was blinded by the sunlight coming through the window. The general, with much beating of pillows, was struggling up in the bed. He wore a tasseled nightcap, but he had done no more than remove his heavy coat weighted with gold lace, and his trousers, and then slumped into bed. He wore a cambric shirt, and the lace was all wrinkled.

"I've had two hours of sleep, Oliver, and I must be grateful for that."

Oliver handed him the letter without a word. His hands were shaking. The general opened it, fixed his square glasses carefully, rubbed his hand along his cheek where the first bristles were beginning to appear and read it steadily, sometimes holding up one hand to shield his eyes from the sunlight. As he read, his face grew graver.

"I suppose someone slipped it into your hands when you were out on a promenade," the general commented after he had read the letter twice.

Oliver blushed, nodded, mumbled, "Yes, sir," and continued to stare out of the window. He wondered why the general had not troubled to draw the curtains.

"Thank you, Oliver," the general said a moment later. "It's from Dr. Warren—and he's the worst of them. I dare say you've never met an American rebel." He carefully folded the letter. "You've come at the right time. By God, you have! You may even see some action, Oliver." He was about to put the letter on the nightstand beside the bed when something in Oliver's manner made him pause. "Who gave you the letter?" he asked.

Oliver blushed again, shifted from one foot to the other and then said, "A woman—this morning."

"The women are the worst," the general commented. "We have enough trouble with the men, but when we've dealt with the men we still have to face the women. I won't ask you any more about her, Oliver. I trust you enough to know you'd have no dealings with these rebels." Then, with a curt "I'll see you at noon," the general dismissed the young captain, rearranged the woolen skullcap on his head, turned over and went to sleep again. Clearly, he had given orders to be awakened at noon, and was determined not to be interrupted further.

As he came down the stairway Oliver found himself wondering at the contents of the letter. Without having seen it, he could almost have recited it. He knew the precise tones of Dr. Warren, the stern implacable voice. All round him the officers of Province House were going about their affairs, for the house was no longer simply the residence of the royal governor: Haldimand lived there and had his offices there, and a room had been set apart for Admiral Graves. Marines kept

coming and going with messages. There was an air of subdued excitement. Upstairs, he heard a child wailing.

"So you've bearded the lion in his den?" De Bernière
said, stepping out from the closet at the foot of the stairs.

"I've seen him," Oliver said stiffly.

"And you read him the letter?"

"No, he read it himself. It was from Dr. Warren all right.
Do I have to report everything to you?" Oliver went on in
a sudden fit of annoyance.

"It won't do any harm, Captain De Lancey. All intelligences
about the enemy pass through my hands. I'll swear to that,
and you may ask General Gage at your pleasure—or ask General Haldimand. They know what I'm up to."

"What precisely are you up to?"

"I'm engaged in trying to discover what the enemy is all
about, and I assure you it's a full-time occupation, Captain
De Lancey."

"Well then, there's nothing to tell you except that General
Gage read the letter through twice, or perhaps three times,
and said nothing about it—not even a thank-you."

"That's all?"

"I've told you that's all."

"I do believe you, Captain De Lancey. God knows, I have
respect for you, and if I ask questions, it isn't out of disbelief.
I have a hundred other questions to ask if you'll give me
time. Can you tell me where Dr. Warren is?"

"So that you can arrest him?"

"I'm not sure about that. We may have to arrest him. We
need to know these intelligences. Tell me—you were taken
to a secret meeting with him, isn't that it? Do you know
where the meeting took place?"

"It was near Summer Street, I think."

"How do you know?"

"I saw the name of the street."

"And you'd recognize the place?"

"I doubt that. I could recognize the house from the garden, but not from the street. No, De Bernière, I've told you all I know. I'm not a criminal in the dock. Leave me alone now for pity's sake! Not that I feel in a mood for pity, but I can see advantages in not being questioned."

Saying this, Oliver smiled. In an odd kind of way he admired the man's persistence. De Bernière was stocky, dark-faced, with a casual directness, and Oliver was now aware that if De Bernière was a plague, he was also high in the councils of the governor.

Leaving De Bernière, Oliver went to see Haldimand. The general was sitting at a table, industriously writing a letter, his heavy hand holding the pen as one might hold a trenching tool. In one corner of the room a black kettle was boiling over a charcoal stove; there was the smell of a thick brew of tea in the air.

"Haff the gootness to sit down," Haldimand said gruffly without taking the trouble to look up.

Oliver waited five minutes, then coughed politely. There was an alarming rumble from Haldimand.

"Cough is not goot," the general said sharply. "Patience is goot."

So Oliver remained patient, waiting until the moment when Haldimand in his thick, spluttering handwriting had composed his letter, had sprinkled sand over it, had read it through and carefully buried it inside an envelope. There was a sense of massiveness about the general as he sat at the table, every seam of his uniform about to burst. He looked as fresh as massive people can look after only a few hours' sleep. Oliver hoped he would not be asked to relate what had happened in General Gage's bedroom. He decided to take the attack to the enemy camp. He would ask Haldimand questions before Haldimand began to cross-question him.

"Do you think it is war, sir?" Oliver asked at last.

"I do not think," Haldimand answered.

"No war?"

"That is what I said. See, Oliver, how could there be war? Are the rebels ready? No. Are they united? No. Two thirds of America is Tory. Four fifths is indifferent. There are thirteen colonies—all of them separate. It is a thing that will pass."

"You are sure of that, sir?"

"I would not say it if I was not sure. As of now, I am sure it is not war. As of tomorrow . . ."

Haldimand shrugged his shoulders. The kettle was boiling, but he paid no attention to it. He kept looking searchingly at Oliver. Like General Gage, he had a habit of roughing his face with his hand so that the skin would be rumpled by his fingers—those hairy fingers which looked as though they were made of iron, so powerful they were, so blunt and straight. It amused Oliver that he should be called by his Christian name. Evidently Haldimand knew that he was the nephew of the royal governor and was determined to take the young officer under his wing.

"I shall place you under Major Pitcairn," Haldimand said, and suddenly, perhaps because he was now wide-awake, the Swiss accent disappeared. "We cannot have you running loose in the town. If anything happens, we must know whom you are serving under. As for horses, I must tell you this: you have come on a fool's errand. There are no horses to spare here. We cannot get them except from the farmers. Plow horses is all you'd be able to get. . . . You're sailing on the *Nautilus* Wednesday?"

"Yes, sir."

"Then make yourself useful to Major Pitcairn in the interval. I can't have you running round doing nothing. Have nothing to do with the people in the town, if you value your life. You understand that?"

"Yes, sir."

"Then good luck to you, Oliver. Report to Major Pitcairn at the barracks on the Neck."

Oliver bowed and went out into the hallway. There was no sign of De Bernière, and for this he was grateful.

The wind was to the north, and all Boston was shining in the sun. It was not warm; neither was it cold. There was the faintest trace of frost on the air as Oliver sauntered out of Province House, oddly content with himself, whistling under his breath. His mind dwelt on the yellow brilliance of the light on this April morning, on the clean sharp faces of the Bostonians who went about their affairs as though there was no rebellion in the air. The houses were clean as paint; so were the roads. The shops were open. Everywhere there was an air of business, and if there were not so many people in the street as there were in London, well, Boston was no more than a small town sitting at the foot of its steeples. A girl passed, and the rustling of her starched skirts pleased him. He smiled at her. She smiled in return, then looked away; but before she passed from sight, he had remembered every detail of her delicate neck, her sharp profile and ringlets of yellow hair escaping from a lace cap. "So help me," he murmured, "they are so clean and fresh they look as though they came from an egg this morning." De Bernière had warned him of the danger of walking about Boston, but he was unaware of danger. Once, someone at an upstairs window emptied some slops into the street, narrowly missing him. It occurred to him that the slops might have been intended for him, but no—the whole street was smiling, the shopkeepers were bowing, and when an officer rode past he thought he saw smiles on the faces of the people. The officer rode on a high-stepping roan, and the sound of the horse prancing down the street was as pleasant as the faces of the people.

Oliver De Lancey was not one of those men who inquire into their own motives. He took life as he found it. He had come off a ship, found a neat town bathing in the spring sunshine, and he was prepared to enjoy it. It was now Saturday: on the following Thursday he would be gone. He might never see Eugénie again, and the thought pained him. Already he was beginning to feel that the ball, the meeting with Eugénie and all the events which happened afterward had occurred weeks, even months ago.

No one told him where the barracks were, but he knew well enough. He had seen them from the ship, tall, squat, ugly buildings looking over the sea, with fresh paint on them, for they had been built only a few months before. Skirting the Common, where the Redcoats were at their exercises, he came to the wharf where some sailors were sunning themselves. They were stripped to the waist. The sun shone on them, and the masts and ratlines behind framed them. The strange thing was that some of them were dancing to a fiddle played by a blind fiddler in a tattered leather coat, and the men were roaring the song as he played, clapping their hands and laughing. They did not pause when Oliver came near them, for Oliver was an army officer and the sailors held the army in contempt. They were singing "Yankee Doodle"; and while the sails flapped behind them and the sunlight ran across the wharf, they looked as carefree as anyone could be. When "Yankee Doodle" was over, the blind fiddler played "Old Mother Margaret," and this pleased the sailors especially, for the words could be used to describe General Gage. The fiddler paused long enough to say, "A health to your lordship," when Oliver came walking along the wharf.

"A health to you," Oliver answered, for the sun was dazzling, there was the smell of fresh fruit on the air and the fiddle was well tuned.

Then the fiddler was playing "It's a Wonderful Day for a Walk in the Hay," and all the sailors were singing lustily, some sailors from the ships joining in.

"What do they pay you?" Oliver asked.

"They pay me a penny an hour and a tankard of ale," the fiddler replied. "It's hard work, your lordship. They have nothing else to do except dance the morning away, and the afternoons, too."

"You're not blind, are you?"

"Blind enough. I can see a bit, but not enough for a livelihood."

There was something in the tone of the fiddler which suggested he was well able to care for himself, and perhaps he wasn't blind at all. Oliver turned to look at the sailors again. Clean-limbed, with the bloom of the sun on them, they were laughing and cheering, paying no attention to the officer who had walked among them.

"Where do you come from, fiddler?"

"Concord, your honor. It's a fine little town. You'll like it well enough when you go there."

Oliver started. There was a hint of menace in the fiddler's words. He looked the man up and down, then he shrugged and walked along the wharf until the notes of the fiddle came faint on the air. He turned when he reached the barracks. Far away he could see the little knot of sailors dancing in the sun.

"Captain Oliver De Lancey reporting to Major Pitcairn," he said to the guard at the barracks, and it amazed him that his hands were quivering when he saluted. For the first time he had felt the menace in the air.

There were some cherry trees in the barracks courtyard. In the restless wind the coiled white blossoms were stirring.

CHAPTER 5

The Alarm

EARLY IN THE AFTERNOON of the next day General Gage summoned his chief officers to the Blue Room. As usual, he had worked through the night and slept through the morning. As usual, he had not slept enough, and the bright sun coming through the open windows made him screw up his eyes. He nodded to Lord Percy and General Haldimand, and made a special point of greeting Colonel Smith and Major Pitcairn of the Marines, whose red hair showed under the white curled wig which was set a little askew. The general smiled at Admiral Graves, and then at De Bernière, who was perched on a small stool behind him, busily writing down the names and titles of the officers who were present in the Blue Room. The names and titles were written in full, but the conversations and discussions would be taken down in cipher. There was something of a smirk on the ensign's face, for in the normal course of events another officer would have been chosen as secretary; but today General Gage had singled him out and asked that he should attend.

General Gage got straight down to business.

"I have summoned you, gentlemen, because the time will soon be coming when we shall have to take measures against Concord. I cannot tell you when we shall march, but it is necessary that I should convey to you my own opinions and hear your views. It is my belief that we should send an ex-

97

pedition solely for the purpose of destroying stores. No
punitive expedition, and not a shot to be fired."

The general's gaze settled on the brown eyes of Major
Pitcairn, whose lips, under the reddish mustache, were pursed
into a smile. There was a long pause, broken by the harsh,
high-pitched voice of Admiral Graves, who said, "I wonder at
your boldness, my lord." There was more than a hint of sarcasm in that sharp-edged voice. "I have suggested before,
my lord, and there are witnesses here, that we have only one
recourse: we should burn Concord to the ground."

Everyone knew that Admiral Graves, who seldom used a
bold course, was forever recommending bold courses in
others; therefore everyone smiled at him, everyone nodded
in his direction, and General Gage, not to be outdone, inclined
his head in the direction of the admiral whose plumed hat lay
squarely on the table before him and who seemed to be lost
in admiration of his own words.

"And how would you burn it down?" the general asked, in
exactly the same tone as he would ask, How would you peel
an apple?

"With rags soaked in oil, my lord," Admiral Graves answered gruffly.

"And the stone walls, Admiral? Your rags soaked in
oil wouldn't harm the walls, would they?"

"I'd bring my six-pounders up and level 'em. It is my
belief, your lordship, that Concord is a misnomer. Far from
being a seat of harmony, the place is a devilish nest of conspirators who should be put to trial and hanged on a gallows
tree."

"Then you insist on a trial first?" the general asked,
amused and frowning at the same time.

"I don't insist on a trial," the Admiral answered firmly.
He would have gone on to make still another of his well-
known speeches on the "devils who are at the heart of this
fearful conspiracy" if General Gage had not raised his hand

sharply, calling on the officers at the same time to look carefully at the maps which De Bernière was spreading over the table.

"As you know," the general said, "I have given orders that the boats should be made ready, and I have asked Colonel Smith to let me know what troops he would advise for the purpose. He has suggested—and I agree with him—that it would be better to take the men over by boat. I don't want them to be seen in Charlestown. We don't want alarm bells all over the countryside."

He turned to Colonel Smith with a quick smile, and went on: "We have the boats made fast under the sterns of the warships, and I think we can say we have very little fear of the rebels employing fireboats. As for the Grenadiers and Light Infantry, they have been off duty for some days and would be fresh for any such journey we have in mind. Meanwhile we have received information that the Committee of Safety is about to move a great part of its supplies from Concord, and we know now exactly what they intend to move and where they intend to move it. They have four six-pounders which they propose to transfer to Groton, and they have ordered the two four-pounders to be mounted. Then there are miscellaneous supplies . . . " Here General Gage opened the leather folder and read with a half-smile through a long list of such supplies as "spades, pickaxes, billhooks, shovels, axes, hatchets, crows and wheelbarrows."

As they listened to this list, all the officers began smiling, and even Admiral Graves, whose customary expression was a kind of worried frown, permitted the slightest of smiles at the corners of his lips. "Wheelbarrows, did you say, my lord?" he asked sternly, and at the same time smiling.

"I said wheelbarrows," the general replied. "I am not of the opinion that these humble articles are to be despised."

"No, sir. But since His Majesty's forces are superbly equipped, and the rebels are equipped with little more than wheelbarrows, I wonder why we allow ourselves to regard them as a threat at all."

General Gage groaned. There seemed to be no way in which he could put an end to the insults of the admiral. He rather hoped that Major Pitcairn would help him out, and so he threw the major a look of appeal.

"If I may be allowed to say a word, my lord, it seems to me that a wheelbarrow serves on land exactly the same purpose that a boat serves at sea: it carries things along."

The general was pleased, and sat back in his chair to watch the effect of Major Pitcairn's thrust. Admiral Graves shot a look of extraordinary venom at the major, but said nothing.

"We shall need to take six or seven hundred men across," the general continued. "My dear Admiral, how many journeys shall we have to make, how long will it take and how would you advise us to conduct the operation?"

"My lord, you have my communication on this subject. We have thirty boats which can be depended on, and each boat can hold about fifteen men fully equipped."

"Then we shall need to make two trips across?"

The admiral nodded. General Gage pointed at the place on the map where he wanted the Grenadiers and Light Infantry to embark. There followed a long discussion about the exact route to be followed. The men would arrive on the Charlestown-Cambridge shore when it was still dark. They would avoid leaving Boston by way of the Neck and Roxbury. The exact time of their departure would be kept secret, for fear of alarming the people. Then there was the question of what provisions they would carry, who would lead them, and what they would do in the case of opposition.

Gage had long ago decided that Colonel Francis Smith should be in charge of the operation, but he needed someone younger and quicker to lead the advance. If there was any trouble, it was likely that the advance would meet it. He said: "I have debated the matter most carefully, and I feel that Major Pitcairn should be entrusted with the advance."

There was a polite murmur of approval.

"You have no objections, Pitcairn?"

"None, my lord."

"I have given you a place of considerable danger, and one which, even if successful, will bring you little credit. It will be difficult, dangerous and unrewarding. There must be nothing spectacular in the mission you are asked to perform. You will be charged with the destruction of the weapons of the rebels at Concord—nothing else whatever—and your success will be measured by the quietness with which the operation is carried out. I want no one hurt, no one killed, and I want that clearly understood."

"You do me honor, my lord. Why, sir, we'll play the fifes and drums through every street of Concord."

"You will?" Admiral Graves asked incredulously. "Well, then, it seems to me you will be lucky if they only throw stones at you. Why, sir, you talk of going on the expedition as though you were contemplating a little frolic. One cannot frolic with rebels, Major. You'll learn better."

Pitcairn smiled. He knew, as well as anyone, that the admiral was likely to see monsters where there were only shadows. He knew too that the expedition was fraught with dangers. He would give a good account of himself. That was all, and it was more than enough. And he knew that Gage had confidence in him. They would treasure those faint smiles across the table in the Blue Room. "When does the expedition set out?" he asked.

"Soon."

"You mean, my lord, that the exact time and date are still undecided?"

"I mean exactly that."

Shortly afterward the meeting broke up. It was now late. They had spent four hours around the table, and long shadows were already darkening the town. Lord Percy had taken

almost no part in the discussions. He had listened carefully,
his eyes on General Gage. At dawn he had drilled his men
on the Common, and now it was late and he intended to dine
later with Admiral Graves on board the *Somerset.* He decided to go for a brisk walk. The air was fresh and clear,
sparkling as it sometimes is on windy days in late spring. He
saw Oliver talking to Ensign De Bernière in the great tiled
lobby of Province House, and it occurred to him that it would
be pleasant to have Oliver as a companion. Oliver agreed
readily.

"We'll go for a walk—anywhere," Lord Percy said. "The
truth is, my dear boy, that there is so much fog of talk in the
Council Chamber that a man would go insane if he did not
breathe fresh air occasionally."

"Then the discussions continue . . . Your Grace?" Oliver
said, remembering just in time that Lord Percy was an earl
and therefore entitled to a very special mode of address.

"They continue interminably. I will tell you a secret. We
discussed the use of wheelbarrows by the rebels, and we came
to the conclusion that wheelbarrows are dangerous imple-
ments of war."

The earl wore a drab cloak over his brilliant uniform, and
it pleased him that he passed unrecognized down the street.
They crossed to the Common. Lord Percy's long neck and
long, sharp nose gave him something of the appearance of a
bird, and he even walked with something of a bird's quick,
eager stride. He smiled continually, and Oliver flattered himself that Lord Percy was happy in his company. The starlings
were wheeling among the elms. Little knots of people were
playing bowls. There were some fishermen standing on the
banks of the little ornamental lake. Lovers were walking
hand in hand beside the flower beds.

"You should pay attention to the Common," Lord Percy
said. "It is an excellent example of the benevolence of our
administration. In the early mornings we use it as a parade

ground. In the evening the young people of Boston take it over. All the artifices of war are demonstrated in the morning, and all the artifices of love in the evening."

They were watching some old men playing bowls when they heard a voice saying, "The British will march, but they'll miss their aim."

At once Lord Percy cocked up his ears, thrust his way through the group of men watching the bowlers and said, "What aim?"

"Why, the cannon at Concord," said an old man in a black homespun suit and a broad-brimmed black hat. "I dare say they'll try to get our cannon, but they are not counting on our resolve."

"And when do you think the British will trouble to go running after a few pieces of cannon?"

"I've heard they are going tonight, sir."

Astonished, Lord Percy tried to give the impression of the utmost calm. He had come only ten minutes before from the Council Chamber. All the high officers had left, and General Gage had been standing beside the window, looking out over the harbor. He had asked Lord Percy to remain for a few moments, and the young colonel had obeyed without any profound feeling of satisfaction. Then the general had said very quietly, in a voice which would not have been heard on the other side of the room, "Well, we're going tonight. I haven't told them yet, and they won't know until the last moment. I may have to send you later with the reserves."

"Then you expect trouble?"

"I expect none. I have full faith in Pitcairn."

The general had said nothing more. His face was expressionless as he gazed out the window. He and the colonel were the only people who knew that the Grenadiers and the Light Infantry would be sent out of Boston to seize the rebel guns in Concord.

And now, Lord Percy thought, here were some men playing bowls, and every one of them, most likely, was aware of British intentions.

"Confound it," said Lord Percy. "You have no trust in the British. Why don't you trust them? They're not after your hides."

"No, sir," the old man said quietly, "they are after our guns." Then he turned away and resumed his playing at bowls.

Lord Percy was disturbed and angry. He had hoped that no one would recognize him, but the old man had evidently seen through his disguise. He had hoped the secret of the British expedition to Concord would be kept, but all of Boston shared the secret. He decided to return at once to Province House.

"They're damned clever at their inventions," he said with too much heat. "They'll take a rumor and embroider it and hammer it into reasonable shape, and then half the town believes it."

Dusk was coming on. Long black shadows lay over the Common. The men who had been playing bowls departed, and the lovers remained. The starlings were no longer chattering.

"Then it's pure invention?" Oliver asked.

"I won't say it's pure invention," Lord Percy answered. "They'll take a fact or a rumor and twist it out of shape. They're good at spying, but they're not so good at making reasonable deductions from the evidence. And they're at the mercy of hotheaded and unscrupulous men."

"You don't think there will be a fight, then?"

"Fiddledeedee!" Lord Percy replied, and then said something about an invitation to take dinner on board the *Somerset* and the need to hurry back to Province House to change his uniform.

Oliver was not impressed by the sudden alteration in Lord Percy's countenance. There was a hot rage burning underneath the surface. It occurred to Oliver that the old man

playing bowls had found a chink in his lordship's armor. As
Lord Percy strode away, a long, lean black shadow against
the gathering darkness of the Common, he looked more than
ever like some handsome and predatory bird.

"God help us if they know all our plans!" Oliver muttered,
and made his way toward the barracks overlooking the tidal
river.

He was about to enter the barracks when a man came out
of the shadows. Oliver could not recognize him, for he wore
some kind of scarf over the lower part of his face. Some
Grenadiers were marching in columns of four just outside
the barracks gate.

"The chair is waiting, your honor," the man said.

"What chair?"

"A chair to take you to see Eugénie de Malmédy."

Oliver's first impulse was to order the man's arrest. All he
had to do was to summon the guards. It might even be simpler to arrest the man himself. The man came closer and
whipped the scarf away, and then Oliver saw that it was the
same man who had been playing the fiddle for the sailors on
the wharf.

"We've met before," the man said. "It was a very pleasant meeting, I remember."

"I suppose you got a great deal of information from our
sailors," Oliver exclaimed heatedly.

The man covered his face with the scarf. "No," he said.
"I don't find the sailors very informative. No one ever tells
them very much. . . . I like to fiddle for them. I'm a cordwainer by trade."

"And you play to amuse the sailors?"

"Exactly."

"And they tell you what they know, even though it isn't
very much?"

"Every little bit helps," the cordwainer said, smiling.

It was now nearly dark. Oliver could hear the men singing in the barracks, and the solemn tread of the guards. Above the sea the stars were coming out, and there was a hint of rain in the air. All the time the cordwainer was watching the expression on Oliver's face, studying him carefully, smiling to himself; and Oliver, in turn, was studying the cordwainer, whose eyes were close-set and whose nose was a little like Lord Percy's, very long and sharp. There was something indescribably comic in this young man who had the temerity to stand near the barracks gate and talk with an officer of the Crown in full view of the guards, and when the scarf slipped away again Oliver was aware of the man's comical mouth. He was altogether a humorous fellow, and perhaps he had some training as an actor; for somehow he gave the impression of taking to disguises easily and delighted in wearing them.

"Then will you come, your honor?" the cordwainer said after a long pause.

Oliver nodded briefly.

"The chair is round the corner."

"Where? I can't see it."

"Use your eyes and walk a bit. You'll find it when you go up the street."

The cordwainer accompanied Oliver a little way and then disappeared. Oliver looked around. There was no sign of him. Perhaps he had flattened himself against the shadows of the wall. It was dark, and the air smelled of musk. It was very silent except for the sounds of singing in the barracks. The strange thing about the cordwainer's disappearance was its surprising suddenness: one moment he was walking beside Oliver, the next moment he had disappeared, and there was no sound of footsteps. It was as though he had been swallowed up in the ground. Oliver was tempted to return to the barracks, and he was already turning round when he saw the chair and the four Negroes flattened against the wall beside it. The Negroes bowed. They were evidently expecting

Oliver, for they made haste to open the door of the chair.
Oliver stepped inside, and at once he was aware of Eugénie's
perfume, the rustling of her taffeta dress. She uttered a faint
cry as he took her in his arms and kissed her on the mouth.
He was still kissing her when he became aware that the chair
was traveling unusually fast, and it was rocking from side to
side.

"Damn those Negroes!" he whispered. "I can't bear it
that they should be shaking you up so."

"You shouldn't damn anyone," Eugénie replied, "and least
of all the Negroes. They are going fast because I told them
to. We thought you would be coming to the barracks an
hour ago."

"So you have been waiting for an hour?"

"More than an hour."

He kissed her again, trying once more to imagine her face
in the unchanging darkness.

"I wonder you dared to stay near the barracks, Eugénie.
It's dangerous—terribly dangerous."

"Oh, you're wrong, Oliver. It's never dangerous. The
Boston women go in and out of the barracks as they please,
and they come every day and no one disturbs them." She
laughed quietly.

"I can't bear to think of you going to the barracks,"
Oliver said impetuously.

"You can't bear the Negroes and you can't bear the idea
of a woman going to the barracks. There are too many things
you can't bear tonight, Oliver."

"I don't want anyone else to kiss you," he said, and the
warmth of his words, the sudden violence of them, shook
him. They were unnaturally loud, and it occurred to him
that the Negroes must have heard him. In a softer voice he
said, "Tell me that no one has kissed you."

"Have you ever kissed anyone else, Oliver?" Eugénie
asked quietly, and there was a kind of menace in her voice.

"Never."

"What a heaven-born liar you are, my darling."

"I beg you to believe me," Oliver said earnestly, one arm around her shoulders and one hand desperately clutching at hers.

"No, Oliver, I must tell you the truth—we must both tell each other the truth. When I saw you I wondered why God had kept us apart for so long. I do love you with all my heart, believe me, and now more than ever, but I love my country too."

"Then we must be eternally apart, because England and America are at war."

"Not at war—at loggerheads."

"Then you don't believe there will be war?"

"We don't know yet, Oliver. We'll know soon—perhaps tonight."

Oliver frowned in the dark. Her scent was overpowering. There was the same thick, musty odor of the curtains. The Negroes were striding at a tremendous pace, so that there were times when he felt the whole chair was being hurtled savagely through the air. When she said, "We'll know soon— perhaps tonight," he had an impulse to hurt her. She was a spy! She was nothing more! He had known all the time that she was a spy, and still he had felt for her only a sense of wonder and adoration. He was seething with anger, and at the same time he knew that it was unreasonable to be angry. He loved her, he would always worship her, and always there would be an abyss between them. He said coldly, "You want me to give you secret reports."

"No, Oliver, I want your help," Eugénie answered slowly. "We have our own ways of getting secret reports. We want peace on honorable terms, and with God's help we shall have peace, but we shall never give in to the British demands when they ask too much of us."

Oliver was about to ask what she meant when he noticed

that the Negroes were slowing down their terrific pace. He
heard their boots scraping against gravel. Evidently they
were going up a path toward a house, for a faint light began
to shine through the curtains. Then the chair stopped so
abruptly that they were thrown into each other's arms, and
a moment later the door was pulled open.

A man with a white wig, a white cravat and a blue silk
coat was standing there with a lantern. He smiled, showing
two ivory teeth, and said, "Lord, lord, I thought you were
never coming back, Eugénie!... I'm grateful to Billy Dawes.
He came ten minutes ago."

"I waited an hour for Oliver," Eugénie explained, "and I
think our Negroes lost their way in the dark." She smiled at
Oliver and then at the man in the blue coat.

"I'm glad you have come, Captain De Lancey," the man
said, holding the lantern above his head as he led them to a
small house surrounded by elms. "I'll tell you the truth. We
have been trying desperately to find you all afternoon." He
pushed open the door which led into a sitting room, plainer
than the one in Summer Street, with only a table, some chairs
and a cupboard full of surgical instruments which gleamed
through the glass case.

"I presume I have the honor of addressing Dr. Joseph
Warren," Oliver said, recognizing the doctor, who was now
preparing a cordial.

"Yes," Warren said, looking up and smiling.

A young man with a red face and a sharp nose came
through another door into the room.

"And here's Billy Dawes," the doctor went on. "I understand you have met before."

Here was the cordwainer again. Oliver nodded, and Billy
Dawes's comical face suddenly wrinkled into a smile. Oliver
was now sure that Dawes must be an accomplished actor who
could assume many parts. God knows what part he would
assume next! He stood there smiling, a little drunk, waving

his hands in a generous salutation. He was out of breath, because he had ridden from the barracks on horseback and had not yet recovered from the pace of the journey. Oliver had the curious feeling that he had been kidnaped only to find himself among old friends. He said, "I can tell you nothing, gentlemen, you don't know. You must understand that I can provide you with no secret information, and indeed I am in no position to possess any."

"We happen to know that the Light Infantry and the Grenadiers are marching to Concord tonight," Warren said.

"You may know it, but it is the first I have heard of it."

"Then you don't believe they will go?"

"You misunderstand me," Oliver answered slowly, looking straight into the doctor's eyes. "I've told you that I know nothing about an expedition of this kind."

"You haven't heard them talking of it?"

"I've told you I haven't."

"It is a strange thing," said Dr. Warren, "when an officer of the British Army knows nothing about a venture which all Boston is talking about."

"Strange or not, it happens to be the truth."

By now they were sitting round the table. From a drawer in the table the doctor removed some maps. They were not unlike the maps used in the Blue Room at Province House.

"I'll tell you this," Dr. Warren said, drawing his thumb across the tidal river and then in a straight line to Concord. "We know what the general will do, because he has already made certain that we should know. He posted outposts on Tuesday, to cut the road to Concord. He has no desire to provoke rebellion if he can help it, so he will march secretly. And the best way would be for him to row his men across the widest part of the river. We know he has not enough boats and may have to make the journey two or three times, and we can guess how many men he will send out."

"How many?"

"About twenty companies."

There was a smile on Dr. Warren's face, but there was no satisfaction shown there. He was desperately earnest. Billy Dawes was sucking at his pipe, and Eugénie was gazing at the map like someone lost in a dream.

"Then what do you want me to do?" Oliver asked. He added sarcastically, "Since you know the plans of the commander in chief, why should you trouble yourself to arrest an officer who is not even a member of the garrison?"

"Because you are the nephew of General Gage. There is no other reason, Captain De Lancey. We still think you may have some way of gaining his attention. Go to him. Tell him that we know his plans. Tell him that the Committee of Safety is concerned that the Grenadiers and Light Infantry should not march out to Concord. Tell him there is nothing to be gained. We cannot promise that your soldiers will return to Boston."

"You mean you will arrest them as you have arrested me?"

"We haven't arrested you. You are free to go where you please. We beg you to go to the governor and tell him . . . You know what we want you to tell him. There is no need to go into details. Simply this: the soldiers must not leave. It would be pure provocation. We cannot promise a safe-conduct to them. Tell him that the Committee of Safety will meet with him tonight, if necessary. We want peace. We don't want war. I have said this before, and it is true. You *must* believe us."

"I gave your letter to him," Oliver said helplessly.

"And there was no reply," Dr. Warren answered quickly. "He treated us with contempt."

"He treats no one with contempt. Of that I am sure."

"He gave us no answer, and that is the same as treating us with contempt. No, Oliver, there is only one solution. He must be told how affairs stand. I would to God we could *arrest* him too, so that he could see the temper of our people. He doesn't suspect our strength."

"Please tell him," Eugénie said, looking pale and even feverish in the candlelight. "It's the last chance for a reasonable peace."

"I'll do my best," Oliver said. He rose, and shortly afterward went out with Eugénie alone to the waiting chair which would take him to Province House.

"What will happen to you?" he asked when they were standing in the darkness outside the house.

"What will happen to all of us?" Eugénie answered. "God knows. No one knows."

He kissed her, holding her so savagely that he could feel her bending under the weight of his embrace. A Negro with a fowling piece was standing in the shadows beside the door.

"Please God you convince the governor!" Eugénie whispered. "Behind every rock and bush you'll find the rebels waiting for the Redcoats."

In the darkness of the chair Oliver felt the loneliness of a man who carries destiny in his hands. All his life he had wished only to be left alone, to pursue his own adventures. When the chair was let down, grating on the gravel, he felt stunned and sick. He got out, to find himself some distance away from Province House, for the Negroes had no intention of taking him up to the doors.

Lights were shining at Province House, but there were not so many as usual, and there was a heavier guard. When he passed the guard he had every intention of knocking at General Gage's door and delivering a kind of ultimatum, but he had no idea how he would phrase it. More than anything else he wanted a drink.

"Well, Oliver, it's pleasant to see you looking so well," Haldimand said as he crossed from one door to another.

No, it would be useless to discuss the plans of the rebels with Haldimand, Oliver thought.

De Bernière had a little office downstairs. He was writing up a report, with a single candle fixed in an iron support beside him. As soon as Oliver entered the room he rose to his feet, carefully concealing with a lead weight what he had written.

"You're the last person I expected to see, Captain De Lancey," De Bernière said.

"I must see the governor at once," Oliver announced, breathing hard. He glared at the maps pinned on the wall and at the corner of the letter which emerged from under the lead weight.

"Useless," De Bernière said quickly. "He's dining with Admiral Graves on the *Somerset* tonight."

"I can row over to the *Somerset*."

"They wouldn't let you on board, even if you came from the rebels with a letter of surrender."

"I've got something worse than a letter of surrender. I've come from Dr. Warren. He says they'll fight."

"Well, then, they'll fight," De Bernière said calmly. "The minds of their lordships in London are made up. There isn't a thing you can do about it. You should know better than to attempt the impossible."

"If I could see General Gage——"

"I've told you it's impossible. He's not here. Try to get a boat if you like, but I have a feeling they will be using their boats for other purposes than conveying messages to the *Somerset*."

"You won't help me?"

"If I thought there were any advantages, I would, but they've worked out their plans to the last detail, Captain De Lancey. There's nothing to be gained by changing the plans at the last moment."

"Then they are leaving tonight for Concord?"

"I don't know. No one has said so. But I have a feeling that they won't delay much longer."

Oliver left Province House like a man in a nightmare. The shadows wheeled in the streets. Except for Haldimand there were no high officers at Province House, and he knew, or thought he knew, what Haldimand's answer would be if he said he had been consorting with the rebels again. He made his way to the barracks, keeping close to the walls. The streets were strangely quiet. The barracks were in darkness. He was challenged three times at the barracks gate. He was going to his own room, lost in thought, when he saw Major Pitcairn hurrying ahead a little in front of him. Oliver caught up with him. He had complete trust in the redheaded major and blurted out: "I've just seen Dr. Warren, sir. He says the rebels are preparing to rise against us if we send an expedition to Concord."

Pitcairn had smiled the moment he saw Oliver. Now he looked grave, and his eyes clouded with anger. "You've been having correspondence with the rebels, then?"

"I couldn't help myself, sir. They kidnaped me. I was taken to Dr. Warren's house—I think it was Dr. Warren's house."

"He lives in Hanover Street."

"I didn't see the name of the street. I saw Dr. Warren. He wanted me to deliver a message to the governor."

"It's no use, Oliver," Pitcairn said, shaking his head from side to side. "I ought to arrest you for having correspondence with the rebels, but I won't. There are things you don't know. We've thought it out. The truth is, we haven't any alternative. They have their stores in Concord, and we can prevent them from rising against us only by taking over their stores. We simply have no alternative."

"When are we leaving for Concord?"

"Soon."

"You mean tonight?"

"I didn't say that," Major Pitcairn replied, gazing at Oliver with the look of a man who has no love for keeping secrets and would prefer that there were no secrets anywhere in the world. "I can't tell you when we are leaving, but you'll learn soon—soon."

Oliver learned half an hour later. At ten o'clock the men in the barracks were awakened by their sergeants, who put their hands on them and whispered that it was time to go, and the men chosen for the expedition were led out of the barracks by the back way so that even the sentries on guard at the barracks gates did not know what was happening. The men walked through the frosty streets in silence. When a dog barked at their heels it was swiftly killed with a thrust of a bayonet. The long column marched silently to the beach in the shadow of the new powder house. Boats from the *Somerset* were ranged along the beach in the dark, and the oars were muffled with blankets to prevent sound. In some of the boats provisions for the journey were being piled up; on the large whalers there were horses for the officers.

"I have a spare horse," Major Pitcairn was saying as he watched the dark boats leaving for the opposite shore.

Oliver nodded. He knew now that he would have to go with them. There was dead silence among the men. He had been standing with Pitcairn for half an hour, watching the boats disappear into the darkness, when he saw the tip of the moon rising; but by this time most of the men were across. Colonel Smith was among the first to get over Cambridge Marsh, and Pitcairn was the last. When they came to shore they had to wade up to their knees in marshy water for a while. There was a farm some distance ahead. All the men, about six hundred, were grouped around the farm. It was strange to see them so silent, so uncomplaining. Pitcairn and Smith were together in the farmhouse, but no word came from them until two hours later. It was one o'clock in the morning when the orders were given to march.

Little tufts of mist rose from the corn stubble, and all round them there was the long, dreadful, creeping silence of the night: no houses, once they had left Phipp's farm behind, no roads, only the field paths, trees, and the moon flooding the landscape with a silver light, yet leaving so much in shadow that the world looked ghostly—very black in places and bright silver in others. The reins and the side arms rattled, and there was the heavy plodding sound of soldiers, some cursing under their breath because they were wet from the journey over the tidal reaches. Though spring had come a month before its time and the leaves and blossoms were well out, this night was cold, so cold that the men's breath hung silver in the air.

"God help us," Oliver whispered. "Delays and delays. If we have any more, it will be the end of us. . . . What time do we expect to reach Concord?"

"With luck, by daybreak," Major Pitcairn answered, and galloped off to round up several soldiers who were preparing to strip some trees of bark to light a fire; they were wet through, and you could see their uniforms sticking to their skins.

Oliver was left alone, the huge moon above him, the boats behind him, and in front of him lay the unknown territory of America. He wondered what he was doing here, alone at night, a little separated from the rest of the soldiers, the bridle slack in his hands, while the long serpentine column made its way across the empty fields. Somewhere, far away and up the slope, he could see another winding column. Soon the last of them disappeared over the brow of the hill. *They're all going into the dark,* Oliver said to himself with a shudder, not because he was frightened, but because he was appalled by the strangeness of the landscape at night. *How will it end?* he asked himself. *How can a thing like this ever end? Surely it cannot end peacefully.* . . . He closed his eyes. His mind went out to the house on Summer Street, Eugénie lying beside him on the couch, warm and sweet-smelling, the pale face of Warren, the heavy red face of Billy Dawes, the Negro

with the fowling piece. What did it mean? What did anything mean? Luck or mischance had thrown him for a brief
moment among the rebels; now they were going out in a long
column toward a rebel stronghold, and Oliver could not tear
his mind away from the thought that they were going like
innocents to the slaughter. *Behind every rock and bush you
will find the rebels waiting for the Redcoats. . . .*

Savagely he dug his spurs into his horse, feeling the cold
damp round his legs, the sweat dripping on his face still—
strange that you could sweat so much on a cold misty
night!—and he was glad when he came upon Major Pitcairn
again, sitting bolt upright on his mare, his handsome face
clear against the moonlight.

"There's too much dawdling!" Major Pitcairn was shouting. "Come on, men. Keep in line." He turned to Oliver.
"Come and ride with me, son. You know, you needn't have
come out with us. I can tell you this. There's nothing but
boredom ahead. I've done the same journey a score of times,
and I know there's more boredom in wandering round the
fields of the province than any other task appointed for us. I
often march out with our battalion six or seven miles into
the country. Well, the people swear at us sometimes, but
there's no harm done. If I could get my hands on the rebel
leaders—men like Hancock and Adams—I'd think the journey was worth while, and there'd be some excitement for our
pains. Why, I've marched into a town where they were all
assembled, and simply nodded to them—that's all politeness
could demand—when I'd have liked nothing better than to
put a rope round the necks of the impudent rascals. So you
see there's only annoyance and vexation ahead."

"Then it's your belief, sir, that they won't fight us?"
Oliver said, and it was as though he were asking a question
in mathematics.

"God Almighty, no! Why should they fight us?" Major
Pitcairn answered. "Do you believe they've got the spirit or

the readiness to fight? They're Englishmen and they have courage, but you need an army to fight with—not a rabble of minutemen."

That was all. Major Pitcairn was a man of long silences and sudden long sentences. He would talk at length when he was in the mood, but now as he rode ahead, listening to the minute sounds which he always listened to on the march— not the sound of marching feet, but those other noises which tell you about the temper of the men, whether they are following willingly and what kind of spirit there was among them—he listened to these sounds carefully, evaluated them; his sharp ears could pick up a muttered curse at the end of the line.

Oliver was left alone to contemplate the white road across the field, a road which shone now like the color of bone. He was content with himself. It was not fear but strangeness which had moved him; and now as he grew accustomed to the look of a Massachusetts field at night, even the strangeness evaporated.

It was half an hour later, when a chill easterly wind was coming up, that Major Pitcairn broke the silence again. "I've told you I'd like to hang the rascals," he said, "but the truth is I would take no pleasure in it. Do you know what's best for them? Put them all on a ship and send 'em back to England." A cloud covered the moon, and in the darkness he laughed quietly. "They hanged Old Mark on Charlestown Neck," he said, referring to a Negro who had been hanged for stealing, "and it did no good to anyone. Admiral Graves is all for hanging them. I've had polite arguments with him, and the more he thinks of hanging, the less I like it. I'd prefer that we hold out the hand of friendship, but I suppose, while they keep making bullets out of pewter mugs, there's no hope for it."

"Then it's neither war nor peace," Oliver commented. In the moonlight there were great black lunging shadows over the fields, and he thought he heard some alarm bells ringing.

"Yes, neither war nor peace," Major Pitcairn answered, and then he stood up on the stirrups and listened to the faint sounds coming in the wind.

There was no doubt of it—there were alarm bells, clear and sharp and yet faint on the frosty air. It had been a clean winter, very warm and mild for Massachusetts, with hardly a trace of snow or frost through February, and the major remembered how sharply sounds had pierced the air as he went riding through the villages surrounding Boston. To-night, with the white sumac glinting on the ridges, the farm-houses shuttered and black in the shadows, sounds carried less sharply than usual, but there was no mistaking this particular sound. By now they had reached the Lexington Road. They were not marching down it, but skirting it, keeping it in sight. He had hoped that the rebels would know nothing about the night patrol, at least until he had reached the out-skirts of Lexington, for then it would be only a short progress to Concord and he would be able to fall upon their concealed guns without giving them time to hide them too carefully. He said: "They're a noisy lot with their damned alarm bells," and he thought he saw far away some lights flickering on the horizon. "The whole place is awake tonight," he murmured, and rode back along the column to see how the men were faring, while Oliver followed at a distance.

It's all riddles now, Oliver told himself. *Neither peace nor war, and the alarm bells ringing out. What kind of land-scape is this?*

"Rebels of hell!" one of the Grenadiers was shouting. "The whole place is full of them!"

BOOK TWO

Concord Bridge

CHAPTER **6**

A Journey to Concord

"WE'LL NEED two men to get to Concord at once," Warren was saying, and then he stared round the empty room. Billy Dawes had slipped away, and Eugénie was with Oliver outside the door. He heard their low whisperings, the grating of the Negroes' footsteps on the gravel pathway. Presently Eugénie was once more beside him. "We'll need two men to go to Concord at once," Warren repeated. "Where in thunder did Billy go?"

"I'm here," Dawes said, pushing open a door, smiling at Warren. There was a pleased expression on his face, for he had gone out through one door and come in through another.

"You don't have to play tricks," said Warren. "Play them on the British, not on me. . . . Will you ride to Concord?"

"It's a good night for riding."

"Then you'll do it?"

"Of course I will. What made you think I wouldn't?"

"You're damned useful, Billy. You're tricky as the devil. You can do it, can't you?"

"I've told you before . . . "

Warren frowned. He wanted Dawes to make the journey, but yet there was something undependable in the young cordwainer. He was a strange madcap adventurer, with a taste for getting into scrapes. Only a few days before he had engaged in a battle with a Redcoat, who had made some

facetious remark about his wife. There was little enough
reason for the quarrel, but Dawes had hammered the Redcoat's face until it looked like raw beef.

"I don't want you quarreling on the journey," Warren
said. "We've had enough quarrels with the British, and
there's the biggest one of all on our hands now."

"I'll go."

"No quarreling, mind."

Dawes laughed his full-throated laugh, and then winked
at Eugénie.

"Ride to Concord and tell 'em a brigade of twelve to fifteen
hundred men are very likely on their way, and find Sam
Adams and Johnny Hancock at Lexington. Tell 'em to run.
And that's all. No embroidery, Billy."

"He won't get through," Eugénie said. "They've got patrols on all the roads."

"We have to risk that," Warren answered slowly. "We'll
always have to risk that. I'll ask Billy to go one way and
Paul Revere to go another. Billy should go over the Neck
and then through Roxbury. It's a long way." He looked at
Dawes. "And tell 'em to ring the alarm bells."

"And you think he'll get through?" Eugénie asked, standing straight in front of Warren and smiling down at him as
he ran a pencil across the map. "It won't do. They're bound
to be caught. You'd better send a woman."

"I couldn't send a woman, Eugénie. There isn't a woman
who could make the journey tonight."

"And I tell you there isn't a man who could make it without the help of a woman, Joseph. You'll have to let me go.
I'm in a mood for riding tonight."

"I won't allow it," Warren said without looking up, but
he knew he was incapable of breaking her determination.
"Oh, Eugénie, I couldn't sleep if you went. Don't do it. We
can have a hundred riders at night, and one of them at least
will get through."

"Then let me go."

Dr. Warren had never been able to oppose Eugénie's will. There was something flint-hard in her, but there was no logic. He had told her he could not do without her, and still she was determined to go. Her cheeks were glowing. He looked up at her and smiled, saying, "If you must go, go with Billy. He has the devil's luck."

"Then you'll come as my lass," Dawes said, winking again.

"I'll go as your lass, if that's the way it is," Eugénie answered.

"And you'll let me put an arm round you?"

"Yes, if that's the way it is."

She looked very solemn, standing there in candlelight, wearing her taffeta dress and with a string of pearls round her neck.

"I'll be a farmer coming home from market, and you'll be my lass. You'll need a shawl, my dear, and as for me, I'll be a farmer with a bag of meal slung over the rump of my horse, and we'll fool the British at the gate. How's that, Doctor?"

"I don't care how you do it as long as you get through," Warren said, and all the time he was looking up at Eugénie with an appealing look in his eyes. He seemed to be saying, You can still escape from the journey. It won't do you any good, and I won't sleep tonight, thinking you are gone.

"I'm going to do it," Eugénie said, and then she followed Billy Dawes into what he called "the tiring room," where he kept all the odds and ends of the disguises he was accustomed to wearing in Boston. Except for the shawl, he offered her nothing to wear. For himself he put on a grizzled beard, a corduroy coat such as farmers wear, corded leggings, and he thrust a farmer's heavy wooden saddle under his arms. Then, as he walked out of the house in Hanover Street, he looked a farmer, and Eugénie, in her shawl, looked like a farmer's wife.

"We've been wedded a month," he said when he helped

her up into the saddle. "Remember that, my dear." He patted the bag of meal which one of the Negro servants had fetched from a grain merchant. Less than ten minutes after leaving Warren they were riding their horses through the darkened streets of Boston.

When they came in sight of the gates of the Neck, Dawes turned his horse into a side street. Eugénie followed him.

"We'll wait here," he said. "It's no use passing them when they have time on their hands. You're riding a pretty roan, and they'll suspect you at once. But if the soldiers march out on a routine order, it's devilish certain that the sentries will be in good humor and let us pass."

Eugénie trusted Dawes as she did few men. His humorous face was always twisting into wry smiles. He had a way about him, and if he said a thing would happen, it usually did. So it was now. They had been waiting in the darkened side street hardly five minutes when they heard the tramp of marching soldiers. Dawes jogged her arm and laughed quietly, as though to say, Watch me. And when the line of soldiers was passing by the sentries, he came cantering out of his hiding place to join them, shouting drunkenly, "Halloo, boys! It's a raw night for a march, eh?" A sentry held a lantern up to Dawes's face. Saliva was dribbling over his recently acquired beard, his eyes were rolling, and he turned from the sentry to Eugénie. He had no need for words. Everything about him suggested a farmer eager to take his wife to bed. There was something altogether fetching in this old farmer with his young wife, a thickset man who leered and winked and dug the sentry in the ribs. The sentry asked him to open the bag of meal. The farmer obliged, and when a bayonet was driven into the bag through the top the sentry said, "It's meal all right. Well, you're a lucky fellow. It's a raw night for the poor bloody sentries as well."

"You have my sympathy, boys," Dawes said, leering again.

"It's more than sympathy we want," the sentry replied. "A man needs a fat little wife and a roof over his head."

Then the sentry thwacked the rump of Dawes's horse with the butt of his firelock, and soon the old farmer and his wife were jogging along the Roxbury Road.

Once they had passed the sentries they came to the open roads. The air was fresh and pure. The fields of rye lay dark beside the road, and the shuttered farmhouses showed no lights. Sometimes Dawes would ride off the road and go up to a farmhouse. Still sitting on his horse, he would shout, "Halloo! Light your lamp, boy. The Redcoats are coming!" As likely as not, a face in a stocking cap would peer from an upstairs window, saying, "Lord, ha' mercy, which way are they coming?" and then Dawes would give them a very brief account of how General Gage was determined to seize the Concord weapons and the British were on the march. "Are they coming right away?" they would ask, and Dawes would answer, "We rightly don't know their journey, but they're coming—don't make any mistake about that."

So they rode to Lexington, with an hour of darkness before the moon rose, riding through the mysterious landscape where every tree resembled a shelter for a Redcoat patrol. Sometimes they would jump over a low wall and ride across a field, if they suspected a patrol along the road. Dawes had a great deal of experience in taking messages from Boston to the villages in the countryside. He never troubled to knock at more than one door in any village they passed. It was enough to let every village captain arouse his own minutemen. A lonely man, he derived comfort from Eugénie's presence, and sometimes when they were ambling along he would tell her droll stories.

When they came to Lexington lights were shining in all the houses around the green. A lantern shone from the church steeple, there were lights in all the windows of Buckman's

Tavern and there were bonfires on the hills. The meeting bells were ringing.

"Revere must have raced us to it!" Dawes exclaimed, coming to a halt outside the tavern.

"Only by a few minutes," Revere said, coming out of the tavern and waving his hands about his head. "Jump down into my arms, Eugénie. . . . Lord, what monkeys we are! We race and tear ourselves into tatters, and I dare say the people knew the news before we reached Lexington. Man, man! Listen to the alarm bells."

Revere was tall, thickset, and he wore his hair like thatch. He wore a deerskin coat and carried a brace of pistols at his belt. He stood there with his feet set apart, smiling broadly, his head cocked to listen to the sound of the bells.

"There's cheese and ale all served for you," Revere went on. "Tell me, did you come upon the patrols?"

"Not one."

"Then you're luckier than you deserve to be, Billy. I came upon two. The devils were standing under the shade of a tree on Charlestown Common near enough toward Cambridge. I could see their holsters and cockades, and they started their horses toward me. I had to ride them out along the Mystic Road. I'd thought they were tiring, and they were, but my poor bloody mount fell into a clay pond. . . . They say the women are gathering the children and the silver, and then fleeing to the swamps. I've had my fill of swamps today."

Saying this, he laughed and led them into the tavern, where a full meal was being prepared for the riders. Revere was rested; Dawes and Eugénie were exhausted, and they were still hoarse from shouting, "The Redcoats are coming" and "The Regulars are out."

"So you did it in style, with no bloody patrol ever gettin' in your way. And you have the most beautiful woman of

Boston as your companion of the journey, and you're never thrown back. I don't believe it, Billy. You must have flown through the air, eh?"

Dawes was in no mood for joking now. He said, "Where's Hancock and Adams?"

"They're running free," Revere answered. "I found seven men guarding Mr. Clarke's house, and they wouldn't believe I had come from Boston until they lifted a lantern close enough to my face to blind me. Mr. Hancock had given orders not to be disturbed. So I hammered on his door and shouted, 'The Regulars are out, and if you don't get out of your comfortable bed, you're a dead man.' He was up and about in the time it takes for a flash of lightning to fall through the sky. Man, I've seen the British rowing across the Charles—the river was black with them—and neither Mr. Adams nor Mr. Hancock was of the opinion that the British were on the way. 'I just can't believe it,' Mr. Hancock said. I told him I could use my eyes to better advantage at night than during the day, and I counted a thousand of them. 'Do you believe me now?' I said, and Mr. Hancock coughed and said he was prepared to believe it. *Prepared!* There he was, in the finest of silk nightgowns and Moroccan slippers, looking like one of the Seven Angels of Revelations—and it was very likely, yes, indeed, maybe and if you please, and that's a fine good thing you've done tonight, Mr. Revere. . . . What do you think of that, Billy?"

Dawes was stuffing cheese into his mouth, but he nodded his head in approval. "Well, are you off to Concord?" he said. "We could ride together."

"What's this about Concord? Dr. Warren said to get to Lexington."

"Not a word about Concord?"

"I don't recollect that he ever mentioned Concord to me, but I'd as well go with you as go with anyone. It's a fine night for a ride." He smiled and clapped Dawes on the shoulder.

The tavern keeper came up and offered Eugénie his wife's cape, saying it was cold, and if she was mad enough to ride, why, she had better keep warm. Eugénie was coming out of the tavern door when she saw a man with a lean face and a hint of a stubble beard who was asking whether there was anyone at the tavern who proposed to make a journey to Concord. "I'm Dr. Prescott," he explained, "and I've had some business at Lexington which kept me late."

"Most likely he's been courting his girl." The tavern keeper winked at them, and the young doctor blushed and then threw back his head in an imitation of a full-throated laugh. "He comes every night," the tavern keeper went on relentlessly. "Fair weather or foul, you'll find Dr. Prescott riding out to meet his girl."

"You're welcome to come with us," Dawes said pleasantly.

Soon the four of them were on their way, while the alarm bells rang deafeningly in their ears. They were halfway down the road when they saw a house where no light shone. Dr. Prescott knew the farmer well; he might have slept through the ringing of the alarm bells. Revere went on ahead. He had gone two hundred yards up the dark road when they heard a shout: "God damn you, stop! Go an inch farther, and you're a dead man!" Dawes held back. It was young Dr. Prescott who went riding ahead, using the butt of his whip in an effort to get through the patrol of four Redcoats who stood across the road.

"They've caught me," Revere shouted. "Go free if you can!"

The moon was blinding in the sky, but the road was so thick with trees that only a faint light came through the leaves. They heard Revere arguing with one of the Redcoats; they were both out of temper. Then Dr. Prescott came riding back, shouting at the top of his voice, "Get over the wall," and Dawes and Eugénie raced across a plowed field. When Eugénie reached a clump of elms she realized that Dawes must have turned back toward Lexington, for there was no sign of him. She was alone now among the creaking branches of the elms, but soon the wind died and the elms were silent as the fields, all burning-white in the moonlight. If she left the clump of elms, the Redcoats would see her soon enough. The stars were shining, and faintly on the horizon she saw the lights of Lexington.

She had been sitting quietly on her roan for about ten minutes when she heard Prescott's voice, not loud or deep, but like a whisper coming from somewhere beside her. She looked, but there was no sign of him as he came slowly through the trees.

"You don't have to hide from me," Prescott was saying. "Stay still—that's the best thing."

Eugénie was near to being panic-stricken. Blood was racing in her veins. She kept saying to herself, *No, it is not the young doctor. It must be a Redcoat. And why is he trailing me?*

"I knew you by your throat," Prescott said when he came riding up beside her. "You hold it so proud, and some of the moonlight touched it. I'm not talking poetry, I'm talking fact. It's a pretty throat for the moon to touch, and I wouldn't have seen you otherwise."

"So many shadows everywhere," she whispered. "You'd think they'd see you, but they don't."

"Why should they?" Dr. Prescott said slowly. He reached out to smooth the roan's mane, but Eugénie held his hand away. Then he said, "We'll wait five minutes and run for Concord. You want to breathe your horse, don't you? You don't want to arrive in a flurry."

"I don't care how I arrive," Eugénie answered, tossing

back her head. "We have to wake them in Concord and tell
them the Regulars are on the way, and there's nothing else
matters. I'd as well arrive in a flurry as in a coach." It was
a feeble kind of pun, but she heard him laugh softly.

"There's spirit in you," he said. "The last thing I expected
was to see a girl out on a night like this. . . . Can you hear
the bells?"

She heard them faintly, cocking her head to one side.

"That means," he said, "they may know already in Concord that there's a patrol out."

"So it does, but this is more than a patrol. This is a thousand men going straight for Concord, and we don't know
yet—and we won't know till we get there—whether Concord's prepared. We've got to warn them, bells or no bells."

Samuel Prescott told himself he was simply testing her, to
see how much spirit she had. He had caught only a glimpse
of her at Lexington, as a door opened and closed again, and
she seemed no more than a slight figure then, with yellow
hair flowing loose from a hood and a brown cape wrapped
round her. Better to wait and see her in daylight, but he
knew for certain that when the sun rose he would be elsewhere; it hurt him that they should race together in the
moonlight without his ever setting eyes on her. He said,
"We've been riding together, and yet I wouldn't recognize
you in the sunlight. We may be fighting the Regulars tomorrow, with blood all over these fields, still I wouldn't be able
to recognize you."

For him the two ideas went together, but Eugénie dismissed them both from her mind, saying, "Dr. Warren is
against a war, and so am I, but that's a different thing than
being prepared for war."

"Yes," said Samuel Prescott. He began to urge his horse
toward the edge of the clump to see whether the land was
clear, craning forward as though in this way he would be

able to hear better. But there was no sign of any patrol on the road, no lights showing anywhere, and the only sounds were the creaking of the branches in the rising wind.

"I'll go to Lincoln over the fields," he said when she came up with him. "You can go to Concord down the Lexington Road."

"No, we'll go together."

"I don't see any advantage, ma'am. It's best to go our own ways, and Lincoln will need waking as much as Concord does."

For Eugénie, Lincoln was only a place on the map. She had never been to Concord, but she knew all about the meet-ings of the Committee of Safety. Warren had spoken about the place in such detail that she had only to close her eyes to imagine the lay of the streets.

"Listen," she said, "it's better to go together, for there may be patrols close up to Lincoln. It doesn't matter what happens to the other so long as one gets through. We could play the same trick we've played before, and send the Regu-lars in a dither by riding our different ways. I'd swear the night is full of them. I'd see a patrol under every tree if I rode alone."

"Then we'll ride together," Samuel Prescott said, and for the first time he leaned over and took hold of her bridle.

The stars were hanging low, clear and frosty, as they made their way over the chalk ridges to Concord, jumping the hedges, keeping for a while away from the main road. Some-times as they rode, and more especially when they were rid-ing in the shadows of trees, Prescott would turn to look at her, telling himself that there was more of the panther than of the woman in her look, but he had never seen a panther silver with sweat and riding into the moon. "God's gift, it's pure lunacy," he whispered once, thinking how easily he got lost riding through the fields at night, and then he laughed.

"What are you laughing for?" Eugénie asked while they were making their way down to the road.

"I'm riding like a witch on a broomstick," he answered. "I've never known such a night. It's all a witch's brew, isn't it?"

After that they rode steadily down the open road, not pausing but ready to pause at every turn of the road, for the British patrols were often to be found at the turnings and sometimes a sparkling leaf would look like a man's eyes. It seemed to Eugénie that more than a week had passed since she had left Hanover Street; almost she felt she had been riding all her life in a strange white landscape of hillocks and shining elms. The place was haunted. They rode fast, but she breathed easily. She had ridden with Dawes, and then with Revere, and now with Prescott. She could see black smudges of houses beyond the fields, and sometimes, for no reason at all, there would be a light moving across a cornfield.

"We're coming to Concord," Samuel Prescott whispered, "and now for love's sake take care of yourself, for if there's a patrol anywhere tonight, we'll find it here."

There was no patrol, only the long winding road deep-carved among the hills with flashes of whiteness on the hedgerows, a road of mud—it had rained earlier—and starlit shadows and the soft echoes of the horses' hoofs as they came tunneling down the road which seemed to wind in a maze, sunken beneath the level of the fields. They saw the first houses, the first plows abandoned in the fields, the first gleams of light and the first sentinels, men standing on the hillside, dark and silver, with fowling pieces at their side; and suddenly, when they thought they were about to enter the town, two bearded minutemen came running out from the shadows into the moonlit road, both gaunt and straight and unbelievably thin, so that they looked like two clothed and bearded skeletons standing there, throwing down long tapering shadows.

"Halt!"

Eugénie could not bring the roan up in time. One of the skeletons clung to the bridle, and at the same time he pointed his fowling piece at her, shouting at the top of his voice, "I told you to halt, didn't I?" His voice was sharp as the splinters of frost on the air. Now that the roan was brought to a stop, he laughed softly to himself. "A woman, eh? And what the devil be you doin' on a night like this? Why, I thought it was one of the Redcoat boys. They've got officers as pretty as women."

For some reason Eugénie felt only a wild horror of this gaunt and bearded stranger on the lonely road. Prescott was some distance behind. "I've come from Dr. Warren," she explained, catching her breath.

"So ye've come from Dr. Warren," the man said dubiously, stroking his chin. "I'll tell you this, you're not the first Redcoat to come disguised as a woman."

The argument was interrupted by Prescott, who came riding up with the other minuteman. "I'll ride to Lincoln," Prescott was saying. "Eugénie will ride into Concord. You'd better take her to Colonel Barrett, men. And hurry! There's a hundred things that will have to be done before sunrise."

That was all. Without saying good-by, without a single glance, Prescott rode his horse up the slope and made his way across the plowed fields to Lincoln, leaving Eugénie alone with two gaunt strangers. They did not speak to her. They even kept her at a distance, muttering to themselves, as though they were annoyed by something in her appearance. She wanted to say, Why don't you let me hurry? What a waste of time this is! But it occurred to her that they were country men, their minds moved slowly and they did not trust her. For a while she heard the faint hoofbeats of Prescott's horse cantering across the hard, spring fields to the west, and then there was silence, broken only by the heavy breathing of the men who marched by her side.

She had heard so much about Concord that she imagined it was a large town, but it was hardly more than a small whitewashed village with a Town House and a village green and a low-walled cemetery sloping above the green; and in the moonlight the white gravestones, all small and close to the earth, flickered and dazzled. Above the stones the pine-tree flag was waving, whipping in the wind. The village was silent, deathly still, with only a few lights showing and a few shadows moving along the ridge. It was the kind of landscape she had seen more often in dreams; and even those heavily bearded men who walked like shambling bears, silent, their faces lifted to the moonlight and the stars, resembled the people you see in dreams.

They walked her first to the Town House, where a small cluster of minutemen were standing in the shadows. They asked for Colonel Barrett, and soon they were all arguing at once, some saying he was at his farm, others that he was at Wright's Tavern; and all the time Eugénie was thinking, My God, in four or five hours the lobsters will be walking through the village, and nothing is prepared! . . . Candles were burning inside the Town House, and she heard the creaking of a stairway. Her temper was rising. She had ridden like a mad woman from Boston. Why did they treat her in their slow, country fashion? Surely they had more sense than to distrust her. She was about to shout at them when she saw an old man riding across the green toward her, approaching in a half circle. Even in the moonlight she saw that he carried himself with casual dignity, though he was old and grizzled. He wore a heavy mustache, and his gray beard bristled. He had a queer rolling look of the eyes, and his cheeks were dark and wrinkled like leather.

Suddenly tiring of the men arguing round the Town House, Eugénie spurred the roan and rode toward the old man on the green. "Are you Colonel Barrett?" she asked breathlessly.

The old man nodded.

"I've come from Dr. Warren. The Redcoats are on their way to Concord. We left at eleven and saw some of 'em making their way to Charlestown. We don't know what they're coming for, but Dr. Warren believes they're out to destroy all your ammunition. He asks you—begs you—to take all precautions. I rode with Dr. Prescott from Lexington, sir, and he has gone to warn the men of Lincoln."

The old colonel listened to every word in absolute silence, then he said, "You say the English are approaching. How long do you think we have got?"

The answer came like a flash. "Four or five hours at most."

"And then?"

"You'll have the Redcoats parading on the green."

Colonel Barrett tossed his head in a way which left Eugénie in doubt whether he accepted her story. Then she remembered the letter Warren had given her, and she thrust it into his hands, saying, "Goddamit, no one believes me. I've ridden through a hard night, and your men look at me with suspicion. If Revere had come . . ."

"Did Revere come?" the man asked sharply, narrowing his eyes. They had ridden right up to the gathering of armed minutemen outside the Town House.

"He was forced back halfway between Lexington and Concord," Eugénie answered. "We met a British patrol. We rode together."

"You and Revere?"

"No, there were three of us. Dawes and Revere and I, and then there was Dr. Prescott."

She knew she wasn't telling her story properly, but she was bored with explanations. What did it matter whether she had ridden with Revere or with Dawes? She alone had made the journey to Concord, for Prescott had slipped away for Lincoln when they were still outside the town. Why didn't they believe her? She turned to the colonel, all her anger blazing, and exclaimed, "You should get to work now, sir! There's no time to be lost. And whether you believe me or not, you should have the sense to prepare for the worst." She turned her horse away and would have ridden off if the colonel had not placed a restraining hand on her bridle.

"So ye were goin' away?" he said, winking at her. "I can see you're a woman who never takes things easily."

"This isn't a time for taking things easily," Eugénie replied hotly. "They may take things easily in Concord, but we are not countryfolk in Boston."

"I see ye haven't much experience of countryfolk, ma'am. We ain't flustered easily. We take time for thought. I suppose you were thinking of riding back to Boston. Well, we could make a bed for you at Wright's Tavern, and you could get your breath back. How would you like that?"

He spoke kindly, though there was a trace of bitterness in his voice. He disapproved of her and admired her at the same time. He kept looking her up and down as though he did not quite believe in her presence, and then, with surprising agility, he jumped from his horse and lifted her down from her saddle.

"Come with me, ma'am," he said, and led her toward Wright's Tavern, which was all shuttered and dark, a stone's throw away from the Town House. "You'll need something to eat. You'll find us hospitable to strangers, ma'am."

"So you treat me as a stranger, Colonel?" she asked, wondering how anyone could ever regard her as a stranger. "Is there war between the town men and the country men?"

"There's no war, ma'am," the colonel replied, "but when a beautiful woman comes riding out of Boston—yes, even with a letter from Dr. Warren—and brings us news of importance, then you must admit we're tolerably perturbed how to please her. This is only a small town. We ain't got many comforts for ye."

Saying this, he began to knock on the tavern door. At first there was no answer. Suddenly the bell on the Town House began ringing, a good heavy bronze bell with a wonderfully sweet tone, and at the same moment the door opened. An old man with a short-cut beard, wearing a nightgown, came with a lantern to the tavern door.

"Mr. Wright, I've brought a lady from Boston. She's ridden through the night and I dare say she needs a rest."

The small man craned forward, holding the lantern close to their faces, standing there in his nightgown and bare feet. "It's a terrible thing, Colonel, to wake a man up in the middle of the night."

He said this very slowly and accusingly, and he jumped into wakefulness only when the colonel said, "The Redcoats are coming, Abraham Wright, and the young lady has come from Dr. Warren."

"From Dr. Warren?" the tavern keeper said, his face lighting up.

"That's right. Give her a bed and let her rest for a while, and whatever she asks for——"

"I'll do as you say, Colonel," the tavern keeper interrupted.

Shortly afterward Eugénie found herself in a small musty bedroom hardly larger than a cupboard, with a feather bed and an iron washstand, and a window overlooking the green. She threw herself on the bed. In her sleep she heard the sound of hoofbeats on the Concord Road, a sound like eternal waves beating against the shore.

CHAPTER 7

The Dark Farm

THE TAPROOM at Wright's Tavern was a small room with a long, narrow table down the length of it. Fumes of smoke rose from a log fire to nestle like cobwebs near the rafters; the dark wainscoting was full of squeaking mice. Eugénie made her way down the stairs. The house had been silent a few hours ago; now it was filled with men singing, drinking, eating, shouting at the top of their voices. They were drinking rum and cursing the British.

When the men in the taproom saw Eugénie standing by the door, looking very slight and small among the heavy farmhands, her face flushed, her lips parted in a smile of perplexity and alarm, they all shouted at her; from every corner of the room there came bursts of happy laughter. None of them except old Colonel Barrett had set eyes on her before. "Let's drink to her, men!" someone shouted, and an old man threw her an admiring glance and suggested that she was "pretty as a newborn speckled pup." The wild laughter broke out again.

Eugénie frowned and would have given them a piece of her mind if Colonel Barrett had not come hobbling up to her. On his old, crafty and careworn face she saw an unexpected look of pleading. "I see you're angry, ma'am," he said quietly in that rumbling voice of his, "and I dare say I know what angers you."

"You're all nothing more than bumpkins," Eugénie said,

her anger mounting, for they were shouting at her louder than ever and calling for toddy and ale and rum.

"That's one way of looking at it, ma'am," the colonel replied, "but there's another and simpler way. They've been working hard, and it was my order that they should come to the tavern for a drink. They've been out in the fields, most of 'em, and it's a chill night, as you know. So there it is! They've been making bullets and hiding the guns, and the work's not done yet, but they cannot work without rest."

"With a war coming to Concord?" Eugénie said, the corners of her lips turning down.

"Who spoke of war?" the colonel asked sharply. "You said the British were coming, and we're indebted to you for that, but it isn't war yet. I don't believe in war—never did! We're brothers beneath the skin. Do you expect brothers to fight brothers?"

Now the men were banging the mugs on the tables and shouting in chorus, "Tell us her name, Colonel," until at last he turned on them and exclaimed, "For pity's sake, let me talk to the young lady. Why, for sure I would tell you her name if I could get my tongue round it, but she has a French name."

In a loud, clear voice Eugénie said, "My name is Eugénie de Malmédy, but it is of no matter. What matters is that the British are on their way, and I've come from Dr. Warren to warn you. Do you propose to sit in a tavern and wait for the lobsters to crawl over you?"

She spoke with fire, her eyes flashing, but they still listened to her as they might listen to some actress on the stage. Flushed with the long journey, exulting in her physical beauty—she could no more avoid being conscious of her beauty than she could avoid breathing—knowing that she had accomplished the journey from Boston against every obstacle and hardly able to believe in her own good fortune, she stood among a crowd of men who could not quite believe in her existence. They would have believed her more if she had looked more commonplace. Even her name was against her. It occurred to her that they were shouting and cheering and raising their eyebrows, generally behaving as they would toward any pretty girl who invaded the taproom; and when she spoke of Warren or the British coming across the mud swamps of the Neck, there would be that unmistakable air of incredulity about them.

"How's Dr. Warren?" someone asked from the other end of the table, and immediately a cheer was raised. "Good old Warren! Three cheers for Warren!"

"That's right! Three cheers for Dr. Warren!" Young Lemuel Shaw put one foot on the table, raised his tankard toward the ceiling and began to cheer at the top of his voice.

While they were all cheering, someone struck his head against an iron bracket which supported an oil lamp, with the result that the lamp was set swinging. This made the taproom look strangely sinister, for great black shadows went wheeling round the timbered walls. They were still moving round the wall when the cheers were repeated for Hancock, Adams and Church, and then there was more cheering for old Colonel Barrett and a final cheer for Eugénie—— No one cared about the rest of her name.

"Now that you've finished shouting, I'll have you pay attention to the young lady's words," the colonel said, his voice like a low rumbling in the awkward silence. "I've said I don't believe the British will go to war. They're after our guns, and we've hidden 'em. And they may pass through Concord, but we've got no reason to think they'll do any harm. They're our own kith and kin. But when Redcoats come marching in our direction, why, we have to have our eyes skinned, though for all we know they may be going to Menotomy and not to Concord. It's my feeling that they're thinking hard about Menotomy, and they may have more to say about Colonel Lee than about old Colonel Barrett. . . . Well, gentlemen, I suggest we soon leave the taproom and get going about our work. There's still a deal to be done." He removed his watch from his fob. "It's getting on for three o'clock, gentlemen, and if you'll kindly excuse me, I'll return to my farm. Amos will stay with you. He's a cool-tempered boy, and I reckon you'll find him of the calculatin' sort. He's not the sort of boy who will get excited unless there's cause for it."

The last sally of the colonel was greeted with applause. Captain Amos Barrett, shockheaded, broad-shouldered, was about twenty-five. He had his father's bottle nose and broad mouth, but he was a full head taller than the colonel and carried himself with a swagger. The colonel was placing the minutemen under the command of his son. There was good reason for it. Most of the guns, much of the hoard of flints, musket balls and cartridges belonging to the Committee of Safety were hidden on his own farm, and thither he was determined to go if the British came to Concord. He had sworn an oath to defend those supplies with his life. He had spent the day hiding the cartridges in casks, then covering them with feathers and hiding them in the attic. As for the best cannon, they were buried in the fields behind the farmhouse, and the fields were plowed over. The British knew his farmhouse well enough. If they arrested anybody in Concord, they would arrest him and maybe transport him on a prison ship to England for public trial. So he decided to return to his farm, riding on his gray mare. Perhaps, he thought, it would be safer if he buried the musket balls. He whispered something to his son. Flames roared in the fireplace, and a row of pewter mugs set against the wall beside the fire gleamed red like bronze.

"Another drink before you go," a bulletheaded man shouted across the table.

"No, Amos Hosmer, though it's kind of you to mention it," the colonel answered, beaming at the group huddled round the near end of the table.

"It's a chill night," said Hosmer. "You wouldn't think it over, would you?"

"No, I've nothing against drinking on a cold night, but it seems to me if we go into battle in an hour or so—and most of you are thinking of going into battle—well, sir, I wouldn't like to have my bladder full when I'm in battle." The colonel laughed and waved his stick at them.

Everyone understood that there was almost no danger of a battle. The danger lay in the possibility that they might lose their heads, the colonel had warned them, talking to them very soberly and without heroics, telling them to get to work—that was the important thing. But now that he spoke laughingly of going to battle, they sat back and pondered. Perhaps it would be a battle; perhaps it was too late to avoid an engagement; perhaps Hancock was right when he said before the Committee of Safety that the first blood might be shed somewhere near by.

Eugénie was still standing on the stairs. She was watching a man cutting a map on the wooden table with a jack-knife, and without studying the map she knew it represented the roads taken by the British on their way to Concord.

"As for you, ma'am—" Colonel Barrett turned and gravely bowed to Eugénie—"I've thanked you before and I gladly thank you again, and it's in my mind that you would care to accompany me to my farm. You'll be in better company with my wife and daughters, and I dare say we could toss down a bed for you."

Now, for the first time, Eugénie felt fully confident in the colonel. She smiled at him, and when he offered her his arm she took it happily. They were about to ride off to the farmhouse when the colonel remembered she had left her cloak upstairs.

"Lemuel, you get her coat, and maybe you'd like to ride with us," he said.

Lemuel Shaw was one of Colonel Barrett's farm boys. He jumped to his feet and fled up the stairs. When he returned, blushing to the roots of his hair, running down the stairs, the men applauded him, and this made him pause at the foot of the stairs exactly as Eugénie had done. He glared round, made a mocking face, and then plunged through the crowd of men until he was outside the tavern, just in time to join Eugénie and Colonel Barrett on their ride to Ponkawtassett, the wooded hills where the farm lay.

The night was still crisp and cold, with a frost thickening. It seemed as though there were men moving cannon wheels and sacks of powder out of every house in the town, with shadows everywhere. High up on the Town House a lamp was shining. On the ridge above the tavern the pine-tree flag was waving, but it looked like a black flag fluttering there; sometimes the wind would snap and whip it, and then there would be a cracking sound, almost as loud as a pistol shot.

The roan had been rubbed down and was still frisky. Eugénie decided to ride sidesaddle, though the saddle was not made for such riding and she found it difficult to keep her seat.

"In Concord we're a companionable lot," the colonel was saying. "We go to bed early and rise with the sun." Then he laughed quietly to himself. "The men have been working hard, ma'am. They've been taking our ammunition and hiding it in towns as far away as Stow and Littleton."

"You're sending everything away?" Eugénie asked in alarm.

"That's right, ma'am, as much as we can. It's in my mind that you can start a war with the best of intentions simply by having too many muskets around. I'm not going to start anything."

They were cantering past the cemetery. A huddled group of lantern-jawed men in homespun came down the narrow lane beside the cemetery wall. "Good evening to you, Colonel," someone whispered hoarsely, pausing on the side of the road to let the colonel pass.

"Where you from?" the colonel asked.

"From Acton, sir. It's a long haul."

"Well, so it is. God rest you. They say the Regulars are coming."

There were minutemen at all the approaches to the town. They would jump out of the shadows and demand the password—dark men whose voices were harsh, for they had spent too long a time in the cold. Colonel Barrett knew them all, of course, and they in turn recognized the old man with the broad-brimmed hat and queer rolling eyes.

"The pine-tree flag hangs high!"

That was the password, and the colonel said the words like a man saying his prayers, with tremendous force.

"Pass, Colonel," they answered, and the old colonel smiled to himself, recognizing each man by the tone of his voice.

They wound along field paths until they came to lower ground. The moon was sinking now, a hint of coppery moon wreathed in blue clouds. The wind was springing up. Young Lemuel Shaw, taking up the rear, cursed under his breath at the thought of accompanying the girl and the colonel to the old weather-beaten farm at the top of Ponkawtassett Hill. The one thing he wanted was a talk in the dark with Eugénie. But the girl paid no attention to him, and he was left to his own resources until they came to the river and a wooden bridge which shone dull gold in the moonlight.

"Tread carefully, ma'am," the colonel said. "She's a rickety bridge if ever there was one. Needs mending, too," he added, more to himself than to Eugénie. "It's my opinion that we'd best walk the hosses over it."

Hearing this, Lemuel Shaw jumped down from his horse and stood beside Eugénie to lift her down. Her instinct was to refuse him this solace, for since she was riding sidesaddle she had only to slip down to earth, taking care that her skirts covered her knees. But there was a desperate appealing look in the boy's eyes, and she could not deny him. She jumped down. Lemuel caught her and planted a kiss on her neck; and if there had not been so many shadows round the bridge, and if the night had not been so cold, she might have slapped his face.

"That's the last you'll have," she murmured, glancing up at him, smiling and tossing back her hair.

"And I'll pray it's only the first," Lemuel said, taking the roan by the bridle. "God's love, it was a sweet thing to do, sir," he answered when the colonel barked at him, saying there were more important things to attend to.

The bridge was well guarded. They knew how well guarded it was when they came close, for immediately eight or nine men carrying their guns appeared out of the bushes beside the river and demanded the password.

"The pine-tree flag hangs high."

"That's right."

The colonel turned to face them. "Upon my soul, there are good men among you. I wish you all well. We've heard the Regulars may be coming up the Lexington Road. You'll do your duty, men."

He stood there blinking in the moonlight, looking more like Isaiah than a stiff-boned farmer. It was on the tip of his tongue to tell them why he was going home, but instead he waved to them, asked about their families and whether they had enough powder and flint; then, while the planking creaked under them, the small procession made its way across the rickety bridge. Below them the reed-banked river was more like a millpool than a thing that sometimes roared

in a spate. No sound came from the slow-flowing river—
only a brisk murmur among the reeds. But walking slowly
across the bridge, running her hands along the twined osier
supports, Eugénie told herself, *Now at last I am a million
miles from Boston, and this is a place where I could stay
forever. . . .*

Eugénie did not know why the bridge made so great an
impression on her. Perhaps it was the loneliness of the place,
the softness of the shadows in this forgotten stretch of river,
the knowledge that it was remote from human destinies. In
Wright's Tavern you felt you might be in Boston; there
were a hundred villages like Concord. But there was nothing
like this bridge on the edge of darkness, soundless water beneath a sheltering hill.

How beautiful it must be in daylight, she thought, *with
the green reeds waving over blue shallows.* . . . Breathing
deeply, remembering some other river in France in some forgotten summer, she imagined the river in the quiet daylight,
no shadows anywhere. "Truth is, we can't tell sometimes
which way the river is flowing," the colonel was saying.
"She's a quiet river. . . ." The words were like a benediction.
"Quiet, quiet," she murmured as they rode up the hill toward
the dark farmhouse.

Once they passed a darkened cottage from where there
came the sharp smell of pewter being melted down into bullets. All over the Province of Massachusetts there were the
same hot smell, the same whispered voices in the dark, the
sound of footsteps on the brittle grass. The old colonel struck
a flint and lighted his long pipe under the stars. The little
flare of flame startled her. And when they came along the
winding road toward the dark farm outlined on the rounded
crest, there rose the sharp crack and hiss of the wind, and
she shivered violently. Soon—for the wind was coming in
her direction—she heard whispered voices, people stamping
the earth, the ringing snaffle of a horse and then some other

sound like a crackling; but it was no more than the noise of the high wind in an elm grove behind the farmhouse.

"We'll put you to bed soon as we come to the house," the old colonel said. "It's more comfortable there than at the inn, and you won't be troubled by noise."

"I'm in no mood for bed," she answered.

"I can see that," he said, his eyes twinkling. "But you'll need a rest, ma'am."

"I couldn't rest on a night like this," she said, half turning on her saddle and looking back over the way they had come.

There, in the moonlight, the whole valley shone silver and black, glowing like something beaten out of metal. The stars were growing dim, and all the radiant whiteness of the sky was disappearing. But the earth was silvery still; and smoke came from the cottage chimneys where they were melting pewter, and the smoke was silver, too. You could put your hand on that landscape, she thought, and find it softer than snow, there, among the sleeping valleys and the river wandering among birchwood coppices, as soft and quiet a place as any she knew; yet it was all ringingly alive, and men with guns were hiding in the shadows.

"God help them all!" she said aloud, and blew a kiss at the long streaming valley. And when she slipped off the roan, only to fall once again into Lemuel Shaw's arms, she was already asleep. . . .

When she woke she found herself lying before a log fire; the sparks were crackling. The warm comfort of a blanket enveloped her, and red flames were shooting up the white-brick chimney with such a roaring that she was deafened and wondered how she could have slept through it all. Lemuel Shaw was lying beside her in the farmhouse, his chin cupped in his hands and a fowling piece between his legs.

"There now," he said as she attempted to rise, "lie down an' git some sleep." When she frowned he said, "You come from Boston, and I'm from the town of Concord, which is no more than a village as you see, but I'll show you a man of Concord has as good a heart as any of the gay blades of Boston. I'll show it in battle, if need be."

She knew the signs: the face alight with love, the eyes glowing, the lips quivering. He was golden in the light of the flames, a tallow-haired boy with very light, bright blue eyes and leather breeches and a leather coat with the sleeves rolled up, showing sunburned arms. Yet she had no desire to be close to him, no feeling for him, no love.

"I see I don't please you," he said bitterly; then more quietly: "I never worshiped anyone so much as I worship thee."

She turned her head away and tried to sleep, but the huge shadows of the fire kept spinning across the rafters. She had no recollection of being brought into the kitchen: Lemuel Shaw must have carried her. Somewhere outside, perhaps in the courtyard or in another room, men were talking in heavy whispers and there was the tramp of hobnailed boots, the crack of a gunstock on the floor. The colonel had drawn up a rocking chair near the fireplace and was sleeping in the shadows a little behind her. In sleep his face assumed an appearance of majestic repose. He looked older now, with his head falling forward over his chest as he dozed, and though he looked majestic, he also looked helpless. He snored occasionally. She wondered what dreams he was having. "God give you pleasant dreams," Eugénie whispered, and then she drew up her knees and flung her arms round them as she gazed into the roaring fire.

Old Colonel Barrett was not the only one sleeping in the kitchen. Huddled against the wall, their voices drowned by the roaring flames, were perhaps twenty minutemen who rested, slept, snored, talked to one another and then went back to their cold sentry duty outside, where they watched the two rivers winding below and all Concord peaceful under the glory moon, with no sign of the Regulars approaching.

They came in for half-hour rests, complained of the rising wind, spoke of the other things they would like to do on a freezing April night and swore under their breath.

"See here, git yer legs off my stummick, Ammi White," one of the minutemen was saying to a boy sprawled out in slumber, a boy who could hardly be more than fourteen, though he was sturdy and red-faced and had the shoulders of an older man.

"Who yer talkin' to?" Ammi White woke up, shifted his legs, coughed, nudged his neighbor viciously with an elbow; then, seeing that the minuteman by his side was twice his own age, a heavily bearded, gaunt-cheeked farmer with a fowling piece across his knees, he frowned and looked away.

"Who am I talkin' to?" the old farmer said casually. "I'm talkin' to Ammi White—Mr. Emerson's kitchen boy."

"I ain't no kitchen boy!" Ammi White said defiantly.

"You ain't got no fur on your cheeks. You're Ammi White, and you ought to be tucked into your bed nights, with that milk round your mouth. We don't want babies in this-here war!"

The boy was now white-faced with fury, trembling all over. He dug the farmer in the ribs with another vicious push of an elbow. "Ain't no kitchen boy," he shouted, waking all the other men in the kitchen.

Even the old colonel, his head falling forward so that he was in danger of tumbling out of his rocker, awoke and growled, "No foolin', men. Git some slumber when ye can."

"Ain't no kitchen boy!" Ammi White shouted again, no longer in control of himself. "I'm willin' to fight the lobster-backs, and I'll show you——"

"What will you show us, cuss?"

"I'll show all you men here how to fight. God a-Heaven, you all treat me like I was unripe coz I got no fur on my chin. I got fur other place. I ain't no kitchen boy. You wait and see."

The boy cursed silently to himself, all white and shivering. The old farmer was Obadiah Jess, a man with six ugly daughters, and it was on the tip of Ammi White's tongue to talk about those daughters, but he held his peace.

Once awake, Colonel Barrett could not sleep again. He got up from the rocker, stiff in the joints and a little lame, and went outside. He said he was going to see what the men were up to, but he really went because he had a full bladder. Pock-marked, grizzled at the temples, his nose bright red like his cheeks, his beard gray except under the chin, where it bristled white, he looked like an old prowling lion as he made his way outside.

"He's a good war horse," Lemuel Shaw said, and suddenly he drew a sharp breath, for Colonel Barrett had left the door open and a cold draft had penetrated the room. "He's lame," Lemuel Shaw went on. "It's the water on the farm that dries up the knobs of bones. You'll find many of us lame hereabouts."

"He's a good man," Eugénie said. "There are not many faces you can read goodness in."

"No, ma'am, but I dare say you'll find more of such faces in the country than in Boston. As for the colonel, there isn't nothing we wouldn't do for him, or for Amos."

"Who's Amos?"

"His eldest son. There's Nathan, too, another son, married to the Kennicks' young daughter just a week ago. I'd say Nathan was the smarter, but the old colonel disagrees. Said we should put Amos in command of the minutemen and Mr. Buttrick in command of the militia. We allowed him Amos, but we put Abijah Pierce in command of the militia. That's freedom."

"Freedom?" Eugénie asked, raising her eyebrows, for he said the word as though all freedom was contained in the business of choosing one's commanders.

At that moment Ammi White crept forward to be nearer

the fire. He came close to Eugénie and peered at her as one might peer at some completely incredible and marvelous piece of furniture. He looked like a child, with his red cheeks, blue eyes and sandy hair, a small-boy's face set on a farmer's shoulders, and as he stared first at Eugénie and then at the fire his lips trembled. He was trying to smile, but a quivering nervousness tugged at his lips.

"What's bothering you, Ammi?" Lemuel Shaw asked kindly.

"Nothin'," the boy answered, staring at the leaping flames; then in a louder voice he repeated, "Nothin'."

"You're not afraid, are you?"

"No."

"Then why tremble? You're warm enough, aren't you? Get some sleep—that's all that's necessary."

The boy could not sleep. He tried. He shut his eyes tightly, but little fits of quivering fear would come over him. "I'll show 'em I'm not afraid," he muttered between clenched teeth.

Eugénie threw her arm round his shoulder. "Why, that's being sensible," she whispered. "There never was and there never is anything to be afraid of."

Then the boy smiled and fell asleep with his head on her shoulder.

Now at last the flames died down, and the kitchen grew cool with the coming of dawn. The men slept. The colonel had been out for perhaps a quarter of an hour when he returned, his boots muddy, his nose redder than ever, his face pinched with the cold air. Once again he settled himself in his rocker, and he would have fallen instantly asleep if at that moment there had not been a faint tattoo of a horse's hoofs along the slope. The sound grew fainter as the horseman rode past the farm, but shortly afterward they grew louder— so loud that Eugénie was surprised that the men still slept. Presently a man wearing a black cloak and an enormous black hat, sweating and out of breath, strode into the kitchen, making enough noise to wake the devils in hell. But the men had come to the point in the early morning where sleep becomes a necessity, not easily put away, and they lay on the floor in ungainly positions, completely unconscious of the presence of the stranger.

"A word with you, Colonel," the stranger said, smiling nervously and quickly, and there was a strange gleam in his prominent eyes. He had high cheekbones, a firm chin which thrust out and a pendulous upper lip which was pink in places from sores resulting from an inexpert use of a razor.

Eugénie shivered when she saw him: he looked like a messenger of doom.

The colonel half rose from his rocker, put a finger to his lips, motioned for the stranger to draw up a chair. He might have gone on to speak in sign language if the stranger himself had not broken the silence by exclaiming in an unnaturally loud voice, "They're all asleep, Colonel, every man jack of them! I passed through the lines and no one asked for a password. They're all sleeping at their sentry posts and the Redcoats are on their way!"

"I've known it a long time," the colonel answered. "And for God's sake, lower your voice, Mr. Emerson! These men need to sleep."

"They need to make themselves ready for battle, sir!"

There was feverish defiance in the Reverend Emerson's tones. He had little respect for the old colonel. The sight of the sleeping men made him want to vomit.

"And how better can they make themselves ready for battle than by sleeping, Mr. Emerson? I suppose you would prefer them to be singing hymns?"

"I would indeed! Don't you realize the Redcoats could have made their way up this hill without any opposition? There's not a man on sentry duty who isn't asleep."

"You've said that before."

"I'll say it again! Why, it's a disgrace, and I'd have the men shot for it! It is only the great mercy of the Lord which has saved us so far, but the God of battles is a very jealous God—I'll have you remember that, Colonel."

"I'll remember it well enough," the colonel said hoarsely, "but I have full confidence in the Lord. If our men sleep, it must be that they are very tired. When you're as old a man as I am, Mr. Emerson, you'll know that a man needs a good night's sleep when he's young."

"Then you approve of sentries sleeping?"

"I don't approve or disapprove. It's something I understand. I'd never shoot a man for sleeping on sentry duty. There might be times when I would be tempted to it, but I'd never do it. We're fighting for our lives, and I wouldn't be one to throw a life carelessly away. I believe the Lord watches over us when we sleep, and if I might offer you some counsel, you'll take a nap with the rest of us."

The Reverend Emerson was not easily convinced he was wrong. With his eyes rolling toward the ceiling he talked of the colonel's sins of omission. Everything was wrong. He had found people carousing in Wright's Tavern. He had seen a pair of lovers scuttling across the cemetery. He had found two sentries playing cards by the light of a lantern. These sins were serious enough, but there was worse to come. Here on Ponkawtassett Hill there was hardly a man awake, yet the farmhouse could be transformed into a fortress. The cannon were buried in the fields, plowed under, seven or eight of them, and it was done at Colonel Barrett's orders. The cannon should have been set up to defend the fortress, but instead the colonel was behaving as though he were ashamed of them.

"If I didn't know you well," Mr. Emerson went on, "I'd say you had no intention of defending Concord from the Redcoats. You sleep the night away and expect the protection of the Lord of Hosts. What you do, you do in the sight of the Lord. God watches you! Yes, the very eye of God looks down on you! Have you thought of that?"

"I've thought of it pretty near every moment of my life, Mr. Emerson."

"Then for God's sake, *do* something! Prepare a fortress! Dig up the cannon! Set your men to watchfulness! I've heard the Redcoats are coming up the Lexington Road. For God's sake, ambush 'em and let the sound of our cannon be heard, or you'll have all our wives and children dead in Concord. Pray for your sins and get to work, or we'll all be dead by noon."

The old colonel solemnly lighted his pipe, puffed at it and then smiled up at the reverend gentleman.

"No, we'll not die," he said at last. "We'll live. Take those gloomy thoughts of death away, Mr. Emerson, for they do not clothe us well when the Redcoats are on their way. You say we'll all be dead by noon. Well, God disposes of us—I've heard ye say that in your sermons—but when you're as old as I am you'll know that one can die as well in one place as in another. I don't intend to dig up the cannon. I don't intend to fight the Redcoats if I can help it. I know what I am doing. I'm in no mood to take advice from anyone except the Committee of Safety, and it was Hancock himself who signed the order to have the cannon buried. If you'll attend to men's souls, Mr. Emerson, I'll attend to their earthly lives. And now let me counsel you to rest awhile."

The Reverend Emerson muttered something to himself, cast a last despairing glance at the sleeping men and then subsided. Some of the men had awakened when they heard him invoking the Lord of battles, but they had heard Mr. Emerson invoking the Lord of battles ever since they could remember; and so they slept again. . . .

Dawn was coming up. The first pale-blue splinters of light came over the horizon. The wind blew and the birds began singing and all the church bells for miles around were pealing, the bells and the cocks singing madly to one another. One by one the men awakened, rubbed their eyes, talked in whispers together and gazed in the direction of Colonel Barrett, who was sleeping like a child.

Eugénie wandered outside, to feel the first cold wave of wind against her face. The grass was sprinkled with frost, the hills were yellow in the sun and the beech copses were throwing down long smoky dawn shadows. Down below, spread out before her as on a map, lay the town of Concord, and Great Meadows and the two arms of an ink-black river. It seemed to her that every blade of grass and every leaf was instilled with life that morning. *How wonderful it all is!* she told herself. *The bells are pealing as though summoning everyone to church. Lincoln hears the bells of Concord. Carlisle and Bedford and Chelmsford hear one another. Acton sends a peal to Littleton. There must be pealing bells right up to the walls of Boston. The whole air and firmament of this dawn is swelling with the frosty sound of bells, and everything is peaceful beyond words, with the curlews in the sky and the small white clouds gathering. Yes, I am sure the colonel is right. There must be no blood on these fields, nothing must dispel this quietness. . . . ,*

Lemuel Shaw came toward her out of the farmhouse. "The colonel sends his compliments, ma'am, and invites you to breakfast. It's bread and rum, ma'am. The colonel says he's sorry, but if ye care for 'em, he'll be pleased to entertain you with 'em, and he has a room set aside for you to spend the day in."

"I don't intend to spend the day in a room," Eugénie said. "I hope I'll be more useful in the open."

"That's for the colonel to say, ma'am," Lemuel Shaw replied, and he held his head high and whistled under his breath as he led Eugénie back to the kitchen.

CHAPTER 8

Lexington Common

As THE sun rose over the long leafy lanes on the outskirts of Lexington, Major Pitcairn was riding with Oliver at the head of the advance. The dawn turned from gray to green and then to silver, but afterward a gray shutter swept over the sky, as though a cloud had hidden the sun. Pitcairn cursed under his breath and said, "It's the false dawn. I've always hated the false dawn, Oliver, and I always will."

Oliver smiled. He was wrapped in his own affairs, thinking of Eugénie, wondering whether he would find her in Concord, for he was certain she was there. Sometimes he found himself shivering. A quarter of an hour before, a sudden shower of rain had fallen. It was hardly rain—the briefest of showers, no more than a hint of a downpour. Like everyone else in the column, he had welcomed this freshness on his uplifted face, but afterward he felt a chill in his bones. There had been mutterings all along the line and Pitcairn had ridden back to discover the cause of them, only to return with the usual complaint: "The truth is, Oliver, they want to know what they are out for, and I can't tell them. General Gage has ordered secrecy, and there's nothing to be done about giving the men information until we pass Lexington. . . ." He was not dispirited; he was simply stating a fact. Oliver remembered afterward that in the starlight the major's face had taken on a look of unfathomable misery. But when

158

the first splinters of sunlight rose through the trees the major looked gay and serious at the same time, his face tilted forward a little as he rode, and the soft lines of his mouth under the yellow mustache were curved into a smile of astonishment and delight in the world around him.

"I see you're pleased with yourself," Oliver said to taunt him, though he knew well enough that the major was not pleased; and though his lips smiled, there was a grave look about his eyes.

"I'm not pleased," Major Pitcairn snapped at him. "Why should I be pleased? I've thought a great deal about war, and it seems to me there is no pleasure in it except in dying for one's country and fighting for the things one believes in."

Oliver pondered the remark for some moments as they rode together in the dawn. He was full of admiration for the tall officer who, with his reddish mustache and clear sunburned cheeks, sometimes looked no more than twenty-five, though he was over fifty.

"The greater pleasure lies in peace," Oliver murmured.

Major Pitcairn turned to him with an extraordinarily pleasant smile and said, "No man knows why he goes to war. We think we do, but we never find out the reasons—the *real* reasons. Why are we sent out today? A thousand intangibles have gone into the making of this column. General Gage gave the orders, but why? What moved him? What impulses worked through him?" He paused, sighed, drew his long blade slowly out of the scabbard and just as slowly replaced it, and said, "It's too mysterious for words, and that's why I believe that everything is in God's mercy."

Shortly afterward Major Pitcairn sent out some scouts to see what was happening in Lexington, for one of the patrols had announced that the minutemen were gathering. He called for a halt. The men stopped and began whispering together. The rolling of drums could be heard from distant villages, and sometimes they heard bells. Suddenly, from three or four places in Lexington, there came the loud pealing of alarm bells.

"They hide in the dark, but at sunrise they come flocking on every hill, so God help us!" Major Pitcairn was saying, straining forward through the gray of the early morning as though he thought he would see better if he were a few inches nearer to Lexington. "I'll tell you this, Oliver. When they ring all their alarm bells and roll their drums, then it means trouble, for they have never rung their bells like this before. So keep a sharp lookout, and let us pray for God's guidance in the coming trials."

Oliver had never heard an officer speak like this before. He was shivering-cold, and he wished he had brought gloves. They had marched sixteen miles through the night, and the men at least had kept themselves warm; but the officers on horseback, slowing to the pace of the infantry, were all blue with cold, impatient for a stiff ride down the road to Concord, down those shadowy sunken roads between the coppices. Bells were pealing; the sounds were coming from all directions. Though he had heard them at intervals all night, they were louder now than ever, so close that the sound seemed to come up from the earth under the horses' feet.

"Then you think they're in arms against us, Major?" Oliver asked innocently.

"I don't know what to think," Major Pitcairn replied gravely. "It's not a question of thinking, probably. It's a question of faith and the honor of our arms. We can't turn back now. We've got to see this thing through. But we're four thousand men at most—that's including every soldier in the barracks, and most of 'em are still in Boston for all I know—and we're up against a mass of villagers from all over New England. I'll tell you one thing. I thank God we have disciplined men. They're not to fire a shot unless fired on, and they won't."

He said this firmly and decisively, as a man will say his

prayers, and urged on his horse to meet the outriders who were returning along the sunken road. The sun was rising. A faint green light dappled the long road wet with dew, while the trees on either side shone with the flickering whiteness of an early morning frost. The wind blew in their faces, and behind them came the solemn tramp, tramp of the line of infantry in the advance. Somewhere far behind came the Grenadiers under the command of Colonel Smith.

The men who had ridden out from the advance were two young lieutenants. They both rode black mares, and held themselves wonderfully erect. They looked fresh and untried, as though they had simply ridden out of Lexington five minutes before. These officers of Light Infantry had chosen the most dangerous course: they rode ahead, scouted the land, returned at intervals to report to Major Pitcairn. So far they had reported nothing unusual. Now for the first time Major Pitcairn recognized from their expressions that something had gone amiss.

"Well, what is it?" he said quickly when he had returned their salutes.

"There are rebels on the green, sir."

"You mean Lexington Green?"

"Yes, sir. About a hundred rebels on the green, and maybe a hundred more on the slopes. They're armed, sir. They'll dispute passage."

"You're sure of that?"

The younger of the lieutenants shrugged. "Perhaps not, sir," he said, "if we make a show of force. I think they're surly and cold."

"What the devil has surliness and cold got to do with it?"

"They're muttering together, sir. They're worried and don't know what to do about us."

"You said they're armed?"

"Yes, sir, with muskets and fowling pieces. They've broken ranks, sir, and there's a group of them standing out-

side Munroe's Tavern. I'd say the leaders are in the group
there, and I'd say, too, sir, the leaders are not controlling
the men."

"How do you know?"

"I didn't hear any orders given. I think they're just waiting, sir, to see what we are up to, but they are all armed."

Major Pitcairn could make no sense of these statements.
He had almost decided to send another party of scouts ahead
to make a further report when a messenger came up from
Colonel Smith to say there was no sign of any reinforcements
from Boston. The messenger was a small dark man with a
lovelock falling across his forehead. Major Pitcairn took an
immediate distaste to the man, muttered something under his
breath and turned to Oliver with the remark, "Are the lambs
ready for the sacrifice?"

"What lambs?" Oliver asked, feeling stupid and ill at ease.
He wondered whether the major was referring to the long
column of Redcoats or to the minutemen parading on Lexington Green; or perhaps they were not parading at all. Perhaps
they were like the Redcoats, standing there forlornly on a cold
spring morning, waiting for something to happen and wishing they were in their beds.

All along the line the men were complaining. They were
wet and cold, and they still had no idea why they had been
sent out. The infantry complained most. They were hungry
and rebellious, and they cared nothing at all for the long
march which would take them, they knew, to Concord and
back again; and what they would do in Concord no one
among them knew. Some of them had taken part in patrols.
They knew the temper of the country people; they had received more harsh insults than they cared to take. Now there
were further delays. Why didn't Major Pitcairn order them
to march on and get the job done with? He was forever
pausing, surveying the land, waiting for the reports of the

scouts. Was he afraid? He was not a man who ever showed fear, but they could find no explanation for his hesitations. And so they sulked, standing there in column just outside Lexington, whispering oaths and wishing to God the major would make up his mind. A sharp wind came racing through the trees, and the heavy bell clanging from the church tower at Lexington sounded like a slow requiem for the dead.

The sun caught the blade of the major's drawn sword, and then they knew the time of waiting was over.

They marched now for the first time to the music of the fifes and drums, holding themselves erect, for they knew they would be seen by the country men. The sun was rising, but it was still misty-dark on Lexington Green. Dusky groups moved across the grass. The dull glow of a taproom fire shone dimly through the windows of Buckman's Tavern, and here and there they saw the flicker of guttering tapers in the silent houses facing the green. It was very quiet except for the steady tramp of the Redcoats and the soft running of the minutemen of Lexington who kept hurrying backward and forward to the meetinghouse, their bronze faces catching the light of the sun though their feet were in shadow. All round the green the branches of the elms were weighted with the silver of dew and the recent rains.

Riding a little apart from the others, quietly confident in his own strength, Major Pitcairn surveyed the scene. He found nothing to perturb him in the spectacle of the minutemen running across the green. There were two groups standing there, and all together they would number hardly more than a hundred. Most of them were spectators who had left their guns at home; a few carried fowling pieces at the trail. They were hard-bitten, scrawny men with a look of defiance in their eyes, but they were not fighting men; and if they showed hatred, the major was hardly aware of it. A small group near the church attracted his attention. These were the men running back and forth to the meetinghouse—presumably to get powder. Well, he would give them no time to take up positions. He would pass by the edge of the green and continue on his way to Concord. He was sure he would not need to fight them, for there was not a man among them who seemed to know what he was doing. There was no order among them: they ran, they scattered, they jostled together, and they were getting in everyone else's way. "They're good men," he murmured, "but there's no sense of military order in them." When he heard someone near the church shouting to the minutemen to disperse, the major smiled again. It was not a smile of satisfaction; it was simply a smile of approval at their good sense in dispersing before his own column of Light Infantrymen. And so he bowed and waved a gloved hand to some of the spectators on the edge of the green, and turned his face toward the long leafy lane which led to Concord. . . .

From behind a low and rambling wall a gun flashed in the pan. Another shot was fired, and then another. Blood spilled from a wound in the white neck of the major's horse. Pitcairn wheeled round in time to see one of the Lexington men who had been close to the edge of the road lifting a firelock as he retired. Flourishing his sword, Major Pitcairn shouted, "Throw down your weapon, you rebel!" Somewhere behind him an officer was shouting, "Damn them, we will have them yet!" Pitcairn turned with his sword above his head and brought it down heavily as a sign that the company should listen to him. Without paying any attention to the minuteman with the firelock, he screamed, "Don't fire—for God's sake, don't fire!"

It was too late. The Redcoats had turned to face the green, and some were already kneeling and taking aim. Others were shouting, and most of them were raising their muskets to their shoulders. Already there were puffs of black smoke rising from behind the walls, those low stone walls which rambled on the edge of the green. The minuteman was running backward and still taking aim. "Lay down your arms, damn you, why don't you lay down your arms!" Major Pitcairn shouted at the top of his lungs. But he knew it was too late, for firing was breaking out everywhere, and every soldier of the line on the edge of the green was huzzaing and taking aim.

"Come on, Oliver," the major shouted over his shoulder, and together they began to race through the English line, striking right and left with their swords against the leveled muskets, both of them cursing the day they were born.

This was not war: this was the beginning of misery, with the dawn coming over the elms and the long shadows falling on the green, and dispirited men were firing at one another because they were frightened and weary of waiting. All this Major Pitcairn understood, as he felt his sword shivering at contact with a musket. He saw the strange appealing and panic-stricken look in an infantryman's eyes, the look of a man who wanted only to defend himself and found that his officer was preventing him from doing even that.

"I told you to lay down your musket."

"I thought you were ordering the rebels, sir."

"For God's sake, for God's sake . . . "

His breathing came with difficulty. Long yellow streaks of light, like illuminated shadows, came creeping across the green, and he was blinded by them. He turned away, wondering when Colonel Smith's Grenadiers would come up. They shouldn't be more than a ten minutes' march behind, but there was no sign of them. A man wearing a deerskin cap was standing on the other side of the green, and he too was shouting at the top of his lungs, saying over and over again, "Come over the wall . . . don't fire, men . . . hold off . . . hold off. . . ." It was like a cry of despair.

Major Pitcairn joined Oliver, who was bleeding from a gash in the cheek received by a bayonet stroke, and together they kept moving up and down the line, saying, "It's all over . . . hold your fire . . . let the rebels go . . . there's nothing to be gained by fighting. . . ." It was all hopeless, because there were Regulars huzzaing now in every corner of the green, and some of them were even chasing the rebels over the walls. There were not many of these Regulars at their bloody work, but there were enough of them. Major Pitcairn sent men off to corner these infantrymen and bring them back into line.

"We're cursed, that's what it is. We were cursed from the very beginning."

"You can't blame the Regulars," Oliver answered hotly. "They were fired at first."

"That's what they say," the major answered, "but God knows the truth of it. It seemed so. I saw a flash in the pan by the long wall."

"The men say there was firing from the windows."

"It doesn't help, it doesn't help," Pitcairn replied. He dug his spurs sharply into his horse's flanks to head off some Redcoats who were firing from the cover of the elms at the north of the common.

As he rode across the edge of the green, it seemed to him that time was moving at an uncommonly slow pace. A leaf bending in the wind swung as slow as a pendulum. All the excitement, all the frustrations, all the noise of a long day of battle had been concentrated in a few minutes; and though he knew that only a few minutes had passed, those minutes had been stretched out beyond endurance.

"Hold your fire!" he shouted when he came in earshot of the men taking cover behind the elms. He saw now that there were only three of them, and they were aiming at the windows of Buckman's Tavern.

"I've caught one there," a towheaded boy said, smiling and looking up at the officer.

"I told you to hold your fire."

"But they fired first."

"I don't know who fired first, and maybe we'll never know. I told you to hold your fire."

"Are you Major Pitcairn, sir?" the boy asked dubiously.

"Of course I am, and you know I am. Are you all mad? You've seen me a thousand times."

"There are rebels disguised as Regulars, sir," the boy went on, and now the other two rested their muskets and came slowly toward the major's horse.

"It hasn't come to that yet," Major Pitcairn said. "Have you killed people in the tavern?"

"We hope so."

"Oh, you fools! Hold your fire—those are my orders," the major said, and then he rode back toward the lines.

In war there are times when the mind takes on wings and seems to soar above the battlefield. As Major Pitcairn rode back to his troops, it seemed to him that he was at a great distance from Lexington Green. He was there in the flesh, but his soaring spirit was elsewhere, established in some vantage point where everything became suddenly clear. And there was no smoke of war lying on the grasses, and no dead men anywhere—only the living. He heard dogs barking, and this was real. He heard a woman's voice, high and shrill and clear, and this too was real. He heard Oliver ordering the men back into formation, and this pleased him. He saw little flakes of yellow light making their way across the common, creeping up each grass and leaf like a benediction, and perhaps this was the most real. "The rains will wash the blood away," he heard himself saying. He looked with pity at the battlefield, nearly deserted now, and from there he looked toward the tavern, all shuttered and bleak in the cold sunlight.

When the major returned to his own lines he saw that there was still a little fighting. A white horse was rushing toward the belfry across the common. The major shouted after the rider, but something in the movement of the horse told him that it had bolted; there was nothing to be done. To his own men he shouted, "The rebels are falling back. Hold your fire, men!" There were three or four rebels lying on the grass. One had been bayoneted and another had the top of his head blown off, his bright yellowish brains falling over the grass and his arm shaking and quivering; he was beyond help. "Poor devil, rest in peace. Lie quietly, don't shake so," the major murmured, making the sign of the cross.

Down the long avenue of shade Colonel Smith's Grenadiers were coming up, with fifes and drums. Hearing gunshots, they quickened their steps. By now all the rebels had dispersed, and the clouds of black powder smoke drifting across the common were vanishing in the wind. At the head of his troops, riding his dappled mare, Colonel Smith looked in the heavy early morning sunlight like a figure out of legend. His rein jingled, his polished buttons caught the sun, and he rode his horse at a prancing pace.

"I heard gunshots, Major," he said, and it was the voice of a man who has been out hunting grouse and suddenly hears the sound of firing on a following wind.

"So you did, sir," Major Pitcairn answered sharply, and for some reason he wanted to strike the man across the face.

"I suppose the rebels tried to hold up the advance, Major. Well, I see you've cleared them from the common. I suppose you fired above their heads, sir?"

For reply Major Pitcairn pointed at the four bodies lying on the green.

"Then there has been fighting," the colonel said slowly, his voice low and hoarse.

"Yes, sir."

"Against the orders of the governor and commander in chief."

"Yes, sir."

"And you will probably be court-martialed."

"Yes, sir."

"You were ordered to hold your fire, and it is quite evident that those poor devils over there didn't commit suicide. They were killed by our own men. You deserve to be cashiered, Major. I shall see that there is a full investigation."

With that the colonel rode off to inspect the infantry. He saw them shambling into line, and some men were still returning over the walls. All of them were murmuring, comparing their own adventures or simply standing in the shadows with the surly, frustrated expressions of men who have been hurt and who have only with the greatest difficulty avenged their hurts. Colonel Smith was not a fool. He saw now at a glance that there had been an attack on the Regulars. He had been unfair to Major Pitcairn, and since he prided himself on his fairness, he felt the need to apologize. He asked a few questions of the men, and then rode back to where the major was standing beside his horse, attempting to plug the wound in its neck.

"I owe you an apology, Major," he said quietly, and then ordered the officers to assemble on the green with their men. Afterward he ordered litter bearers to pick up the rebel wounded and dead and take them into the tavern.

While the men were assembling, Colonel Smith summoned his staff and as many officers of the advance as his orderlies could find. He noted that the windows of the tavern were opening, that the wind was still coming from the sea, that a cold windy day lay ahead of him and that a desperate silence came from the American houses on the edge of the green. Four hours before he had sent a messenger to Boston to call for reinforcements. No one had come from Boston to tell him that reinforcements were on their way. A huge portly man, suffering from gout, possessing the methodical mind which often goes with obesity, he noted in pencil in his diary:

At about six of the morning arriving Lexington Common to find Maj. Pitcairn very saddened by a brief engagement with rebels, his men restive and much put out.

Having briefly discussed with the officers the engagement with the rebels, he rode out to take up a position facing the advance, which now occupied the line of honor on the common. In a clear, high-pitched voice he said, "I pray your attention. The orders of the governor and commander in chief are that you continue the march to Concord and there seize the stores of the rebels. That's all we are up to. There isn't anything else in the world you are asked to do. I tell you once again that all engagements with the enemy must be avoided to the best of your ability, and you are not to fire unless fired on."

That was all. There was a brief cheer, and the colonel smiled in the direction of Major Pitcairn, who came riding up only in time to hear the last words spoken by the colonel. Ten minutes later the long column resumed the march to Concord.

"God help us all!" Major Pitcairn said as he took a last look over his shoulder at the sun shining on the trampled green. "That's not war, Oliver—that's the negation of war, and I don't want a fight like that again."

Oliver was deep in his own reflections. It occurred to him suddenly that all the alarm bells were silent now, and no fifes and drums were playing. Half an hour had passed since they arrived on Lexington Common. In silence the long scarlet line was making its way to the green hills of Concord, and high above his head the starlings were singing.

CHAPTER 9

The Way to the Heart

IN COLONEL BARRETT'S kitchen the bread and rum were being handed round, new bread and boiling-hot rum with the sweet sugary fragrance of molasses. The Reverend Emerson had ridden down to his manse overlooking the North Bridge, and with his going the atmosphere of the kitchen was less strained. Men laughed and joked, swore and engaged in pleasant fisticuffs, or else they sat together in small communities, picking out the touchholes of their fowling pieces, knapping their flints and cleaning the barrels. Young Ammi White, his face shining, all his courage returning with the dawn, was busily occupied with a powder horn given to him by the old colonel. It was engraved with the face of Amherst, and when Ammi White had finished spitting on it and rubbing it smooth, it shone as white and pure as a bleached bone. Eugénie was still huddled by the fireplace, dreaming her long dreams, living in a world apart where the voices of the men entered only at intervals.

"The farmhouse is all yours," the colonel said, smiling down at her. "No doubt you'll make yourself comfortable, ma'am."

"I won't stay," Eugénie answered, looking up at him with a detached and wondering look.

He said nothing. He imagined she meant that she had no desire to impose on him, and he dismissed her from his mind.

It was now nearly six o'clock in the morning, with a low

mist hanging over the valley and long shadows on the grass.
The men were already beginning to gather by the farm gate.
Eugénie followed them like someone in a dream, hardly
knowing what she was doing and hardly caring, for it had
occurred to her that these young farm hands would soon be
thrown into battle against the British. At the thought of battle her mind rebelled, grew numb, but the thought was suddenly extinguished: there was only a girl shivering in the
wind under an apple tree and watching men with wide-open
eyes. Here, on the high slope of a hill, with the blue bay of
Great Meadows below her and the elms clinging along the
yellow ridges, with woodchuck and sparrows flying across
the grass, and the buds of the apples and cherries scenting the
air, she felt as if she were a million miles from Boston. She
could see men parading on the green amid the spires and the
spaced barns of Concord, and in all that silence there was
nothing to comfort her—no comfort in the dark river winding
below, and none in the sunlit uplands.

"Are you crying to see the menfolk going off to war,"
Lemuel Shaw asked, "or because the cold is nipping you?"

"Because the cold is nipping me."

"Then you should wear my coat, ma'am," the boy said,
instantly removing his coat, which was cut from deerskins.

"I wouldn't take the coat of a soldier," Eugénie said.

"I was hoping you would, ma'am," Lemuel Shaw said
politely, "for then I might be brave enough to demand a kiss."

"It's too early in the morning for kisses."

"Are you sure you're not cold, ma'am?" Lemuel Shaw
said a little later, removing his coat and wrapping it round
her shoulders. But when he saw there was a kind of dreamy
film over her eyes he walked away to where Colonel Barrett
was talking to the men under a great elm near the farm gate.
The old colonel sat barrel-chested on a black mare, a woolen
scarf wrapped round his neck. He looked like a man who had
freshly risen from bed, his eyes clear and his beard bristling.

"I've told you before, men, and I'll tell you again, the Committee of Safety has ordered we are not to fight the Redcoats unless they force us to it. They're better armed than we are, and by God they're better soldiers! They are trained for fighting, and as for us—well, they say the best range for a rifle is fifty yards, but your fowling pieces there, I wouldn't reckon they'd fire with any accuracy more than twenty. You'll have to see the whites of their eyes and the cross-webbing of their belt before you fire, and that's no more than twenty feet. And I don't want you to fire unless you have to. We'll hold on to what we've got, and that's the better part of our lives."

So he went on, on that brisk morning, leaning forward sometimes to stroke the horse's mane or to fish for a lump of sugar in his pocket, while the wind whipped the scarf and the leaves whistled above his head. He had been talking for about five minutes when he saw they were all turning toward the rider coming up the long winding slope. The mist was clearing. All over the hills they could see little groups of men making their way toward Concord Green. They were bronze in the sun, and they all carried flintlocks or fowling pieces. Somehow the presence of these men, coming from all directions, moving silently among the shreds of grayish-white mist, made nonsense of the colonel's words; and the rider coming up the slope of the hill, dark and terrifying, with the sweat streaming from his face, his arms flailing the air, looked strangely like a portent of doom. They knew before he arrived that he brought bad news. It was something in the way he rode, the way he held himself, but most of all in the billowing of his cloak and the urgent flailing of his arms. He brought his horse to a halt beside Colonel Barrett, for the men opened out as soon as he came among them. He was a tall man with a reddish beard, and his red hair was damp on his sweating forehead.

"I've come direct from Lexington," he said, and then

paused, waiting for the air to return to his lungs. "There's
been fighting on the green, sir, and seven or eight of our men
are dead. I know some of their names, sir. Ensign Robert
Munroe, Jonas Parker, Jonathan Harrington, and that's not
all. The Redcoats came and they were out for murder, and
they're coming here—straight for this farm, sir. You're
Colonel Barrett, aren't you?"

The colonel nodded, and once again he fished in his pocket
for some sugar to feed his restive mare. The red-bearded
man from Lexington was gazing round him with a look of
extraordinary wonder on his face. He had ridden across
pastures and stone walls to Concord, talked to Amos Barrett
on the green, and then had ridden up to Barrett's farm. He
expected to be believed, but instead there was a look of incredulity on the face of the old colonel.

"You mean there's been a pitched battle?" the colonel
asked quietly.

"It doesn't matter what I mean, sir. The facts are there.
The dead are there. The devil will have to pay for it. I've
seen the boys lying dead in their own blood on Lexington
Green, and some were bayoneted where they lay. The Redcoats show no mercy, sir."

There was cold anger on the man's face as he sat there on
a shivering horse.

"You don't believe me, sir," he said sharply, "but there are
others who will believe me better. I tell you, sir, our men
were on the green, going about their legal purposes, and we
didn't fight them—we didn't open fire. It was the Redcoats
who opened fire, and they'll do the same in Concord. For
all I know they'll murder every man, woman and child among
you, and it won't be long before they're here."

"Then we must go on our way," Colonel Barrett said in a
hoarse voice, "and meet the British where they are." He said
these words slowly, thoughtfully, as though all the weight of

all his experience lay behind them, and still he did not spur his mare. Instead he looked down across the valley in the direction of Lexington. There was no sign of any Redcoats there, but on the hills all round him were scattered groups of men coming in from the neighboring villages.

"Yes, we must go down and meet them where they are," the colonel said a little later, and there was a faint cheer from the men. They would have cheered louder had they known the colonel a little less well. He was not a man who delighted in heroics. The men looked at him more than they looked at the red-bearded stranger from Lexington, and in a strange kind of way they even distrusted the messenger, as the colonel distrusted him. They began to believe, like the colonel, that whatever had happened might have some other explanation than the one given by the red-bearded man, who never gave his name, never identified himself, and seemed possessed, like the Reverend Emerson, of a personal hatred against the enemy.

There were two fifers and a single drummer among the men on Ponkawtassett Hill, and the colonel asked them to play as the men strode down the curving hill with an old pock-marked colonel at their head. The air was now fresh and sweet, with the last lingering taste of frost dying in the hot sun. The apple trees were shaking in the wind, and all the houses near the road were filled with chattering women who waved them on.

Once over the creaking bridge, they turned into Great Meadows as though they were marching straight to the Bedford Road; but on the ridge above Meriam's Corner they paused, for all the minutemen from all the towns around seemed to be congregated there. It was a little after half past six on a bright morning. Church bells were pealing. Every hill and every valley was crowded with minutemen, and most of them carried silken flags. These men rarely spoke aloud.

They whispered together, and sometimes an order was barked.

Colonel Barrett, leaning forward on his horse, gravely stretching out his hand toward their officers when they came to report, for they all saw him on the rise and recognized him at once, kept saying, "It's a fine morning, gentlemen— a fine morning," as though the armed colonials had come to Concord to see a fair or a horse show.

"You wouldn't think there's an ounce of perturbation in his spirit," the Reverend Emerson commented as he drew back to make way for the leader of the men from Acton.

"Nor is there," Lemuel Shaw answered, and he received a glare from the bushy-bearded parson in the black ministerial clothes, who had ridden over from the manse after seeing that the women and children in the place were well protected.

It was ten minutes later before they heard the fifes and drums of the British coming down the Lexington Road. It came at first as a thin, faint sound on the sparkling air, followed by the drumming sound of tramping feet. It was like music, the same music they had been hearing for the last half-hour, only this time it was more incisive. There was more than a hint of sternness in the unchanging military pace of the Redcoats as they marched under the lea of the long hill, along a sunken road, invisible to the men at Meriam's Corner. Along Brook's Hill, overlooking the road, some minutemen, black against the yellow fields, could be seen retiring.

Amos Barrett, red-faced like his father, clambered up the hill. His beard was black and full, he wore no cape, and he had a fowling piece slung over his shoulder. He looked tired, worn out, for he had been working through the night, hiding the military stores and even going himself to wake the minutemen in the outlying houses.

"We're waiting for orders, sir," Amos Barrett said. He held himself straight, looked at his father with the same expression he would have used if he were looking at any superior officer.

"March out to meet them and play your music, boys," the old colonel answered.

There was a gasp from the Reverend Emerson. He had been standing there with his coattails wrapped round him, a queer smile on his face. As soon as he had heard the fifes and drums of the Redcoats his face had lighted up with a savage smile, and immediately he had looked in the direction of Colonel Barrett, hoping to catch the old man's eye. But the colonel had deliberately disregarded him. And now the colonel was behaving insolently, madly, absurdly. There was no sense in it. The minutemen from miles around had come to ambush the British, and here was the old fool ordering them to march out with flags waving and music playing.

"I tell you it's an impossible thing to do!" he shouted in his high-pitched, nervous voice which carried better than any other voice on Meriam's Corner.

"No, it's not impossible," Colonel Barrett answered, waving a gloved hand at the minister and smiling. "Nothing is impossible. And I tell you this, Mr. Emerson, there's only one man in command of our militia. I can't have you arguing against my decisions. They'll go out to meet the British with all their flags flying, and if you say a word against it, I'll have you . . ."

The old colonel did not complete the sentence. He was watching his son giving orders to about thirty minutemen to form in column and march down the road. The music of the Redcoats was growing louder, piercingly sweet, and now the Americans were marching down the road between the stone walls. Few of them were in step, and even the fifers and drummers were playing out of tune. They looked like a brave little rabble of men going out to spend a morning in the fields, without uniform, and the fowling pieces they carried on their shoulders might be mistaken for pitchforks. They were playing "The World Turned Upside Down," the British were playing "Yankee Doodle," and somehow the two tunes made a pleasing combination.

"This is outright idiocy," the Reverend Emerson said, planting an old gnarled walnut stick firmly in the ground in front of him.

"It's nothing of the sort," Colonel Barrett answered.

At that moment, at the turning of the road, the British came into view: first, two officers on white horses, followed by the musicians and then the scarlet-coated men marching with incredible precision, their heads held high, their bayonets glinting in the sun. It was the startling redness of the uniforms which sent a wave of unconcealed admiration through the Americans. How neat they were! How precise their steps! They were as pretty a sight as anyone had ever seen in Concord, and they came forward possessed of the momentum of a relentless machine, a gorgeous scarlet snake winding along the deep road toward the upland. It was a sight none of the minutemen of Concord would ever forget— the stone walls still glinting with dew, the shreds of mist on the earth, the quiet barns, the smell of sap in the meadows, and then the marching column of Americans going out to meet the long red serpent of the enemy, whose bayonets were on fire, their red coats blazing, their brass buttons and silver gorgets glinting.

The Americans marched steadily on; so did the British. They were within a hundred yards of each other when Captain Amos Barrett shouted to his men, "About face!" The Americans immediately turned to face the ridge, and with the Redcoats close behind them, they marched in step, fifes and drums still playing, toward Meriam's Corner. Neither the Americans nor the British gave the slightest sign that they were unaccustomed to such displays. The officers on their white horses rode as naturally and calmly as they had ridden before, and so did the infantrymen who followed them.

They were all marching exactly as though they were on parade.

Colonel Barrett had not the slightest knowledge of what would happen next. He had given the order that the Americans should go out to meet the British, and he had watched the two columns marching toward each other without excitement, completely certain that no harm would befall his son or any of the men with him. And when Captain Amos Barrett gave the command "About face," this seemed to the old colonel the most natural thing in the world. The Americans were leading the British into the town. It was a sign that they possessed no animosity against the British, and at the same time they did not fear them. He was pleased with the decision he had made. With his gloved hand he waved to his son in exactly the same way he would wave to Amos on any ordinary day.

But Amos misinterpreted the waving hand. He assumed it was an order to disperse, and at the place where the road to Bedford turns sharply right he shouted, "Run for the hills, men!" Shortly afterward the small column had scattered along the loose sandy ridge which follows the road until it dips down into Concord Green.

Immediately all the Americans at Meriam's Corner began to run toward the cemetery as though they were all solemnly engaged in an unspoken desire to protect the liberty pole which lay a little above it. The flag and the pole were the symbols of their resistance: it was a natural meeting place and it was dangerously close to the center of the town. At most, if they ran fast enough, they would find themselves with seven or eight minutes to spare before the infantrymen were parading on the green.

Above the burying ground, with the green pine tree floating above his head, Colonel Barrett rested his horse and surveyed the scene. The sun was striking hot on his face; the grasses were steaming. The hill was a blaze of yellow, and the minutemen were scrambling all over it. He had raced his horse to the flag with the same unconscious desire to protect it which moved the men, and now that he had reached it, he wondered whether he had done well. The sight of Mr. Emerson advancing over the rise, his coat flapping, his face stiff with outraged anger and pride, made him feel reasonably certain that he had done the best he could; and when Mr. Emerson croaked, "Well, how is it now, Colonel? All talk and no work?" Colonel Barrett felt that everything was happening according to some destined plan which would be revealed to him later.

"By God, we are doing our best!" he shouted impatiently, for the first time raising his voice.

"So you think we are doing our best when we run like flies?" the minister commented. It was not a question so much as a bitter statement of fact. "You have the advantage of me, Colonel," the minister went on, more bitter than ever now that he had got his breath back. "You have a horse, and you can see better. But it is my feeling that we should stand our ground. We've run far enough, and we've put on a ridiculous display to amuse the Grenadiers. Music! I never thought I would have to listen to our men playing music to the British! No, sir, we should stand our ground, and if we die, we should die here."

There were a few murmurs of agreement, but most of the minutemen standing beside the liberty pole had long ago made up their minds to trust the old colonel rather than the fiery minister.

"You may take care of the men's souls, Mr. Emerson," the colonel said tartly, "but let me take care of their young bodies."

"The souls and the bodies of men are indivisible," the minister answered.

Colonel Barrett whistled under his breath. For the first time the old, pock-marked face showed signs of anger. Always red, his cheeks were now the color of the scarlet uniforms of the British.

"We can't dabble in theological arguments at a time like this," he said quickly, paying no attention to the minister but addressing the men. "If there are any of you who would like me to retire from the command, I will do so immediately. I am an old man. There may be younger men with better ideas."

The minutemen were still running and stumbling toward the liberty pole, and the British were still playing their fifes and drums as they turned toward the green.

Young Major Buttrick, thin and tall, with high cheekbones and a sallow skin, walked straight up to Colonel Barrett and said in a loud voice, "We don't change commanders when we are crossing a stream. We have faith in you, sir. We think you'll need an adjutant to help you."

"You're talking of adjutants on the edge of hell's fire," the Reverend Emerson interrupted.

"I'll choose Lieutenant Joseph Hosmer as my adjutant," the colonel said quietly, "and as for the men here—all of you—I have a hard demand to make. We'll retire in good order. Every man must be on his best behavior. I've told you before, and I'll tell you again, I won't have a shot fired in anger. We'll retire over the bridge, and we'll do it in style!"

Everyone knew he meant a general retirement over the North Bridge, toward Ponkawtassett Hill, the place where the larger number of cannon were buried under the plowed fields. They knew the colonel was determined to protect their lives, and they knew they would follow him against any enemy. He did not give an order to retire; it was more like a suggestion. Major Buttrick said, "I'll have lookouts posted," and then someone came with a pitcher of water and offered it to the colonel.

There were four hundred men gathered near the bridge,

and most of them were silent and perplexed. There was no more music from the British, who were now parading in front of Wright's Tavern on the green. By this time the Americans had reached a deep saddle on the ridge behind the burying ground, facing the ripe slopes on the farther side of Concord River.

"We'll go to the long slopes," the colonel said, pointing to the fields of rye lying in the summery sun.

White clouds were trooping over the heavens in a stiff easterly wind.

All this time Eugénie, wearing Lemuel Shaw's coat, had kept close to the colonel without being observed. The long deerskin coat gave her the appearance of a minuteman. She had carefully avoided attracting the colonel's attention, but now he saw her and was angry.

"We can't have women in the militia," he said sternly. "It's against all the rules of war."

"No one said I was a woman when I rode from Boston," Eugénie replied.

"It's a brave answer, but the rules of war are strict about it. I won't have it. Get to my farmhouse. You'll be safe on the journey. The British won't mistreat you, I promise you."

Along a narrow road buttressed with a low stone wall the men of Concord, Acton, Middlesex, Bedford and Lincoln were making their way toward the farm. In the dust of the road one could still see the footprints they had left less than two hours before. They were itching for a fight, but they knew they were outnumbered more than three to one. There were four companies of Concord men, three from Acton, two from Bedford and one from Lincoln at full strength, with half a dozen more companies at half or quarter strength. But they were ill-equipped, mostly with fowling pieces, and only the men from Acton came armed with bayonets. As they marched they would sometimes fall out of line to clean their flintlocks: there was little discipline among them. When they came to the river there were some who waded out into the stream beyond the reeds and splashed water over their faces; others took off their shirts, shouting to the men on the bank that there was more virtue in fighting near-naked, until Joseph Hosmer called to them, saying it was no way to fight a war—why, their deerskin coats were their best protection of all, allowing them to hide among the trees.

"And who are we to hide among the trees?" the men wading in the river asked impatiently. "We've hidden enough, haven't we?"

There was silence again when Colonel Barrett appeared, looking older than ever, his mare picking her way delicately in the sandy gravel.

When they had all crossed the bridge the colonel called them all together again. "I've heard you whispering, men," he said, "and I've nothing against it, but you've made me your commander and now you'll have to listen to me. You keep whispering we've retired too far, and we're always doing what the British want us to do. That may be true, and it mayn't. I don't know. But I know this—they've stacked their arms by now and are searching out our stores in the town, and it's not a good or a pleasant thing to contemplate. As you know, they're after our stores more than they're after us, but our stores are all we've got to defend ourselves with. Well, we have a reasonable faith in our good right arms, haven't we? We know we have a right to bear arms, don't we? But by the looks of them there are more than a thousand men against us, and we're not much more than three hundred. We can't fight them yet on open ground, so don't expose yourselves, men. Keep cool and calm, and don't fire unless you are fired on."

"God's glory, have we got to fight by retreating, Colonel?" the Reverend Emerson exclaimed. "We climb hill after hill, and where's the end of it?"

"I'll tell you the truth, sir. I don't know where it will end."

The minister snorted. "We're not goats!" He was so outraged that he walked away toward the bridge with his head held high in the air.

His manse, facing the river, was not a stone's throw from the North Bridge. It was an old timbered house like a Dutch barn, with a stubble field in front of it, a large house standing against the sun. The river bent there, turning into a reed bank, the leaves all yellow and shining, the river blue as steel. Flowers grew on the water's edge. Mr. Emerson walked straight across the stubble field toward the door of the manse, where Mrs. Emerson and her children were huddled together. "Get indoors," the Reverend Emerson shouted. "Get right in, for God's love!"

"There's no harm in him leaving us," the colonel muttered, and then led the men to higher ground.

The sky was cloudless, very clear and blue, like the blue of a kingfisher's wing. As they came up the hill into the clover they saw that a detachment of Redcoats were already on the heights, coming over the edge of the hill. Then they disappeared. Evidently they were making for Colonel Barrett's farm, or the other farms hidden behind it. For the first time the Americans were caught between two enemy detachments—the one on the hill and the other in the town. Very faintly on the wind they heard the Reverend Emerson shouting, "Phoebe, Phoebe, get into the manse, and take the young ones with you, for God's love!"

Colonel Barrett had done many strange things that morning, but the strangest of all occurred when the men were halfway up the hill. Leaving them behind, he quietly spurred on the mare and began to ride straight toward the place where the British had last been seen. The men debated among themselves why he had left them, without a word to anyone. Was he climbing the hill to meet and parley with the British? Did he want to make sure of the safety of his wife and grandchildren on the farm, or did he simply want to survey the scene and see how many Redcoats were there? They watched the black horse disappearing into an apple orchard, and he could not have been more than a musket shot away from the Redcoats. There he was, delegate to the Court of Massachusetts, member of the Provincial Congress, Superintendent of Public Stores, Commander of the Concord Militia, and God knows what else, and he had simply deserted his men without a by-your-leave.

"I reckon he knows what he is doing, and there's nothing to do but wait for him," Lieutenant Joseph Hosmer said. He was a handsome man, tall, ruddy-faced, and he carried himself easily. Eugénie thought he was the most handsome of them all, and she saw how fire gleamed in his eyes and misery twisted the corners of his lips.

"What do we do now?" one of the Acton men shouted.

"I reckon we stay where we are," Lieutenant Hosmer answered, and all the time he was looking toward the spur of the hill and the white blossoms of the apple trees.

Colonel Barrett could not have told himself why he left the men. Afterward, whenever he came to think about it, he remembered that he had some plan to head off the British. The greater part of the stores were buried around his farm. There were guns, all oiled and wrapped in cotton cloth, laid in the soft, rich earth under the sage and parsley of Mrs. Barrett's kitchen garden, which was the pride of her eyes. As the ox teams fashioned the spring furrows, rows of muskets were laid in them. There were barrels of powder hidden behind the false walls of the cellars, and more barrels lay concealed under brush in the swamps of Spruce Gutter, behind the farmhouse. There were gun carriages, leather bags full of shot, bayonets, a whole treasure put away there.

As he rode slowly with the apple boughs brushing softly against his face, he watched the Grenadiers as they poured across the farm. Once he saw his wife's face at an upstairs window and waved to her; he even made a gesture as though summoning her to run away, out of the farmhouse into the woods, but she shook her head. By this time the Grenadiers were already under the great elm at the farm gate. He watched them march up to the door, and suddenly Mrs. Barrett was there, wiping her hands on her apron. The officer at the door was saying he had search orders, and Colonel Barrett distinctly heard his wife say, "Very well, sir. I'll expect you to respect private property." The officer bowed.

Grenadiers were posted at all the entrances to the farmhouse and even beneath windows. There was a long silence. No one moved about the fields. Then he saw some of the Grenadiers wheeling a gun carriage out of a shed. It had been hidden under straw, but they had found it without any trouble. The old colonel, hidden among the apple boughs, smiled to himself. Everything was happening as he wanted it to happen. Against everyone's advice he had deliberately left the gun carriage in the shed, as a sop to the British. They would find it, burn it, and then perhaps they would go on their way. And so it happened.

The Grenadiers were preparing to burn the carriage under the barn when Mrs. Barrett came running out of the farmhouse, saying, "If you burn the carriage there, maybe the whole farmhouse will go up in flames."

"Then we'll burn it in the road, ma'am," an officer said. Though the straw was already alight, the flames were put out and the carriage was wheeled into the road.

By now one of the Grenadiers posted under a window had caught sight of the colonel. He was waving vigorously and pointing in the direction of the orchard. The colonel decided to spur the mare and rejoin his troops. As he came over the top of the hill, he saw three small fires burning in Concord. They had just been lighted, for there was still little smoke: the fires resembled three small pools of gold. By the time he reached the men, the flames and smoke were mounting into the blue sky.

"They're burning the whole town down, sir!" Lieutenant Hosmer shouted, pointing to the spiraling smoke rising above the elms. He could not see the town halfway down the hill. "Can't you see the smoke, sir?"

"Smoke, eh?" the colonel answered. "Eh, what's that? I don't see any."

"It's true enough," Major Buttrick interrupted, running back from the rocky edge of the curving field. "They're setting fire to the center of the town, curse 'em. We can't stand for that, Colonel Barrett."

"Well, that's serious," the colonel said, stroking his beard. "They're setting fire to a few stores, that's nothing to worry about. We're rich in stores, Major."

"Then you think we should stay here?"

"I'm waiting on events, Major. I don't propose to fight the British for the sake of a few stores."

"I tell you they're burning the town, sir! We've had enough of retreat, sir. We've got a score to settle with the lobster-backs, haven't we? Let me lead the men down to the town. We'll fight it out. We don't want them burning the place down over the heads of our women and children and committing other desecrations and horrors, do we?"

"Steady, gentlemen," Colonel Barrett said, speaking over the major's head to the restive men all looking toward the three black columns of smoke rising over the elms.

"I tell you it's smoke, and they're burning the town!" Major Buttrick shouted.

He lived on a farm close to the Barrett farmhouse, and there had always been a feud between them.

"And I tell you they have found a few stores—Wright's Tavern, and the meetinghouse, and some at Mr. Meriam's house. I've seen it, Major Buttrick. I rode up the hill to see what they were up to. Listen to me. You don't trust the

British to behave decently, but I do—I have to. There isn't any rule of thumb in war, but you've got to believe in decency."

"We shouldn't take these things lying down, sir. If I had my way, I'd cook all those lobsters in grease!"

The old colonel smiled down at the red-faced major. It was the same battle he had fought with the Reverend Emerson. The Americans were out of temper. He knew that. They were itching for a fight, but there was no evidence yet that the British were of the same mind. He was holding the Americans back with all the strength at his command, but it was a losing battle: in the end they would reach the flash point.

He said, "I've been listening all this while for the sound of musket shots, but I haven't heard one yet. We mustn't think of our hates. We must keep our powder and our tempers dry. We're safe enough now——"

"We don't want safety," Major Buttrick interrupted. "We're not chicken-livered!"

He said this in a loud voice, appealing to the men. There was a burst of applause, but it ceased when the colonel raised his hand for silence.

"I say we're safe on this hill, men," he said, leaning forward and stroking the mare's neck, "and a hill's as good as a fortress. The best way we can live through this day is to avoid the British and make them understand they had better avoid us. They won't tread on us, you can be sure of that!"

"Then what else are they doing when they burn our houses to cinders?" Major Buttrick said angrily. This time there was a note of explosiveness in his voice.

It was growing hot, though the wind was still coming from the sea, and more minutemen were making their way over the river. Colonel William Prescott's minutemen came up from Westford. They said they had seen the Grenadiers raiding Sam Barrett's gun shop. The Grenadiers had also broken into Ephraim Brown's saddlery and found the trunnions of three twenty-four-pounders. These they smashed and carried to the pyre they had lighted under the liberty pole.

"Yes, and they're even put fire to the Town House," someone said.

"You're not talking seriously," the colonel said doubtfully.

"I saw it, didn't I? Got a gold cupola and a gilded vane, hasn't it? I saw the flames reaching up."

"I won't believe it till I see it with my own eyes," the colonel said, more to reassure himself than for any other reason. Then louder: "Well, men, it's time we went trampin'. We ought to get a bit nearer to see what they are doing." Waving to them as he made his way down the slope at the head of the men, he added, "It's a nice morning for a ride."

It was like an act of defeat. Colonel Barrett still hoped the Americans and the British would keep away from one another. The Redcoats on the hill had disappeared. Presumably they were searching all the farmhouses behind Spruce Gutter. He hoped the men would cross the bridge and take up positions on Great Meadows. There they would be nearer the town, and their presence would frighten the Redcoats from any more burning. He was still thinking in this way when he observed that the greater part of the men had already passed him.

Major Buttrick came up to him and said, "May I lead, sir? Have I permission?"

"You have," the colonel said, "but whatever happens, don't let anything happen in anger."

At this moment Captain Isaac Davis, a gunsmith and the leader of the Acton men, came running up. "We're better armed than the rest, sir," he said. "Every man of us has a musket and a bayonet. For God's sake let us have the advance!"

The colonel looked down at the tousled gunsmith who still wore a leather apron, the sign of his trade. "You'll have to settle that with the major," he said. "I've promised him the advance. You're not afraid to take this charge?"

"No, sir, I'm not, and there isn't a man in my company who is," Captain Davis answered.

Presently the men of Acton wheeled out of the road and doubled through the elms to reach the advance. Now, they told themselves, they were an army on the march. Sunlight glittered on the blue bayonets of the Acton men, and at last they possessed a purpose: they would reach Great Meadows and face the British and scare them out of the town. Their blood stirred in them. The long hours of uncertainty were over. As they came down the hill through the elms and the cherry blows, the drums were beating and the fifes were playing; never had a morning seemed so green and full of life. The fifers were playing "The White Cockade" to taunt the British. Black smoke from the fires was winnowing away. It was half past nine now. Quietness was beginning to settle on the Concord valleys and smoke rose lazily from the farms, and the men were hungry. Swallows were flying madly in their paths, and the hungry men on their way to the North Bridge kicked up so much dust they hid the light of the sun.

As they came close to the bridge they saw that the Redcoats were coming down the lane on the other side of the river; some of them had already crossed the bridge and others were pulling up the planks. There were British in the copses on either side, and one could see the reflections of their red coats in the slow-moving water.

"For God's sake put the planks down!" Major Buttrick shouted, and then he unbuckled an old hunting knife at his belt and waved it over his head as a sign for the men to move faster. "It's our bridge, men. Don't let them destroy it!"

Eugénie found herself being carried forward in the wave of minutemen. The drums and fifes were being played louder than ever. She saw a girl standing by the low stone wall and some of the men darting out of the ranks to kiss her, but she remembered neither the face of the girl nor the clothes she wore. There was the taste of salt air on Eugénie's lips.

The apple trees trembled as the minutemen passed, and old Colonel Barrett, behind the men, was shouting, "Boys, don't shoot unless you're fired on!"

Then, before they knew where they were, the road had come to an end and they were standing knee-deep in the wet grass, and there were the Redcoats in front of them.

CHAPTER 10

Concord Bridge

FROM HER place behind the wall Eugénie
thought she could see the gold lace of the officer's epaulets—
each thread and twist of it—and even the engraving on the
gold handle of the sword he carried at his waist. There was
the slow-moving river below, no longer blue but green, and
the rotting hulk of a boat lying in the shadow of the bridge.
A steep path led to the water's edge. The Redcoats were all
on the other side, and she could hear them talking among
themselves. There were perhaps three hundred of them
jostling together, on one another's heels, crowding the narrow
road, their scarlet coats gleaming like oranges on a tree, and
they looked as unconcerned as the Americans. They were all
young men, their faces tanned a deep brown by the spring
sun. Now they were less than fifty yards away, so that you
could just see the whites of their eyes. The elms shading the
river were rustling in the high wind, and ripples were forming on the green scum of the river.

Eugénie remembered how she had ridden over the bridge
in moonlight and how white and silent everything had been.
Even now it was like a dream, though the Regulars were
forming into street-fighting order to defend the bridge, with
the front rank down on their knees—four men with their
flintlocks at their shoulders, and behind them four more
standing, and others behind and above on the rising ground.
It was the strangest thing in the world to see the British at

the bridge and ready to fire, but taking their time at it; and there were two officers jumping over a wall and trampling Mr. Emerson's grain field, as if they were going to make a call on the minister. "They're going to kill one another," Eugénie said. She knew in her heart of hearts that all the wandering over the hills, all the hiding of gun carriages and bullets and powder and cold steel, all the debates of the Committee of Safety ended at the small wooden bridge over a country stream, where the wild weeds grew and the reeds were shivering.

In front of the flooding tide of minutemen Captain Isaac Davis and Major Buttrick were standing close to the bridge, so close that their shadows fell on the planks. They were saying something to the officer on the opposite bank. In answer there came the crack of an officer's pistol aimed at the middle of the river, and a little waterspout jumped up where the warning shot hit. Then a second and a third shot were fired, all into the river, and still Eugénie could hear the voices of Captain Davis and Major Buttrick, though no separate words could be distinguished.

"Hold your ground, men, and don't fire unless you are fired on," Major Buttrick said, loud enough for the British to hear.

He accented the word "fire" and perhaps the British thought he was giving the order for an attack. Immediately there came a volley from the Regulars nearest the bridge. The Regulars were good marksmen, but they aimed wide.

"By God," someone said, "they're firing with ball! Fire, men, fire!"

Captain Isaac Davis said, "They have begun it now, and it's their fault. God damn them!"

"Swear not at all," someone said, standing by the captain's side. It was an older man with a fringe of iron-gray hair.

Captain Davis turned to him and said, "I didn't mean to swear, and as God will forgive me——" But he said no more, for he was hit in the chest. He jumped two or three feet in the air, and then fell on his side without a word more, not far from the wall. He was the first to fall, but a moment later an Acton drummer boy, not more than fifteen, who had been drumming faintly beside the bridge through all the long silence, fell with half his face shot away, as though it had been sliced in half, neatly, cleanly, with an immense stroke of a hunting knife.

A farmer turned over the body of the Acton drummer boy. The farmer's mouth opened, closed, then fell open again. He screamed at the top of his voice, "Are they fighting with jackknives?"

"They're fighting with ball," Major Buttrick replied, "and there's nothing to be done except to answer them with the same kind of fire."

He shouted: "Fire! Fire! Fire!" and now all the Americans were firing from the shoulder. The men on the hill were firing above the heads of the men below, and some were taking cover behind the low stone wall; others stood in the open.

A shot grazed against Eugénie's shoulder. She could see the Redcoat taking careful aim at her, and what made it worse was that he smiled with assurance and seemed to fling a greeting as he raised his musket to his shoulder. He was a handsome man with yellow curls and a sunburned, childish face. She could almost hear the words forming on his lips, "Why, sir, here's a present for you. All rebels go to hell!" There was a kind of whispered conversation between them, the Redcoat smiling and Eugénie gazing at him as one might gaze at any stranger seen in a sunny field; then he swung the barrel of his musket round and aimed at the river. The river was white with little waterspouts peppering the green scum of the surface.

In some way which it did not occur to her to think about or try to understand, Eugénie knew that the men on both sides of the river were fighting in spite of themselves. They fought to kill, but just as suddenly they put their killing moods away. Black powder smoke wafted over the river. Though they had been firing continually for nearly five minutes, surprisingly few people had been killed, and Eugénie could see only one Redcoat lying dead on the bank and a few others lightly wounded. The Americans had fired with every flintlock and fowling piece they had, and men running down the road had broken ranks and huddled on the little strip of bank. They had all fired their guns, and the bullets had either gone wild, or their guns were defective, or they had fired without aiming to kill.

It was a strange war, and for Eugénie the strangest thing of all was the silence of it, the hush and the solemnity which descended on them all; there was no yelling, even by the wounded. She saw how, as the exchange of shots went on, everything took on a deeper light. All colors became richer, and the scarlet coats of the enemy shone with a deeper hue than any scarlet she had seen before. The young Englishman was still there, smiling at her on the opposite bank: he was a ranker lost in some kind of dream, his head cocked a little to one side. His scarlet coat looked neat and well-trimmed, as though he had put on his uniform only a few moments ago.

"No, this cannot go on," Eugénie said aloud, smiling to herself. She saw the reflections of the men in the river more than the men themselves, everything clearly mirrored in moving water. As she leaned forward she saw that the moored boat among the reeds was beginning to sink, water swelling up through three shots in the stern sheets. It sank slowly, without rocking, as calmly as though the boat itself was a hand falling smoothly in water; and as she watched it disappear, she wondered what it was doing there among the reeds and why men should waste ammunition on so useful a thing as a boat.

Lemuel Shaw had returned to be by her side. He was

hopping up and down and shouting angrily, "God in heaven, what makes our bullets go wide?"

The Americans fired without order, impulsively, and yet without hatred. The British Regulars fired in order, the front rank of four men kneeling, then running behind when they had fired, so that there was something in the mechanical precision of their movements which reminded one of mechanical dolls. And when they turned, they turned abruptly, quickly, mechanically, and they did not run into the cover of the elms: they marched.

"They're not made of flesh and blood," Lemuel Shaw muttered.

"Then what are they made of?"

"I wouldn't know, ma'am. I wouldn't know. . . ."

Major Buttrick was the first to make his way across the bridge. He had a flintlock in one hand and a sword in the other, and he walked the bridge as unconcernedly as though he were taking a stroll. The British paid no attention to him. Behind him the Americans were clambering on the bridge, shouting at the top of their voices, "We've turned the lobsterbacks away, hurrah!" and some were weeping with joy. And when they reached the other bank it seemed strange to see them there instead of the Redcoats.

Colonel Barrett came riding down to the bridge. "How many have we lost?" he shouted.

"No more than two for sure, sir," Major Buttrick answered.

"And wounded?"

"Seven or eight, but some lightly."

There was a short pause. Colonel Barrett kept looking from Major Buttrick to the men running across the bridge; then the major turned away and the old colonel shouted after him, "I don't want them pursued. It's no use. Make for Windy Ridge."

The major wheeled round. "Why, Colonel, we have them in the hollows of our palms. They're in full retreat, aren't they?"

"Yes, and likely as not they will lead you into an ambuscade."

Saying this, the colonel, all his vigor returning to him now, led his horse down into the water and made it swim across. He had spent the last twenty minutes on the slope above the bridge; he had seen nothing of the engagement, though he had heard the shooting. And now more than ever he was determined to follow his original tactics: he would bring the Americans over Great Meadows and somehow thrust the Redcoats out of the town by coming down from high ground. It was the advantage he wanted; no other was worth the having. He would not fight them on level ground; he would not allow any more frontal attacks; he would bite and goad at the British, force them out of town, and send in a bill to the governor and commander in chief. Meanwhile it was still his duty to protect the lives of the men of Concord.

He rode warily in the hot sunshine, glad when he reached the long avenue of elms. At the very end of the avenue the British were marching in formation, as though on parade, and from somewhere far away he heard the command, "Turn right, steady, hep, hep, steady," and knew they were on their way to the green.

The dying and the wounded were left where they were. Here and there he could see smears of blood on the grass, and in the shadows of the elms he saw a Grenadier lurching, clutching a broken arm. At first the colonel had no intention of riding up to the wounded man, but suddenly he found himself swinging to the left and racing up to the fellow, who was leaning against an elm now, his worried face blanched with pain.

"Take it easy, lad," the colonel said sorrowfully, seeing

how the boy's eyes were like little blue slits. "Go over to the manse—they'll bind you up again." Then he rode on to join Major Buttrick at the head of his men.

While the colonel was racing through the tunnel of elms, never far from the retreating Redcoats, Eugénie was being carried forward in the flood of minutemen crossing the bridge. It occurred to her that if the British had taken it into their heads to rightabout-turn and then charge the Americans, they could have mowed them down as hailstones mow down a field of autumn grain.

Beside her came Lemuel Shaw, grunting and wheezing a little from a ball which had ripped the flesh of his left shoulder. He was breathing heavily. He said, "I wish we had grape, Eugénie. If we had grape, we could have made a furrow through the Redcoats and walked straight through."

"You ought to rest, Lem. You can't fight with a wound. You must rest now and let me bandage it up."

"It's no more than a grazing wound," he said, "and I'll fight as long as I can."

At that moment, twenty yards away across the cartway, Eugénie saw a Grenadier lying in a pool of blood beside the road, the white blaze of his coat glinting in the sun. He had one hand pressed to his stomach, his white and pointed hat, like a bishop's miter, askew. He looked like a doll once threaded together with strings, but now all the strings were broken. She recognized him. He was the yellow-haired boy she had spoken to, whispered to, across the stream.

It was quiet on the edge of the cartway—quiet and shady. Above them floated the wispy black smoke of battle with its acrid tang. There came to her the smell of flowers and weeds and the sunlit leaves of the elms, but she had no sense of being on a bank where small flowers pushed through the grass. She had eyes only for the wounded soldier under the tree. He had a delicate, clean face, a long chin, a mouth cut clean and red as a fresh wound; and now that he had opened them wide, she saw that he had the largest blue eyes she had ever seen. The wound must have been deep: his fist was buried in it. The wind ruffled his yellow hair. He showed no fear, but seemed to make a salutation with his free hand as she advanced toward him. There was about him, as he rested there beside the road, a strange composure, as though he thought that pain would never harm him.

Eugénie was ten yards away from the Grenadier when she saw Ammi White running toward the dying Englishman. He carried a hatchet in his hand, and he was flailing his arms wildly, his face beet-red and his eyes shining with a curious light. She had seen him among the Americans at the bridge, shouting himself hoarse, urging the men to kill, getting in everyone's way, with an absurd powder horn hanging from his neck. Even then she had noted the bitterness in his face. He wanted to be a hero, but everyone was urging him out of the way. Now he saw his opportunity. He stood beside the Grenadier, who was painfully attempting to rise to his knees. The face, so calm before, became livid and ghastly, like something in a nightmare, the face of a soldier who had reached the limit of suffering and could bear no more. He made not the slightest appeal. He simply rose as though to confront the boy, as though to reduce the boy's advantage; and then Ammi White smashed down with his hatchet, again and again, using all his strength, his legs apart, the hatchet gripped in both hands, and he attacked the soldier exactly as though he were chopping firewood.

"I didn't miss a lick, did I?" Ammi White said when Lemuel Shaw came running up; then he looked down at the soldier's broken head, the blood mushrooming up, the brains spilling, a face that looked like an orange squashed underfoot, and gave out a long roar of quivering laughter. "Didn't miss a lick, did I?" he repeated.

"No, you didn't," Lemuel Shaw said quietly.

"He's dead, ain't he?"

"No, he's not dead."

"Then maybe I ought to give him another licking," the boy went on, pleased with himself, while the breath came out in loud slow sobs from the soldier's broken mouth. "He had it coming to him, didn't he?"

It was then that Lemuel Shaw sent the boy sprawling against a tree with the hardest blow he had ever delivered with his fists. Eugénie was crying. She was staring at the dying soldier, unable to do anything to comfort him, lost in the terrible dream of a face from which all expression had gone.

"There's nothing left to do," Lemuel Shaw said, attempting to take her arm.

"Oh, but there is—there always is," Eugénie answered, and she leaned forward and kissed the forehead of the dying man whose breath came like a long low whistling.

Then, with Lemuel Shaw beside her, she went to join the minutemen on Windy Ridge.

CHAPTER II

A Battle Begins

DARK AGAINST the sky line, wearing on his head an old stocking cap he had found in the pocket of his cape, the old colonel was riding along the ridge. He looked lonely there, riding the black mare in sunlight, detached from his troops, sometimes waving his gloved hand at the minutemen, all the youths and old men he had known since they were many years younger. Sometimes he mopped the sweat from his face, sighed, turned round on the saddle to watch the minutemen coming over the low hills; then he would smile briefly, as though he suddenly remembered something he had long forgotten.

Through the thickets of sumac and dwarf oak Colonel Barrett could see very faintly the Redcoats marching below, and sometimes there would come the voice of a British officer. "In step, men, steady, hep, hep, hep." It was the same voice he had heard when he crossed the bridge, but now it was louder and more assured, the voice of a young man in the prime of life. It amused the colonel to imagine the appearance of a man who took defeat with such singular nonchalance.

He had ridden for about ten minutes when he came upon Major Buttrick and a group of young officers from Framingham who had only just arrived on the scene. They were fresh and well-armed, and they were established behind a low wall which gave them cover from the enemy. There was

a stretch of turf below them. At the foot of the turf, within
the range of their firelocks, the Redcoats were parading toward the common. There were ten or twelve of them, led
by an officer. They had evidently returned from a search, but
they marched as though they were being reviewed by the king.

Major Buttrick said, "We could cut them to pieces if you
would give us the word."

"I won't give it," the colonel said.

"I've no quarrel with you, Colonel," Major Buttrick said
hotly, "but you've held us on a leash longer than any man
of us can stand. We could pick them out, couldn't we?
They've killed our men, haven't they? They've burned our
houses."

"I can't see a house burned anywhere, Major Buttrick,
and even if they did, why, one can build a house again. But
you can't build anything out of a dead man."

Major Buttrick was almost weeping with frustration.
"Why, sir, we must fight them, mustn't we?"

"All in good time."

"In whose good time?"

"In yours and mine."

"I see you have no desire to put an end to their insolence
and murder."

"I have as great a desire as any man to put an end to insolence and murder, but I'm holding you men back of set
purpose. There's a time to attack and a time to rest. I've
thought and thought again, and I don't see how we can meet
them on their own terms. We must go warily."

"We've been wary enough, it seems to me. There's blood
on the bridge, Colonel."

"So there is, and I want no more of it," the colonel said,
and for the first time the major noticed that there was a new
voice, a new emphasis in the colonel's words. They came
crisp and clear. His mind was made up, and there was no
fighting him.

"You'll hold your fire," the colonel said, "until I give the order for it. I'm waiting for reinforcements. There's more to come. When we have a thousand men under arms, then we can talk of cutting them to pieces."

"He's a lonely man," the major said when the colonel had ridden away.

"How old is he?" an officer from Sudbury asked.

"Sixty-five," the major answered, "and that's too old by thirty years."

He sounded snappish, but he could not help himself. He crouched down on the turf and gave a sigh so hefty it sent the grasses flat.

"We could make a run for it," he went on a moment later. "The men are awful restless."

"You mean disobey Colonel Barrett?"

"We might find a way to do it. It wouldn't take much to get the men down on the common."

"And you'd do it?"

"I'd think of some way," the major said slowly, but he knew he would never dare to lead an attack in defiance of the colonel. "I'll say this for Colonel Barrett. He has the gift of silence and the gift of waiting. I've seen him standing in the field and looking at a bank of mint or an apple tree or a long furrow, and he doesn't move for fifteen minutes, half an hour, even an hour—just stands there thinking, and God knows what he's thinking about. Afterward he will be sort of puzzled for a while, and go about as though he doesn't know where he is, smiling to himself."

The major dug up a lump of turf and flung it away as far as he could. He often quarreled with the colonel, who was known to snore through Mr. Emerson's sermons, talked more of pigs and cattle and foaling and manure than politics, and cared not a damn what people thought of him. The men of Concord loved him blindly and told stories of how he had been a ship's captain with a house in Nantucket in his youth;

then he had settled in the Bahamas, owned a plantation, and returned at last to the place of his birth. There he was, an old, tired man against the sky line, a loose woolen cape flowing and flapping behind him, his eyes watery, his eyebrows so bushy that in profile they stuck out farther than his beaked nose. He spoke rarely, refused to lead an advance or even order it, while the Redcoats paraded below, and it was like a perpetual affront to the Americans that they must wait for his orders, even though they loved him.

Major Buttrick was not the only man who disagreed with the colonel. All the time Colonel Barrett was riding along the ridge, men would come up and say, "Can't we charge, Colonel?" and he would answer, "We've got our long wall, haven't we?"

"What wall, sir?"

"Why, the wall to fight from. Walls everywhere, if you use your eyes. Take up your places behind the walls, and they'll never dare to attack up the hill, for with every wall you have an ambuscade. That's one thing they are frightened of— an ambuscade."

The wall! There were hundreds of walls. Which one did he mean? There were the low crumbling walls between the farms, walls of rock slabs heaped on one another, with moss and ferns growing on them, and the silvery traces of snails. There were the walls of houses, walls along the roads, walls everywhere. Every wall was a fortress.

Down below, the Regulars were behaving like men in a conquered town. Outside Wright's Tavern there were officers sitting under the blooms of a cherry tree, drinking ale, and not far away the wounded soldiers were being wrapped in quilts and put into waiting carts. The British behaved as unconcernedly as though they were in Boston. They did not know they were surrounded by fortresses, and they did not know that the clans were gathering; for now, hidden on the other side of the ridge were the American reinforcements, another two or three hundred men from Framingham and Sudbury and farther afield. The colonel had given orders for them to rest. If there was battle, here were fresh troops to be thrown in. Meanwhile he would wait, as he had waited so many times before.

The British were in no hurry. You could see them more clearly from the top of the hill than from below, the scarlet facings and the silver gorgets, and you could hear the clink of bit and spur chains. Eugénie expected to see Oliver riding among the horsemen who were cantering past Wright's Tavern, but there was no sign of him. What if she saw him? What in God's name would she do if she confronted him face to face? She had picked up near the bridge a long, beautifully made fowling piece which must have been abandoned by one of the Americans after finding a British flintlock. She held it gingerly, having no desire to fire it, admiring the sleek hickory ramrod, the maple stock and the delicately carved brass butt plate. It was very light in her hands, though it was more than five feet long. What would she do if she came upon Oliver? Would they smile and pretend that neither had seen the other? "I know we shall see each other," she told herself, "and so there is no reason to hasten the meeting by thinking too much on it. I must prepare myself." She hardly knew what she was saying. The sun glittered unbearably, and somewhere down below, Oliver, she knew, was wondering at the same thoughts.

"You're always dreaming away and mutterin' to yourself, ma'am," Lemuel Shaw was saying. "I reckon you need to bed down."

"I'm wide-awake—never been more wide-awake," she answered.

"Then you're thinkin', ma'am. I reckon that's a dangerous thing to do in war, Eugénie." He smiled to himself, roughed his chin with the knuckles of his right hand and burst out laughing.

"I don't know what I should rightly do, Eugénie," he said when she asked him why he was laughing. "I ought to turn you over to the housewives of Concord, but I won't. Wearing a taffeta dress, ain't you? And my deerskin coat, ain't you? And some poor fellow's fowling piece? You're a Jacob's coat—a bit of this and that."

"Yes, a bit of this and that," Eugénie agreed.

Suddenly her attention was attracted to a young minuteman who was pushing a Redcoat up the slope through the dwarf oaks. The Redcoat kept stumbling. Every time he stumbled the minuteman gave him an extra push. "Git up, red belly," the Redcoat was told every time he fell. "Git up and show your damned face to us." The Redcoat was wounded, for there was blood all over his leggings and he dragged his feet. He was round-cheeked and cockaded; there was a stubble of wiry gold hairs on his chin and blue pouches under his eyes. "Git up, git up, you blundering———"

"I'll get up in my own time, you damned rebel!" the Redcoat said as he dragged himself slowly to his full height, and turned to look back at the minuteman, who was now beginning to prod him with the stock of his fowling piece.

It was a stupid move, for the Redcoat instantly caught the stock and fired point-blank at the minuteman, whose face was immediately covered with a black powder burn. Before the Redcoat could shoot again the minuteman was wrestling with him, and they were wrestling to kill, with their hands on each other's throats. The Redcoat had the advantage of height and weight; the minuteman had the advantage of more powerful hands. They might have throttled each other to death if Lemuel Shaw had not pounced on them. Even then the Redcoat managed to disengage himself, and he was half-way into the scrub of dwarf oaks when Lemuel Shaw brought him down with a shot from his fowling piece aimed deliberately at the man's legs. When he ran up, the man was hopping about on his one good leg.

"You damned rebel! You damned rebel!" the Redcoat shouted. "Why don't you shoot for the heart, you damned rebel?"

"I'll tell you why, my pretty pigeon," Lemuel Shaw said heatedly. "You're too pretty to shoot—that's the trouble with most of you. You're mighty good at wrestlin'—I could see that—and I'd like to wrestle with you someday. And that's not all. I've never shot a man in cold blood when he wasn't armed. Yes, and there's another thing."

"Well, what is it?"

"I had a mind to shoot you in the thigh, but someone pulled at my arm. I reckon you must have a smashed ankle."

"I can walk," the Redcoat said, placing his bleeding leg firmly down on the ground. His face contorted with pain, and he gave a little scream. The pain must have been intense, for he began to sweat like a stuck pig. "Jesus, Jesus," he kept muttering, and then he locked his teeth together as he hopped there in the sunlight, making a sound like a kettle boiling as he prevented himself from screaming with pain.

"Take my arm," Lemuel Shaw said.

The Redcoat obeyed, and Lemuel Shaw gently helped him to lie down.

"You'll have to bandage up the wound," Eugénie said, coming closer. She bent over the Redcoat and held up his head.

"And where shall we git bandages when there aren't any?" Lemuel Shaw asked. "This ain't a hospital, Eugénie."

The blood was coming in thick streams from the two leg wounds. Already the Redcoat's face was growing pale. He had laughed at the wounds, but now he laughed no longer.

Eugénie kept thinking of the boy who had been struck by Ammi White's hatchet. She said, "Turn the other way, Lemuel," and pulled up her taffeta skirt and reached for her cotton petticoat, tearing a large strip from it. Then, with Lemuel Shaw's help, she bandaged the wounds tightly, till the color came back to the Redcoat's face and he sat up.

"You surely bind bandages tight, ma'am," he said.

"That's better," Lemuel Shaw told him. "There's more politeness in your voice now."

Seeing Eugénie standing and reaching for her fowling piece, the Redcoat gazed at her with a puzzled expression. "So we have to fight a pack of young women," he said ruefully.

They were helping him to stand when Colonel Barrett came riding up. Deliberately the colonel seemed to be avoiding any meeting with Eugénie's eyes. He looked down at the Redcoat, raised his bushy eyebrows, thought for a moment and said, "We'll have to take ye to Jones' house and get ye cared for. . . . What's your name?"

"John Hopkins, sir."

"And your regiment?"

"The King's Own."

Perhaps it was the memory of his own regiment which made the Redcoat suddenly stiffen, though he was standing with difficulty. He looked directly at the colonel and said quietly, "God save the king! God damn the rebels!"

"God may save the king," the colonel replied. "I am not so sure he will damn the rebels."

"He will. He'll damn 'em to hell!"

"You're mighty strong in your opinions, Mr. Hopkins," the colonel said. "I'd like to have you and Mr. Emerson debating together. Good day to you, Mr. Hopkins."

The colonel rode away, and once again Eugénie had the curious feeling that he had deliberately avoided meeting her gaze. A little while later Lemuel Shaw and the minuteman carried the wounded Redcoat into Jones' house.

By this time there were signs that the British were beginning to move out of Concord. The column which had been conducting a search on Ponkawtassett Hill had joined the

Regulars outside the tavern, and on his white horse Colonel Smith was addressing the men on parade. The carts with the wounded soldiers were drawn up in the dappled shadows of the elms on the green. Some women of the town could be seen bringing jugs of water to them; evidently they had been ordered to perform this service. Though the Redcoats were on parade, they could be seen turning their heads in the direction of the armed militia on the hills. There was a curious buzzing air of activity all round the common. They were forming into columns, ready to march away, and some of the officers were coming out of doorways and hastily mounting their horses. All the fires had been extinguished. With the Redcoats in formation, their scarlet uniforms showing up against the green grass, the town looked, as Lemuel Shaw said, "as pretty as it has ever been." Then a trumpet blew, and with a group of officers riding leisurely at the head, the whole column began to march across the green and then down the hill below the sandy bluffs, with very slow, steady steps, without music or a word spoken.

For the space of three or four minutes there was complete silence on both sides, but the silence was followed by a full-throated roar from the minutemen on the hills. The roar was taken up by the men in the hollows behind the hills, and suddenly all the minutemen were running toward Meriam's Corner, where the bluffs came to an end and the road to Lexington turned sharply to the north toward Bedford. They came over the breasts of the low hills, over Great Meadows, a thousand men against the sky, some bringing their farm carts with them and some on horses, and most of them were getting in one another's way. They carried the banners of their towns, and shouted at the top of their lungs; none of them knew what was expected of them. They had heard that the Redcoats were moving away, and they wanted to see them depart—perhaps have a jab at them. And the British, seeing the men crowding on the hills, would look up and then turn away, keeping in formation all the time, their pipe-clay trousers and black leather boots and scarlet coats glinting in the sun. They were as neat as new pins, and they had nothing but contempt for the minutemen on the hills.

A Framingham man, a giant in corduroy, came running up to Colonel Barrett. "Sir, I have a count, sir."

"A count? What's that?"

"A count of our men. We're seventy from Framingham, sir. We're here to fight, and there's more coming."

"Give my compliments to the men of Framingham, Captain," Colonel Barrett said, and then for the first time that morning he raced the black mare along the hills.

There were men everywhere. They seemed to have sprung fully armed from the ground. He tried to make a rough count of them, but either they flashed too much in the sun or else they came so thick they were like the shadows of clouds. There they were, more than a thousand men, perhaps fifteen hundred, all clamoring for battle, and on their banners he saw the names of Billerica and Reading and Stow and Westford and Lexington. The strange thing was that these men, racing and shouting along the hills, would sometimes stop and shake hands with one another, and exchange news of their crops. Listening to them was like being among a crowd of men at haying.

Lemuel Shaw turned to Eugénie. "Hurry, ma'am. Don't you want to see the slaughter? We've caught 'em now. We'll put 'em in a box and wrap 'em up and send 'em in a dory to the King of England."

Eugénie was frowning. She was out of breath. She had caught a last glimpse of the Redcoats through the trees, and then they had vanished from sight. She wanted them to be punished, but she did not want them to be hurt. Oliver was somewhere there. She hardly knew Oliver, and in her heart she wondered whether she loved him. There were six miles of road from Concord to Lexington, and from every field for miles around the minutemen were springing up.

"Do you think it's war, Lemuel?" she asked.

"I'm sure of it, ma'am, and not a quick one either. They won't get back alive. We've been waiting for this—we've been waiting for it all our lives, some of us. Concord couldn't fight the Redcoats on its own stick, but it's not a battle with the Concord men any longer. It's the whole Province of Massachusetts."

"We'll fight them to the end, is that it?"

"I reckon so. Yes, I reckon so," Lemuel Shaw said.

They came out to the head of the bluff. There were a hundred men on each side of them, and the long scarlet column was winding below. They could see the road to Bedford branching to the left, the rye fields shining in the wind, a yellow-stacked farmhouse nestling against a red barn, and Brook's Tavern, with the smoke coming quietly from the chimney, half a mile down the road.

"It's time we had a go at them," Major Buttrick was shouting, waving his bayonet above his head. "Damn it all to hell, you can't deny us a prize this time, Colonel."

"You'll hold your fire," Colonel Barrett answered.

"What, and let them pass out of the net? We can spring it whenever we want to. They're at our mercy. Give me this prize, Colonel. For God's sake give us this prize!"

Suddenly the old colonel felt more weary than he had ever been. He had held them off with all the strength at his command, but now his strength was failing. The roar of the men on the hill was deafening. Those bronze men had tasted blood at the bridge, and they had an account to pay. He closed his eyes. From down below there came to him, like crystal bubbles rising from the bottom of a well, the voices of the British officers, not sharp and frosty any more, but quiet and sonorous. Even now he thought of holding the men back, and he sat there, hunched and thoughtful, the stocking cap pulled down low over his forehead, gazing sorrowfully over the sunlit landscape. He knew every stone, every brook, every

hill and hollow. He had seen war and men dying at sea, and
he had no wish to see the fields of Concord littered red with
blood and entrails and scraps of bloody uniform. It was like
a nightmare.

"No," he said slowly. "Let them go. They've had their
lesson."

"Yes, but they need a better one," Major Buttrick answered.

At that moment the armed people at Meriam's Corner,
where the sandy heights fall away, gave a shout louder than
any they had uttered before. It was a shout which seemed to
come straight out of the earth, as the men themselves seemed
to come from the earth, and it thrust out against the sky and
reverberated in the hollows of the low sandy ridge above the
road. Entirely unexpected to the men on the hill there came
along the Bedford Road a small company of minutemen,
perhaps no more than twenty, but something in the way they
marched suggested that they would drive straight against
the Redcoats. They were bearing down on the British flankers who were about to cross a bridge, and they were waving
their arms, summoning the men on the hill to come down
and tear the Redcoats to pieces. At first the men on the Bedford Road marched in column, then they suddenly fanned
out and took cover behind the walls; little red spurts of flame
came from their muskets. The British went on, marching in
compact groups, ten to a row, and when a man fell in one of
their rows, the others would swerve and reform the lines.
Very faintly from the distance came the whistle of ball and
the shouts of the men hiding from the enemy behind their
stone walls. Still more faintly came the voices of the British
officers, "Steady, men, hep, hep, hep."

"I can't hold them back any more," Colonel Barrett said.
"It's no use. I've done the best I could. Every man is his
own colonel now."

He said this regretfully, even sorrowfully. He watched the

tides of minutemen clambering down the hill like a swarm of midges or mosquitoes ready to bite the flanks of the long red snake winding down the sunken road. Shots cracked from the meadows. The Redcoats kept in line, though sometimes one would turn, kneel, fire into the hills or at someone firing from Meriam's farm, and then march on. They were unbreakable. They seemed not to know what fear was. Their columns shivered, but remained steady; and while the minutemen shouted at the top of their voices, "Alarum! Alarum! Alarum!" making a sound like the rolling of thunder on a winter's day, the Redcoats began to play their fifes and drums and even to sing. Some officers were now riding up and down the lines, attempting to stop the men and form them in ranks two deep. The men marched on. They had been taught to march through fire, and by God they would march through fire to the very end, hardly troubling to turn their heads any more.

For a long while the old colonel remained on horseback on the brow of the hill. He followed the Redcoats till they were out of sight. There were no more minutemen to be seen, for they were all running across fields and over walls in the hope of being able to cut off the enemy. If they could, they would catch the tail of the snake and whip its head to the ground. A column of dust rose over the road. The sun shone on the blazing rye fields. Here and there he saw the dead, and here and there the road was bloody.

CHAPTER 12

A House in Menotomy

THE SUN was yellowing the white caps of the apple blows, and the smell of spring came thick on the following wind. All the spring scents were there—the grasses and the cherries, the plowed earth, the rows of apple trees and the hot knee-high rye waving in the wind—and all these smells came welling over the banks into the sunken roads where the gasping, sweating Regulars were marching. Men on the hills were trying to pick them off, but the flintlocks of the British had more range than the fowling pieces of the rebels. So they marched on, blinded by the sun, with their fifes playing and their drums beating, their shakos shaking and swaying, and sometimes a gleam of blue sunlight would sparkle along the length of their bayonets. If the rebels came too close, they would pause for no more than three or four moments, to kneel and reload their weapons.

"They're like painted dolls on a painted day," Lemuel Shaw said admiringly.

"Well, that's poetry," Eugénie said, riding beside him.

"I don't know whether it's poetry or not," Lemuel Shaw said. "No, ma'am, it's goddam reckless bravery. I thought it was all over at Meriam's Corner, with a thousand or maybe two thousand of us scamperin' over the fields, but they shrug us off. I didn't think they could do it, and I don't believe it even now."

From one of the farmhouses they had obtained horses, and from somewhere else Lemuel Shaw had found a pine-tree flag, which now waved behind him. They had raced across the hills and over coppices, keeping in sight of the gorgeous snake marching below, moving in and out of shadow. There were whole fields black with minutemen racing after the Regulars. The minutemen would divide up, break into small groups, clamber over walls, disappear into farmhouses for water, for the sun was strong, and emerge a little later exhilarated and fresh, ready to take on the Regulars; but by this time the Redcoats had marched a little farther on, always in step. The rebels came hard after them, pressing through the fields, taking cover in the woods and orchards and behind stone walls, racing ahead to take up places in the houses on the roadside. But the snake, with all its baggage trains and carts, marched along the exposed and fire-swept roads as though it were taking an afternoon stroll through the New England countryside.

"The snake has fangs," Lemuel Shaw said when he saw a small column of Redcoats breaking away from the line and marching into a farmyard.

The minutemen had been scrambling all over the yard, taking positions behind the walls. From there they had fired at the retreating British, but now the Regulars had had enough. With the precision of machines they wheeled into the farmyard, breaking down the gate, fanning across the yard, kneeling and shooting at point-blank range. When they had gone there were six or seven minutemen lying about the yard, all sprawled out, looking from the hills like spread-eagle birds, those birds which have their wings nailed onto a barn door. Among them, in the center of the yard, was a solitary Redcoat lying in the sun.

All through the long afternoon the attacks went on, and all afternoon the Redcoats kept to the winding road, rarely firing unless they had been fired on.

"I don't know how they do it," Lemuel Shaw was saying. "By Jesus, I don't know how they do it."

"They're British, and they know how to fight," Eugénie said.

"We haven't begun to learn yet," Lemuel Shaw said helplessly. He was watching some men making for a low wall, crouching there, firing and then running helter-skelter, frightened because the British had veered round, knelt, and sent a few neatly aimed balls in their direction.

He wondered whether he shouldn't send Eugénie away. She was determined to fight, but they had never been close enough to the Redcoats. Like hundreds of other minutemen he was enjoying the pursuit, enjoying being out of danger, but at the same time hurt and bewildered because there was no place to get close enough to the enemy. The sweet-smelling earth has a flavor of its own when you ride over it in the early morning, and another in the noon sun, and another in the afternoon; and though it smells sweetest at night, it looks richest in the afternoon. Then every ridge and furrow and farmhouse glitters with sunlight and purple shadow, and every trembling flower is seen sharply by the eyes, till you think the stubble fields are flooded with oxeye and dog rose, fritillary and sweet Susan. And there was the scarlet snake crawling away to Boston, where it would be out of harm.

"Let's get at them," he said, and shouted to some minutemen wandering lost across a corner of the rye field.

"You can't do it on horseback," someone said. "They'll outrace you. We're not playing with Indians."

"Jesus, I know we're not, but I've seen the Indians raiding. They go straight through. I've seen them. We could ride them down with our horses, couldn't we?"

"They'd crawl over you like fleas."

The more he thought of it, the more the idea pleased him. At a low sloping curve of the hills, where the rye fields met the road, there was a place where he thought twenty horsemen could break through the British ranks. There were not many horsemen in sight, perhaps eight or nine. He rode over to them, to tell them about his plan. They would have to hurry, and be sure they were well-armed, and they would need a sword as well. They would break the British column behind Malt's farm, and have minutemen converging on the road afterward to pick off the British stragglers.

"We could go through 'em and cut 'em down, and then ride up the road there and turn again. Are you men enough for it?"

He knew it was dangerous, but what else were the minutemen for unless it was danger? He was sick of seeing the column making its relentless progress, sick of being blinded by the sparkle from the blue bayonets, sick of hearing their fifes and drums, sick of wandering the fields.

Altogether there were ten horsemen making for the bend in the road, men of all sizes and shapes, beardless boys and old farmers. Most of them came from outside Concord, but Lemuel Shaw recognized Abijiah Evans and Makepeace Jones of Concord, one a cordwainer and the other an apprentice saddler.

"Think we'll make it?"

"We'll come down the hill so damned fast they won't see us until we are on top of them."

"And take the woman with you?"

"Why not? She rides pretty, don't she? She's a good hand with a gun."

This was almost a lie. He had never seen her firing. She was determined to take part in the raid, and that was all there was to it.

"Be careful of the flankers," Lemuel Shaw said, pointing to the curve of the hill beyond the road. A sunken road led up the hill, and there might be flankers there, waiting for an attack. "They move a hundred paces from one another and go in pairs. They're dangerous. Keep your eyes open, and wait till the last line comes by."

They came now through the copse of black birch a little above Lincoln. The main columns of the Redcoats were already entering the town. The small white houses glittered, and you could see the smoky yellow dust rising from the Redcoats' feet. The flankers fanned out so that they would be behind the houses and in the farmyards when the procession made its way through the town. Altogether there were no more than about fifty Regulars in the last line that came down the road. Lemuel Shaw hoped to pick them all off in revenge for the dead minutemen in the farmyard, those poor spread-eagle, colorless things they had seen less than an hour ago.

"Are you ready, men?" he said, waving his fowling piece above his head as though it were a sword.

Lemuel Shaw never knew whether they answered his challenge in words; they answered it well enough in deeds. The horsemen came thundering down the slope, concealed from the Regulars by the high banks, and when they came to the road they sliced through the line, scattering the Redcoats, wounding a few with the butt ends of their fowling pieces. They moved too fast to do any great damage, but went riding up the opposite hill, content with themselves, the wind hot on their faces. Until they were hit, they did not know that the Regulars were kneeling in the road and firing after them. Lemuel Shaw, gripping his horse with his knees, suddenly lurched forward and would have toppled off his horse if he had not somehow caught his elbow in the reins: and so he was dragged along. He was screaming but he did not know he was screaming. He looked like a waxwork bobbing up and down, his face turned to one side, and blood was pumping out of a wound in his back. Of the ten horsemen who made the attack on the road, three were wounded severely and two others received grazing wounds. The Redcoats were kneeling in the dust of the road and firing up the hill. "Poor Lem, poor Lem!" Eugénie cried. She would have brought them to a halt if she could, but the impetus of the charge, the whistle of balls, the shouts of the Redcoats in the road and of the minutemen as they rode up the hills sent them over the rise. The Redcoats did not follow. Lem was still screaming when they took him off the horse, but soon the sounds faded away; he died in Eugénie's arms, in a green hollow in the hills, his head in Eugénie's lap. Some flankers were near by; there was no time to bury him. And so they rode on, cutting across the fields, toward Menotomy. . . .

By chance Oliver found himself in the rear line. He hated this exposed position, but steeled himself to it. Weary and haggard, he had watched the minutemen raging up to the stone walls like a wave, only to be thrown back again. In Concord he had seen none of the fighting at the bridge; all he knew of the fighting was that the Regulars had lost three or four men, and it was said that most of them were scalped. He had spent his time in Concord with Colonel Smith and Major Pitcairn in Wright's Tavern, and it was only when the minutemen attacked along the Bedford Road below Meriam's Corner that he realized he was engaged in a fight to the finish. Early in the morning, at two o'clock, Colonel Smith had asked for reinforcements. None had come.

Oliver was bitter, exhausted, and in no mood to be merciful. Then out of the blue, while he was concentrating on the road ahead and wondering whether the rebels were entrenched in the houses in Lincoln, there were horsemen riding down a hill into his own line, and he recognized Eugénie. He had sometimes thought she might take part in the fighting as a minuteman; he had never dreamed that she would be on horseback. He could have shot her easily, for his pistol was cocked and she passed straight in front of him. He gave orders to the men not to fire at that group of wildly fleeing horsemen up the hill. The Regulars disobeyed his command, but they fired ineffectively.

"Oh, my God! What in God's name is she doing there?" Oliver shouted aloud in his grief, for three of the men in the line lay on the dusty road, trampled by the horses. He had looked for her during all the journey to Concord and back again, and it broke his heart that when he saw her, she should pass through the British lines like lightning, in a desperate and futile desire for glory. "The little beautiful fool," he said, and then rode on with his column.

Ravaged and nearly broken, at the mercy of every stone wall, the column made its way toward Lexington under the hot sun. The fifes no longer played, but occasionally there could be heard the mournful beating of drums. The Redcoats were out of patience. If they caught an armed minuteman, they clubbed him to death; they broke into the farmhouses on the way and clubbed everything in sight. They were out for blood, but they dragged their feet wearily. Tattered and bleeding, they were so nervous that whenever they saw a wall or a tree large enough to provide cover they blazed away. They were reeling from the gadfly attacks of the minutemen, but they marched on, though there were continual pauses, sudden inexplicable halts, interminable conferences among the officers. It was only six miles from Concord to Lexington, but it took them two and a half hours.

Oliver had long ago given up any hope of reinforcements, and he expected that at Lexington the whole weight of the minutemen would fall on the Regulars. It was important to avoid Lexington, yet the place could not be avoided because it lay on the only road to Boston. The men were crying out for water, and then for revenge. Suddenly he heard a shout, then a vast noise of cheering. As the Regulars swung slowly into Lexington they saw something they had never hoped to see. A whole army of Redcoats, battalion on battalion, was spread out across Lexington Common, and four or five houses were already in flames. For the first time the Redcoats who had fought their way out of Concord broke their ranks. The scarlet battle line of the First Brigade lay in front of them, with the banners and standards of three regiments waving in the wind. The clouds of smoke billowing above the treetops and the roaring six-pounders echoing in the woods proclaimed that the Royal Artillery was in the field. Lord Percy, leading his men out of Boston, had saved the day. For five minutes the cheers of the Regulars could be heard echoing across the common. The sun came out full and strong, and there on the rising ground shone the golden cannon. Once again the six-pounders roared and reverberated in the New England hills.

"There were delays upon delays," Lord Percy was saying, "and all of them were inexcusable. I received Colonel Smith's message asking for reinforcements as late as nine o'clock this morning."

Lord Percy looked like a man still grappling with a nightmare. The muscles of his lean, handsome face kept twitching. He asked few questions. He could tell at a glance what had happened. The First Brigade, which he commanded, had been over five hours on the march, but it was comparatively fresh and there were no casualties among the officers; Colonel Smith had been wounded by a ball in the leg and had to be carried in a litter; Pitcairn had had his horse shot from under him and had walked the last two miles to Lexington. Lord Percy ordered the wounded to be cared for in Munroe's Tavern. Seeing some minutemen congregating near the meetinghouse, he ordered it destroyed by cannonfire. The fieldpieces were barking, and the round shot was splintering through the walls of the meetinghouse where Hancock and Adams had stayed the previous night and many other nights.

To Lord Percy the spectacle of the buildings all round the

common in flames gave no pleasure. He had to hold up the
minutemen, and this was the only way he could do it. And
when the stench of burning came to his nostrils he took out
a scented handkerchief and said, "Have you noticed, Pitcairn,
that a house can smell like a corpse?"

"How long do we rest here?" Major Pitcairn asked.

"We shouldn't rest a moment. I've ordered the Light
Infantry to retire from the right of the companies by files.
They are out of harm's way when they reach high ground.
I tell you, they shouldn't rest, Pitcairn! They've got to fight
their way through Menotomy, and that may be the worst."

Though reinforcements had reached the Regulars, they had
also reached the minutemen in Menotomy. It was dusk when
the Regulars came to the town. They discovered that the
minutemen had transformed the houses into fortresses and
were hiding behind walls, behind trees, within houses. Somewhere down the street a roof was burning. Oliver saw a boy
with a small pock-marked face like a bruised apple running
behind a wall with a fowling piece in his hands. A Redcoat
was stalking him. When the boy rested against a tree and
the Redcoat crept after him Oliver wanted to shout, "Boy,
boy, look out!" He was too late. The Redcoat stabbed the
boy in the back, then calmly wiped the bloodstains off his
bayonet.

"It's plain murder, sir," one Redcoat was saying, pulling
at Oliver's bridle. "Let us get at 'em, sir."

"You'll have to ask Colonel Smith. You can't go into the
houses."

"If they're allowed to fire from the houses, sir, they'll murder us all."

A window opened, and as it swung open it caught the
gleam of the flames farther down the street. The Redcoats
were breaking ranks. They were pouring into the houses,
grim men with hatchets at their belts. They broke down
doors, smashed in windows, broke up furniture, shouted

wildly; and if they found anyone with a fowling piece in his hands, they threw a grenade at him or cut his head open with a hatchet.

"They're hell-birds, aren't they?" a Regular shouted at Oliver when he ordered them back into line.

It was no use. He could not order them back. There were dead and bleeding Redcoats lying on the side of the road. He saw one man all doubled up, his face like a burst grape, his hands spread out over the muddy earth; the hands caught the faint glow of flames. Oliver's face turned dark and sullen. He wouldn't hold them back any more, or even try to. A window opened opposite him, and a gun was pushed out of the window. He could see the point of it turning toward him. "They'll be sorry they stayed at Menotomy," he said aloud. "Before we have done with them we'll have burned every house to the ground." He rode his horse over a low wall, and then through a garden to the back of the house. He would do what the others did. He would batter down the door, not because he was hungry to kill, but because a man's hands were spread out stiff on the moist earth. He heard sharp screams down the road, the sudden hissing burst of a grenade, and somewhere a gun carriage was rattling down a street not far away—perhaps the same street. The garden smelled of lilacs, and so did the house when he had opened the door, leaving his horse tethered to the pump. He strode through the door and into the darkness beyond, not caring what sound he made, not caring any more whether he was killed, conscious only of the awful silence in the place and the minuteman upstairs with the gun pushed through the window.

He almost hoped to see the minuteman confronting him on the stairs. Downstairs there was a table laid for dinner; there was even a pot, red-hot now, with all the water boiled away, on the iron stove. Though he searched the room quickly, he knew by the look of it that there was no one hiding there. He went up the stairs, keeping flat against the wall, his pistol cocked. The stairs creaked. His blood was racing, his breath came loud; he felt lonely and vulnerable without his horse, without the men round him. Once his foot slipped, and he heard the whole staircase quivering. There were pictures hanging on the stairway wall, and though it was dark he could see they were pictures of country scenes, mostly engravings, with milkmaids and gallants, and some shepherds bringing their sheep home. There was a burst of shooting just outside the house, and the gunshots kept echoing in the empty house. Oliver had half a mind to go running down the stairs, for there was something ominous in the echoing of the shots, in the gathering darkness, in the terrible squeaking of the stairs.

Upstairs there was no sound. He crept along, his back to the wall, until he came to the only door which could lead to the room where the minutemen had thrust open a window and fired on the column. He felt for the door handle, but the door was locked from the inside. He cocked the hammer of his pistol, stepped back until he was touching the banister rail, fired at the lock and almost simultaneously kicked at the door. There was a sound of splintering wood. The door swung open, and Oliver saw the thick gray light of a room with dormer windows. In the middle of the room stood a woman with a fowling piece in her hands, wearing a tattered deerskin coat and some kind of deerskin cap on her head.

He said: "I should have known you were here, Eugénie."

Oliver was gazing at her with such dumb desperation that she recoiled in horror. Somewhere in the dark interior of his mind a candle was burning and crackling; he was trying to shield it, but the flame was about to go out. He walked steadily toward her, having forgotten to prime his pistol, not caring what happened, caring least of all that there might be others in the dark, shadowy room.

"You mustn't come nearer, Oliver," Eugénie said, and all the time she was covering him with the fowling piece in her hands. "Not nearer, Oliver!"

He came closer. She wanted to scream, to bury herself in the wall. There were hollows under her eyes. She passed her tongue over her lips, for she had suddenly grown unbearably thirsty. "Please don't come nearer, Oliver," she said pathetically, and then, because he refused to obey her, she fired at his hand to make him drop the pistol. A yellow flash, and smoke filled the room.

He held up his bleeding hand, and watched the blood dripping down on the floor boards. There was as yet no pain, and this surprised him.

"You're damned, aren't you?" he said, coming closer to her.

She still held the long fowling piece, and it was still directed at him, shaking a little, for she could no longer hold it steadily.

He said: "The way to the heart—we never found it, did we? We tried. There isn't anything else one can do except try. It's a long journey. From the heart to the heart . . . "

"It's the longest journey there is," Eugénie said quietly. Her voice was close to sobbing, and she could not hold the fowling piece; it clattered to the ground.

He was still coming closer to her, inch by inch, holding his hand up almost as though he wanted to blot out her face with his bleeding hand. When she was up against the wall and he was almost standing against her he shuddered, dropped his hand by his side and said sorrowfully, "It's dishonorable to fight behind walls. Don't tell me there was no other way. You could have met us in the open. We've burned houses and smashed people's heads in, because we had to. When they fired out of windows, did they expect us not to reply?"

He did not know why he was talking like this. The shadows were darkening. He heard musket fire farther down the street, and the voices of women, and then there was a sound like a crackling. Eugénie was not cringing against the wall; she was simply standing there, in thick shadow, smiling at him. There was no reproach in her smile.

She said: "You must let me bandage the wound."

It was like something he had heard long ago and wanted to forget. There was no answer.

She shuddered and heard herself making a little low moan of pain. For all she knew, Oliver would stand there forever in the shadows, gazing at her with hunger and hatred and defiance, smiling at her while the pain began to travel up from the wound into his arm and from there into his brain. She had never thought war would be like this. War was shivering in fear and watching a pane of glass crack while a woman fed her child. War was waiting. War was a morning spent in the dwarf oak, a boat sinking in the green scum of a slow-flowing river, an old colonel riding along the crest of a flowering hill. War was being sick and running into the shade to be sick again, the loneliness of waiting and the fever in the blood, riding through the British lines and not knowing why—dark clouds, dark sky, and the swallows sailing along the marshes and someone whispering beside you, saying, "You're damned, aren't you?" over and over again, or perhaps they were only the echoes of words which would reverberate forever in her brain.

Again she said: "You must let me bandage it. It must hurt terribly."

"The strange thing is that it doesn't hurt at all," he answered, but his voice was unsteady.

"That's not true."

"I swear it's true. There are things which hurt so very much more. You must believe me, Eugénie."

It was the second time he had mentioned her name, and at first she wondered at the sound of it—a name which no longer seemed to belong to her. He said the word caressingly, quietly. His hair was beginning to shine with the sweat coming up through his skin, and even in the gathering darkness his face was silver.

"I love you," he said. "We're both damned. It's no use fighting it any longer."

Then she was in his arms, and he was holding her to him with all his strength; even the mangled hand was pressed against her deerskin coat. He was not conscious of pain as he kissed her, or of any emotion except his love for her. He said, "I believed everyone has his enemy, but I never knew the enemy could be the only friend. You go through life, and it is destined that you should meet your greatest enemy and your greatest friend. I've known that for a long time. Perhaps the greatest enemy is always the greatest friend."

"You're so wrong," Eugénie said. "It's not friendship— it's love. And there is no enemy within love. Love destroys all enemies. Yes, and it is the same with our countries. There should have been love, not commands, not the desire to keep us in chains."

He could think of no counterarguments. Perhaps she was right. These were not things to be decided in a darkening room while the distant sound of gunshots faded in the evening air.

"We must not talk of these things," he said. "We've gone through too much to be able to see what is happening to us. It's best to be quiet."

She led him to a gooseneck rocker near the empty fireplace. He kept staring at the wound in his hand, the blood pumping out from a dark hole in the flesh, while she rummaged for clean linen in a closet. Finding some, she tore it into strips and bandaged his hand firmly. The pain was beginning to mount in a pulsing wave through his arm, until he could

almost bear it no longer; then, simply because she had bandaged it, or because he had grown accustomed to it, it became
bearable. He rose and stood by the window.

"You mustn't stand there," Eugénie said. "If they see us
together, they will shoot at us."

"Then there is no escape?"

"There never is. And you must go soon."

"Why?"

"If they find us, they'll shoot us both. There's no sense in
dying together."

"We could hide," he suggested, smiling at her with a
desperate look of appeal.

"There's no place to hide in. Menotomy is full of minutemen. They'll learn sooner or later."

He thought of hiding in the closet and then dismissed the
idea. There was nothing to be done. He said, "You will
always be my friend, and always my enemy, and I shall always
be your lover. I can't help myself. In the end we shall find
each other."

Eugénie was crying. Long silver tears poured over her
face, and when he kissed her, his face was wet from her
tears. He held her hand for a moment; then, without caring
what sound he made, picking his pistol off the floor with a
curious grace, as though he were picking up a handkerchief,
he left the room and ran down the stairs, making a sound
like thunder with his heavy boots. He found his horse in the
garden where he had left it, jumped on the saddle and raced
over a low wall. . . .

When Eugénie said Menotomy was filled with minutemen
she was wrong. They had gone in pursuit of the British.
Except for women, children and old men, and some members
of the Committee of Safety, the town was empty. Oliver's horse
was rested. Darkness was thick over the hills. He heard the
crackling of musket fire and followed it. Sometimes he was
shot at by the minutemen who had not caught up with the

Redcoats, but by riding hard he was able to avoid them. It was nearly dark when he reached the long winding column of haggard, cursing men.

Sunset came at half past six with a ghostly rain falling. Along the thinly wooded heights to westward the sunset fires were burning out, and soon enough they would be in view of Charlestown. "The worst is over," Oliver told himself, but he knew in his heart the worst was only beginning. With no banners, no cannon, no generals, the Americans still pursued, hiding in ditches and behind trees, picking off the weary men who staggered along the winding road, shouting in the gathering darkness their defiant songs:

> *Shot the Redcoats in the road;*
> *Scalped 'em neat and handy!*
> *Going back to scalp some more!*
> *Yankee Doodle Dandy!*

So the Redcoats wandered down to the sea. Sometimes they would look over their shoulders and see the thin flames of the sunset descending—the yellow moisture-laden sun, more like the sun of autumn than of late spring, with a froth of clouds bearing low over it; and then the froth turned momentarily to bloody red, then to the palest watery black, and there was no comfort in it. A sharp, cool wind came from the sea. "Hep, hep, hep, steady, men, keep in step," an officer was saying, but few paid attention to the orders uttered in the dark. Oliver rode down the dark lines, searching for Lord Percy, but there was no sign of the young colonel whose guns at Lexington had done no more than hold up the American advance. The worst was Menotomy, and he would remember this to the day he died.

Night fell, the fog froze round them, and the six-pointed star of Venus rose through the evening mists. Now there were no lights to be seen except the low reflected light on the clouds, which showed that Boston was still many miles

ahead. *The night,* Oliver thought, *has a love for throwing its arms round a man, but tonight it is hugging us altogether too close.* He tried to look through the darkness
and the mist, and it seemed to him that he saw shadows
leaping out of the banks of the road; sometimes a horse
reared, and sometimes a nervous soldier would shoot wildly
into the dark, the glare of the flash sending a scarlet flame
over the man's face. Then the darkness seemed greater than
before. When the mist rose he could see more easily, for the
stars were shining. There was no moon, though it would
rise later. He hoped they would reach Boston before moon-
rise, for then the battle might begin all over again: once
again the British would be picked off by hidden minutemen,
and there would be no way of seeing them in the dark.

Along the wooded heights the Americans were attempting to group their forces under General Heath. Warren rode
beside him, a head taller than Heath, his coat torn by branches
and his shirt covered with blood from a grazing wound. From
their place on the hill they could see the British winding toward Charlestown, toward the protection of the *Somerset*
and whatever soldiers Gage could still afford to throw out to
defend their flanks.

"We could go on and fight them to the end," Warren said,
"but the darkness is against us."

"The darkness is a friend," Heath answered quietly. "It is
a friend to both of us. We couldn't go on fighting much
longer. We think we could, but the truth is we are no more
than a disorganized rabble."

"And the enemy?"

"The same."

"You're being too hard on our men," Warren said. All
the time he was listening keenly for the sound of musket
shots in the distance, but for some minutes everything had

been quiet. "They've fought in the only way they know, and they've fought well. You must admit that."

"Well, yes, but every time I gave an order it was disobeyed, and every time I told them to follow a plan they argued like farmers on market day. We'll have to beat some sense in them. They'll have to learn to fight like the British— in formation—before the day is won, and they won't do it easily. . . . The mist is rising and it's gettin' to be plain dark. There's no sense in following 'em farther. Tomorrow will be another day."

Then the two generals rode back over the dark fields toward Menotomy in the hope of finding the Committee of Safety in session.

Oliver rode on until he reached the head of the line. His injured hand was aching, and sometimes he would find himself about to scream with the pain of the wound. All round the wound the skin was hot and swelling. Shadows were still coming out of the dark, and beyond the hills there lay the menace of the Americans. "God help you, Eugénie, wherever you are!" he whispered. "There's no way out, not even the way to the heart. You see, it was all blindness and misery from the beginning. We should have talked it over— not round a table, but during a country walk under the elms. We shouldn't be fighting each other. We are not Cavaliers and Roundheads—it was insane of you to think that we are. No, it's not too late—there must be some other way."

He found Lord Percy at the head of the column. In the starlight the colonel's nose seemed longer and more pointed than ever. But the extraordinary thing was that the colonel looked as immaculate as when Oliver set eyes on him at Lexington, and his voice was steady. "Tell the men to be of good heart," he was saying to an orderly, "and tell them, too, they have fought well, and after Charlestown they'll be safe enough and can rest for a while." He said the words as precisely and as leisurely as he would say, Have the goodness to pass the port, in General Gage's dining room.

"Then the battle is all over?" Oliver asked.

The colonel must have noticed the pain in Oliver's voice, for he looked steadily in Oliver's direction and in a lower voice said, "How should I know, my dear fellow? God knows, I hope it is."

"But you don't know?"

"Of course I don't know. For all we know, the good people of Charlestown are sitting out in the streets with muskets in their hands, or erecting barricades and taking up positions in their upper windows."

At that moment a scout came riding up with news that armed irregulars were massing in the streets of Charlestown and Cambridge as well.

"They'll learn better," the colonel said grimly.

He said nothing more for some time, riding in silence. There was still very little light. Some shooting had broken out on the flanks—perhaps some flankers had come upon a group of irregulars. Soon enough, when the road turned, they would come in sight of the lights of Cambridge.

Oliver was far in the rear when he heard the burst of cannon fire which put an end to the fighting at Cambridge. He heard that some of the citizens had come out with old matchlocks, intending to hold up the British advance. Lord Percy ordered the cannon to be set up, saying, "It was the same thing at the battle of Minden. Now we'll scare 'em." Then he ordered the columns to wheel to the left, so taking the shortest road to Charlestown. Some houses were burning. In the red glare the army swung toward the marshes, not halting until they came to Breed's Hill. There Lord Percy negotiated an agreement with the selectmen. He offered safety to the people as long as the womenfolk were kept indoors and his soldiers were furnished drink.

By eight o'clock the troops were moving down to the village. They were haggard and bleary-eyed, with no strength left in them. The fifes and drums were silent at last, though they had played at intervals during the long march. It was dark still, for the moon did not rise until ten o'clock. In the distance came the shouts of the rebels taunting them under cover of darkness: it was like the laughter of a cracked bell. Dark shapes moved in the water—boats from the men-of-war—and the great hulk of the *Somerset* stood out against the dark sky. And then all the darkness would be burned away in a silvery-green explosion from their naval guns, as the dull booming of the ships' cannon kept the rebels at bay. The lights of Boston hung low over a silvery lace of water, till one by one, as the British came to land, the lights went out. By the time the moon rose, nearly all their wounded were safely in Boston.

All night the slow-moving boats went backward and forward over the white water. The moon was a thick white glare in the heavens. From the shore the rebels could see everything that was happening. They could do nothing to follow up their victory, for the *Somerset* was able to rake Charlestown Neck.

Oliver rode through the encampment on Breed's Hill in the glare of the moonlight. He saw that the wounded soldiers were given drink, and sometimes he would come upon a forgotten officer who was clenching his teeth on a lead bullet to forget the pain of his wound. His own wound was no longer aching; it had gone beyond aching altogether. The wounded looked unbelievably white and ghostly on their crude litters, those soldiers who had made their ragged way down the country lanes of New England. "Where's Gage?" they muttered. "Where's the old general? He isn't out, is he? Sleeping in a comfortable bed at Province House, most likely."

Oliver knew it wasn't so. The general was sitting in the

Blue Room with Haldimand by his side, gray-faced, poring over the reports which were continually being handed to him. By now Lord Percy had been rowed ashore, and probably they were together, the old general and the young colonel, and perhaps Pitcairn and Colonel Smith were with them.

"God bless them!" Oliver said, and then turned to look over the moon-flooded landscape, which looked now like a great salt desert of intense whiteness.

Somewhere out there, in the white desert of the moonlight, Eugénie was looking up at the moon. In Menotomy, or in some other village, wearing a deerskin coat all bloodstained over a taffeta dress, she too was dreaming her dreams. "It can't go on," Oliver murmured. "We need a new fresh wind, a wind of sweetness between us, a wind of love. There will be no peace until it comes."

At midnight Oliver decided to take to the boats. There was still some rain in the air. At the embarking point he met Pitcairn, who had been wounded in the leg, but not seriously.

"We had the devil's luck," Pitcairn said. "Another hour and they would have surrounded us and picked us off as they pleased. Thank God, we're still holding."

"We'll hold to the end, sir," Oliver said, but only because the words were demanded of him.

They relapsed into silence. They could hear the water whipping against the strakes, the slow rhythmic pulsing of the oars in the white water, while the tiller squeaked and the white-faced men looked across the ever-widening gap of water to shore. Here, at sea, the air was fresh and pure, and a soft wind came from shore. "The wind of love," Oliver murmured, and then he heard himself singing under his breath:

> *"O western wind, when wilt thou blow?*
> *The small rain down can rain.*
> *Christ, that my love were in my arms,*
> *And I in my bed again!"*

CHAPTER 13

The Conspirators

THERE WERE five men sitting round the table in Menotomy. It was near midnight, but even here, in the cellar, the smell of gunpowder trickled down from the streets. A small pine-cone fire was burning, but neither the fire nor the oil lamp hanging on a long stretched wire overhead gave much light. When the men leaned forward over the table their faces were in shadow.

"Better put more oil in," Samuel Adams said, turning in the direction of Eugénie, who was brewing tea in a corner of the cellar.

"In a bit, in a bit," Eugénie said, gazing at the pale, strained faces round the table.

They sat in silence for a while. The wind rustled the documents on the table. They had fed on cold roast ham. John Hancock was lighting his pipe, and Samuel Adams was frowning at the blue smoke which began to hover over the table. Then Eugénie came to trim the wick and pour oil into the lamp from a small porcelain cruse. The warm smell of oil penetrated the damp cellar, and the lamp began to flare.

"Better turn the wick down," Samuel Adams said impatiently. He was aware that in some strange way this trimming of the lamp, the sudden bright flare of yellow, the stern faces round the table, the pattering of Eugénie's feet on the bare stone-flagged floor, all these were part of the revolution and all possessed a precise significance. He could not have

said why they had chosen the cellar in which to debate. The
last Redcoats had passed many hours before. A few stragglers had been rounded up; they were now being guarded
in Hickenberry's store. The wounded were being attended to.
Then he remembered that it was Dr. Warren who had ordered them to take refuge in the cellar, fearing or half fearing
that the British would return and put fire to the town.

John Hancock thought it "a peck of nonsense." The British were licked, weren't they? All these documents, these
tallies of the dead and wounded, these lists of the men who
had participated in the fighting, went to show that there was
no more fight left in the British. So John Hancock glared
at the documents, impatiently biting at his fingernails, and
sometimes he complained they hadn't allowed him to fight the
British, though there was no better way of dying than in battle. He gazed across the table at young Dr. Warren—broad,
smiling face, thick lips, an expression of extraordinary sweetness and repose. From Dr. Warren he let his eyes rest on
Dr. Church, who was older and thinner and seemed never to
know a moment's repose, for his face was continually twisted
into strange, meaningless shapes, his mind forever at work
and his face forever reflecting the pursuit of his mind. John
Hancock distrusted Church, but he did not hate him. Samuel
Adams abhorred him. There was always a terrible flare of hate
between them, and it took all Warren's diplomacy to keep
them from each other's throats.

When Eugénie came with the pot of tea Dr. Warren said,
"Well, Eugénie, you serve the revolution in a most admirable
way. We thank you for the *shu-shou*."

"Did they dredge it up from Boston Harbor?" Dr. Church
asked with a weak smile.

"It's a bit left over from the store," Eugénie said.

"I believe *shu-shou* is a Chinese word," John Hancock
said nervously, more because he wanted to break the heaviness in the air than for any other reason. "I dare say the

Republic of America will soon be dealing in tea directly with the Empire of China. It's a prospect which, I confess, gives me pleasure."

The words hung empty on the air. In this cellar in Menotomy the Empire of China seemed so infinitely remote that no one had any heart to pursue the thought. Eugénie hovered over the table, whispering to Dr. Warren. Suddenly Samuel Adams' patience snapped.

"We can't trust a girl to listen to our deliberations," he said, and glared round the table.

"We can trust Eugénie perfectly," Dr. Warren answered. "She has helped us to win our victory."

"I don't doubt it, but I think a lady should be absent from the councils of war."

"That's a matter of opinion," Dr. Warren said, waspish now, with a deep flush riding his cheeks.

Dr. Church was amused by this exchange. It was not the first time he had been amused by Samuel Adams' behavior. Like many others, Dr. Church called Samuel Adams "the psalm singer," not because he composed psalms, but because he had a voice like a dirge heard through a winter fog. He called John Hancock "Dopey Jack" because he rarely opened his mouth and generally contented himself with stating the obvious. *They're unstrung fiddles,* Dr. Church told himself. *They don't know—they could never guess—what I am going through. . . .*

After they had all sipped the tea, Dr. Church turned to General Heath, who was sitting beside Dr. Warren, and said, "We must go through the tallies and examine them, I understand that. But the important thing, gentlemen, is that we make provision for the future. We must know where the blow is going to fall. Rest assured, the British will not take this defeat lying down." He paused and observed with satisfaction that Samuel Adams was listening intently. "But before we make any provisions for the future, we have one pious duty to perform. We must celebrate the valor of our country-men. *Homo sum et nil humanum ad me alienum est.* Which I translate, I am a man and therefore I celebrate human valor. So I say, gentlemen, that even in this cellar, on the day when our countrymen signally enriched themselves with honor, there is reason for celebration."

"Wheels within wheels," General Heath said, puffing at his pipe and gazing at the ceiling. The doctor was always making these little speeches, and General Heath had long ago come to the conclusion that they could be ended only with a piece of calculated rudeness.

"I see you don't agree with me," Dr. Church said, raising his eyebrows.

"It is not a question of agreeing or not agreeing," General Heath answered. "Let's get to business."

"Yes, indeed," said Dr. Church, and he threw his head back and covered his eyes with his long yellow fingers.

Dr. Warren unrolled a map. The map, hastily drawn dur-ing the late afternoon, showed the roads on which the Regu-lars had traveled. There were little red crosses wherever en-gagements had taken place. Beside the red crosses there were figures indicating the numbers of men involved, and in the case of the Americans, the names of the towns from which they had come.

"An admirable map, very well and carefully constructed," Samuel Adams declared, only to be silenced by a withering glance from Warren. "I see you are in untoward mood, Doctor."

"I've been in the fight," Dr. Warren said simply. "Not much of it, but still I was there, and it did my heart good. But sometimes I shudder when I think of all the fighting we yet have to face. This is the main question. The war goes on. I have heard that General Washington has some ability and is likely to be elected commander in the south, but the war won't be fought in the south. It's a matter for the Prov-ince of Massachusetts to decide. This is the battleground, not

Virginia. And then there is the question of stores and what's left of the stores. I contend, gentlemen, this is the most pressing problem of all. You must make your decisions. I am not hurrying you. It is simply that we must decide on the matters before us while there is still time." He paused and then added quickly, "I hope, gentlemen, you are not of the opinion that General Gage will sit quietly in the fortress in Boston, licking his wounds."

There was no answer. Dr. Warren shuffled the tallies, as though he were about to distribute a hand of cards, and then went on.

"You must know, gentlemen, what we are up against. We damaged 'em, but we didn't hurt 'em, didn't tear 'em apart. Every minuteman had a pound of powder in his horn and forty bullets in his pouch, but he had neither enough equipment nor enough knowledge to fight a war. As you know, there's a law in the province which says that every inhabitant has to be furnished with a firelock, a bayonet and a pretty considerable supply of ammunition. They must drill in the evenings and help to cast bullets or make cartridges. And in spite of all that our men were nothing but a mob! They had absolutely no rendezvous for gathering of battalions or regiments. They didn't care a tinker's damn about strategy. They didn't know how to meet an attack or cut off a retreat. They didn't know how to co-ordinate their forces. They were in possession of cannon and didn't use 'em. And whose fault was it?"

Dr. Church smiled, stroked his eyebrows with his long yellow fingers and said, "I remember Sam Adams and John Hancock giving orders to bury the guns. It is not, of course, the first time they have made mistakes. The truth is, I believe, that Mr. Hancock has been much engaged recently in the pursuit of a young lady of Lexington. We cannot expect Mr. Hancock to pay full attention to the needs of the minutemen or of the army."

The fat was blazing. Samuel Adams struck the table and

shouted, "For God's sake, Dr. Church! Why, I've known him five years and always known him to be an impudent, untrustworthy fellow. Yes, sir, I am talking to you, Dr. Church. I don't understand what you are up to. You are forever trying to riddle the Committee of Safety with your doubts and hesitancies, and at the same time you are forever going backward and forward to Boston in the most open manner. I've heard enough reports that you are consulting with the king's men."

"Of course I consult with the king's men," Dr. Church said in his most sweet-tempered voice. "How else can I obtain news of their intentions? I admit the charge readily, Mr. Adams. I hope you are not imputing——"

"You know perfectly well what I am imputing, Dr. Church. I will say this : I have the gravest doubts about your loyalty."

"Poor Christ!" General Heath exploded, then buried his head in his hands. But a moment later he had jumped up and was about to go and throw an arm round Dr. Church's shoulder when he heard Warren's low whisper, "Let them fight. It's better for them."

There was no fight. Quivering with anger, Samuel Adams thrust his head forward like a bulldog faced with a piece of raw beef just out of reach, while Dr. Church smiled at him, taunting him, saying over and over again, "I was not responsible for burying the cannon, sir. No, sir, I was not responsible."

"Admit you have had correspondence with the British," Samuel Adams roared.

"I've admitted it," Dr. Church answered pleasantly. "I would have correspondence with General Gage if I thought it suited the purposes of my country. I will not live in a vacuum, sir. I will weigh information wherever I can. To the best of my recollection, I remember saying that the cannon should be placed at the crossroads and wherever the damned Redcoats might be expected to pass. You impugn my loyalty, gentlemen. I impugn your virtue—your intellectual virtue. In my opinion the Committee of Safety has shown a complete disregard for the safety of our noble warriors—those embattled men who have crowned the day with honor and who have received no assistance from the province. We all know that Mr. Adams is a past master of psalm singing. Let him sing a hymn to intelligence, and let him see to it that the war against the British is fought with the weapons of the mind as well as with fowling pieces."

"I don't trust you, Dr. Church," Samuel Adams went on doggedly, "and I don't believe the use of cannon would have altered our victory today. It might have been a greater victory, a more bloody victory, but I hold that we can use our cannon another day and inflict a grievous wound on the British from which they will never recover."

"You hold to that?"

"I do."

"Then I must say that I regard you as a simpleton, Mr. Adams—a poor fool of a simpleton. We have enjoyed a great victory, and we could have enjoyed a greater. You called it a running skirmish, and so it was, and it is your fault that it was not more. Myself, I was in this battle. I helped to support a poor boy shot in the stomach, and I have blood on my stockings to prove it."

Saying this, Dr. Church rose and put one leg on his chair. There was a great splash of scarlet on his white stockings.

"If we had had cannon," he went on solemnly, "the poor boy would still be alive. I had not intended to mention this matter. I pride myself on my discretion. There were ninety to a hundred barrels of powder at Concord, enough to level Boston to the ground. With half of it we could have destroyed all of Colonel Smith's forces—oh, with much less than half of it."

"I don't trust you, Dr. Church," Samuel Adams repeated,

wagging a finger at him. "I don't trust a word you say."

"Gentlemen, we are all brethren surely," John Hancock murmured. "I do believe Mr. Adams is being unwise in making these unfounded allegations. We are not fighting one another. God forbid! We should behave with respect toward one another, and therefore I propose that Mr. Adams and Dr. Church make peace with each other. We must be united, gentlemen."

Dr. Church smiled, and even Samuel Adams shook himself out of an inexplicable rage. The long night wore on. The sudden flares of temper subsided. Occasionally they heard the whispers of the guards outside the room, and once a rider came with a long-delayed report from Colonel Barrett. The maps were brought out, and they sat hunched over them, talking in low voices, not looking up even when Eugénie poured tea into their empty glasses. . . .

Toward dawn, Dr. Church rose from his chair and said, "With your permission, gentlemen, I shall now leave. The sun will be up soon, and I am determined to go to Boston."

There was a moment's silence, then Warren leaned forward and said, "Are you serious, Dr. Church? They will hang you if they catch you. The day before yesterday you might have gone with impunity. They were in no mood for hanging, then."

"I am serious, and determined to go at all adventures," Dr. Church said quietly. "I am the best judge of my actions. You must believe me there are good reasons for the journey."

"Then if you are determined, let us make some business for you," Warren said, a puzzled look in his eyes. "We shall ask you to get medicines for our officers and also for theirs, for we have a few of them on our hands. I shall write a letter to that effect."

"I need no letter," the doctor answered, offering a particularly sweet smile to Samuel Adams, who raised no objections and accused him of no crimes.

It was still dark when Dr. Church left the cellar. The oil lamp was flickering again. Eugénie continued to fill their glasses. She was not tired. She felt, like many people when they have been awake for more than twenty-four hours, extraordinarily exhilarated and at the same time very quiet, subdued and contented. In the strangest kind of way, while listening to them disputing round the table, she had entered into their quarrels, now taking the part of Dr. Church, now of Warren, now of Hancock, Heath or Adams. At the same time she was wondering whether the journey to Concord had really taken place. Was it something she had dreamed? Where was Oliver? She had seen him twice during the day, but it was not Oliver who filled her imagination. The bridge of Concord! She closed her eyes and tried to imagine it as she had seen it during the morning, but she did not see it in the sunlight. She saw it in the moonlight, shaped like a curved bone over a silver river. There was no sign of the dead, no bloodstains anywhere: only the sunken boat was still there, glassy-green under a silvery wave.

"What are you dreaming about?" Warren asked her.

"The bridge."

"Where?"

"At Concord."

"There seems to have been a bit of fighting there," Warren said, unrolling the map. "Well, you'll have to get some rest. I'll have a bed made for you upstairs. A few hours' rest, and then we'll have to go and find somewhere to hide."

He went to the foot of the cellar stairs. Eugénie ran up to him and put her hand on his coat.

"You don't have to come with me, Eugénie," Warren said. "I'll get the bed ready for you."

Eugénie was silent for a moment, her face shining in the light of the yellow lamp. Then she said, "I'm coming with you to the end of the war."

BOOK
THREE

*The
Fantastic
Mountain*

CHAPTER 14

The Blue Room

TEN DAYS after the battle of Concord Bridge, General Gage was sitting alone at the head of the table in the Blue Room. Rain was pouring in torrents outside, and sometimes there were a peal of thunder and a blue smear of lightning across the heavens. The gilded lion and unicorn painted on the high-backed chair flickered blue and green in the lightning flashes. Maps lay in disorder on the table. The general's three-cornered hat, with its gold-lace trimmings and cockade of red, white and blue, lay at his elbow, as though he had come into the room for only a few moments and would soon take up his hat and depart.

As he dipped the long slender goose quill into the ink, the general was no longer thinking of the engagement and the retreat. His mind was on his sick child, on the terrible expression on Margaret's face when she heard the news of the battle, and on Oliver's injured hand. These were the perfect and intimate signs of his failure. He had been writing for some minutes, copying from some notes by his side, when an unusually loud explosion of thunder made his hand do a dance on the page. The ink ran out of the quill onto the paper; the letter he had been writing to Lord Dartmouth was ruined.

The general was not angry because there was a great splash of ink on the page. He quietly tore up the sheet of paper and went to the window. He enjoyed the spectacle of lightning, the clean rain-swept roofs, the silvery-blue streets deep in water, the ships bobbing in the white waves. He smiled grimly when the lightning blazed in front of his eyes, hiding the whole town in a blue flare of fire which seemed to be edged with gold, though this perhaps was no more than optical illusion. The earth rumbled. The sea was all white spume. Someone was hurrying down the street below, leaving a white furrow in the watery road, the man's blue cloak beating in the wind.

"Poor devil," the general muttered, and then went back slowly to the table, thinking of those other poor devils who had gone out to fight. "There would have been no fighting if there had been a storm," he muttered. "The god of battles hides when the elements fight among themselves."

Hardly knowing what he was doing, he picked up a list of tallies showing the number of men, together with their equipment, who had gone out to Concord. The names of the dead and missing were underlined. Altogether the casualties totaled nearly three hundred. He told himself he could have prevented them from going out. He remembered how he had commanded Major Pitcairn to hold his fire. *Not a shot must be fired, do you understand?* And Pitcairn, with his red hair and long, narrow face and deep-set blue eyes, had nodded his head and smiled gently. *We'll play the fifes and drums through every street of Concord.* . . . It had not happened like that.

As he sat down once more in his place at the head of the table, facing a clean sheet of paper, the general murmured, "God help them to bear the knowledge of defeat!" And with his quill poised in mid-air he gazed out of the window at the ships riding like corks in the bay, the sea a dull boiling green whipped with whitecaps and the rain flashing silver on the roofs. He was still gazing out of the window half an hour later when Lord Percy entered the Blue Room. He had knocked, and received no answer. All the ink from the poised pen had fallen on the paper.

"The whole town's under water," the young colonel said, only because it was necessary to say something to startle the general out of his nightmare. There was a terrible fixed, glassy look in the general's eyes.

The general turned toward Lord Percy, then shuddered. He realized now that he had been wasting his time, surrendering to inexcusable emotions.

"The whole town's under water," Lord Percy repeated.

"Well, yes, so it is, and the ships too if they are not careful." General Gage smiled, gazing at the colonel whose face turned a startling blue in the lightning flash. "It will give Graves something to think about," he added maliciously.

"The admiral is working in his office downstairs."

The general smiled again. "I thought he would be. I can't see him running for shelter in a bobbing boat. You'd think the devils of hell have made their home in Boston."

"They have!"

"I know they have, Percy, but I know too they won't be here for long. We have other devils to worry about. Storms pass, especially spring storms. I'm writing to Lord Dartmouth. I'm determined to tell him the truth—every mortal thing, no fear or favor. If they deprive me of rank or benefits, I'll never squeal. God knows there are times when a man can act in only one way. They say the whole province is rising against us. Well, we have done our best. I try to think what else I could have done, but I still don't know the answer. I pray for guidance."

"I'm sure it will be given to you."

"I hope it will be given also to our enemies."

There were blue pouches under the general's eyes; his skin was drawn and the long razor cut on his cheek was like a raw gash as he leaned forward to keep Lord Percy in focus. To add to his other miseries, he was having trouble with his eyes. Lord Percy was still standing at attention.

"Dear Percy, don't weary me with civilities. Sit down. Make yourself at home. I'll need a report from you. I'll send it as a separate document, and I'll see that their lordships give you a mark of their favor. I promise that. You fought an action such as no Englishman ever fought before, and you fought it well."

"I'm not beggin' for compliments, sir."

"I know you're not, but I'll tell you this. Whenever they write about the battle, I want them to remember that you saved the day."

The general's voice was husky, but strength was coming back to it. The blue lightning flashes had seared his eyes, but he was growing accustomed to the changing shapes of things, the faint golden edge on everything he saw. He felt better now that Percy was in the room.

"Are the new dispositions in order?" Lord Percy asked.

"God knows!" the general answered. "We're doing the best we can. For all I know there may be ships trying to make for the harbor now. We're making plans to bring in reinforcements from Canada, and then, as soon as the weather settles, we'll throw up fortifications on Breed's Hill. Then, too, I have agents seeing to it that the Indians fight for us if the rebels persist in their madness. We'll raise Negro troops, too, if we have to. If we can get 'em, we'll throw the Regulars of East Florida and the Bahamas into the battle, and all Dunmore's loyalists in Virginia as well."

Lord Percy raised his eyebrows. "Then you expect another battle?"

"I expect many," the general said grimly, "unless we can scotch the thing at its source. It will be worse if Howe takes over. It is my belief he will take over. I don't trust fighting dogs, and he's the fightingest. I'll tell you what I'd like. I'd

like to see Warren here. He's the only one of the rebels who
is a gentleman, according to my way of thinking."

"What about Church?"

"He's not a gentleman, but he has the considerable virtue
of not even pretending to be one. I've never trusted him.
I've tried to. No, I would like to have Warren here and see
whether peace couldn't be patched up. If we don't patch it
up, it's war all over the Americas. It's an affair of diplomacy
now, though His Majesty's government is hardly likely to
resort to diplomacy."

"And you have hopes for diplomacy?"

"I have no hopes at all," the general answered, and once
more he gazed out of the window, where the rumbling of the
storm was still going on and the sea was a milky white under
the gray pelting sky. For some time the center of the storm
had been in the bay; now it was coming closer to the town,
and the general could have sworn the thunder was breaking
over Province House itself. He could hear the rafters creaking and the rain water gurgling and swilling down the over-
loaded drainpipes.

The general corrected himself. "I say I have no hopes,
but the truth is I have slender hopes—very slender hopes.
I've sent De Bernière to search out Warren. I'll deal with
Warren, but I won't deal with anyone else."

"Then you believe he has authority to trade a truce?"

"I believe nothing. I only hope he has. He is a man, and
the rest, it seems to me, are monkeys. I'll deal with a man."

Lord Percy felt obscurely uncomfortable at this grasping
of straws. He possessed none of Gage's faith in Warren,
pretended to no understanding of diplomacy, saw no way out
of the conflict except a fight to the death. He had been pleased
when the general spoke about throwing in the East Florida
Regulars. He had hope in Dunmore's loyalists. For the rest
he pinned his hopes on fortifications, on making Boston an

impregnable fortress which could be supplied permanently by sea.

As the center of the storm grew closer to Province House, windows began to bang and the voices of servants could be heard in the long corridors. They were unnaturally loud and curiously changed. Indeed everything on this day of storm was curiously changed. And while the general was trying to shout above the storm, there was a loud, insistent sound of hammering on the door. At first he paid no attention to this hammering. It was absurd that anyone should so forsake the customs and habits of Province House to batter against the door. At last he could stand it no longer. He rose, swept to the door and swung it open. Trembling, very red in the face, De Bernière was standing there with an extraordinary expression on his face, an expression which was at once timid and proud. The young ensign's mouth was open, his eyes were rolling like a Negro's, and he held himself in such a way that if you blew on him he would probably fall over. Dr. Church had told him that he had news of momentous importance to convey to the general and for some reason De Bernière had believed him.

"Your lordship, I was knocking——"

"So I understand. It is the habit to knock gently at Province House."

"My lord, I knocked for ten minutes. I thought something was amiss."

"I suppose you thought I was dead."

"It crossed my mind, sir, that you might be ill."

"I'm never ill, De Bernière," the general said, wondering why he should detect himself lying so openly.

De Bernière found himself ushered into the Blue Room only because the force of the wind in the corridor was so great that the general soon wearied of holding the door open.

"Well, what is it?" the general said.

"Dr. Church is here, my lord. I've bundled him into a closet for fear that someone might see him."

"An excellent place to put the doctor," the general said, smiling at Lord Percy. "I hope you fastened him with a key."

"No, sir, I simply begged him to pass the time of day in the closet, hiding among the uniforms. He threatened to leave unless he saw you at once."

"Yes, I remember he threatened the same thing before, and little good did it do him. I'll make an exception this time. I'm ready to receive him at his pleasure."

In less than five minutes Dr. Church was in the Blue Room. He was very red of face, for there was little air in the closet, and he had been gasping for breath. He insisted on wearing his rain-soaked cape, and as he stood in the Blue Room, still gasping for breath, his thin legs supporting with difficulty his heavy and ungainly body, he resembled a spider which had been hung up in the rain. His black hair lay creased over his forehead, his hands fidgeted with the brim of his wide-brimmed black hat. He looked from General Gage to Lord Percy with a mixture of incredulity and relief: incredulity because there were only the two high officers present, and relief because he had been received so quickly; hardly more than half an hour had passed since he slipped into the side entrance of Province House. General Gage realized that the doctor was the man he had seen running down the street, leaving a white furrow behind him, his cape swirling in the wind.

"I took the advantage of the rainstorm to pay my respects to your lordship," the doctor said. "I do not believe I have been observed. As your lordship must realize, this is not a risk I would lightly undertake. If it were not for the consummate obligation I have to your lordship, I would not have attempted to come here."

The general begged the doctor to sit down and remove his

cloak, glancing at De Bernière for having shown so little
consideration for the doctor.

"Pray tell me if you have news," the general said when the
doctor was comfortably settled.

"I have a good deal of news, your lordship, but it is for
your ears alone."

"Lord Percy is my brigadier."

"Nevertheless it is for your ears alone."

The doctor was enjoying his role. It pleased him that he
could order Lord Percy and De Bernière out of the room.
For the first time the general remarked that Dr. Church possessed two faces: one youthful and eager, the other wise,
crafty and old. The strange thing about Dr. Church was that
these two faces were presented simultaneously; he did not in
the least resemble those fat men whose swollen faces conceal
a minute, wrinkled face within.

"I am at your service, Dr. Church," the general said pleasantly when Lord Percy and De Bernière were out of the
room.

The doctor sighed. "Believe me, I have come at intolerable
risk to myself."

General Gage was growing impatient. He had swung the
ornate gilded chair round, the better to face the doctor, and
now the doctor saw the nervous crisping of the general's
fingers as they rested on his knees.

"We all live in a state of risk," said the general, "but of
course no one knows that better than your honorable self.
Do not let us insist on risk. The face of danger is remarkable,
but one should gaze on it steadily. . . . I observe that the
storm is dying down."

"All the more reason for me to give you my news quickly
and then depart. I hope I shall have your considered attention."

"You have it always."

"Then I will be brief. My lord, I have attended the Provincial Congress. I have in fact attended four meetings of it since you last honored me with a summons to your presence. I find only confusion among them—confusion and worse, for they have only a poor supply of equipment and are hard pressed to obtain even a modicum of powder. As for artillery, they have no more than six three-pounders and one six-pounder in Cambridge, besides sixteen pieces of poor quality in Watertown. They talk of fighting a war barefisted. My lord, it is all talk, nothing but talk!"

"I'm glad to hear you say that. I hope you are right."

"They are firebrands without purpose, lost in their own dreams, and desperately attempting to gather ammunition from all quarters. They have, as you know, sent to New York, where there are no more than a hundred pounds of powder for sale, and I even doubt whether they have the money to buy the powder. The truth is they have scarcely five thousand pounds of currency to meet all expenses. They tell me—I was present at the conference—that they propose to issue certificates of six pounds and upward, and they have thought up some scheme of legalizing the paper money of Connecticut and Rhode Island. They are without money, without soldiers, without weapons, without ideas. And with all this lack of essential supplies they believe they can oppose the king's majesty."

The doctor paused significantly, for he had even more exceptional news to impart. The storm was abating. For the first time a glimpse of pale-blue sky could be seen through the window.

"They have nothing, but they have faith," the general suggested quietly.

"Fiddlesticks! They have not even faith! They are all at one another's throats! They are allowing themselves to be led by old General Ward of Cambridge, who is so infirm he is not fit to appear on horseback and who has nothing but the virtues of an aging magistrate to commend him."

The general smiled. He knew he could always discount the bitter personal opinions of the doctor. Knowing little concerning General Ward, he was content to believe that the magistrate knew his duty.

"But there is worse to come," the doctor went on, keeping his voice deliberately to an even monotone. "My information is that at the next meeting of the Provincial Congress, which will take place on May 5, a resolution against your lordship will be offered and no doubt will be accepted."

"Against me?" General Gage said, with the slightest lifting of his eyebrows.

"Against your lordship, named as the inveterate enemy of the people of Massachusetts."

"Well, if that amuses them . . . "

"I see you have not remarked upon the perfidy of the revolutionaries. They have named you, sir, of deliberate intent. You will become their blackest enemy. They will say that the government of His Majesty in London is peaceful: it is being misled by General Gage. They will paint you in terrible colors, write street ballads about you, turn the whole force of their fervor against you."

"They know I am their friend," the general said stubbornly.

"They may know it, but they won't care to say it. You will become in the minds of the common people the scapegoat, the evil thing, the prodigal son of the devil. When they raise their flags they will say they are fighting against you, not against the government. They will say—God help them!—that there is no mercy at your hands, that you inflamed the soldiers against them."

"They will be lying if they say that," the general said sadly. "Have you the text of the resolution they will pass?"

"No, sir, but it was generally discussed among the members of the conference. I think it will go something like this:

'General Gage has disqualified himself from serving the colony in any capacity, and therefore no obedience is due to him and he should be regarded as an unnatural and inveterate enemy of the people.' "

"If it gives people pleasure to believe such nonsense, I shall not object."

"I see you are still unaware of the seriousness of the charge they have brought against you. Clearly, they will try to assassinate you."

"My dear Dr. Church, please control yourself and do not give way to emotional outbursts. I have lived among Americans for many years, and I am the last man to fear assassination at their hands."

"You don't know them in their present mood," the doctor insisted, looking older, wiser and more crafty than ever.

The general stood up abruptly. He had a mind to show the doctor to the door, but it occurred to him that the doctor might have more information to offer him.

"What do you expect me to do?" he asked, gazing benignly at the doctor as though he had set eyes on him for the first time.

"I expect you to fight, sir! I expect you to nip the revolt in the bud. A general rebellion throughout America is coming on suddenly and swiftly, led by intemperate men who haven't counted the cost and know nothing of modern warfare. There's your opportunity. Fight now!"

"You say they know nothing about modern warfare?" the general said quietly.

"Yes, I said that, my lord."

"You're quite sure you know what you are saying?"

"Perfectly sure. I've listened to Dr. Warren discussing strategies and tactics like any ignoramus. He knows nothing, and General Ward knows less. I listen to them with pity and incredulity. There never was such an arrant mob of ignorant hotheads. Ignorance is their watchword, ignorance their banner, and in the name of ignorance and ingratitude they will die!"

The phrase was nicely turned, and Dr. Church permitted himself a smile of triumph.

General Gage was not sure whether the triumph was well earned. He very rarely smoked a pipe. Now he removed the pipe from a drawer under the table, lighted it, gazed at the smoke reflectively, puffed out his cheeks and said, "I'm not so sure of their ignorance, Doctor. I'd like to believe it. I don't."

"Good heavens, are you doubting my word of their ignorance? I attend their damned conferences. All ignorance!"

"On military affairs?"

"On military and all other affairs," Dr. Church said with extraordinary determination.

"Then please explain to me, my dear Dr. Church, why it is that Charles Beaker, our Boston bookseller, has sold more books on the art of war during the last six months than in all the sixty years he has been selling books here. You must admit there has been a good deal of reading in the art of war by members of the *soi-disant* Provincial Congress. I have examined Mr. Beaker's books, and I remember very clearly coming upon your name."

"I am a great reader. Everyone knows that."

"Particularly interested in the art of war, Dr. Church?"

"It's one of my hobbies."

"Well then, let us assume that it is only a hobby for the other members of the Provincial Congress and leave it at that," General Gage said, hiding behind a puff of blue smoke. "Rest assured, Dr. Church, that I do not hold it against you that you read books on war. Indeed, I hold the opposite opinion. I believe it is the mark of a civilized man that he reads widely."

Dr. Church was never sure he could detect the general's

irony. He thought he knew the general well, yet there were moments when he realized he did not know the general at all. It was the first time since the battle at Concord that he had shown himself at Province House, yet General Gage had not once asked about the American forces who fought in the battle. The general appeared, in fact, to be astonishingly well documented concerning the revolutionaries. Who would have thought, for example, that he had examined the lists of the Boston booksellers?

"I have one further piece of information to impart to your lordship, though I fear you will receive it as coldly as you have received the rest."

"On the contrary, my dear doctor, I receive all your news with great warmth and gratitude. You must believe that."

"I do, my lord. It was a slip of the tongue. I was thinking of the extreme danger in which I am placed by my own recklessness and loyalty to the Crown. My news is this. The delegates from Massachusetts and Connecticut are already on their way to New York. I believe great decisions will be made in New York. I fear the hotheads will be in the ascendance. That is why I ask you to fight now."

"I will hold your opinions in mind."

"Opinions! They are more than opinions, sir—they are facts. If you don't fight now, everything is lost. Every moment spared to them is a hostage to fortune. Remember that! I have given you warning."

General Gage could not say afterward how it came about that he began to believe Dr. Church. Now for the first time he trusted the man, observed the minute passions, the bitternesses, the homely revolts, all congregating to form one intense, searing passion—a passion not of revenge, but of pure hatred. Dr. Church hated the rebels as George III hated them, without knowing why he hated them and without caring. They were the blind wall against which he battered with a desperate longing to break through.

"I see you are determined on their destruction, Dr. Church, and I can only commend your earnestness."

Dr. Church shook his head. He knew now that he had only just begun to convince General Gage. Perhaps the seed would flower; it would need a deal of watering.

"Please believe me, your lordship. I am the servant of the Crown, only of the Crown."

"I know that."

"And if I say these things, it is because I feel that time is running out. You must act now—today. Tomorrow is already too late."

In the years that came afterward General Gage often thought back to this conversation. How shall one know when to strike? Not all the midnight bells strike in unison. The general looks at his watch, announces that an attack will take place at such and such an hour, prepares everything for the combat, calculates the most remote details, and then—this is exactly what happened at Concord—a message which was supposed to be given to Lord Percy at four o'clock in the morning fails to reach him until nearly nine o'clock, at a time when the main battle is almost over.

"Time will not wait for your lordship," Dr. Church said sententiously as the general led him to the door. "Time waits for no man."

The general smiled. "I believe this is particularly true in America." He gave a little bow, and this pleased the doctor so much that he burst into a short nervous laugh.

"Thank Heaven the rain is still blowing," the doctor said. "With any luck I shall be able to return to my house unobserved."

When Dr. Church had gone, the general sat down at the table for a few moments, wrote some notes in his clear, rounded handwriting, unrolled a map, drew a circle round the town of Charlestown, and then resumed the writing of his letter to Lord Dartmouth. He had half finished the letter when the luncheon bell rang, and after collecting his papers together he made his way downstairs. He had hoped that Margaret would be well enough to have luncheon with him, but she was indisposed. At his table there were only Haldimand, Lord Percy and Oliver. The storm was still driving down the Boston streets, but its fury was abating. Soon there would come, in the place of the boiling murk of the storm, a clear blue evening with every tree sparkling in the sunset.

"Storm or no storm," said the general, "I've never seen such a gluttonous lot of sorry faces!"

The remark was addressed chiefly at Haldimand, who looked like an old peasant as he gazed at his soup plate, his heaviness and silence giving him the appearance of misery.

"Well, Oliver," the general went on when he saw that his sally had failed to hit the mark, "I am accustomed to General Haldimand's silences, but not yours. Out with it!"

"Out with what, sir?"

"With whatever you are thinking, boy. I won't have silence at this table, nor glumness either. One would think the British arms had been licked, by the looks on your faces."

Oliver, who was having difficulty holding his fork in his bandaged hand, dropped the fork and threw a smile of deep affection toward the general. "I was thinking, sir, I should return to New York by the next ship."

"You are longing to escape from Boston, is that it?"

"I like Boston, but I believe I could be more useful in New York. I came for horses, sir, and there are no horses to be got. Major Pitcairn is an admirable man, but he has no need for my services."

"Then you're a fish out of water?"

"Yes, sir."

"I'll find something for you to do, by God I will!" the general exclaimed suddenly, dropping his knife and fork on his plate. "We've all got jobs to do. We're a town under siege, whether we like it or not, and there's work enough for every man. I'll see you have something, Oliver."

For the rest of the luncheon Oliver mused on the fate the general had in store for him. Conversation revived. There was some discussion on the general's announcement that he would raze Charlestown to the ground if the Americans brought up batteries there. Haldimand spoke about food supplies; it was a subject close to his heart. Lord Percy spoke of the Americans who were languishing in the Boston jail; he wanted them placed on trial.

"A trial by their peers?" General Gage asked, stroking the gash in his cheek.

"No, sir, a drumhead trial."

"You mean a drumhead court-martial, followed by an immediate hanging?"

"A few hangings won't do any harm," Lord Percy replied bitterly. "You're too lenient with them."

"I won't have any more hangings. There are people who keep on telling me I should string Hancock and Adams up on the mast of the *Somerset,* but I won't. When a country is suffering from wounds, you need the balm of Gilead, not the hangman's knot."

"And you are supplying the balm?"

"No, my lord, I am supplying no balm, but at the same time I am not rubbing salt into the wounds."

Afterward there was another of those prolonged silences which fell now at more and more frequent intervals on the dining room at Province House.

Most of the rebels had gone from the town when General Gage promised them a safe-conduct, provided they left their arms with the selectmen at Faneuil Hall. For several days the road to Roxbury was thronged with these wretched exiles, who joined the milk boys and farmers in the surrounding country. Now Boston was a shell of itself, curiously silent, a town of whispered rumors and counterrumors. Samuel Adams had called it "that prison, Boston," and all the high officers, from the royal governor down, were aware that they were building a ring of bars round themselves. Beyond Boston lay America, the long valleys, the wooded fields, the walls where the minutemen scampered to unload their fowling pieces on the unsuspecting Redcoats, who could never convince themselves that a stone wall could conceal an armory. The silence at Province House was the silence of perplexity, the silence of men who do not know where the next blow will fall.

After luncheon Oliver rose, intending to return immediately to the barracks on the Common.

"Come to the Blue Room, Oliver."

Oliver was surprised. The words had been whispered to him, as though the general had no desire that Haldimand or Lord Percy should overhear them. In silence Oliver followed him up the carpeted stairs. He observed that the general walked very slowly and stiffly, deep in thought.

Once they were in the Blue Room the general said, "I don't want any more of this damned ceremony, Oliver. Sit down. I'm weary of men who stand at attention. Tell me, when did you last see Mademoiselle de Malmédy?"

"Who is——"

"You ought to know perfectly well who I mean. Eugénie de Malmédy. When did you last see her?"

"At Menotomy," Oliver said, blushing furiously, looking down at his bandaged hand.

"I see you have cause to remember her. There were at least twenty women fighting with the rebels. They say she is Warren's mistress."

"It's not true!"

"I'm not concerned with the truth of the statement. She knows Warren, doesn't she?"

"Yes, sir."

"I want you to find her, Oliver. I want you to find Dr.

Warren. His morals don't interest me and neither do yours. De Bernière has been trying to find the doctor for the last ten days, but he has failed. It may be a dangerous mission, Oliver, but he must be found. The whole future of British power in America may depend on a meeting with Dr. Warren."

There were still a few silver ropes of rain dripping from the leaden gutters of Province House, but the sky was clearing. As Oliver walked down the stairs, he felt annoyed and confused. For the first time he realized that General Gage knew his own secrets. Once, long ago, he had given the general the opportunity to meet Warren. Then the general had refused the offer. Now he desired it more than anything in the world. Why? Was this a sign of defeat? How much had De Bernière discovered?

"What fools they are!" Oliver muttered. "They won't end this war by talking. Hang the rebels! It's the only language they will ever learn!"

CHAPTER 15

Nightmare

THE HEAT of May was something that could hardly be believed. No one had ever known such heat so early in the year. At night storms came; then there were long summery days without a breath of wind blowing through the narrow streets, and every evening the skies were a soft liquid blue, like the sea. The white tents, erected on the Common, empty now though the reinforcements which were expected daily would soon fill them, glowed like campfires in the sunset; the trees sparkled. Sometimes a cloud of dust, arising inexplicably, would travel like a whirlwind down the streets; afterward, even in the evenings, there would be a hush like the hush at high noon.

Oliver walked the streets in search of Dr. Warren, some sign which would reveal where the rebel was hiding. He had no liking for the task and hardly knew how to go about it. He could not leave the town for fear of being arrested by the rebels. He saw little of General Gage. He still took luncheon at Province House, still reported every evening at the barracks, still attended the early morning parades on the Common which were commanded by Lord Percy; and he did this out of a sense of duty and loyalty, knowing that the rebels might enter the town unexpectedly, forcing the gates. He made inquiries in the taverns, wearing civilian clothes, but

265

everyone recognized him: he was Margaret Gage's nephew, the officer who had brought instructions to General Gage on H.M.S. *Nautilus.*

In the taverns the Tories drank rum to drown their sorrows, complained against the taxes and the lack of food, made sly remarks about the inadequacy of the royal governor. Sometimes, in the oddest manner, they would break out into empty cheering, calling for three cheers for the king, then three more for Lord North, and then there would be three damn-'em-to-hells for the rebel leaders. The state of siege was slowly breaking their nerves. They must have guessed whom Oliver was looking for, for they would nudge him and talk about Warren's whore until Oliver would turn scarlet and threaten to knock the head off the man who spoke so disrespectfully against the woman he adored. But he was never able to find the man who spoke against Eugénie: mysteriously he would have disappeared into the crowd. What tormented Oliver more than anything else was that everyone knew his business, and he could no more conceal it than he could conceal his own military manner.

"You won't find her by sulking," De Bernière said, meeting him one day when he came out of the dining room at Province House.

Oliver had avoided De Bernière deliberately.

"I didn't ask your advice," Oliver said, moving quickly away.

De Bernière tugged at his sleeve. "For God's sake, don't take it amiss, Captain De Lancey! Why treat me as an enemy?"

It was a hot day, with the heat striking up from the marble floor and the air deathly still in all the corridors of Province House.

"Won't you come into my office?" De Bernière went on. "We can talk quietly there." He dropped his voice to a whisper which was almost a whine. "I don't know why the

devil you avoid me, sir. I could be of some help, if you chose
to use me."

Oliver found himself in the small cubicle which De Bernière called his office. Afterward he had no idea why he had
accepted his invitation. De Bernière had changed. Like
everyone else at Province House he had begun to look older,
and there were deep lines of anxiety under his eyes.

"Well, what do you want?" Oliver said, feeling trapped.
It occurred to him that he might have to fight his way out.
The heat in Boston was bad; in this small office it was worse.

"You won't find her by sulking," De Bernière repeated,
with more insolence in his manner than Oliver had a taste for.

"I'm not looking for her."

"I know. You are looking for Dr. Warren. But you
wouldn't mind finding her, would you?"

"I won't have you talking about her!"

"All right, I won't talk about her. I'll talk about Dr. Warren. There's only one way to find him. You have to go in
disguise through the villages. They'll know where he is in
Roxbury or even in Cambridge. I know it's more than an
Englishman's life is worth to go there, but still it's the only
way. The royal governor sent me out on many missions
through the country. I made reports. He was good enough
to commend me for them. Warren is somewhere around. I
know that. As for Eugénie de Malmédy, there are rumors
that she is in New York, in Baltimore, in Philadelphia. The
bird has flown."

Oliver resisted the impulse to crash his fist against De
Bernière's face.

"You will refer to Miss de Malmédy more civilly," he
said. He wondered why the heat was stifling him, forgetting
that the cubicle was only a few feet square. "If you know of
some way of finding her, that's another matter." He was
determined not to use brute force on De Bernière, but the
temptation remained.

Suddenly De Bernière's whole expression changed. He had deliberately angered Oliver, to discover how much Oliver knew. Now he saw no further purpose in the ruse. "You must forgive me, Oliver," he said quietly. "It's the heat. We're all out of our wits here, and I suppose we will continue to be until General Howe arrives. The truth is, his lordship is more afraid of war now than he ever was. When the reinforcements come we shall be able to show a brave front to the world, but not now."

"Then you expect them to come soon?"

"They're on their way—that's all we know. When they come we will be able to mount our defenses. Now we are wide open for attack. Even the general does not know how close we are to disaster. Why, man, the rebels have only to march into Boston and take over the town. We're so powerless that an army armed with broomsticks could force a way in, as long as they didn't mind losing a few men to our sixpounders."

All this was new to Oliver. He had believed that Boston was well defended; he was certain there was no immediate danger. The rebels were talking, threatening, assembling. They were jeering the royal governor and printing handbills which showed the Redcoats as grotesque beetles and cockchafers; if they only jeered and printed handbills, there could be no harm in their maneuvers. Obscurely, Oliver was aware that the kettle was boiling over, but every time he saw the British flag flying from the masthead of the *Somerset* he felt a strange sense of the permanence of British power. When General Gage said that everything depended on a meeting with Warren, Oliver told himself that the general was suffering from strain. Now he realized that the general was speaking no more than the truth.

"So we're in desperate case?" Oliver said.

De Bernière nodded. "Much more desperate than the government knows. We have to find Warren. He's the only one of them who is open to reason. I don't mean he can be talked into surrender, but he carries prestige, he knows what he is about, he is devoted to the revolution. No one would ever dare question his motives. He's a worthy antagonist."

"What about Hancock and Adams?"

"They're talkers. You won't find them on the battlefield. I doubt whether they would die for their beliefs. Warren would. I've thought and thought, Oliver, and I've come to the conclusion that he's the only man who could lead the Americans against the British and win."

They were silent for a few moments.

"I don't know how to find him," Oliver said. "I've tried. I believe he's still in the town, still coming in. The guards at the Neck have orders to arrest anyone who resembles him. I've stood for days on end with the guards, but I haven't set eyes on him. I've sent messages to him through people going out. There's no reply. Sometimes I have the damnedest feeling that he is here, watching me, knowing everything I am doing, smiling with those two ivory teeth of his."

"Have you been to Hanover Street?"

"Yes."

"And you found nothing?"

"I haven't been through the house. I've had it watched—watched it myself. I'm sure he's not there. I believe he comes to Boston, stays in a different house every night—perhaps every two or three hours he slips away into another house—and then vanishes like the wind."

"It won't do any harm to go through the house," De Bernière said.

"Will it do any good?"

"Maybe it won't do any good at all, but it's worth trying. You could leave a letter there."

"Leaving a letter in Warren's house would be like leaving it in a hole," Oliver remarked, but he had already decided that there was little else he could do.

That night, with three men borrowed from Pitcairn's regiment, Oliver went to the house in Hanover Street. No lights shone. The house was some way back from the road, with a gravel path leading to the door, and two immense elms beside the iron gate. Oliver had not seen the place since he was taken there by Eugénie. With the three Marines beside him he knocked firmly on the door. As he suspected, there was no answer, only the hollow echoes of the knocking in the empty house. The sky was clouded; there was a sea mist blowing in. With their lanterns held above their heads, their pistols leveled, the Marines resembled conspirators. Oliver wanted to laugh at the absurdity of his task: one does not discover a rebel leader simply by knocking on his door.

"We'll have to make our way to the back," he said.

He was about to lead the Marines over the fence which separated the house from the kitchen garden when one of the Marines said he thought he heard someone stirring inside the house. They all crouched beside the door, listening.

"I don't hear anything," Oliver said.

"I heard it plain as daylight," the Marine answered. "It was softlike. He's standing there, just behind the door. I could shoot him dead with my pistol if you'd let me."

The Marine, a Welshman named Sergeant Evans, Sergeant being his Christian name, stepped back and would have fired straight into the door if Oliver had not twisted the pistol out of his hand. The pistol clattered onto the stone steps. Immediately there came from inside the house the sound of scampering feet. Ruefully, Oliver realized that Sergeant Evans was right. Perhaps the man had been watching them casually through the keyhole. Someone suggested breaking the door down.

"No, there's another door at the back. We could break that. I'll leave one man at the front."

Crossing a garden fence, they came to a tradesman's entrance. There was still no sound in the house. Oliver pressed

a bayonet into the side of the door; there was some splintering of wood, then the lock was forced back and the door
opened. With the two men left to him, holding his storm
lamp at arm's length, Oliver went into the kitchen. There
was a musty smell in the house, as though it had been unused
for a long time. He was convinced that the sound they had
heard before was some kind of hallucination. The house was
empty; he was sure of that. He went from room to room,
his right hand cocked on his pistol, his left holding the storm
lamp. He could hear the Marines breathing hard, for they
were frightened; there was something in the darkness of the
house which encouraged their fears. Sergeant Evans was by
Oliver's side.

"I swear there's someone in the house," he said. "I can't
hear, see or smell anyone, but I'll swear it all the same."

"You're dreaming things," Oliver said, and then he
jumped, for quite close to him, standing against the wall,
naked to the waist, his bronze body glistening in the light of
the storm lamp, was a huge and powerfully muscled Negro.

"Who the devil are you?" Oliver said, relieved because
the man was unarmed.

"I'm Hannibal," the Negro said, his voice rich and full.

"Where's your master?" Oliver peered at the Negro's face,
sure that he had seen him somewhere else before.

"Ma mastuh's in Cambridge, suh, and ma Missie is with
him."

There was something so transparently honest in the Negro's face that Oliver asked him no more questions. Warren
and Eugénie were in Cambridge. Well, he had expected it.
Without further ado Oliver and the two Marines left the
house. . . .

The search for Warren was an unequal one, for all the advantages were on Warren's side. Halfway through the month
of May he announced publicly he had been four times

in Boston during the previous six weeks. Then the British
began to make plans for securing for their own troops the
fodder and hay from the islands along the coast. The plans
were secret, but on the morning when the British troops
landed on Grape Island, preparing to remove the hay in their
own barges, they found that the Americans had reached the
island during the night. The farmers said that Warren had
led them. That was on May 21. Six days later the British
led an expedition for cattle and hay, sheep and horses on
Noddle Island. They found that the Americans had taken
possession of over three hundred sheep, rounded up the cattle, and were drawn up on Chelsea Neck with two small four-
pounders and eighty men with fowling pieces. Late that night
the Marines were dispatched from a schooner, and a sloop
engaged the Americans in the dark. At daybreak the British
counted twenty of their men killed. Once more Warren had
been in command, according to the farmers.

"I know enough about him to know that he would be useless as a raider," General Gage said. "Anything that is
done well, they say is done by Warren. It's all the more
reason for trying to find him, Oliver."

Then, on May 25, a whole flotilla of ships sailed into Boston harbor with reinforcements, and there were three new
British generals in command of them. . . .

One day at dusk, on an impulse, Oliver went alone to the
house in Hanover Street, breaking the door open without
anyone's help. It was very dark in the room. There was no
sound except the elm leaves brushing against the high window, and somewhere some water was dripping. Oliver made
his way across the room, shielding with his cloak the storm
lamp he was carrying, stifling in the midsummer heat which
seemed to be all the greater in the shuttered house, as though
the house, so lonely, so enclosed, had somehow absorbed the
heat of all the surrounding houses. He did not know what
led him into the house or why he should trouble to go to such

lengths in concealing the light of the storm lamp; above all, he did not know why it had occurred to him to enter the house alone. The floor boards creaked. Once he knocked against a wall, and only with difficulty did he retrieve the lamp which had fallen from his hands. His heart pounded. He was afraid of meeting Hannibal, but more than anything else he was afraid of meeting himself in a mirror. Once, when he was a child, he had been walking with a candle down a dark corridor. Suddenly he had come upon another child walking steadily toward him, holding his candle high, smiling his own puzzled, mysterious smile; in sheer terror he had dropped the candle, having recognized his own solemn smile of greeting in the smile of the child who came toward him out of a dark mirror.

He walked slowly, craftily, pausing from time to time to wipe the sweat from his brow. There was no air in the house. His uniform was hot, choking him. He told himself he would simply go into the room where once—it seemed long ago— he had talked with Warren, and leave the letter on the desk. It was an act of sheer desperation, inexplicable, and therefore perhaps tolerable. At any moment he expected Hannibal to step out of the shadows.

When his sword banged against the edge of a chair he groaned; the sound of the groan echoed through the house, seeming louder than the sound he had made. He hardly cared when, passing from one room to another, the storm lamp caught against the wall, fell with a clatter to the ground and then went out. Hot oil was pouring across the floor. For a few moments he was in pitch-darkness, his eyes still unaccustomed to the dark. Then he saw that the summer lightning flickered faintly through the curtains: there was still enough light in places to enable him to make his way through the house.

When at last, having blundered into the kitchen twice, he reached the study where he had last seen Dr. Warren he was

aware that there was someone else in the room. It was not
Hannibal. It was someone who breathed lightly and gently—
someone lying on the couch. He was so certain that the
person lying there was Eugénie that he said, "I never thought
I would see you again."

There was no answer, only the light gentle breathing of
someone lying there, quite close to him. The silence made
the hair bristle at his neck. His hands were clammy with a
cold sweat. He said aloud, almost shouting, "Eugénie!"

"What is it?" a voice said, coming out of the dark from
somewhere beneath the long window. "What are you looking for?"

"I'm looking for you, Eugénie."

Then there was silence again while something moved in
the dark. She came toward him. He could see her faintly
whenever the sky flared up with a blue lightning flash. She
walked uncertainly, peering, stretching out her hands toward
him, as blind people walk. It occurred to Oliver that she must
be ill, or dying, or perhaps she was a ghost: only the faint blue
wraith of Eugénie was coming toward him.

"I didn't expect you here," she said softly.

He knew this was a ruse. His heart was beating violently.
Now he was no longer hot; his blood had turned cold, icy.
He said softly, "Eugénie."

"I was sleeping," she said.

Now her voice was rich and strong, and his heart leaped
at the recognition, at the knowledge that she was really there,
no longer a ghost or a wraith. He struck a tinder match and
gasped when the sulphurous blue flame rose with its cloud of
black smoke. Eugénie was gazing at him, her face terribly
vivid in the light of the match. Then the match went out, and
there was only the smell of sulphur in the room.

"It's all dreams," he said, laughing. "You're not there—
you're your ghost."

"No, Oliver, I'm here. I didn't think you would find me."

"Then you expected me?"

"Yes, I came into Boston three days ago. I wanted to see you once again, perhaps for the last time."

"Why the last time?"

"There is always a last time, Oliver," Eugénie said sadly. "There was a last time at Menotomy, too."

He could not understand her. It was part of the nightmare that she should talk like this. Even when he drew her into his arms and kissed her, seeing her long and beautiful face uplifted in the blue flares of lightning, he could not believe she was real. He said, "For God's sake, let us light the candles! I cannot endure this darkness any more."

"Nor I," Eugénie said, and busied herself with finding the candlesticks.

When they were lighted he saw she was wearing a taffeta gown, perhaps the same one in which she had ridden to Concord, and there was a red scarf twined negligently round her neck. On her face there was the dreaming expression of someone who has been sleeping; on her upper lip there were gleaming bubbles of sweat.

She settled herself on the couch, threw a smile at him and then said quietly, "You are mad to have come. It's so dangerous."

Frowning, she turned her head away, while thoughts raced one another across her brain; every frown was a thought, and every relaxation from frowning was the passing of a thought.

"Do you forgive me?" he asked.

"Yes."

"Do you love me?"

"Sometimes I think I love you more than anything in the world."

"Is that true?"

She threw out her bare arms and touched his knees. "You know it is true," she said softly. "I've hidden nothing from you, nor from Warren. All my spirit, all that I call my spirit, is in love with Warren. His wife is dead. He loves his children tenderly, but he cannot talk with them, cannot plan a revolution with them. So we are together spiritually. Then I saw you coming toward me and I knew there was another kind of love. I think he hates me for it now. He has had a fever. He is sick. He keeps telling me there is nothing to be gained by any other love except the love people share in the spirit."

"And you believe him?"

"No, but I honor him, and I'll go with him whenever he needs me."

"But I love you, I need you!"

"We have this evening," she murmured, turning her face to the wall.

She was shaking with grief. He knelt beside her, having long ago forgotten why he had come. Then he embraced her, and stroked her face and shoulders until the tears came freely. He tried to imagine her secretly entering Boston three days ago simply to see him. She told him, between sobs, that she knew he would come. Hannibal had told her of how Oliver had broken down the door with three Marines and then patched it up so well that no one would have known it had been damaged. For Oliver the pain of her suffering was too intense to be borne; he wanted to carry her away, far away, out of the world of wars. Suddenly, while she was brushing the tears from her eyes, she said the one thing he had not expected her to say.

"Do you want to see Warren?" she asked.

Oliver was torn between the desire to serve General Gage and the desire to stay with Eugénie.

"No, why should I?"

"There are reasons."

"What reasons?"

"Everyone knows you want to see him. De Bernière has sent messages, and you've made it clear enough you want to

see him. Tell me truthfully, did you come here to see me or
to see Warren?"

"To see you. I prayed to see you."

"Even if it is the last time?"

"Yes, even if it is the last time."

"The last time," she murmured, and smiled to herself, as
though there was some secret in her she would never reveal.

As often happened on these hot nights, the moisture in the
air made the candles sputter. He envied her her cool dress,
her look of quiet composure, now that she had finished sobbing. He kissed her again, burying his head in the cool curve
of her soft breasts, and all the time he was planning, trying
to think of some way in which they could both leave America. But when he spoke of his plans she said sadly, "It's no
use, Oliver. We belong where we are until the wars are over."

"Then you won't come with me?"

"No. I told you this was the last night together."

"Let there be many lasts," he said hopefully.

He blew out all but one of the candles; then he undressed
her. And when she lay at full length on the couch he knelt
beside her again, gazing at her for a long time, until he blew
out the remaining stump of candle and took her in his arms.

They slept for a while, to be awakened by the chimes of
Christ Church ringing eleven o'clock. As Eugénie dressed
in the dark she said teasingly, "If I went to Warren now,
would you come with me?"

"I would go anywhere in the world with you."

"Then dress quickly."

During the next half hour Oliver hardly knew where he
was. Hannibal came into the room with a three-branched
candlestick. Eugénie had disappeared on mysterious errands;
he heard her running up the stairs and then down again. She
was gay and happy, humming under her breath: it was as
though their love-making had brought new life into her. Her
face was flushed, her eyes shining, and there was a mysterious

smile at the corners of her lips. Hannibal gave him an old gray cloak which smelled of moth balls, and shortly afterward they were in the garden, the elm trees gently waving overhead.

"We'll go by canoe," she said. "Hannibal has made the journey many times. Six days ago he brought Dr. Warren into Boston by canoe. There's a moon. We won't lose the way. You are sure you want to come?"

He embraced her fiercely, crushing her in the shadow of the elms, thinking she was leading him to his death and not caring. With Hannibal leading they went by deserted alleyways to the river, then ran quickly across the patch of moonlight to some stone steps leading down to a canoe. There were oars wrapped in cloth already in the canoe. Several frigates were in the river, their lamps shining, and sometimes voices were heard coming from the decks, very clear and resonant in the quiet night. Hannibal pulled the oars, keeping in shadow. Though the moon was shining, there were enough clouds to soften its glare. With the light of the sky almost gone, the landscape took on false contours. Oliver could not recognize whether he was on the Mystic or the Charles River. When the moon disappeared at last and Hannibal took the opportunity of branching out into midstream, everything was gray—the spires of Boston, the curving banks and bushes, the ships standing against the sky.

"Where are you taking me?" Oliver whispered once.

She pressed herself against him. "To Warren. He wants to see you as much as you want to see him."

CHAPTER 16

The Dark Tide

"WHO IS IT?" the voice said at the end of the corridor.

Eugénie answered gaily, as though it were something she said every day of her life, "Eugénie and Oliver."

"Good God, woman, are you mad?"

There was the sound of someone grunting, and then the door burst open. Warren faced them with a lamp behind him, with such a look of perplexity on his face that Eugénie burst out laughing. He had not shaved. He wore a dressing gown which reached to his feet, and the silver buckles on his shoes glinted in the lamplight. He looked older than when Oliver had seen him last, but perhaps this was a trick of the light.

Then Warren smiled, lifted Eugénie's hands to his lips, kissed them, and said, "You're a devil of a woman, Eugénie. I should have you shot for communicating with the enemy."

"But you won't."

"At least I'll consider it."

He led them into a small spare room where there were only a bed, a bookcase, a Chinese screen and three or four chairs. Books were crammed into a bookcase without order. Others lay all over the table in a way which suggested he had been searching hurriedly for some passage and still had not found it. There was a heavy smell of tobacco in the room. It was the room of a man who lives alone in complete seclusion, or perhaps it was a hiding place. For the life of him Oliver could not remember how he had reached the place; he remembered only that they had beached the boat somewhere on the outskirts of Watertown, climbed some stone steps, slipped down a dark alleyway and come into a narrow clapboard house through the garden. All the time Hannibal had led the way.

When they were in the room Oliver saw that he was suffering from a fever. In the harsh light of the lamp he was almost unrecognizable—white-faced and taut-lipped. His eyes were immense and brooding, and there was about them a look of utter weariness. His dressing gown was damp with sweat. He moved about the room like someone in a dream, collecting the books and papers together to make the place appear more habitable.

"I won't say you are welcome, Oliver," Warren said after a pause, "but I'll say this: I've thought about you often and planned to meet with you. It is not on my account that there were so many difficulties." He thrust some books back into the bookcase and then settled on the edge of the bed. He said, "These damned fevers come at the wrong time. I can medicine everyone except myself." Then he smiled, looking absurdly youthful.

There was something so frank and boyish in the smile that Oliver thought for a moment that the fever had magically passed. Unshaved, sitting on the edge of the bed, he hugged his dressing gown to him and gazed at Eugénie with an expression of extraordinary tenderness, perhaps forgetting that Oliver was in the room.

He said: "The worst of all the battles is the battle against pride. I've fought against it, and I think the enemy is dashed to the ground. I mean to cleanse myself completely. They offered me everything—every kind of honor, every kind of testimonial, even the command of the American forces—but I won't lead."

Tears were springing from Eugénie's eyes. She shook her

head from side to side and grasped his damp hands. "They worship you—you know that," she murmured.

"It's enough reason for not leading them," he answered quickly. "I hate the look of worship in their eyes. If we rebel against the British, there must be no worship of the commanders. We must fight as a united people and for ourselves, not for the sake of the commanders, however able——"

"Why fight?" Oliver interrupted. "God knows the British don't want to fight you. A few hotheads perhaps, but if you give us time, we will throw the hotheads into the ditches where they belong."

Warren said sorrowfully, "There are hotheads on both sides. Have you counted on that?"

"I know that General Gage is not a hothead. He wants to put an end to the fighting."

"Then he should come over to our side."

"You know he won't—you know it's impossible. He has sworn an oath of loyalty to the king."

"The oaths don't bind any more," Warren said, and a flash of light shone in his eyes. "The oath binds only when the king protects. Surely he knows that if he comes over to our side he will be treated with honor, and generations of Englishmen will bless his name. That is one way—the best and simplest way—of ending the fighting."

"And you know he can't do it?"

"I know that."

"Then let us think of some other way, General Warren."

At the mention of the title which had been given to him by the Provincial Congress Warren frowned, not as a man will frown when he is annoyed, but with a kind of comic helplessness, as though he wanted to convey his own unworthiness, his desolate sense of his own unimportance.

While they were talking Oliver had a feeling that time was running out. Here, or somewhere close by, desperate decisions were being made—perhaps had been made already. It was now past two o'clock; the night was close and still. Beyond the elm trees in the garden he could see the river below flowing quietly in the moonlight.

"General Gage proposes that there should be a secret meeting with you to discuss the terms of a truce," Oliver said, leaning forward. "He was never more earnest than when he said he desired this above everything else."

"And could he keep the truce?"

"He is his own master," Oliver said, bridling. "Make no mistakes about that."

"Yes, but the king . . . "

The words hung in the air, chiming like distant bells, the echoes softening until at last all sign of the words melted in the moist air.

"The king's hand can be forced," Oliver said, not knowing what he was saying. "None of the king's ministers understands what is happening in America. We must force his hand. I swear to you that General Gage will do everything to force the hand of the king, provided you give him assurances."

"What assurances?"

"The assurance that there will be an end to the rebellion."

Warren stroked his cheeks, smiled, gazed at Eugénie, then fell to wondering again why Eugénie had brought Oliver, though she had threatened to bring him several times in the past. What would he gain? No; he would gain nothing. He had come because he sincerely desired peace, because he was in love with Eugénie, because he was prepared to serve General Gage loyally—for a hundred reasons. He had come too late. Perhaps it had always been too late. In a strange way Oliver resembled the lone survivor of a tribe which had once flourished on the earth, a survival out of the archaic past, a man who thought that reason could rule, when the time of reason was over. Seeing the way in which Oliver leaned forward, so anxious to serve peace, so desperate in his desire to accomplish miracles, Warren smiled compassionately.

"What are these miracles you talk about?" he said bitterly. "You talk as a soldier, Oliver. Well, if it were a matter for soldiers alone, there might be peace. But the king's ministers demand war, and now the American ministers demand war. Who shall have the last word?"

"We must keep the peace," Oliver said stubbornly. "Too much blood has flowed already."

"And how will you keep it?"

"I've begged you to consider General Gage's offer."

"Listen, Oliver. I am no one. I have stripped myself of titles. I won't command. I'll fight with the people if they have to fight, but I won't lead them into battle, because it is more than I can bear to have such a responsibility on my hands. I'm a doctor by trade. I won't be a butcher. A month or two months ago I might have given you a different opinion, but it's too late now."

"It's never too late," Oliver said desperately, leaning forward, his eyes blazing.

"Tonight it's too late," Warren said, and then there was a long, heavy silence like the silence of the sea.

Somewhere below, perhaps at the bottom of the stair well, a clock chimed, but no other sound disturbed the air. Warren was listening for sounds coming from the street, but none came. Once he smiled weakly at Eugénie and wrapped the dressing gown still more closely round him.

In his loneliness and misery Oliver found himself looking at the books which were spread out on the table. Straight in front of him was a small book bound in red leather. Idly he turned the pages and saw that it was an old and well-thumbed prayer book, dated 1559.

"I see you read our prayer book," Oliver said, more out of nervousness than for any other reason. "It's very old—older than almost anything in America."

Warren smiled. "Yes, older than any of us. There is truth

in prayers—that I am sure of. But beyond prayers, what is there? I know a few truths—no more than a few."

"What is the greatest of the truths you have found?"

"I can't tell you, Oliver—I don't want to tell you. You would think it was madness if I did."

"I wouldn't think anything you say is madness, sir."

"Well, then—it's death. There's such a peace in death men would be envious if they knew it. I keep thinking, *Must I lead them? Have I the right to lead them? Better to die with them than to put oneself in a position of power.*"

"They *must* be led," Oliver said.

"No, they must lead themselves. They must learn. And as for me, I have so great a love for them that it would be nothing to die for them."

Oliver was thunderstruck with horror. It was the last thing he ever expected to hear from a rebel leader. Warren was gaunt and ill, but he was not so ill that he had no desire to live. The room seemed to tremble, and at the same time it was breathlessly still. Warren was smiling his enigmatic smile, his lips pursed together. He looked younger than ever, with that youthfulness which people in high fever sometimes show.

"I see you don't agree with me."

"No, I'll never agree with that."

"That's because you're young. Your whole life is before you. Mine is coming to an end."

Eugénie had turned white. Her mouth was open. She wanted to speak, but no words came. She thought he was speaking of his fever. She wanted to hold his head on her lap, but she could not move from her chair.

"Two months ago, when we asked you to send a communication to General Gage he spurned it. Now, Oliver, you ask me to arrange a meeting with him. You could not have chosen a worse time or a more useless man. I have finished with the revolution. I no longer think of it. The people raised me to high office, but now I have gone back to be with the people again. I have not done this lightly. I've prayed and prayed again. Believe me, if there was anything I could do, I would do it, but the time we live in is out of joint. I prefer the people to the generals, though I am a general. And it is the people who die in war. So I shall be with them, and I shall die with them." Then he said savagely, "I hope I shall die up to my knees in blood!"

Eugénie screamed and threw herself on him, but he only smiled at her, holding her in his arms. She was trembling violently, her eyes suddenly bloodshot. He saw her red-veined eyes and utterly empty face, and kissed her lightly on the forehead; and when she had composed herself a little he said, "I didn't mean to frighten you."

She put her hand over his mouth. When he gently disengaged it and held it in his own she sat beside him on the edge of the bed, shivering.

"There mustn't be war," she whispered.

"Too late, Eugénie," he answered, shaking his head again. "They've started for the hill already."

"What hill?"

"Why, Breed's Hill, what else? They're setting up fortifications there for fear that General Gage will set them up instead. They're ready for a fight."

Seeing that Eugénie was still pale, he poured out some red wine from a bottle near the bed and gave it to her in a small glass tumbler. Eugénie pushed it away.

"I don't want it—it looks like blood!" she exclaimed.

"It will do you good, Eugénie. It will bring the color back to your cheeks."

"You don't care about the color of my cheeks. You care only about fighting."

"We are at war," he said slowly. "What else is there to

care about? Come, Eugénie, drink a glass of wine with me, for I am going on the hill tomorrow and I may never come off again."

Eugénie swung round and faced him. There was some madness burning in his eyes, or perhaps it was fever. He was strangely calm, strangely relaxed when he talked of dying.

"You must promise you won't go," Eugénie cried. "Promise! You're too ill! You have a fever, and you ought to be under the care of a doctor. It's madness for you to speak of going up the hill, when you are too ill to hold a gun. If you expose yourself, as surely as you go there you will be killed."

"*Dulce et decorum est pro patria mori*," he murmured.

"And what's that?"

"A Latin tag. It is sweet, and pleasant, to die for one's country."

"I don't think you know what you are saying. You are sick. You must let me nurse you."

He drew her hand to his cheek and kissed it; then he said, "You are forgetting the guest of honor. You must look after Oliver. God knows, we must keep him a prisoner for a little while longer. The British know nothing about Breed's Hill yet."

For the first time they heard the sound of footsteps in the street.

"What's that?"

"Our men going out to build the earthworks, I suppose."

"Then it's war," said Oliver quietly.

"Yes, it's war."

"Then God help you, and God help us all! You know what will happen if Charlestown is occupied?"

"Yes."

"God have mercy on you, Dr. Warren! You have started this thing, and you won't be able to bring it to an end. The war will blaze across the whole continent. There's still a hope of peace. Call the men off. Tell them—tell them anything, for anything is better than war."

"Too late," Warren said. He poured out another tumbler of wine and gave it to Oliver.

Outside, the dark tides of men were making for Breed's Hill. In the darkness, with the moon covered with clouds, they dragged fieldpieces across the Neck and set to work raising earthworks on a small spit of a hill facing Boston. They worked hurriedly, against time, with only a little powder in their horns, swarming like beavers under the cold stars in the hot June night. All of them knew that if they were captured, they would be hanged with a cord. All this Warren knew. At first he had fought against the adventure, then he relented and gave it his blessing.

"Isn't there some way you can prevent them?" Oliver said despairingly.

"There's no way, Oliver. The men out there are terribly united. I've fought against their plans, but I can't fight against them any longer. They have their own ways of doing things."

"They are not your ways?"

"No. If I had to fight this war, I would begin in some other way. But it's their war, and they've spoken. I'll have no part of the leadership. They must do what they know best."

"Aren't they frightened of the consequences?"

"Why should they be? Do you think they were born in the woods to be frightened by owls? No. They know they will win, and that's enough for them."

"You think they will win?"

"I know it, and that's why I'm prepared to die with them. How humble they are when they die!"

To Oliver it seemed that the air was shivering, cut through with strange wavering silver ribbons. The earthworks were not important—the ships' guns could blast them to powder—

but the consequences were important. He tried to imagine the men working on the hill—breaking up rail fences, ringing themselves with battlements of stones on a hill so small it was hardly larger than a hay cart brimming with hay.

Warren was saying, "I must ask you to be my prisoner for another hour."

"I've realized that."

"You can go now if you give me your word of honor you won't inform on us."

"Then I would prefer to stay."

Oliver had his pistol with him. No one, not even Hannibal, had tried to take it away from him. He could kill Warren and fight his way out. There was a desperate look in Warren's eyes which said, *Why don't you kill me and get it over with? . . .* Once Oliver's hand went to his side, but the journey to the pistol was never completed. How, under what conditions, does one kill a man determined to die?

They stayed there, looking deep at each other, while the air shivered and beat against them and time flowed through their hands. As the minutes passed, Warren's face looked more and more drawn. Eugénie seemed in control of herself, but occasionally her lips quivered and the blood rushed to her cheeks, only to fall again like a wave. Warren sat on the edge of the bed, staring straight in front of him, as though he had been there since the beginning of time. Suddenly, with a scratchy pen, he began to write in a ferocious handwriting on a sheet of paper which he pulled out of the pile of books on the table. He wrote:

> *The bearer, Captain Oliver De Lancey, has my permission to pass through our lines.*
> *Joseph Warren, General.*

"You can go now," Warren said. "You won't reach the British lines before dawn."

Warren held out his hand. It was a long, pointed hand,

very white, with thick knotted blue veins. It did not tremble.

"I wish your health, dear Oliver," he said. "I wish this most humbly, most devotedly."

"And I—I desire God's blessing on you."

Then Warren gave a little nod, and Eugénie took Oliver by the arm. Hannibal was standing just outside the door. He had been there, patiently guarding his mistress during all the time Oliver had been there. The door closed, and they went down the creaking stairs. Soon they were in the garden.

"I'll leave you now," Eugénie said. "Hannibal will take you back to Boston."

The stars were shining. There were no longer any clouds over the moon.

"Shall I see you again?" Oliver asked.

"Oh, God, I hope so."

"Then why don't you come with me?"

"I'm needed here."

She looked white in the moonlight, very quiet, withdrawn into herself. When Oliver kissed her she clung to him. It was as though there was nothing separating them, and under the elms they were closer together than they had been in bed. There was no sound of anyone marching in the street; the houses were shuttered. In the garden there was only quiet.

"I love you," he said. "I know that. We'll find each other again."

When Oliver followed Hannibal down the path and then into the sheltered side streets she stood there listening for a long time. Then she returned slowly to the house. She had expected Warren to be at the door to welcome her. When she reached his room she found that he had fallen fast asleep on his bed.

CHAPTER 17

The Mountain

THAT NIGHT, according to a long-established custom, General Gage had worked in the Blue Room, reading reports, writing marginal inscriptions on them in a neat, rounded hand; sometimes he just stared into space. Late in the evening there had been a trying interview with General Howe and another with General Clinton. They had spoken heatedly. Both of them were of the opinion that General Gage was not directing the full force of his energy against the rebels. The general reminded them that he had proscribed Samuel Adams and John Hancock. Wasn't that enough? And the two generals, recently landed from England, had exchanged glances and kept their own counsels. When they had gone the general said, "They can go to the devil. They know nothing of American affairs, and they'll never learn!"

Usually at the first stroke of dawn the general went to bed. As a rule he would no sooner fall on the bed than he would be sleeping soundlessly, deeply, "diving," as he said, "twenty thousand fathoms deep." But this morning he had no desire to sleep. The presence of the generals who accompanied the reinforcements had unnerved him. They were always offering advice; they were insolent. He wished them in hell.

It was one of those calm New England mornings when even the sun seems to rise gently. There was no outpouring of golden spokes, no sharp and brilliant radiance. The sea's color passed from black to purple and then to blue, with infinitely gentle gradations of color. A few flat-bottomed barges were moving out in the bay. Small straggling wisps of summer mist, seeking to escape the mounting sun, were driving inland, and overhead a convoy of wild geese was winging its way south.

All this the general observed from the windows of the Blue Room. Though he had worked hard during the night and had strained his eyes, he saw the bay and the glittering roofs clearly; the very effort of looking out the window after reading so many papers calmed the nerves of his eyes. Suddenly he saw something which startled him. He blinked and rubbed his sleepy eyes, ran his hand over his forehead and then exclaimed, "God in thunder! What the devil makes them so bold?" No. It was completely incredible. He went to the bookcase, where he knew a telescope was reposing among the books, and then returned quickly to the window, put the telescope to his eye and whistled under his breath. He saw that a yellow parapet had been raised a little way in front of Bunker Hill, jutting out into the tidal river and facing Boston. It was no more than a low bank of earth, but the earth was bright yellow, almost white in the sun, and there were people working feverishly behind it. Even as he looked, the general saw some men throwing up that bright earth with their spades, and others were scurrying at the foot of the mound and bringing up rail fences. Still others were gathering great heaps of mowed hay and stones. They were like ants scurrying up and down the hill. A few wisps of summer mist still clung to the hill, but already these were drifting away, dying in the blue air.

"By God, they've done it!" the general exclaimed. He then went to the door and shouted at the top of his voice, "De Bernière!" The guard standing outside the Blue Room, a Grenadier in full uniform, a blaze of scarlet, gold and silver, was so startled by the general's appearance that he dropped his musket.

The general turned on him icily. "You fool! On a day like this . . . "

He said nothing more. From downstairs there came a scurry of boots. De Bernière came running up, wearing his boots, his trousers and his shirt. The general led him to the window.

"For someone who calls himself the head of the British secret service in America, you are remarkably unobservant and remarkably useless," the general snapped.

De Bernière took the telescope, peered through it, then muttered stupidly, "They were not there last night."

"Nor the night before?" the general asked, his voice cutting sharp on the warm air.

"No, nor the night before," De Bernière answered. . . .

General Howe had spent the night in a small house at the foot of Summer Street. One of his staff officers, who had observed the parapet from the shore, ran to wake his commanding officer. Some twenty minutes later General Howe stormed into the Blue Room shouting, "Have you seen where the damned rebels are driving?"

"I've seen them," General Gage answered coolly.

"And you do nothing—you sit there and bite your thumbs! Why, they're not in uniform," he went on, peering through the telescope, assuming exactly the same expression which De Bernière had assumed, an expression of incredulity, horror and rage. When he put the telescope down he muttered, "Damned if these herdsmen should be allowed to point a sword at us, General. They shall observe what a good drubbing means. On my honor, I'll see that they hang on Gallows Hill!"

General Gage had been alarmed. Now that he had time to contemplate all the possibilities of the rebels' actions he was far less alarmed. He said softly, "It's a small mound—a very small mound. A few hotheads."

"It's not a mound, sir," General Howe said, the blood rushing to his face. "It's a mountain."

"I beg to differ. A few fools—I doubt whether there are more than a hundred of them all told—have entrenched themselves on a slight eminence and you call it a mountain. I assure you, there is nothing to be alarmed about."

"There is everything to be alarmed about," General Howe replied hotly. "If you are not alarmed when the American rebels hold a sword to our hearts, then—— No, sir, they have only to bring up their guns and you will find them commanding the whole of the inner harbor of Boston. They must be smashed, sir—smashed to a bloody pulp, or we shall not hold Boston for the king!"

Even as General Howe was speaking the ships moored in the channels of the Charles and Mystic rivers were approaching the hill, their sails flying white in the sun, or else shadowy blue, rippling in the faint summer wind. The sea was glassy, without a wave in sight. The *Lively* fired a broadside, with great puffs of streaming black smoke from the gun ports, but the balls fell short, bouncing on the soft grass below the hill, doing no damage. The moment the ships came up to take position the yellow parapet was deserted, with no sign of any Americans. They had disappeared as silently and mysteriously as they had come. Silence, and the yellow earthworks like some strange flower sprouting from the hill, and the drumming of the cannon balls in the grass.

"I see they are not being smashed to pulp sufficiently quick for your taste," General Gage observed, and then General Howe lost his temper.

He was a florid man, with a large mouth, deep-set eyes and the look of a bulldog. He rode well, he liked rotund phrases, and he was cursed with a singular inability to tolerate the opinions of others. He possessed no tolerance of sarcasm, and when General Gage took him gently to task he cursed blindly and solidly for three whole minutes. When the exhibition of cursing was over he said, "God help us! There is Admiral Graves incapable of throwing a cannon ball on a molehill, and there is you, my royal governor, incapable of making up your mind!"

"I have made up my mind," General Gage said quietly. "I have made up my mind to excuse your ill temper."

"Thank you."

"The next time you lose your temper, my dear General, I shall have you put in irons, for while I am here I am the representative of the king, and the respect you pay to me is the respect which is due to the king. Now let us argue no more. We are both determined that the rebels shall cease rebelling."

As the morning wore on, the cannonades from the sloops and the floating batteries grew fiercer. There was Breed's Hill all green and velvety, and then the hills of the Neck, with Charlestown huddled at the foot of the largest hill. To prevent the Americans from sending reinforcements to the parapet, the Neck was raked with fire. Through telescopes one could see that the parapet remained untouched: it was too small a thing to be damaged easily. The nine hundred men who marched by starlight over the nose of Bunker were employed on a mission uncommonly like the goading of a giant.

Gage prayed that a few cannon balls would smash the parapet; then there would be an end to anxiety. With General Howe he went down to Copp's Hill where a battery had been installed, but still the balls fell too short or else they sailed above the parapet altogether. Below Breed's Hill the orchards were glowing in the sun, and some smoke sailing over the brick kilns suggested that the brickmakers were still at work. Deep down below the parapet the Americans were waiting. Behind them lay the high cone of Bunker, very still in the hot noon sun. Still farther behind Bunker lay the mainland, and this too was quiet and deserted. But in Boston every tree, every steeple and every roof was thick with people looking toward the ships shooting at a small yellow ridge of earth which was sometimes lost in the drifting smoke.

General Howe scowled. "You would think they are on a holiday." Shaking his clenched fists he said, "With your permission, my lord, I shall lead our Grenadiers against the hill."

"You have my permission," General Gage answered. "You have it willingly."

When Oliver returned from Watertown the sky in the east was a pale yellow. The cocks were crowing, as they always were, with such a wild, raucous display of high-pitched voices that they alone seemed in possession of Boston. Hannibal left him at the wharf. A few shadowy figures were walking down the street in single file. Oliver knew they were guards sent out on search parties, probably at De Bernière's orders. As he stood there on the edge of the street, facing the sea, he saw no sign of activity on Breed's Hill. All was dark and misty, and behind the mist shone the pale sun; the steeples of Boston were wreathed with the same delicate purple mist. On the way from Watertown he had dashed some sea water into his face to keep himself awake. Now, striding toward the barracks, still wearing the cloak which Eugènie had given to him, he decided to see Major Pitcairn at once, tell him what had happened and then make sure that the news was conveyed to General Gage and to Admiral Graves. It would be better that Pitcairn should have the news first, for the general trusted him. An attack on the mound was exactly the kind of thing the major could do magnificently.

Major Pitcairn was awake, sitting over his breakfast. Lord Percy was suffering from a fever, and Pitcairn had taken over from him the duty of drilling the men on the Common. As soon as he saw Oliver, Pitcairn exclaimed, "You look like a man who has seen a ghost, Oliver! For

God's sake put some coffee under your belly, and some rum, too." He poured out a cup of coffee, added three thimbles of rum and pushed the cup across the table.

"I *have* seen a ghost," Oliver replied quietly.

The major laughed. "I hope you laid him. Have you been walking the churchyards?"

"I've seen Warren. He's a sick man. I saw him at Watertown, and I came back this instant on a safe-conduct from a major general in the American forces!"

With a sad flourish Oliver laid Warren's letter on the table. Pitcairn smiled, and all the wrinkles round his eyes grew deeper. He wore no wig. A gentle, warm wind, coming through an open door, tossed his long reddish hair, which was turning gray at the temples. As he held the letter up to the light he whistled.

"It's his handwriting," the major commented, and then pushed the letter cautiously across the table as though there were poison on it. "The devil's own."

"You'll find his handwriting on Breed's Hill, too," Oliver said.

"I don't doubt that," said the major.

"I mean now—this instant. They're building fortifications over there. My God, Pitcairn, they're up in arms! By the way Warren talks about it, they mean business again. It's Concord and Lexington and Menotomy once more."

"You saw 'em building fortifications?"

"No, but he spoke about 'em. I'd trust his word more than I trust my own eyes. It was too dark to see a moment ago, but if you come out now . . . "

There was still some white mist like smoke hanging about the masts of the frigates, and there was mist on Breed's Hill. But through the mist they both saw the gaudy yellow earthworks, brighter than anything else there because it was touched by the sun. Then Oliver and Pitcairn raced back to the barracks. A message was sent by boat to the *Somerset* and another to General Gage at Province House.

"They won't believe it," Major Pitcairn said, "until the guns start firing from the earthworks."

When Warren wakened half an hour after daybreak there was no sign of Eugénie in the room. She had found him sleeping with the lamp burning and had very quietly extinguished it and tiptoed into a room farther down the corridor. For some reason he had expected to find her there. He was annoyed. For some time he stared at the ceiling, and then it occurred to him that she must have accompanied Oliver to Boston.

"She is lost between the two fires," he murmured. Then he sprang out of bed, having said his morning prayers, his brain clear, no trace of the fever left in him. Aloud he said, "We are all lost between the fires, but only in the fires can we ever find ourselves."

Under the bed there was a jug and a large basin. He undressed completely, stood in the middle of the basin and poured the water down over his head. As the cool water trickled and swam over his body he smiled and murmured, "I am baptized for the last time." When he had rubbed himself down there was a warm, pleasant glow over his body. He poured himself a tumbler of wine, opened a tin canister filled with cakes, and then did what he always did in the early morning: he opened the window and sloshed the water in which he had bathed into the garden. The sparrows were chirping in the elms. He saw that it was an unusually beautiful morning. Munching the cakes and sipping the wine, he stared out the window: the elms, the dappled sunlight in the garden, and at the foot of the garden there was a little plaster statue of Apollo on a pedestal. Apollo was flaking away.

He had no idea how long he sat, wearing only his dressing gown, at the window—perhaps no more than twenty minutes. Then, as quietly as possible for fear of disturbing the other people in the house, he dressed. He put on his best clothes— a light-gray coat, a white-fringed waistcoat, white knee breeches. He put a summer rose in the top buttonhole of his coat and slipped the red prayer book into his pocket. He had thought of going out bareheaded, but at the last moment he decided to wear a tiewig. There was a pistol under his pillow, but he decided not to take it. "One should go to war empty-handed," he murmured. "One should be naked—it is always the best way."

When he reached the street he was surprised that there were so few people about. He went down the road till he came to Thompson's Inn, where a horse was kept for him. It was a small roan, one of the smallest he had ever seen. As Warren mounted the saddle, Jamie Thompson came running out, a thickset man with immense reddish freckles all over his face.

"Are ye goin' to the hill, Joseph?" Jamie said. "If ye're goin', I'll come wi' ye."

"There's no time," Warren answered, and dug his heels into the roan.

For a long while afterward, as he made his way toward Cambridge, he kept asking himself what he meant when he said, "There is no time." "There's time enough," he told himself, "all the time in the world." He raised his hands and shouted happily to some farmers making their way to the fields, but afterward he had no recollection of what he said to them. The fever was coming back again. When he reached Cambridge a feverish sweat was streaking down his face and he had difficulty in finding the house.

All the generals except Warren were old men. They were all troubled. They argued bitterly against the decision of putting up fortifications on the hill. Warren listened, and then went to lie down on a chaise longue which was stretched under an apple tree in the garden. Dimly he could hear the voices coming from the council chamber. At last, when he could bear their discussions no longer, he returned and said in a thick, feverish voice, "I pray that when I am in Heaven I shall not hear so much talking. Gentlemen, you talk as though the war were in your hands. It is out of your hands. The people have taken over."

Later in the morning he rode out alone to Charlestown. Asked where he was going, he said, "I am going home, the place where I have always longed to go."

Only a few cannon balls were falling near the Neck. The sun was beating down, and in the dancing sunlight the two hills were shimmering. Warren could see the roofs of Boston glinting sharply in the sun, and there came across the blue and silent water the heavy roar of the guns, the sounds of people shouting themselves hoarse in Boston. And all these sounds were perfectly clear; they seemed to be quite appropriate and entirely expected. Surely it was a holiday! Surely the ships were merely firing salutes! In his weary, fever-laden brain everything seemed unreal and at the same time exquisitely fashioned.

When he reached the parapet, having crossed the Neck completely alone, he was delighted to discover how carefully and tenderly the earthworks had been constructed. The breastwork consisted of a fence of posts set in a low stone wall, extending for about three hundred yards toward the Mystic River. Only the day before, the mowers had been over the meadows, and the grass lay on the ground in cocks and windrows; so the men had woven the newly mowed grass between the rails. They had chosen well, for the hill was steep and slippery with loose bits of grass on the slope. There was an advance breastwork made of posts and rail fences with hay piled between them. On the way up to the parapet Warren found a musket and a cartouche. Instinctively he picked the musket up. He had seen a sergeant running down from the hill, then dropping the musket and plunging into the knee-high grass. He felt no anger at the man's cowardice. The cannonade from the ships had quieted. Suddenly it broke out again with great bursts of smoke from the gun ports, followed by the dull throbbing sound of the balls thudding in the grass or breaking against the fence posts.

As Warren slipped over the parapet he heard a voice saying, "I didn't expect you here, General. Have you come to take the command?"

It was the voice of Colonel Prescott. The colonel was pale, lanky, studious; he wore spectacles. His excitement made the spectacles mist over, and he was continually wiping them on a handkerchief. This constant wiping of the spectacles, even at moments when the ships' guns were booming, gave him a curious air of authority: it was as though he commanded his little fortress sunk on a hill without being able to see the enemy, and therefore there was no enemy worth any man's worry.

Warren looked at the haggard men crouched by the posts and said, "They're the same who did the digging?"

"That's right."

"Then there have been no reinforcements?"

"No." After a moment Prescott said, "The command is yours, General."

"I shall take no command here. I have not yet received my commission. I came as a volunteer to serve with you, and shall be happy to learn from a soldier of your experience."

"Then you mean to stay to the end?"

"Yes—to the end."

"By God, General, you'll see us at our best, I'll promise that," Prescott said. "We have no food, no reinforcements and precious little ammunition, and if the British come by our rear, we're done for."

"I can see that," Warren said, and went to join some old men whose trousers were rolled up to their knees, and some beardless boys, all sweating hard, all with brown hands from the earth they had been digging up since midnight. It was now two o'clock on a hot afternoon.

"I'll join with you, if you'll let me," Warren said to an old man with a grizzled gray beard which resembled coiled wire.

The old man grunted, his hands steady on his fowling piece.

The British had wearied of bombarding the Neck and the hill; they were sending their Redcoats into a frontal assault on the hill, sending them across the river on barges.

"Thank the Lord they come by our faces and not by our arses!" the old man muttered.

Down below, the British had landed on a little bluff and were making their way through an apple orchard, marching in long straight lines like rows of geraniums, the bright scarlet glistening through the leaves. Their fifes and drums were playing. Their white, spotless knee breeches could be seen flashing in time to the music. Suddenly, after a long lull, the cannonade burst again, first against the parapet and then against Charlestown, and at the same moment the British, having reached the edge of the apple orchard, paused. All along the American line could be heard the sound of the clicking of gunlocks, then silence, a deep heaving silence, the silence of men who are waiting for an inevitable blow, a silence broken only by the old man grunting, "Why in thunder don't they come on and have this over with, an' not be shootin' their dinner pots at us!"

Charlestown was burning: the bright yellow flames curled, crackled, blew in the wind and then went soaring into the sky. From Boston came the dulled sound of cheering.

The British were coming into the open. Prescott was

going from man to man, putting his hands on their shoulders and saying, "Hold fire! Wait till you see the whites of their eyes. Then up, and tear out their bellies."

"Where should we shoot?" someone whispered hoarsely.

"At their belts, God damn 'em!"

Warren waited. The fever had in some unaccountable way made him perfectly lucid. He could see better and hear better than ever before. He murmured once to himself, "It is certain I shall die. I'll fall somewhere and not be seen until the crows begin to fly." He was very calm, and he observed with satisfaction that there was no trembling of his hand on the musket. He liked the smell of the new-mowed hay, and most of all he liked the silent company of his fellows, these men with rusty duck guns who were waiting apprehensively for the moment when they could fire their slag and horseshoe nails at the British. Over Charlestown the smoke, white and yellow at first, was turning into dark billows.

Down below, striding at the head of his men with Oliver De Lancey beside him, was Pitcairn. Both were smiling. Both looked like men on holiday. With all the other Grenadiers and Marines they were singing in tune with the fifes and drums.

"They don't know—they'll never know what they're fighting against," Warren muttered, and prepared to fire.

The British came closer, climbing up the hill as though there were no hill, only a smooth terrace. Their swords flashed, their muskets were leveled. They, too, must have been told not to fire until they could see the whites of the enemy's eyes. There they were, streaks of vermilion against the bright grass, with white conical caps, white belts, innocent faces, and not a shot had been fired. Buried in the shelter of the parapet, the Americans saw them through holes dug in the hay with their fingers, and perhaps this made them shine brighter. All the Americans could see was the section in front of them. There was no movement in the air, and the only sound now was the thumping of their boots in the grass.

An American boy, squatting on the hay in a place where the parapet jutted out, pulled on the trigger and killed a Grenadier with a ball through the head.

"The next man who fires before an order is given," Prescott said in a loud whisper, "that next man will be shot!"

The beautiful, slow advance of the British up the hill was coming to an end. Already one could almost see the whites of their eyes. The light gleamed on those strangely fore-shortened bayonets which seemed so small but were actually so long.

"Wait for it!" Prescott shouted. Suddenly, a split second before Prescott shouted, "Fire!" there was a loud crack of gunfire all along the breastworks.

The British, smiling and singing, were within fifteen yards of the entrenchments when the shower of blunt and sharp-edged iron broke into them. They recoiled, stunned. The line did not waver; they simply failed to move, as though some mechanical or clockwork engine inside them had broken down. Those who fell looked as though the strings which once held them together had suddenly been slipped out of them, as though they were toys strung together and the string had inexplicably melted. The strangest thing of all was the innocent surprise on their faces. One could see, too, how the light changed on the roofs of Boston as a shiver went through the people sitting there.

"They'll pay for Charlestown," Prescott said grimly.

All over the green grass there were men squirming in their own blood; some were slipping down the hill and others were running. Officers were shouting, "Form line!" The men knew better. They ran down the hill to get out of range, and then regrouped. Only a few held their position, and these were picked off by the Americans.

Sweat was trickling down Warren's face, along his cheekbones, down his neck and over his chest. The red blood on the grass had a sickly silver tinge to it. Warren looked strange there, with his feverish pallor and fine, silk-fringed waistcoat. It was a quarter of an hour later before the British came up the hill again. This time they divided into three columns and came up the three sides of the hill.

"There's some damn chivalry left in the bastards," the old man said. "They could take us in the rear if they wanted to." There was a strange look on his face, as though he hardly believed there was so much chivalry left in the world.

"There's Willie Howe down there leading his men," Prescott said. "I'll give a fine turkey to the first man who puts a hole in him."

There was some laughter, but mostly astonishment—astonishment at the thought that General Howe should be there at all. But there he was, thickset and burly, his white trousers bright red with fresh blood; but he walked easily, and therefore it was not from his own wounds yet. This time when the British came up the hill they were faced with a third wall—the wall of their own dead who blocked their path. As though in instinctive obedience to some ritual, this time there were no fifes, only the roll of drums.

In the silence, in a very clear voice General Howe could be heard saying, "I shall not desire anyone to advance one step beyond where I am at the head of our line."

"Then he's dead meat," said Prescott quietly, and he aimed his own musket in the direction of the British general.

In the interval between the attacks, more ammunition had reached the Americans from General Putnam, who was beginning to throw up earthworks on Bunker Hill in case they should have to retreat.

There was silence below the parapet. More barges were arriving, but the Mystic River was empty, sweet as a lake in sunlight. On the Charles came the floating batteries. There were thousands of British soldiers in Boston. If necessary, the whole weight of British arms could be thrown against the rebels. So the Americans waited, hoping against hope, wondering how often they could quietly bury themselves in the earth and then emerge to strike the British down. So far not a single American had been killed.

The second wave was like the first. With unbelievable stubbornness the British repeated the maneuver, marching up the hill as though there were no dead bodies there. This time the Americans fired when the British were twenty yards away, aiming at their stomachs. Most of the British fire fell against an apple tree high above the redoubt. For long afterward there was the sound of crackling leaves and branches.

"The seventh wave is the largest," Warren told himself, and wondered whether he would survive even the first six. Putnam had promised reinforcements, but they were slow in coming. "His promises are worse than his requests," Warren muttered. "He always promises." Biting off cartridges, his face blackened by powder, his tiewig askew, his white knee breeches plastered with dust and earth, and wisps of hay all over him, he looked like some down-at-heel nobleman who had taken up a farm boy's occupation.

"You ain't got no place here, General," the old man muttered, more to himself than to Warren. "You ought to be a-leading us, not fighting with the men."

"Fighting with the men is the only place there is, sir," Warren answered, and turned sharply to see that the British this time were racing up the hill on three sides in larger numbers than before. They had recovered from the shock. One could see that by the expressions on their faces, the way they held themselves. This time they charged in columns, not in lines; and because they were accustomed to columns, they knew exactly what to do.

Prescott had been going round collecting ammunition. He gave it to the sharpshooters; the rest were allowed to keep only their bayonets. He could see Pitcairn and Oliver running together. They were grim, determined, with blood smeared on them. Pitcairn was twenty yards from the parapet when he reeled over, shot through the chest. He lay there in the high salt grass while the Grenadiers walked over him. Oliver came running on, looking no longer like a boy but like a full-fledged man, with a hollowness in his cheeks which had not been there the previous night. A sharpshooter, standing beside Warren, was aiming at Oliver.

"Let him be," said Warren. "I've known the man too well."

He had hardly spoken when the British came surging over the parapet, swinging their legs over, dropping down in the soft grass and hay, only to be fought back against the parapet walls. Warren swung his bayonet into a British stomach, and then a sword fell against his hand. When he tried to protect his hand with the other, the sword fell again. For a little while, smiling to himself, he gazed at those two lifeless hands from which flowers of blood arose; and when a ball broke into the right side of his skull, grinding deep into his brain, sounding like the great echo of a bell, he whispered, "Let it come, let it come," and then fell across the hay.

As he lay there, seeing a forest of bayonets shining in the sun above the parapet wall, one bloody hand clapped to the side of his head, a few moments of consciousness remained to him. He wanted to cheer the men on, and when the grizzled old man crawled toward him across the hay, blood on his beard and streaming down his face, Warren had strength enough to say, "For God's sake, pay no attention to me. I'm a dead man. Fight on, my brave fellow, for our salvation." And then, his mind wandering from the noise of battle, hardly knowing what he was saying, trying to remember his prayers, he whispered, "The Lord leadeth us to dark pastures, where our salvation lies. How sweet are these pastures in the shadow of the rocks! How sweet it is to travel among the pastures!" Feeling lightheaded, he cried out, "It is paradise to be among the farm boys when they are fighting for the truth." Suddenly all the truths he had ever sought for were revealed in a single white, blinding flash. . . .

Later in the afternoon, when the rebels had been pushed back across the Neck and the flames of Charlestown were dying down, Oliver returned to the redoubt, hoping to find Pitcairn's body. There was no sign of Pitcairn, but he found Warren. He folded the bloody hands on the silk-fringed waistcoat, took the prayer book he found in the pocket and dug a grave for the body. A British battleflag was lying near by. Hardly knowing what he was doing, Oliver wrapped Warren in the flag and then helped to pile earth on the body. . . .

Eugénie had slept late. When she wakened she found Hannibal by her side.

"Where's Dr. Warren?" she asked.

"Ah, Missie, Missie," said Hannibal, "the devils have killed him dead."

CHAPTER 18

The End of the Road

SUNLIGHT welled through the window, and all the papers on the table flashed gold. Boston was quiet, as it always was at midday. The flies buzzed, and the little paper fan on the table rustled its leaves, for a warm wind came through the open window. The general sat at the table in the Blue Room, his face pale and puffy from the heat. Beside him lay his wig, and round his neck he wore a cambric scarf which absorbed the sweat.

As he wrote, he recalled all the events he had seen from Copp's Hill—the smoke, the fires, the patches of scarlet moving up the hill, the terrible quietness which lay over the tidal reaches at night when only the flames of Charlestown were visible in the black waters. All this he saw clearly and in bright colors, and somehow superimposed on these pictures were others: the faces of people he had known, Pitcairn's characteristic gestures, old Colonel Smith waddling on his horse on the parade ground, Oliver smiling his discreet and mysterious smile, Eugénie de Malmédy making her grand entrance to one of the many balls he had given in Province House. The smoke cleared, and there were the frigates on the Mystic River, low on the water line. The water was a soft blue like the color of English summer skies, the hills were a savage ocher, and all the mainland was parched and a sickly green. The thought came to him that he would soon be leaving America. Howe would take command. Somewhere on

the high seas there was a frigate sailing to Boston with letters
of recall. Not by a word or a gesture had Howe suggested
that the command would be taken away from him, but he
knew now, as he had known long ago, that he had failed. In
some watering place in England, isolated and forgotten, be-
coming more threadbare as the years passed, he would spend
the remaining years of his life.

My Lord, he wrote, *the news I have to share with you is
painful in the extreme.* . . .

He wrote no farther for a while. His mind, so quick and
adaptable at moments of crisis in his youth, had long ago lost
its sharpness. He had fought with Wolfe on the heights of
Quebec and with Braddock in the forests of Pennsylvania.
He had knotted the handkerchief which held Wolfe's jaw
after death; he had spent a night of agony in the forest when
the Indians surrounded Braddock's small column, and in the
morning light the grasses were red and scalps hung from the
branches. In this same campaign he had fought with a youth
called George Washington. Well, Washington was now the
generalissimo of the rebel forces, and it was Dr. Warren who
had called, from his retreat in Watertown, for Washington
to lead the rebel armies. Warren could have taken the highest
command if he wanted it. Then why hadn't he wanted it?
He had thrown his life away, deliberately, remorselessly,
knowing exactly what he was doing, careless of fame, contemptuous of the British and perhaps contemptuous of the
Americans as well, a strange willful man who delighted in
being stage manager, determined never to advance himself
upon the scene, and there was some cold-bloodedness in him.
"Poor man," the general murmured to himself. "He was
restless. Now he rests in God's mercy, and Pitcairn rests
beside him." For a moment grief shook the general, and
with the cambric scarf he brushed the tears and sweat from
his face. Then for a few idle minutes he gazed out the window at the sea hawks circling above the masthead of the

Somerset, and the golden flashing of their wings in the sun.

Half an hour later, when the general had already written the first draft of his letter to Lord Dartmouth, there was a knocking on the door. De Bernière came in noiselessly, left a folder on the table and was about to retire when the general called him back.

"Are they tallies?" the general asked.

"Yes, my lord."

"Of the British or the Americans?"

"Of both, my lord, as far as they are known."

"And General Howe has been given a copy?"

De Bernière nodded.

"Thank you, De Bernière. Thank you. You've done well. I won't say you did perfectly. We all failed in our task."

When De Bernière first came into the room he paid no attention to the expression of the general. Now, as he looked more closely, he saw that the general looked ill, with a curious blue tinge to his cheeks. His hair was white and uncombed, and some of it lay damp on his forehead. The general needed a haircut, but most of all he needed a restorative. His lips were the color of liver, and his flesh hung flabby from his cheekbones. It was on the tip of De Bernière's tongue to ask the general to see a doctor, but instead he said, "Captain De Lancey is waiting in the anteroom for an opportunity to say farewell to your lordship." Immediately there was a change in the general's expression. He smiled, and the light came back to his eyes.

"So he is going?"

"Yes, sir. He has received orders from London to proceed to New York."

"Excellent! He will have something to do besides moping in Boston. Tell him to come in."

In the interval between De Bernière's going and Oliver's appearance, the general poured himself a glass of rum. He felt better. There had been a graveyard chill in his bones; now the chill had gone, the blood was coursing through his veins, he breathed easier. He carefully unknotted the scarf round his neck and hid it in a drawer; then he brushed back his hair and put on his wig. He was standing with one hand resting lightly on the table when Oliver entered. Oliver was in full uniform, with a silver gorget and a thick cluster of golden braid. His boots were polished until they shone like silver. He held his plumed, three-cornered hat under his arm, pressed against his side.

"I see you're rarin' to go," the general said, smiling. "I don't blame you. I hoped we would see more of each other, much more. There were two people I wanted to see during these last weeks, Oliver—you and Dr. Warren. I'm told you buried Warren at the redoubt."

"I helped to bury him, sir."

"He died well."

"Yes, sir, and without pain, so far as I know. We buried him in an English flag."

Oliver spoke hesitantly, afraid of a rebuke, but the general said only, "There's justice in that—a strange sort of justice, but justice nevertheless," and then went on to thank Oliver for some presents he had sent to Margaret. "She's not half of herself yet, but she'll mend. I know you wanted to see more of her, and she asked about you frequently, dear boy. Tell me, you never did find Warren, did you?"

"Yes, I found him."

"When?"

"On the night before the battle."

"Where?"

"At Watertown, two nights ago. Eugénie took me there. I argued with him, but he wouldn't change his opinion, though sometimes he seemed to waver. He was in great pain—spiritual pain. I do believe that in his heart he wanted an end to the war."

A clock chimed. General Gage remembered he had promised to have the letter to Lord Dartmouth ready by midday and still only the first draft had been written. He sighed, sat

down in the gilded chair, and then impulsively grasped
Oliver's hand, saying, "We all wanted an end to this war,
believe me. There's no purpose in continuing it. Good luck
to you, boy."

Shortly afterward Oliver saluted, turned about face smartly
and left the Blue Room. The general went on writing.

When the clock was chiming noon, Lord Percy came to
the Blue Room, looking sterner than ever, his long nose
making him resemble some kind of brilliantly plumaged bird.
It pleased the general that Lord Percy was near, and it pleased
him that Oliver had come. At last he threw down his pen
and said, "Oliver tells me he had an interview with Warren
on the night before Breed's Hill."

"A pity he didn't accomplish the interview sooner."

"I know. He says Warren was in pain. Great God! I've
never honored a man more than Warren, and I envy Oliver
his opportunity. . . . Rum?"

"I'm not drinking this morning. I don't want to sweat
rum through all the pores of my skin. Is the letter finished?"

"It's finished," the general said simply, and he rose to go
to the window after pushing the letter across the table. It
read:

*To the Lord Dartmouth, from his humble and devoted
servant, Genl. Gage.*

*My Lord, the news I have to share with you is painful in
the extreme. The success, which was very necessary to our
present condition, cost us dear. The number of killed and
wounded is greater than our forces can afford to lose. We
have lost some extremely good officers. The trials we have
had show the rebels are not the despicable rabble too many
have assumed them to be, and I find it owing to a military
spirit encouraged among them for a few years past, joined
with uncommon zeal and enthusiasm. They intrench, and
raise batteries; they have engineers. They have fortified all
the heights and passes around this town; which it is not impossible for them to annoy. The conquest of this country is
not easy; you have to cope with vast numbers. In all their
wars against the French, they never showed so much con-*

*duct, attention, and perseverance, as they do now. I think
it is my duty to let your lordship know the true situation of
affairs.*

Lord Percy read on, smiling grimly, the smile of a man
who recognizes the truth when he sees it. He paused once or
twice to read a sentence again, and then there was a great
rustling of paper when he turned over a page. General Gage
went on to describe the death of Major Pitcairn, and spoke
of Warren's death—how he had been buried by the British—
but there was nothing about the English flag in which he was
wrapped. The general had left blanks in the places where
the tallies would be inserted. Oddly, the writing of the letter
was in bold handwriting, but the signature at the end was
cramped, a small spider at the bottom of a folio page.

"It's honest," Lord Percy said quietly.

"That's all I wanted it to be," the general answered, still
gazing out of the window, his hands behind his back. Suddenly he turned round sharply. "You know," he said, "if
there had been a battle we would have known what to do, but
it wasn't a battle—neither the first time nor the second."

"Then what was it?"

"A quarrel between brothers. Do you read Shakespeare?"

"Sometimes."

"Then let me show you something."

At the far end of the Blue Room, beside the locked cupboard where the maps were stored, was a pulpit table of oiled
mahogany, with a large vellum-bound folio of Shakespeare
on it. Walking stiffly, the general went to the table and
opened the book at the place where he had left a leather
marker; then he read in a hoarse voice the words uttered
by Blanche of Castille in the play *King John*:

> *"The sun's o'ercast with blood: fair day, adieu!*
> *Which is the side that I must go withal?*
> *I am with both: each army hath a hand;*
> *And in their rage, I having hold of both,*

> *They whirl asunder and dismember me.*
> *Husband, I cannot pray that thou mayst win;*
> *Uncle, I needs must pray that thou mayst lose;*
> *Father, I may not wish the fortune thine;*
> *Grandam, I will not wish thy wishes thrive:*
> *Whoever wins, on that side shall I lose;*
> *Assured loss before the match be play'd."*

"Well, Margaret read me these words last night, and she told me they described her own emotions. Sometimes I think they express mine. You know, if I hadn't given the order to Colonel Smith to proceed to Concord, there might have been no fighting, or we might have delayed the issue until the hotheads on both sides had cooled down. We could have killed every man on Breed's Hill by attacking from all quarters, but we didn't. We are cursed with mercy, and so are they, in their own way. They fight behind fence rails and walls. We'll have to learn the way. It may be a long time before we learn how to deal with them. Do you know, for tuppence I might have joined them. Now it's out of my hands. They'll fight to the end. There's only one recourse—to make terms—and it's too late for that. Sometimes I think if Oliver had seen Warren in time, if there had been a meeting between us—well, I won't be fobbed off with excuses, my own most of all."

"You did your best," Lord Percy said, turning over the pages of the Shakespeare folio in the breathlessly still air.

"I tell you honestly—I didn't know what to do," the general said. And then more softly, looking straight out the window where the ships were shining in the tidal river and all of Boston shone in the sun, he said, "No one ever knows."

Far away, with streamers fluttering, Oliver's ship was making for the open sea.

THE END

A NOTE AS AFTERWORD

A Note as Afterword

THE BOOK ends with General Gage in the Blue Room at Province House, and this is as it must be. I have hoped you will see him at close quarters, a man past his prime, with no malice in him. Songs were written about him. He was said to be an ogre who ate children for breakfast, but it was not so. I have tried to show him as he was, restoring some color to the faded portraits in the history books, showing him at the prey of doubts, at cross-purposes with himself, a man who did his best to fight off the coming of an inevitable war and suffered only heartache for his pains. If you will read John Richard Alden's admirable book called *General Gage in America,* you will find a reproduction of an oil painting by John Singleton Copley painted in 1769. The general stands under an oak tree, and with one hand he points to a parade ground and the distant mountains; on his face there is an expression of extraordinary sensitivity, courage and resolve. The textbooks have a good deal to say about his folly. The portrait by Copley and the researches of John Richard Alden would suggest that the charge of folly must be placed on the king and Lord Dartmouth. It was not General Gage's fault that he was called to make terrible decisions on the first day of the American revolution.

This book is an attempt to hold the balance between the American revolutionaries and the British government of the Province of Massachusetts. Most of the story is true; I have invented little. Captain Oliver De Lancey did arrive in Boston on H.M.S. *Nautilus* on April 14, 1775, carrying dispatches from the British cabinet; and though it is impossible to discover whether he took part in the march to Concord, it was a likely thing for this young Etonian to do. Oliver De Lancey later became a general in the British Army and was known to be something of a gay blade to the last. Major Thomas Pitcairn and Colonel Francis Smith are, of course, historical figures; so was Colonel James Barrett, who did the work of six men during the fighting at Concord and still gave the impression that he was doing nothing at all. Ammi White, the half-mad boy who killed the British Regular at Concord Bridge, is also something of a historical character, though it was nearly a hundred years after the fighting that scholars learned enough to see him in precise perspective. At a time when his name was unknown he haunted Nathaniel Hawthorne, who brooded on the strange incident at length when he was living in the Old Manse, a stone's throw away from the place where the incident happened. Hawthorne hoped one day to write a book on the boy and to explore his character, the character of a simple-minded youth who must necessarily be haunted to the day of his death by an inexplicable murder. As for the rest—Major Buttrick, Lieutenant Hosmer, General Haldimand, Dr. Church, Dr. Warren and the others—all of them have been described as they were, and I have quoted in many places their reported conversations, altering them only slightly when the words, as they were reported, have the stilted style of eighteenth-century English. That stilted language belonged to the time; there are conversations and statements of many revolutionary leaders which look as though they were delivered on the stage, not in the middle of battle. They were men of their time, speaking the language of the time, which is not ours; and so they have been put into modern speech.

If young Oliver De Lancey, with his red face and swaggering walk and desire to show himself always at his best, belongs to history, Eugénie is, of course, pure fiction. She never rode to Concord, never rode full pelt against the British lines, never wounded Oliver De Lancey in an upstairs room of a cottage in Menotomy and never, so far as we know, attended any meeting of the Committee of Safety. Her name appears nowhere in the roster of brilliant women who helped Dr. Joseph Warren to organize the first stages of the revolution. Yet she might well have existed. The proprieties of that time forbade the mention of the names of many of the women who took part in the war against the British. We do not, for example, know the name of the almost legendary woman who gave her red petticoats to Paul Revere so that he could muffle the sound of his oars. Many girls must have fought the British in various way on their journey to Concord, but for the most part we know the names only of old women who complained—often wrongly—against the behavior of the Regulars. As for Eugénie, I confess to an affection for her which I cannot share with any of the others except old Colonel Barrett and young Dr. Warren. Eugénie, then, must be accepted on her own terms; they are the terms of love and cannot be accurately defined.

I am aware that in attempting to hold the balance between the revolutionaries and the British I am treading on dangerous ground. The aim was to fill the actors of my story with life and purpose, to see that these half-forgotten heroes of another time walked in their proper air and went about their proper business. "History," said a sage of Concord, "is incarnate in each man," and I have tried to show that they were perfectly aware of the treasure which was at stake in the quiet dignity of their lives.

In the writing of a historical novel hundreds of books and documents have to be examined. Among the more recent books which have provided some of the background for this story it is pleasant to name here *General Gage's Informers* and *The Day of Concord and Lexington* by Allen French, Harold Murdock's *The Nineteenth of April 1775*, John Richard Alden's *General Gage in America*, Townsend Scudder's *Concord: American Town* and Esther Forbes's *Paul Revere and the World He Lived In.* They are all histories written with a sense of the humanity of history and with a scrupulous weighing of the evidence.

Boston—New York
1948-1952.

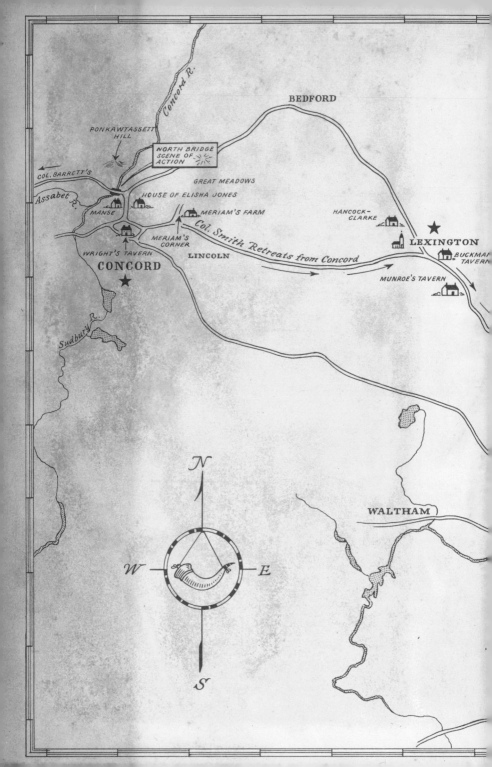